OFF KILTER

BY GLEN ROBINS

To my wife for all of her support and for reading and re-reading and critiquing. And to my kids for putting up with my long hours away, hard at work on this manuscript.

CHAPTER ONE

LONDON, ENGLAND
APRIL 30

Adrenaline made his hands shake, but he forced them to remain steady. Fear made his breathing ragged, but he forced it to slow down. Apprehension made his body rigid, but he forced his muscles to move. When prompted, he stepped forward and gave the uniformed guard at the security line his passport and boarding pass. He had done this dozens of times over the past six months in more airports than he could remember. But today was different. Today he had actually seen them. They were real and they were there, somewhere, hunting him.

James Stevens, as the passport read, was a thirty-year-old Canadian national. His real name, however, was Collin Cook, and he hailed from Huntington Beach, California. He was a man on the run. From many things. For now, he just wanted to get out of London, out of England, and on to the next unfamiliar hiding place. Without anyone following him or recognizing him.

Clad in dark jeans and a black North Face rain coat, Collin did not stick out of the crowd. Standing five feet ten inches tall, he had a trim, athletic build. With two days' stubble on his face, he was just another harried traveler moving through London's Heathrow Airport.

The cold, pale, marble floors were smooth and polished and reflected the bright, white lights from above, filling the space with a sense of cold modernity. A veritable buzz of activity echoed against every hard surface surrounding him. The thick, arching steel beams above were white, clean, and shiny, awash in brilliance from the fist-sized spotlights attached to them. Everything felt high tech, fast-paced, and efficient. There was no darkness, no shadow to hide in. Collin was exposed in open space, so he picked up the pace to catch a group of American tourists ahead of him in line. The blue, stretchy nylon ribbons and the three-foot-tall metal poles holding them in place, though easily kicked over, might as well have been steep canyon walls, transparent and illuminated. There was no subtle way to exit. To do so would surely garner attention.

Collin tugged at his collar and exhaled, keeping his face toward the shiny floor as he inched forward at a sloth's pace. His legs shook. Coaxing them to relax took constant monitoring. He checked his watch repeatedly. That, too, had to stop, so he jammed his hands in his hip pockets.

There were so many faces in this vast transit hub. So many eyes. Which ones were watching him? He never stopped scanning the crowd as he moved forward with the group, searching for signs of recognition or surveillance. His attempts at nonchalance were unnatural, but he had to appear cool and calm. Just another guy boarding a plane. Two faces emerged across the massive corridor. Lots of gleaming marble between him and them. They looked oddly familiar, despite the fact that they were wearing shades. That was it. The shades. Thick, black frames, extra dark tint, square-ish lenses. Fashionable but distinct. And exactly the same. He had seen them earlier this morning as he left the V and A Museum. They were the reason he had felt the sudden need to get out of London. Something about them and the men who wore them wasn't right. One glance at them this morning, and Collin went straight back to his hotel and packed. Now they were here, in the airport. Freely roaming and searching while he was caged by nylon barriers only three inches wide. And they were moving ever closer.

His pulse quickened, as did his breathing. The echoing of thousands of jumbled voices and hundreds of clacking roller wheels and the whirring of dozens of machines added to his nervousness, making it more difficult to think. His shoulders tightened, his back straightened, and his right eyelid began to twitch, as it often did when he was stressed. Ignoring it, he pushed his hands deeper into his pockets. Taking two deep breaths, he turned his face away from the men in the shades.

But he had to know. He pulled out his iPhone, thumbs dancing expertly across the screen. Using one thumb and one index finger, he pushed out from the center, as if he was inspecting something on the screen. The well-groomed men with the fancy sunglasses were closing the distance, examining every passerby. His camera was trained on the first one. He zoomed in and snapped a couple of photos. Finding the second member of the set, he repeated the process. Turning away again, he hastily worked the phone with his thumbs and sent the photos via text message to his friend, protector, and security consultant, Lukas.

10:48 a.m. in London meant 2:48 a.m. in Los Angeles. A normal person would be fast asleep. But Lukas wasn't normal, so it was just as likely as not that he'd be awake, working to keep Collin, and the rest of the world, safe.

The crowded line consisted of a blend of busy-looking European business people, clumps of Middle Eastern transplants, scurrying hordes of American and Asian tourists, and groups of loud and exuberant youth, presumably heading off to some exotic location for holiday. Together they inched forward into an area with a lowered, paneled ceiling, interspersed with evenly spaced track lights.

Light was still abundant, but the space was more defined, less exposed, although more restricted. Collin hunched his shoulders, adjusted his backpack with an elbow, and shuffled forward. He reached the end of a long metal table with stacks of plastic trays of various sizes. It was time to entrust his few possessions to the conveyor belt that fed the scanner.

He had nothing dangerous in his bags, but if searched, their contents could raise some serious security questions. Multiple passports. Stacks of cash wrapped in duct tape. Colored contact lenses. Hair dye. Prosthetic teeth. Being stopped by airport security could spell an end to his freedom and lead to a dizzying barrage of interrogations, none of which he wanted to deal with. He just wanted to get away and hide somewhere else. Hide, that's all he wanted to do right now.

The contents of Collin's pockets, including his iPhone—the all-vital link to Lukas and his protection—were unloaded into a padded, oblong dish; his laptop was pulled out of its case and placed in a black, rectangular plastic tray. He clung to the tray until the woman sitting in front of the monitor said, "Sir?"

Collin uncurled his fingers from the edge of the tray and then laid the computer bag and backpack in tight formation on the conveyor belt. If he walked out of here with nothing else, he knew it would be that laptop and the iPhone. Everything else he could replace, some at a steep cost. But not those otherwise ordinary portable wonders. His obsession with that computer was justifiable. It contained all of his travel plans, passport information for each of his bogus identities, PINs, bank account and routing numbers and balances, as well as a list of trade and transfer orders. That computer held the key to managing his increasingly complex life and the 30 million dollar fortune he needed to hide from the likes of these two miscreants, whoever they were, and the boss who sent them. Without it, he was a goner.

Just as important, though, was the gift contained on its hard drive. The consummate labor of love and the only real gift he could give his beautiful wife.

Likewise, the iPhone provided secure access to Lukas, the only man he trusted to guide him through the dark and dangerous world and help him evade those who would take the only thing of value he had left: his freedom.

Collin watched the two trays like a parent watching a toddler take her first steps. At the same time, he had to keep track of his pursuers. Every fifteen to twenty seconds, he stole a glance back toward the wide-open concourse to see what the two sets of shades were doing. They had split up. One was looking through the lines in front of the ticket counters, thirty yards away. The other was searching the neighboring security line ten yards from where Collin stood. Collin's muscles locked up. It felt like his blood turned to ice and froze in his veins. It was now his turn to go through the body scanner. If his legs would function, he would be through to the secured area, where only ticketed passengers roamed, away from the probing eyes behind the dark glasses.

Hesitating for a protracted moment, his legs came back to life, but not before the ruddy-faced security agent motioned to him a second time. First one step, then another, until he was walking almost normally again. He got through the body scanner and received the nod from the irritated guard on the other side. He started to breathe again. Shaking his head just a few degrees to each side, Collin moved forward and collected his things. He was only a few paces away from the relative safety of the boarding area. The goons with the glasses would need tickets to get to him now. This, of course, was not out of the question. Although one of the men looked in his direction, there was no immediate sign of recognition or movement toward him. Collin strode away from them, fighting the urge to look back. He was now in another immense, bustling corridor. People jabbered and tussled and scurried every which way. Scents of curry, stale cigarettes, and London's unique urban air mashed as it were into a cloud that filled his nose, seeping from the clothes and bodies that scampered around and past him. Everyone was in a hurry, so Collin sped up. As he walked, he switched on the phone, slung the computer bag over one shoulder, the backpack over the other, and adjusted the load. He heard the familiar chime of an awaiting message. It was Lukas.

The message was simple. "Not in db." That meant the faces he'd sent photos of were not in the database, so there was no information on them. Lukas had access to databases used by the clandestine intelligence community, both government and private. There could be three possible reasons these two didn't produce a hit in the database: they were so expert and elusive that no one had yet put together a file on either of them; they were rookies, gaining experience on what they surmised to be an easy target; or they were just two dudes who happened to be in the same place at the same time as Collin—twice in one day. Coincidence? Probably not. At least, it was too risky to assume. He had to evade them.

He hurried to find a lookout spot where he could watch for the shades. Lots of people, random movement, and chaos would provide contrast with the calculated search of the two men he was sure were following him. There were very few places that offered good food at Heathrow Airport, but near the intersection of several corridors, there was a pizza restaurant tucked away from the main flow of foot traffic. A dozen small tables near the front entrance provided just the view that he wanted and afforded him some cover at the same time. Most were occupied. He found an empty table in the corner. A perfect place to hide out and watch the crowd until his flight was ready to board, so that's where he headed.

At the counter, he spoke for the first time that day. "Two slices of pepperoni and a Diet Coke, please."

Finding an open table in a darkened corner, he dropped his computer bag and backpack into one chair and himself into another. No one paid him any attention. Good. He devoured the pizza, the only food he had eaten since early that morning.

Collin opened the first newspaper from the stack he had purchased at the international newsstand. All he wanted was to be left alone, but he had to watch his back. They were out there, Lukas had reminded him, coming for him. Relentlessly. Doggedly. The stress was exhausting. When would it end? Why couldn't they just leave him alone?

After reviewing the third newspaper in the pile, his eyes began to close and his head began to droop. He shook his head from side to side, rubbed his eyes, and took a long drag on the Diet Coke. Maybe the caffeine would help. He returned his focus to his work, scanning every page of every section before moving on to the next paper. It took him nearly an hour and two refills to look through them all. He skimmed each page, occasionally reading the first half of an article under a headline. The newspapers kept his face concealed and his mind working. Two key elements to maintaining control over his fractured mind—staying hidden and occupied. He checked over the tops of the papers periodically to keep track of any developments among the throng, watching to see if the shades had come through security. Nothing. At least not yet.

He turned his attention back to the newspapers. He had to know if anyone was looking for him, still interested in him. At some point, maybe, there would be another follow-up article, perhaps only a small blurb, about him and his story. Just months ago, his saga dominated the local papers in both Northern and Southern California because of his ties to each. If anyone was still writing about his plight, it didn't print on this day in any of the four papers he had bought: *USA Today, The New York Times, Los Angeles Times,* or *San Francisco Chronicle.*

In a way he was pleased, but in another way he was disappointed.

He finished his pizza and took the Diet Coke with him as he worked his way through the crowded terminal to his gate, arriving just in time to hear the boarding call for rows twenty-five through thirty-five, where his seat was located. Before entering the Jetway, he glanced back through the boarding area. His stomach dropped, his heart practically leapt to his throat. The two well-dressed men with the designer shades were walking toward the boarding area, looking determined. How'd they get here? Collin ducked out of sight down the hallway toward the plane, his pulse racing. His eyelid twitched unabated now. With one hand, he massaged it to make it stop fluttering. With the other hand, he steadied himself on the railing, struggling to maintain balance.

The Jetway was full of noisy, bustling people who also wanted to get somewhere. It seemed like a hundred conversations were happening

all around him, but he couldn't hear a thing. Fear of his imminent capture gripped him and forced out all distractions. The line was at a stand-
still. People near him craned their necks and peered down the line to
see what the holdup was. No one paid Collin any mind. Before the line
started moving again, he regained his wits. He stabilized his breathing
and steadied his balance, but his eyelid still contracted involuntarily. He
kept glancing toward the opening through which he had entered this
moveable hallway, but the shades didn't appear. Maybe they didn't see
him after all.

Walking stiffly and with more effort than usual, Collin worked his
way down the aisle of the plane, careful not to bump anyone with his
bags. By the time he arrived at his row, his muscles relaxed enough so he
could bend and crawl into his seat. He settled into place next to the window, unpacking as if following a well-rehearsed script: the music player
from his iPhone on, earbuds in, computer on his lap, and a thick novel
in the seatback pouch. He sat back and closed his eyes. Even though it
was a short flight to Hamburg, he wanted to be unapproachable.

A voice came over the speaker asking the passengers to prepare
for takeoff by stowing all carryon items and turning off all electronic
devices. After obediently switching his phone to airplane mode, Collin
hesitated. Staring at the icons on the screen, his thumb twitched, trying
to fight off an overwhelming temptation. He couldn't resist and opened
the photo album labeled "family." He scrolled through the collection of
pictures, searching for the right one. He knew this was dangerous. He
was flirting with disaster, but his heart yearned for them. It had been so
long; he had to see them again, even if only for a moment.

He paid no attention to anything that was going on around him. He
was lost in his past.

A familiar tension built behind his eyes as he flashed through the
pictures, each one holding a sweet memory. He continued, quickly
swiping the screen with his finger until he stopped at the one he was
looking for. There she was. His beautiful wife, Amy. Her sparkling
blue eyes and dazzling, seductive smile were right there, right in front
of him. She was giggling. The sun lit up her face, as the gentle breeze,
loaded with the warmth and fragrance of spring, tossed her soft, blond
hair behind her shoulders. The red shorts showed off her tan legs. The

white, peasant-girl blouse was tight in the right places and flowing at the end, with thin, white strings that laced up in the front, dangling in the wind. She was posing, cute and bubbly, legs crossed, leaning into the camera. She glowed. Collin recalled that day, that moment of sheer celebration, so long ago. The joy they felt, the closeness they shared, the love that bound them together. They were expecting their first child. She had just taken the test that morning. It was a Saturday, so they had taken a drive together through Sonoma County and found this out-of-the-way park. They had hiked a mile or two, holding hands, laughing, and talking about what their child would be like before stopping at the top of a knoll to take in the spectacular view of the rolling green hills and verdant wine country valleys. In her excitement over being with child, all the cares of the world had melted away and a new-found energy had taken over. She was flirty, romantic, and completely at peace, more so than he had seen since they were first married. How many times did she stop along the way to throw her arms around his neck, kiss him, and squeal with joy? He couldn't count, but remembering those passionate kisses made him miss her badly. Amy had sat on that rock to soak up the golden rays of the sun. Collin had tried to sneak a quick, candid picture to capture the moment forever. She must've known what he was up to and struck the pose that was now the photo he pulled up most often when he felt her slipping away, when the distance between them became unbearable.

The moment the flight attendant leaned over and nudged his shoulder, he realized he was drawing unwanted attention to himself. "Sir, are you OK? Can I get you something?" Her British accent was gentle and low, but laced with urgency.

Collin found himself clutching the phone with both hands and holding it to his nose and lips, eyes shut tightly. With his elbows on his knees, he swayed forward and back in his seat. His breath was drawn through his pursed mouth and across his teeth in quick, short bursts, making a sharp hissing sound. He didn't know how long he had been at it or at what point he had drifted away, but the moment he became aware of what he was doing, he was mortified and self-conscious. Heat welled up from his neck and engulfed his face, pushing out from his eye sockets, causing him to turn away from the concerned flight attendant.

This was the kind of awkward situation he most wanted to avoid.

The woman in the aisle seat reached across the empty space between them. She was a middle-aged woman with streaks of gray in her long, dark hair. Her hand was on Collin's forearm, squeezing it gently.

Collin cleared his throat and surveyed his surroundings, his eyes wide and darting. He shouldn't have gone there. He shouldn't have opened those photos and given his memories a chance to grab control. His safety and freedom depended on his ability to stay sharp.

Against Lukas's advice, he had loaded this digital family photo album onto his phone. This was his first indulgence in a very long time.

"I'm fine, thank you," he lied, shaking his head and wincing with embarrassment. "It's just been a really long week." His voice was thin and wispy. The two women were empathetic.

The woman in the aisle seat peered at the picture on the phone, uninvited. "She's downright beautiful, she is. Your girlfriend, I presume?" More of a Northern English accent, perhaps Scottish, but he couldn't be certain. In any case, her soothing voice and charming accent brought a wan smile to his face, blunting any ill feelings.

Still struggling to re-enter the present, Collin sheepishly nodded toward the phone. "My wife, actually." His voice ragged, barely audible.

"You miss her, don't you? Can't say I blame you at all." Shooting her eyes toward the phone, she added, "Gorgeous, I say. Just gorgeous." The way her words bounced and rolled was almost musical, engaging his mind in their sounds instead of the paralysis brought on by the searing pain his memories produced, unleashed by a glance at his favorite picture.

Smiling now and still very attentive, the flight attendant asked again if she could be of service. He shook his head. She locked eyes with him just long enough for him to know she was concerned, then turned and continued down the aisle.

The business woman added a closing statement before turning back to the computer on her own lap. "Bet you'll be glad to get home now, won't you?"

He just nodded as he pressed the button at the top to lock the screen and put the phone in a pocket in his backpack. She couldn't have known, and he couldn't tell her, that he had no home.

Collin lingered in the moment, mouth open, ready to speak, but rather than start a conversation, he turned away and looked out the window. Better to stick with Lukas's advice: lay low and try not to draw any attention.

He rubbed his hand across his face from his forehead to his chin, smoothed his shirt, and stared out the window. He clenched his eyes and tried to push away the memory. *The deep moaning sound of a big rig's brakes locking up. The squeal of tires. The crunching of metal.*

The business woman was soon re-absorbed in her own world—laptop open, earphones in, keyboard clicking. Occasionally, she looked at Collin as if to check on him, making sure he was OK. Collin opened his laptop and pretended to work. Open in front of him was his journal—a travel log he kept for Amy, chronicling the sights, sounds, smells, and food he had taken in during his wanderings. She had wanted so badly to travel the world with him. It was one of her fondest dreams, so Collin did what he could to share his experiences. This was his labor of love. His show of undying devotion.

He couldn't work. His mind was locked in a battle to push back the pain and he stared blankly at the screen until he gave up and put the computer away. He spent the rest of the flight wrestling with his memories. After the plane landed and taxied to the gate, the business woman leaned over to him one last time and said, "All the best to you now. You take care of that pretty little wife of yours when you're back to the States, won't you? Be sure you don't take things for granted, you hear?"

Collin managed a half-smile and nodded to her, unable to speak because of the knot caught in his throat at hearing those words. They were well-intentioned, he knew, but uninformed.

Collin stayed in his seat, looking out the window, biting his lower lip. *High pitched screams. Rocks slamming against metal. Silence.* His insides went numb. He couldn't move.

He waited until the crowd thinned out so he could maneuver unobstructed through the aisle of the plane. His pace was lethargic until he entered the main corridor. When he noticed himself isolated and exposed in the wide expanse of the terminal, he quickened his steps to catch a group of passengers, walking at the edge of the crowd, keeping pace with them, becoming just another face in an unfamiliar place.

Despite his prior anxiety, Collin easily cleared customs in Hamburg. From the curb outside the terminal, he caught the branded shuttle to the Marriott downtown. He checked in, speaking few words but in perfect German, even using a German name, passport, and credit card. In his room, Collin turned on CNN and watched it for an hour before opening his backpack. Again, no mention of him or of his case. A sigh of relief and a twist of disappointment ran through him.

He could now relax for a short while. He needed rest. He needed time to sort through the myriad thoughts tumbling around his brain. Tonight, he would order room service and read a book—a perfect way to unwind and escape his situation until he could bring his memories under control and push them back into the far recesses of his mind. Sleep would help. It usually did, yet it was increasingly difficult to come by. The memories chased him and frightened him, much the same as the two men in the shades.

But first, a shower.

Dry, warm, and relaxed after his shower, Collin put on his old sweat pants and favorite T-shirt, ready to spend some time with a book. He looked forward to letting his mind go somewhere else. It was only 8:00 p.m., but he was physically and mentally drained.

Just as he stretched out on the bed, book in hand, his phone rumbled on the wooden nightstand. A text from Lukas. "Get out. Now. The two guys from Heathrow just landed in Hamburg."

CHAPTER TWO

She sat still in the high-backed, Queen Ann wing chair. Her back was ramrod straight, and her aqua blue eyes were fixed on her hands, which were clasped together and perched atop her knee. They caught her attention. Maybe because she needed a distraction. The conversation had grown so tense and so heated she needed an outlet, something else to concentrate on. For the moment, the age spots appearing on the backs of her hands filled the need. But, at age sixty-three, Sarah Cook determined she was allowed to start showing her years of experience.

Despite the recent appearance of the age spots, Sarah's blond hair had yet to turn gray. Most people guessed her age ten years younger. Her square jaw and deep-set eyes gave her a no-nonsense, determined look to match her personality.

"Agent Crabtree, with all due respect, you are wrong, plain and simple," she said with conviction, her eyes still fixed on her hands.

Across from Sarah Cook, two FBI agents sat on an elegant sofa trimmed with dark cherry wood legs and arm rests. The cushions were covered in silky fabric the color of desert sand. Between them a cherry wood coffee table with ornate bronze foil inlays held up an oversized historical picture book of Huntington Beach. The hardwood floor was partially covered by a plush, Persian rug. A row of rectangular transom windows along the tops of the sixteen foot walls let in natural light that bathed the room.

"I wish I was, Mrs. Cook. I really do. For your sake and his, I wish I was wrong." At fifty-eight, Reggie Crabtree was only three years from retirement. The white hairs adorning his temples showed his maturity. His mustache, however, was still jet black. The skin of his face was a few shades lighter but still taut and lean. He was in fine shape for a veteran agent of twenty-seven years, though more paunchy than he liked.

Reggie's partner, a thirty-four-year-old hot shot recently brought into his unit, was being groomed to replace him upon his retirement. Agent Spinner McCoy spoke for the first time this visit. His Texan accent was tempered by his desire to sound as professional as possible, but it was, nonetheless, unmistakable. "Ma'am, we're not making this up. You saw the photographs. They're real. You identified your son yourself."

"Yes, I did, but ..."

"But, Mrs. Cook, the problem is these photos were taken in the Bahamas ten days ago. Collin flew there the day before under a false ID, ma'am. We believe this meeting was not coincidental. Why else would he travel under an assumed name with a counterfeit passport?" McCoy said. "That does not prove that he is in league with this alleged terrorist as you say," protested Sarah. "I believe with all my heart that he is the victim of an unfortunate misunderstanding."

"Mrs. Cook, if that is true, we need some evidence to prove it," said McCoy. "This set of photos, taken in London two days ago, shows otherwise. That's Pho Nam Penh seated next to Collin." The former football star was a large man. Even his suit coat could not conceal the muscles filling the sleeves. But his voice was kind and the accent endearing. "We're asking for your cooperation. Our main target is the man he is with, but we have had a very difficult time tracking him. We're hoping you can help."

"As I've told you, I know nothing about that man. This is the first time I've laid eyes on him."

Reggie resumed the questioning. "Did Collin ever mention anything about these meetings to you?"

"No, he didn't."

"Did he inform you that he was taking a trip, or did he happen to mention where he was going?"

"No. He hasn't said anything to us about any plans."

"Did he discuss the content of his meetings with his attorney, a Mr. Shane Dupree, or anyone else?"

Sarah sighed. "I have to admit I don't know anything about what he was doing or thinking or who he was meeting. After he was released from the hospital, Collin was a completely different person. He used to be so gregarious and fun-loving. He was talkative and funny. We used to have a very open relationship. All that changed, though. After the accident, he just closed up. He barely spoke to me or anyone else." Sarah studied her hands again, her voice dry and distant.

Both Reggie and Spinner had read the California Highway Patrol report and were familiar with the circumstances surrounding Collin's hospitalization. The CHP had sent Sergeant Terrance Draft to Collin's home when he didn't answer either his home or cell phone. Sergeant Draft found Collin Cook lying on his living room floor in a pool of blood, vomit, and shattered glass from the coffee table. A cell phone lay a few feet away. Collin was breathing but not conscious. A gash on his forehead continued to ooze blood. He suffered a concussion, had his head sewn together with thirteen stitches, and spent three days in the hospital, but most of his wounds were unseen and had yet to heal.

They also knew what precipitated Collin's injury. A thick silence hung in the air as all present reverently reflected upon the events that overturned Collin's life.

Reggie breached the quiet. "That's understandable, considering his loss," he said just above a whisper. "We're just trying to determine why he met with this Pho Nam Penh and what he may have discussed with him, that's all."

McCoy paused, then returned to the business at hand. "I'd like to shift our conversation, if we can, Mrs. Cook, to your last communication with him."

"Agent McCoy, if I may," said Henry Cook as he entered the living room from a foyer behind Sarah's chair, the sound of the garage door closing behind him. Henry was tall and trim, with a full shock of white hair. This was the second meeting between the Cooks and these two FBI agents, and the first time they had visited the Cook home. The first meeting was in early December, nearly six months prior, and the agents did more listening than talking that time. The Cooks had requested that meeting after Collin no-showed for Thanksgiving. No RSVP. No phone call. That worried Sarah and Henry. When Collin's closest friend, Rob Howell, informed them that Collin was even avoiding him, their concern reached the level where they felt it necessary to bring in the federal authorities to help find him.

In the past two weeks, however, the agents had turned up much unpleasant information regarding Collin and his activities. They came to sort it out with the Cooks in person. Crabtree and McCoy arrived with photos and accusations instead of help and support.

"Of course, Mr. Cook," McCoy said with a polite nod in Henry's direction as Henry pulled the twin Queen Ann chair closer to his wife and reached for her hand.

"We have not heard from our son in over six months. We haven't had what I would call a normal conversation with him since before the accident last July. That accident, as you might imagine, changed everything for Collin. His whole life was sent into turmoil and he has not yet recovered, it appears."

Reggie looked at Sarah, then back to Henry. "That's what we're afraid of, Mr. and Mrs. Cook. Considering that everything changed for your son as you say, we think it's plausible that he is working with Pho Nam Penh, either willingly or not. Penh is crafty, sophisticated, and extremely elusive. We want to know how Collin's involved and why. We also want any information we can get on Penh."

"Our son is not a criminal, Agent Crabtree," barked Henry. "He would never do anything to hurt anyone."

Sarah added, "Everyone who knows him knows he's a peacemaker. You don't know him, or you wouldn't be making these rash accusations." "Mrs. Cook, what we know is that Collin received a $30 million settlement. We also know that within seconds of that money electronically entering his account, all $30 million disappeared, having been routed and rerouted so quickly and expertly there is no way to trace it. The trail dead-ended. The level of sophistication required to do that is extremely high, Mrs.

Cook. Where might your son have learned how to instantaneously hide $30 million?" Reggie studied her face, reading every nuance of her reaction.

Sarah stuttered and stammered and looked confused. She and Henry shared a puzzled exchange. "I don't have any idea, Agent Crabtree."

"We do," said McCoy as he leaned forward, elbows on knees. "Pho Nam Penh's syndicate is known for carrying out this sort of electronic financial trickery. It's very advanced and requires the use of specially devised algorithms. Why do you think your son would go to such lengths? And how did he acquire the know-how to do it?"

Reggie chimed in. "These are just some of the questions that point to your son's involvement with Pho Nam Penh."

"I resent the implications here," said Henry. "This is all highly speculative. Collin is a bright kid with a fair amount of computer experience. Who's to say he couldn't go online and learn this overnight?"

"Okay, Mr. Cook," Reggie said. "Let's presume that's what happened. Let's say he learned the fine art of opening and closing multiple foreign accounts—numbered accounts, the kind that require secure authorization and no identification—online like you suggest. And let's say he learned the intricate programming algorithms required to move large sums of money not once, not twice, but multiple times into multiple accounts spread across multiple countries, without leaving a trail. Now the question is why? Why would he do that?"

Again, Henry and Sarah were dumbfounded. Instead of protesting, they fell silent. Henry's gaze dropped, as did his shoulders. He turned to his wife and squeezed her hand. Sarah let out a sob as a tear formed in the corner of her eye. Both were speechless.

Reggie continued, "Pho Nam Penh is an enemy of the United States, and anyone associated with him is under considerable suspicion. If you've listened to the news or read the paper, you realize how many security breaches there have been at the banks, credit card companies, and other financial institutions over the past several months."

Henry and Sarah each nodded their heads.

"Over the past few weeks, we've gathered some information regarding this man and his organization, but we're still unable to track them or monitor their activities. They like to be invisible. But we caught a break. These photos appeared on the Internet, clearly showing your son in conference with this man. Two days later, there was a security breach at the Royal Bank of Scotland, a bank your son had visited the day before meeting Penh. That's when he became a person of interest and a subject of our investigation. It's our job to stop Pho Nam Penh and his organization before he strikes again and undermines the security of the United States. If you want to help your son and your country, you will cooperate with our investigation."

"None of this proves he's guilty," said Sarah. Her voice was laced with the righteous indignation of a protective mother. "Our son may be going through a very difficult time, but he is not a terrorist."

"Let's focus on what we have in common, Mrs. Cook," said Reggie.

"We all want Collin to come home. We all want to help him put his life back together and move on. We all want to make sure he is not working for, cooperating with, or taking orders from a known enemy of the United States. Help us bring him home. We'll find out what he knows. If what you say is true, and all goes well, you'll have your son back, and we'll have some clues to help us bring Pho Nam Penh to justice. Is that a reasonable request?"

Henry and Sarah exchanged another glance. Henry answered, "What guarantees do we have that he will not be hurt or branded a terrorist with your Chinese friend there?"

"Vietnamese, actually, and you have my word that every effort will be made to safeguard your son's rights and keep him safe throughout the entire process."

Henry let out a sigh, then looked at his wife. "What do you think, dear?"

"I don't know what to think," she said, her voice low and cautious. She reflected a moment and then continued. "What I do know, however, is that Collin could never be guilty of what they are accusing him of. I know Collin is hurting and probably very confused right now. I know he needs help, and frankly, so do we. I just want our son home, safe and sound."

"Very well, Agent Crabtree," Henry said. "We'll trust that you are a man of your word, as you appear to be. What can we do to help?"

CHAPTER THREE

HAMBURG, GERMANY
APRIL 30

Lukas's text warning him to get out of Hamburg arrived just in time. It served as a stark reminder to Collin of why he was on the run, just when he had nearly convinced himself Pho Nam Penh and his gang had forgotten about him. He was mistaken. They were smart, determined, and patient he remembered Lukas saying.

Following Lukas's instructions to leave proved to be more difficult than simply packing up and walking away. Within two minutes he stuffed everything he had back into the only two bags he carried. According to what Lukas taught him months ago, he chose to take the stairs instead of the elevator. But as he entered the stairwell, he heard footfalls clamoring on the metal steps some floors below. Someone was coming up the stairs rapidly. A muffled voice, followed by a pause, followed by another subdued response alerted Collin that this was a synchronized search. He turned and grabbed the handle of the door before it slammed shut. He poked his head out into the hallway. There was a man in a suit marching in his direction. *Damn.* No shades, but that suit and that gait looked all too familiar. He couldn't be sure, but he couldn't risk it, either. As he held the door ajar, he heard the man in the hallway speak to someone. *But he was walking alone.* Not thinking, he let go of the handle and ran up the stairs. The door slammed shut by the time Collin, taking the stairs two at a time, made the next landing. Grabbing the rail, he spun and continued his ascent. The footsteps below quickened, and by the time he pulled at the door of the next floor, he heard the voice from the hallway barking commands in a British accent. "North stairwell. Eighth floor. Close on him. I'm right behind." Collin whipped the door open and sprinted down the hallway, heading for the stairway at the far end of the floor. His speed was track star speed. Always had been. It was something he was proud of, and it was proving valuable. Even with both of his bags over one shoulder, Collin felt like he was practically flying. Must be the adrenaline.

As he reached the tiled corridor halfway to the next exit sign, he noticed the elevator door beginning to close. At the same time, another man in a suit was exiting the stairwell he had hoped to use as his exit. Collin skidded to slow down, then lurched into the elevator car just as the doors shut behind him. To his chagrin, it was going up, not down.

That makes three of them. At least.

Two floors up, Collin bolted out the doors and to his left toward the south stairwell. One of the suits poked his head around the corner from the stairwell door and, seeing Collin coming toward him, stepped into the hallway. Collin was at full speed and didn't hesitate. As the man reached into his jacket, Collin dropped his bags and went airborne. Before the man in the suit could produce the 9 mm Beretta from its holster, Collin's feet kicked out, one landing a vicious blow to the man's chin, the other to his chest. The man flew backward, landing on the burgundy carpet with a thud. His body cushioned Collin's fall, and he let out a pained grunt as something crunched under Collin's backside.

In one fluid motion, Collin popped to his feet and through the door to the stairwell, slinging his backpack and computer bag over his shoulder as he went. He leapt down each flight, touching no more than two stairs between landings, one hand on the rail for balance. For ten floors he bounded downward.

His brain was working just as hard as his body. What started with two guys in London had grown to three that he knew of. He had to assume the three brought reinforcements and that someone would be stationed in the lobby. Therefore, he didn't stop at ground level but continued to the basement, knowing there was a car rental kiosk there.

Exiting the stairwell into the garage, Collin met with a surprise. What appeared to be a high school rugby team from out of town was just loading into a large passenger van twenty yards from him. To his delight, the rear doors to the cargo area were wide open. There was the typical commotion and chaos associated with teenage boys. Punching and pushing and laughing and loud voices and music. With so many bodies and so much activity, no one noticed him slip inside and roll under the back bench. Within seconds someone slammed the doors shut and, speaking German, ordered all those who wanted food to get in and get buckled.

Fifteen minutes later, the van stopped and a group of hungry teenagers and coaches piled out. Collin waited until the voices faded away, then crawled out from his hiding spot.

Thirty minutes after that, he was on a train to Munich.

With his narrow escape from the hotel in Hamburg, Collin knew he would have to step up his intensity and focus to match that of Pho Nam Penh and the Komodos. Otherwise, he was a goner.

It was a long train ride to Munich, giving Collin plenty of time to ponder, analyze, and lament the series of events that brought him to this unenviable state of affairs. He wondered how he had been found and thought back through the previous days and weeks of living life on the run. Time and events and places melted into one another as if his recent memory were more of a soup, void of form or boundaries. Naturally, his mind went back to the beginning, though he begged it not to.

His mind went back to his rather ordinary existence ten months ago. At the time, he thought he hated his life. He hated his sales job. He hated his boss and his insatiable appetite for more. No matter how much Collin sold, it was never enough. He hated his financial situation. No matter how hard he worked, there were always more bills to pay. But he loved his wife and three children dearly. The stress often made it difficult to show it.

Sitting on that Munich-bound train, the lack of sleep and the non-stop tension brought on by the sense of being hunted, memories crept into Collin's consciousness, like a thin line of invading ants, one after the other, searching. Despite his efforts to resist, his mind went back to the funeral.

Unable to move, Collin sat stone still, head down, eyes closed. His breathing was jagged and labored. His fingers were interlaced across his lap as if in prayer. Maybe it was a prayer. Maybe it was just a momentary pause to deal with the weight of the situation. Dozens of pairs of eyes were on him and he knew it. In that moment, he was immobilized.

When his eyes opened, they took in the green artificial turf that stretched beyond his black, patent leather shoes. It was spread out to protect the grass and conceal the mound of dirt just a yard away. The smell of freshly cut grass, mingled with wet earth and a hint of flowers, sat heavy in the warm air of the mid-July morning. Just a few feet from where he sat was an open hole, a full-sized wooden coffin suspended above it. To his right, there were three more holes; they had smaller coffins hanging over them—belonging to his eight-year-old son Max, his six-year-old daughter Jane, and sweet little Eliza, not quite three. Surreal, devastating, and utterly unimaginable was the sight. He closed his eyes again and fought back hot tears.

Though there was a large crowd of people who had come to show love, support, and shared loss, Collin felt little comfort. Though the words spoken during the funeral were meant to bring peace and strength, Collin felt tormented, alone, and unsure. Though thousands of letters had filled his mailbox, he still felt detached and disconnected. In that moment, his life had begun to spin out of control. Normal was forever lost.

His father's meaty hand squeezed his shoulder. Henry Cook rose slowly. Instinctively, Collin followed and felt the large hand steadying him. Blindly, Collin walked next to his dad who, as always, was solid as a rock. Silently, the two men made their way past the hushed crowd, all adorned in black, all appropriately reverent.

His mother, Sarah, his brother, Richard, his sister, Megan, and his best friend, Rob Howell, followed behind them. Rob had been at Collin's house since hearing about the accident, putting his busy schedule on hold for the week to help his buddy make the arrangements. The rest of the family felt it natural for Rob to step in and take over as Collin leaned heavily on Rob's steady, reliable leadership. Rob was like another member of the Cook family. Always had been.

Collin's mind also recalled the monotony and despair that dragged on for months and how it was shattered on a November morning by the arrival of a FedEx envelope and the cryptic note it contained.

Meet me at Graffiti. 6:00 tonight. Take a taxi.
Bring this envelope. It's important.
—Rob

Collin remembered how Rob gave him a quick hug, then ushered him out the back door of the crowded restaurant and onto a boat at the adjoining marina. The back deck was covered by a fitted, canvas tarp. Rob led him through an opening in the tarp and into the leather and teakwood appointed salon.

While Collin's eyes adjusted to the dimness, a man who had been seated on a leather sofa rose awkwardly and put out his hand. After a short pause to focus, Collin peered into the face of a man whose funeral he had attended three years earlier. The handshake became an embrace as the dead man drew him near and said, "I'm so sorry for your loss. I wish I could have been there for you, Collin." As Collin squeezed back, his dear friend added, "I also wish we had managed to meet under more pleasant circumstances." The softened Germanic accent and the icy blue eyes confirmed that Collin was in the presence of Lukas Mueller, the third member of "The Perfect Trio," as they were called at Huntington Beach High. Lukas was the brains, Collin the brawn, and Rob the looks and charm.

When Lukas loosened his bear hug, Collin stared in disbelief. "It's really you," he said, grabbing his friend's shoulders. "I can't believe it."

"Yes, it is. In the flesh. Resurrected, as it were. Sorry about the fake funeral and all. I didn't like putting my friends through that, but it was part of my cover when I went into covert ops with the NSA's cyber-crime response group. Only a handful of people know I'm alive. You're now one of them, so guard this secret as if your very life depended on it," Lukas said.

Collin looked puzzled until Lukas broke into a chuckle. "Geez, dude, you had me scared there for a minute," Collin said as he exhaled.

"Well, it is true. People need to think I'm dead."

The next six hours were spent on that boat, in the marina, listening to Lukas tell his story. He warned Collin about the danger he was in because of one of Lukas' MIT classmates, Pho Nam Penh, and his stated desire to disrupt and eventually end the prosperity and gluttonous lifestyle of western civilization. Lukas and Rob detailed Penh's strategy and known successes in the execution of his plan. Sad tale after sad tale was told of unsuspecting victims and their sometimes-horrific demises.

Since the funeral, Lukas cautioned, Collin and the $30 million he was soon to be awarded from the insurance company had become a target. The insurance company, Lukas explained, was one of Penh's legitimate businesses that hid his nefarious, cyber-terror activities. Every large payout made by this Tranquil Pacific Casualty Insurance Group had been followed by a tragedy, misfortune, or peculiar series of events that left the recipients broken down, hospitalized, imprisoned, or dead. All of their money gone. Lukas had been piecing together the clues and working to bring his cagey classmate to justice for years. But Penh and his syndicate had proven elusive.

Lukas wanted to prevent his dear friend from falling victim to a similar fate and vowed to teach Collin everything he would need to know to run, hide, and out-wit these crafty criminals. A plan for a new life was presented and, with little reason to resist, Collin agreed.

Just after midnight that same night, Rob Howell's boat left the Petaluma marina with Collin aboard. He was never to return to his home again.

Collin stood and walked down the aisle of the train, past all the sleeping passengers, trying to push aside the memories that made him ache and wish he could go back to his ordinary existence. This new life that had begun that night on Rob's boat was not the life he wanted to live. Nevertheless, he was not going to let someone else alter it for him again. Not if he could help it.

CHAPTER FOUR

It was a breezy, cool morning in Munich, Germany. Collin's train arrived at 7:15 a.m. The adrenaline rush produced during his getaway from Hamburg and the hours of reliving unwanted memories had eliminated any chance for sleep. Knowing he was being hunted by the guys with the shades didn't help, either. Who were they? How did they find him? Why now, after months of running? Had he made a mistake? Left a trail? Been turned in? What was going on?

These thoughts replaced the menacing and debilitating memories that had run their course throughout the night. As daylight broke, his mind became occupied with his current predicament instead of with sorrow or guilt or loneliness. That was a good thing. But the fatigue was not. More than anything, Collin just wanted to hunker down somewhere safe and comfortable for a night or two. If only he could be invisible.

Putting his questions aside as he got off the train, he had to focus on getting out of sight and staying there for a while. Getting some sleep would be good, too. The problem was it was too early to check-in to a hotel. Feeling very exposed out in the open, Collin jumped on the first bus that came and rode it downtown. He found a crowded coffee shop with free Wi-Fi and settled into a small booth in the back corner with a view of the front door and easy access to the back door. For two hours he worked on his laptop and scanned every face that walked through the door.

Lukas replied to Collin's instant messages, expressing his gratitude that Collin had made it out in one piece. The Komodos were so quiet that Lukas had not picked up on any chatter and could not track their movements. He apologized for the dangerous circumstances in which Collin found himself and promised to get him out of it. *Gotta go. Be in touch soon with an updated plan* was the last message he sent before signing off the secure IM protocol he set up especially for his dear friend.

Collin finished the pastry and coffee he had been working on and left the bakery to find another spot to hang out until two thirty, the earliest check-in time for the hotel he booked online.

Time dragged on. Collin found it increasingly difficult to remain vigilant and on guard. His thoughts wandered and strayed, the lack of sleep bearing down on him. But all he had to do was think back on the events that brought him out of Hamburg, and his mind clicked back into gear.

Weary mentally as well as physically, Collin finally found the quaint, traditional, German hotel near the river and got a room on the top floor of the three story, cube-shaped inn. The gray stone exterior and the clinging ivy gave the building an Old World feel. The interior also held a centuries-old charm with its towering ceilings, richly colored draperies and rugs, its giant stone fireplace in the center of the lobby, and the antique furnishings. Collin felt as though he had stepped into a time machine. The uniforms of the staff matched the mood set by the architecture and décor.

His room was no less impressive, making him feel lost in the immense space. The ceiling was twelve feet high, with a row of sconce lighting fixtures a foot below the large crown molding. There were three sets of French doors along one wall, each bordered by long draperies, heavy and regal. Through the doors, a small wrought iron balcony clung to the exterior wall, overlooking a manicured garden with pathways meandering through bushes to the Rhine River.

His late lunch arrived while Collin was setting up his computer with all its accessories. In his best German, he thanked the bell hop, asked for his usual collection of American newspapers, and gave him a twenty-euro tip for his eager response. He took his tray to the other side of the room and ate the sandwich slowly, looking through the glass doors at the garden full of flowers and green shrubs. Birds flitted from branch to branch, and squirrels scurried from one patch of greenery to another, following their instinctual need to gather. He watched in envy of their carefree existence. Wispy, white clouds stretched across the cobalt sky, hinting at a shifting weather pattern.

The food went in his mouth without being tasted or considered, so preoccupied was his mind. Before he knew it, there was nothing left to eat. He was neither hungry nor full, but this marked the conclusion of an activity that had kept him occupied. Now what?

He had been in the room scarcely an hour, but already Collin felt like a prisoner under house arrest. He had the comfort of a luxurious suite but dared not leave it. The desire to explore this new place and capture some interesting photos for Amy's scrapbook tugged at his innate tendency to be outside on a beautiful day. He knew he had to resist his native restlessness. Moving about in the open was not an option. Not yet. Despite the dread of confinement, he knew what was best right now. There were too many unknowns out there. No, he wouldn't leave this room until he had a chance to talk things over with Lukas. It had been several days since they had actually spoken on the phone. Collin needed Lukas's uncanny knack for making him feel safe, secure, and on course. He would know what to do.

Collin tapped his phone's screen. His call went straight to voicemail.

Waiting for a return phone call, Collin paced in circles around the palatial suite, rolling the iPhone over and over in his hand. He needed sleep, but he couldn't hold still. Physically, it felt like his chest was filled with concrete, the weight of it pulling him toward the soft mattress. Mentally, the wheels were churning at a blistering pace and the brakes were inoperable.

Thoughts of his friend Lukas streamed through his mind like a dozen video clips. Short snippets from his time with Lukas on Rob Howell's boat replayed in brief segments. He recalled Lukas's familiarity with Pho Nam Penh; Penh's connection to the insurance company involved in Collin's lawsuit; the mounting stack of evidence against Penh and Tranquil Pacific Casualty Insurance Group, which he headed; and the reasons Lukas was sure Penh was coming after Collin's money. Scenes that flashed by included the crash course in all things technical that Collin would need to know, as well as the outline of the plan to run and avoid Penh and his group of thugs, the Komodos. Despite his thorough indoctrination, Lukas had never predicted this many close calls coming this close together. It wasn't supposed to get dangerous. Collin's mind was spinning and he needed more than ever the reassurance that only Lukas could provide.

Collin waited as long as he could, then tapped his thumb on his phone to dial Lukas's number again. It always took several rings for

Lukas's security protocol script to run and verify Collin's ID and credentials.

Lukas answered this time in his customarily calm and assuring voice. "Hallo, meine freunde. How goes it?"

"I guess I'm OK. I just can't sleep. Can't relax. And can't stop thinking about those guys. That was too close a call. I mean, I've never decked someone like that before. I'm not used to it. What if they show up here?"

"I'll check footage from the surveillance cameras in the Munich train station first. Then I'll check the airport." Even as Lukas said these words, Collin could hear his fingers clicking away at the keys of his computer. "It'll take a few minutes, but I'll let you know if there were any hits. But for now, just stay where you are and try to rest. You sound exhausted."

"I am, and I'll give it a try. But I can't stop thinking about it. After all this time, I can't believe they're still after me. Why won't they just leave it alone?"

"That's not how they operate. Pho Nam Penh is a very patient, meticulous man. He won't forget a $30 million payout—ever. If he believes there's a way to get it back, he'll work tirelessly to that end. He's a real son of a—"

"But how did they find me? I mean, it's been months since I've picked up a tail. Why now? Did I get too complacent or something?"

"Well, Collin, this is where the news goes from bad to worse."

"What do you mean?"

"It appears that there is a renewed interest in you and your story. Some pictures of you surfaced on the Internet this week. I didn't want to worry you until I knew the implications."

"What pictures?"

"Pictures of you shaking hands with one of Pho Nam Penh's top lieutenants. I'm sending them to you now."

Collin paused to open the text message and view the pictures. "What? I've never met—"

"Apparently, you did. Last time you were in the Bahamas—what, two weeks ago? And that's not the worst of it."

"It's not?"

"No. Check out the next picture of you seated at a table with none other than Pho Nam Penh himself."

"Really? When was that?"

"London, three days ago. The day before the massive hack attack on the Royal Bank of Scotland. The day after you visited that same bank and transferred money out. Remember that?"

"Wait. What are you saying? Are they somehow trying to link me with this guy? Do they think I had something to do with his crimes?"

"That's exactly what I'm saying. Do you remember sharing a table with a Vietnamese guy in London?"

Collin studied the picture. "I remember this. I was in a crowded pub in Kings Cross, sitting by myself, as usual, just watching TV and eating my dinner when this Asian guy asked if he could share my table. I said sure, since I was just about to leave anyway. I didn't even say anything else."

"Well, my friend, you thought nothing of it, I'm sure, but that picture shows you with your hand out, offering him a seat. The next shows the two of you sitting across from each other at a small table, both leaning inward. Looks like a cozy little conversation."

"I was working on my computer. I didn't say more than two words to him," Collin protested.

"That was enough, though," said Lukas. "They orchestrated this very cleverly. Apparently one of his guys snapped those pictures and posted them for the FBI to find."

"The FBI? So, the guys with the shades are FBI?"

"Probably not. They could have been Interpol, but I doubt that, too. My hunch is that they're contractors for Pho Nam Penh. I can't be sure since the facial recognition software didn't pick up a match on the photos you sent me. The question is: what's next? That's what I can't sort out at the moment."

"Penh must have a network in Europe looking for me."

"Wouldn't surprise me. He's got long tentacles. What alarms me most is that he has now essentially enlisted law enforcement in his search."

"That's not what I wanted to hear," said Collin with a heavy sigh.

"If the FBI believes you are in league with Pho Nam Penh and had something to do with shutting down RBS, they'll get Interpol involved. You'll be a high priority international fugitive. When you add the list of attacks Penh is suspected of launching over the past few months, you'll become one of the World's Most Wanted. Congratulations, my friend." Left unsaid were Lukas's concerns for Collin's ability to hold things together.

"Oh, great. This is just lovely. I'm going to have this Asian mob *and* every cop in the world after me?"

"I'm afraid so. We're going to have to take measures, my friend."

"What measures?"

"Drastic and immediate measures. Let me work on this and get back to you, OK?"

* * * *

HUNTINGTON BEACH, CALIFORNIA MAY 1

At age sixty-three, Sarah Cook had become a Facebooking fool. Her first foray into social media came just a few weeks after Collin's disappearance. After yesterday's difficult meeting with Agents Crabtree and McCoy, she doubled her efforts to use this modern medium to reach out and find Collin's and Amy's friends. She now had 381 friends, but she was not satisfied, nor would she be, until she got these friends to help bring her lost son home. Most had expressed condolences over the family's loss and Collin's subsequent disappearance but provided no useful information.

Tonight, some ten months after the accident and six months since anyone had seen her youngest child, a familiar name and face appeared on an accepted friend request. Emily Burns was practically part of the family at one point in time. She and Collin dated steadily their entire senior year of high school. Everyone thought they would get married. They were so close and always had so much fun together. "Henry," she called out from her desk in the den. "Come here. You've got to see this."

Henry was watching ESPN in the family room, which was on the other side of the wall from her. He muted the TV and pretended to run to her side, shuffling his slippers along the hardwood floor noisily so she would hear his haste. "Yes, my dear," he said.

"Come around here and look at who just became my friend on Facebook," said Sarah, pointing at the computer screen. Emily Burns' radiant face smiled at them. Naturally beautiful, there was hardly a trace of makeup.

"I'll be darned," exclaimed Henry. "Haven't seen her in years. She looks as good as ever."

"Yes, she does," said Sarah. After a pause, she added, "You know, Henry, I don't remember seeing Emily at the funeral. Do you?"

Henry stopped for a moment, scratching the whiskers on his chin. "No, as a matter of fact. I don't believe I saw her there."

"I wonder why she didn't come," said Sarah. "Considering she's the one that tracked us down in Alaska and told us about the accident, I find it very curious that she didn't attend the funeral."

"There were so many people there, she very well could've gotten lost in the crowd. I'm sure she would not have wanted to make a scene or upset Collin," Henry said.

"You would think she would at least come and say hello," said Sarah. She paused before continuing. "That's in the past now, isn't it? I guess the important thing here is that she and I are now Facebook friends. Isn't that wonderful?"

"Yes, dear, it is, I suppose. What now?"

"What do you suggest? I don't want to be too aggressive and scare her off, but I am dying to talk with her. I really want to find out how she knew about the accident." Sarah remained quiet as she scrolled through photos and posts on Emily's Facebook page. "I know she and Collin patched things up a year or two ago. I wonder if Collin has communicated with her since he left. If anyone could get through to him, it's her. Don't you agree?"

"Yes, I agree on both accounts. We need her help, but we can't risk pushing her away by being too eager. Why don't you just invite her to lunch? That's a natural thing to do."

"That's a marvelous idea, Henry. I'll do that."

"And while you're at it, ask her what happened that night on the back patio."

"I'm sure that would be a fantastic way to start our first conversation in over a decade: 'And why is it you broke my son's heart after he spent all day cooking and decorating and setting up that special graduation celebration?' She wouldn't mind that question right off the bat."

Henry chuckled at her quick-witted response. "Yeah, but you're aching to know, aren't you?"

"Darn right I am, but I'm going to be a little more subtle than that, I think."

"That's a good idea. I still think its strange how everything changed so suddenly. The night of graduation they were so happy and playful, full of smiles and hugs. Then the next night, after all of Collin's hard work, she dumps him and tears out of here without a word. I believe that's the last time we saw her, isn't it?"

"Yes, it was, but the mother's network has kept track of her, you know," said Sarah with a gleam in her eye.

"Oh, yeah? You've been stalking her, have you?"

"I wouldn't call it that, but I know she graduated top of her class from Johns Hopkins with a degree in Bio Medical Research and did her doctorate at Harvard. I also know she's working at the Scripps Institute in San Diego doing cancer research."

"Wow, that mother's network knows a lot."

"Well, the last part is right here on her Facebook profile. But Janice and Diane seem to always be in the know about that whole group of kids."

"Whatever happened to her parents? I always thought they were fairly pompous and high-minded," said Henry.

"Who knows? They never associated with us commoners. They were definitely the high society type, born with East Coast money. Wasn't he a cardiologist? I think that's right, from Harvard, and she was a socialite who liked to fundraise for the trendiest charities and attend all the elite galas," Sarah said matter-of-factly. "I think Emily really looked up to her father but was controlled by her mother. If you ask me, that woman had more to do with her breaking up with Collin than Emily did." Sarah's voice was tinged with ire.

Henry read a message from Emily that popped up. "Look, she's asking how you're doing. I think she wants to chat, so there you go. Just be yourself."

Sarah typed a quick response and opened a conversation that began the rebuilding of a relationship long since forsaken. The conversation flowed naturally and without interruption. By the end of their twenty-minute exchange, the two ladies had arranged a lunch date for Saturday.

Sarah was anxious. With the clock ticking, she needed help and was happy to enlist Emily in her cause.

CHAPTER FIVE

MUNICH, GERMANY
MAY 2

Collin shook off the grog that customarily enveloped him in the mornings, trying to remember where he was. The brochure he left on the nightstand served as a reminder that he was in Munich, Germany. He fumbled for the remote and turned the TV to CNN. He watched the news for half an hour to be sure there was nothing relevant. He flipped through the local channels, too, before going to the door to pick up the newspapers he had requested with his breakfast, which arrived at 8:00 a.m. He ate his eggs and toast while scouring the pages of the newspapers.

Nothing. Nothing about him, his family, or the episode in London. Not even a mention of the violence in Hamburg. Nothing about his supposed connection with the assault on the computer systems of the Royal Bank of Scotland. That was good, he thought. A quick check on the Internet produced the same results. *Perfect.*

After showering and dressing, it was time to take to the streets and subways. Lukas had confirmed that he had not been followed to Munich, so he was free to venture forth from his hotel and explore the city. He wore clothes to help him blend into any crowd. A dark, hooded sweatshirt, black running shoes, and jeans.

He spent the day walking the streets, trying to look like everyone else. Only, he just pretended to have somewhere to go and something important to do. With nothing more than a quick glance, he would study faces as they went by, being careful not to make eye contact. He had learned to discern expressions and body language. He looked for anyone who appeared to be looking at or watching him. But no one paid attention to him. Not today. The suits from London and Hamburg were nowhere to be seen.

That was good.

During lunch, Collin managed to read a local newspaper in German and pull out a few more vocabulary words and sentence structures to keep building his language skills, although he rarely used more than the

typical phrases needed to order food, a hotel room, or to buy tickets for
transportation. There was a sense of accomplishment that came with
recognizing words and phrases. He also listened carefully to conversations in the subway, cafes, and at street corners. He almost never spoke
to anyone, but it was comforting to know that he could have a conversation about the weather, current events, or the economy and sound
pretty good doing it.

The small street-side café grew more crowded as he ate. Collin's
seat was against a wall, under an umbrella, in the far corner of the outside patio. Like many of the young people at that café, he had his laptop
out on the table and was browsing the Internet. He was busy planning
his stay in Munich, deciding what attractions and areas of the city Amy
would most like to have seen. Being a fan of old European architecture,
especially cathedrals, he knew his wife would enjoy this city, its ambi-
ence, and the wealth of sightseeing attractions.

After lunch, Collin walked through the streets of the shopping district, taking pictures of the quaint buildings and streets, like so many of
the other tourists he saw. He headed to the famous Englischer Garten,
created in the eighteenth century to preserve the natural wonders of
Bavaria. Miles of walking trails and wide open green space made this a
place worth seeing. Collin strolled along its paths, knowing Amy would
have loved this area, fighting back his emotions as he thought about her.
Maybe it was a mistake to come here. His break down on the plane to
Hamburg left him feeling more mentally feeble than he had in months.
He pressed on for Amy's sake, pushing aside the rising tide of feelings
and focused on photographing the scenery for her.

His efforts yielded little. The flood of memories was building, spill-
ing over his delicate barriers. Try as he might, he could not contain it.
As he walked along taking in the sights, sounds, and smells, his defenses
began to break down. He heard Amy's laughter echoing from a time
years before when they had gone on a picnic together at a similar looking place in the Sierra foothills.

Soon his mind was caught up in the memory, and he felt himself
spinning out of control, unable to stop it. Flashbacks of Amy and the
children laughing and playing in the park and on the swings gripped
him as he watched a young German family. The children were the same

ages as his had been and were frolicking much the same as his had done not so long ago. Collin stopped in his tracks, only ten yards from them, transfixed with a hollow gaze. His mouth half-curled up in an eerie smile as his eyes glazed over. It was a bizarre display that frightened the German children.

Replaying that day in the park in the California foothills took him far away from reality for a few dangerous moments. He was forced to snap out of it as the irate German father approached him—irritated and intimidating with tightened jaw muscles and glaring eyes. Stunned and self-conscious, Collin turned and sprinted away as fast as his legs would carry him.

A quarter mile later, he was well out of danger, so he slowed to a brisk walk and headed toward the downtown area to find a crowd into which he could merge. His eyes darted in every direction and his head swiveled side to side but saw nothing unusual. These types of suspicious actions could draw attention, he knew, so he sucked in a deep breath to calm himself. He ran his fingers through his hair and let out his breath as he struggled to shake the haunting memories that had taken control of him in the park. In his mind, his children continued to run and play, laugh and call his name, hold his hand and look to him for protection.

Like a herd of wild horses corralled in a crowded pen, Collin's memories couldn't be contained. His diminishing control over his thoughts and actions presented a growing peril to his safety and survival. It was time again check in with Lukas for some coaching and reassurance. He needed a friend and wished Lukas was there with him.

"Collin, what's up?" Lukas's voice sounded distracted. Collin had the feeling he was calling at an inconvenient time.

"Sounds like you're busy. Maybe I should call later."

"No, no. This is as good a time as any. I meant to call you to see how you're doing."

Collin explained to Lukas what had just transpired.

"I'm no expert on mental health issues, but it sounds to me like the pressure may be affecting you more than we expected. Maybe you need to get your mind on something else. You know, add some other sensory inputs. Try to distract yourself. Go somewhere crowded where there's a lot of noise and lots of things to look at. Maybe watching a game on

TV would help."

"Right," said Collin. "I'll find a busy sports bar or something."

"All right. Sounds good. Call me later, OK?" said Lukas.

With darkness moving in, enveloping Munich in its chilly grasp, Collin found a teeming sports bar in the bustling downtown district— the kind with several television sets showing different games all at once. The choices were soccer, cricket, rugby, or the news. He settled into a seat near a television, where a dapper anchorman in a fashionable suit talked and smiled. The volume was too low to hear, but the words and pictures on the screen told enough of the story.

He ate alone against the wall at the far end of the restaurant, hunched over his laptop, pecking away at the keys, recording not only the events of the day, but his reaction to them in his journal. He hoped this would provide insight into his meltdowns. As he typed, Collin nibbled on the uninspiring food and monitored the happenings on the TVs. As his eyes scanned the room, they inadvertently locked onto the face of a beautiful woman sitting at the bar with her girlfriend. Her long, silky, blond hair shone in the dim light of the bar. Her cheeks were slightly concave, and her skin was perfect. His gaze lingered on her face a bit too long, and she blushed and looked away. The two girls started giggling and whispering to one another. By the time they looked back, there was nothing but a plate and a few bills on the table.

Collin was out on the street, hurrying to escape an uncomfortable situation.

That face was so sweet, so pretty, so happy. It was hard not to dwell on it, but he couldn't allow it. Her laugh was cute and genuine, and her eyes danced. All of it too much like Amy. He couldn't stay; it was all wrong. Too many memories were already too close to the surface.

Out in the cool night air, he turned his focus on the chill and the wind. He was heading east toward the subway when he noticed the sound of footsteps behind him on an otherwise desolate sidewalk. He turned a corner. So did the footsteps. He quickened his pace and checked his watch. The footsteps were still there. He crossed the street, and so did they, the soft thumping growing louder. The shadowy figure followed him into the subway terminal. Without stopping or looking left or right, Collin walked right onto the train in front of him just before the doors shut, nearly hitting him.

He turned and looked through the window to see a large man nearly collide with the closing door. The man's angry gaze was fixed on Collin. A thick finger jabbed at him against the dingy glass amidst a hail of snarling and cursing.

Collin's stomach rolled over, twisting into a knot, and his face went pale. His knees wobbled, so he sank into the nearest seat and buried his head in his hands, trying to shut everything out.

It felt like the walls were closing in on him and there was nothing to stop them. The forces squeezing him were too powerful.

As the train stopped at the next station, Collin pulled himself together, exited the train, and made his way to the street. He checked his surroundings, glanced at his watch, then headed toward the bus stop. The streets were damp and crowded; the air chilly. He switched back and forth between the bus and the train, looking out for anyone following him, until he was back at the hotel.

Once in his room, he packed without delay, collecting the few personal items and clothes he traveled with, and checked out via the hotel TV. Pulling up a map on his phone, he charted his route.

He was on an express train out of Munich less than forty minutes later.

Next stop: Paris.

CHAPTER SIX

LONDON, ENGLAND
MAY 2

The call came into Alastair Montgomery's London office at four thirty on an otherwise ordinary Thursday, if there was such a thing anymore. Recent events had amped up the pressure. Alastair had just finished yet another meeting with the Chief of Investigations. They discussed, of course, the ongoing probe into recent cyber-attacks on multinational corporations. Urgency was at a fever pitch, thanks to the shrill cries of the British press, not to mention Parliament. The increasing strain on him and his staff was becoming difficult to bear, and he expressed the need for more manpower but was once again politely denied. Interpol's budget did not allow for hiring more investigators. Though only fifty-one years old, his thick hair had gone completely white, complementing his thin, wrinkle-free face. He sat facing the long window of his tiny office, twirling his pen between the fingers of one hand while loosening his tie with the other. His desk was cluttered with files and papers.

When the phone rang, he practically barked into it. "Montgomery here."

"Section Chief Montgomery, my name is Reggie Crabtree, Special Agent in charge of the cyber terrorism task force for the FBI's West Coast bureau. How do you do?"

Oh, swell, now I've got the Americans making demands, too. "I'm quite busy, as it were. There's been a load of activity over here in recent months, as you know. It's keeping me and my team in the office late," said Alastair with a huff.

"I understand, so let me cut to the chase. I think we can help each other out. We have a lead on an organization that we believe was behind several, if not most, of the recent attacks on European and American banks. Who knows? Maybe with some cooperation, we can apprehend these suspects together. What do you say?"

"It all sounds very intriguing, I must admit. What have you got?"

"Ever hear of Pho Nam Penh and his Komodos out of Southeast Asia?" asked Reggie

"We know the source of the RBS attack last week originated out of that region, yes. But Penh and his group cover their tracks extremely well, so as of yet, we have nothing solid to link them to any of these crimes," said Alastair, the tone of his voice betraying his growing interest.

"We have some photos of Mr. Penh with one of our own, a dis-associated American who we believe has gotten himself ensnared in the Komodo syndicate, perhaps naively. We can't confirm his level of involvement at this point, but we have our suspicions."

"And what are the bases of your suspicions, Agent Crabtree?"

"We have photographic evidence that our man met with Pho Nam Penh in London just before the attack on RBS and with one of his top-ranking lieutenants in Nassau, a week earlier."

"Yes, very intriguing." Alastair nodded his head as if Reggie could see it. "Send over what you've got, and I'll put one of my best guys on it. Maybe we can bring an end to the Komodos' reign of chaos. Sure would make my life simpler."

* * * *

SOUTH OF MUNICH, GERMANY
MAY 3

Collin was lost in thought as the darkened countryside whizzed past the window on his left. He didn't know if he was in Germany still or in France. And he didn't care. The gentle swaying and clickety-clacking of the train lulled him into a contented stupor. He felt safer than he had for several days. He was sure no one was following him, and no one on this train cared what he was doing. The stress was working its way out of his system, so he allowed his eyelids to close and his head to rest against the seatback. Time to relax.

At that moment, his phone rang. Only one person it could be. Lukas's voice was strained with urgency. "Collin, you need to go straight to LeBourget Airport when you get off the train."

Collin didn't bother asking how Lukas knew he was on a train to

Paris. "Why? What's going on?"

"The FBI just posted that picture of you and Pho Nam Penh on their Most Wanted board online. They've teamed up with Interpol," said Lukas. "And that's not the worst of it."

"It's not? How can things get much worse?"

"Interpol has taken a lot of heat for all of the recent cyber-attacks. They need to show progress—you know how the European press can be. They're broadcasting your picture all over the airwaves. I'm sure they'll block all borders and do extensive searches, so we have no time to waste. You've got to get out of Europe ASAP. Even then, it's going to be harder to hide now."

"Where shall I go?" asked Collin.

"Don't worry about that. I've got a private jet waiting for you at Le Bourget. My connections in Paris will see to it that you get out of there without problem. You're going to the Cayman Islands, my friend."

"Awesome. Warm beaches, great scuba diving there, right? Sign me up."

"I'm afraid there'll be no time for beaches or scuba. We're not playing around here."

"Yeah, when was the last time I did any of that?"

"I appreciate you keeping a good sense of humor, but I'm telling you, man, this is serious stuff. We've got to change tactics," said Lukas.

"Dude, you're scaring me right now," Collin admitted.

"I know. I wish I had the luxury of being more jovial, but I'm extremely concerned about your safety."

"So, what's the game plan? I mean, beyond just going to the Caymans?"

"I'm working on that. Hopefully I'll have something for you by the time you land."

Collin gulped hard and checked his watch. "I don't even know what time this train is due to arrive in Paris …"

"You'll be there about 6:21 a.m. That's two and a half hours from now. Try to catch a few winks if you can."

"Yeah. Not sure about that."

* * * *

GEORGE TOWN, GRAND CAYMAN ISLAND
MAY 3

Everything had gone smoothly to this point. He had exited the train, walked straight to the taxi stand, and made a bee line for Le Bourget Airport. When he got there, he was greeted by a short, stocky man named Jean Claude, who escorted him as if he were a dignitary straight to the waiting Learjet. Jean Claude raised the stairs to close the door as soon as Collin boarded the plane, and they were taxiing before he even sat down. Two well-dressed businessmen in expensive wool suits gave Collin perturbed glances as he made his way to the back of the plane. But he was on the plane, and they were on their way without a hitch. There were six passengers besides Collin.

Collin was unable to sleep during the long flight. Once again, too many things on his mind. He was anxious to hear from Lukas to learn the new game plan, uncomfortable with his new branding as a wanted criminal. He wondered how he could stay safe with the international police hunting him. These unsettling concerns kept him alert until the pilot's voice came over the speaker, announcing in French that they were making their final approach.

Looking out the window as they descended, Collin surveyed what awaited him on the ground in George Town, Grand Cayman. As the plane neared touchdown, he could see Police cars racing down the run-way, following the plane that landed just ahead of Collin's.

Collin's plane never made it to the gate, instead emptying its passengers on the tarmac, where the confused businessmen collected their bags from the rear cargo hold of the plane as the copilot unloaded them. Since he had no luggage other than his backpack and computer bag, Collin was well on his way to the terminal when the sirens sped toward his plane. Four blue and white police sedans rushed in formation to intercept the bewildered passengers.

By this time, Collin had merged with a group of anxious tourists, many of whom stood slack-jawed and gawking at all the commotion. He turned and watched in stunned horror as police cars screeched to a halt. Uniformed officers jumped out and began to surround the plane he had exited just moments before. He turned back toward the terminal and picked up his pace. He could hear howling and yelling behind him from his fellow travelers. Forcing himself to continue moving forward, Collin reached the glass door of the terminal, stealing a glance back to survey the scene. The small aircraft was a beehive of activity. The passengers and two pilots were visibly upset and agitated, their hands and arms waving in the air. Jean Claude looked toward the terminal and gave Collin an almost imperceptible hand motion to keep moving. The officers were encircling them and moving them like dogs herding sheep.

He moved briskly through the airport. Most locals seemed unfazed by what they saw. To Collin, though, all this activity was bad news. It felt like he had stepped right into a waiting trap. He worked to control his breathing. Nothing on his phone yet, so he called Lukas. No answer.

Collin wiped beads of sweat from his brow. He checked his phone as he walked, expecting a text or call from Lukas, instructing him where to go and what to do. He cursed under his breath but kept moving straight through the terminal to the curb, where a row of taxis was waiting. He stepped in front of a tourist couple and told the driver to take him to the Comfort Suites on the outside of town amid their protests.

As the taxi hurriedly pulled away from the curb, Collin checked the back window. An exasperated police officer arrived at the curb a bit too late. The officer strained his eyes to make out the numbers on the cab and began talking into a radio.

Fighting back the panic, Collin said, "Speed up, please. But don't get in trouble."

He kept checking the back window, then scanning the scene in front of them. Soon the ocean was visible on their left. In the distance, he spotted the tops of the tall masts of sailing ships and changed the destination. Remembering his escape from Petaluma Marina on Rob Howell's boat, he asked his cab driver, a kindly gentleman with more gray than black in his hair, to instead take him to the sailboat docks.

The cab driver nodded his head as a wide grin covered his face. "Ah, yes. Sailing is good for the soul. You made a good choice, man."

The cab wove its way through neighborhoods and past shopping areas. Collin grew antsy. At last, he could see the boats in the marina and began to believe that they might make it there before the cops caught up to them. "Drop me off here, please." The cab had not even come to a stop before Collin jumped out the door. As he did, Collin waved a one-hundred-dollar bill in front of the cab driver and asked him to avoid the airport for a while. With a knowing smile, the driver nodded and said, "Sure, man. Whatever the boss want."

Collin threw another twenty through the window and mouthed thanks as he yanked his bags over his shoulder and strode toward a group of men loitering on the docks. Near them a sign read: *Explore the sea on a private luxury sail cruise.*

As he approached them, he asked which one of them was the captain. They all shrugged and looked at each other. "Can I charter a private cruise, please?"

"Yeah, maybe. How many people in your group?" the oldest of them said.

"Just me. I need a ride to Jamaica."

"When do you need that ride?" came the incredulous response. "We do mostly sunset cruises, you know."

"Like, now would be good," said Collin as he glanced toward the road.

After the chuckles died down, the leader of the group said, "I can do that, but it's gonna cost you, man."

"How much?"

"Well, I need to take my crew here. I can't go that far without a good crew."

"Fine. How much?"

"Well, that's gonna be $20,000."

"Are you kidding? $20,000? Jamaica is not that far away. $10,000 and you got a deal."

"No way. It's gonna take me and my crew more than two days to make that round trip. We need to get paid for such service."

The wailing of sirens fast approached. Collin tensed and turned away from the street. "I'll give you 12,000 US dollars if we can leave right now and none of you breathes a word of this to anyone. You never saw me, you understand?"

The sirens grew closer. Collin checked his watch and moved into the shade where the men were congregated. The man noted his movements with a raised eyebrow.

"Make it $15,000 and you got a deal."

Screeching tires and blaring horns no more than a block away.

"Fine. But can we go *now?*"

The Captain eyed Collin warily. Collin shifted and squirmed as the noise from the approaching police cars grew louder. "I need time to reschedule tonight's passengers. We can't take off just like that."

Collin reached into his backpack and produced what looked like a thin brick made out of duct tape and tossed it to the Captain. "That's $10,000. I'll pay you the rest when we get there."

The Captain tore at the duct tape. A broad smile spread across his face. "Yeah, man. Get on the boat," he said as he pointed to a beautiful sixty-foot schooner parked in a slip thirty yards away. One of the men hopped to his feet. He fumbled for a key card in his pocket and swiped it in front of an electronic reader to swing open the painted wrought iron gate for Collin.

Collin practically ran down a grated, steel ramp and across a faux wood deck to the waiting boat, glancing over his shoulder as he went. The sirens approached and brakes screeched. Collin jumped aboard and ducked through the narrow passage into the quarters below decks.

The Captain ordered his men to double time it and cast off now. One of the men gave the boat a mighty push and jumped onboard as the Captain started the engine and steered his way into the channel. As they backed away, a police officer came running toward the dock. By the time he reached the locked gate, the boat was swinging around. Determined to do his duty, the officer found a nearby maintenance worker to open the gate. The men on the boat busied themselves and pretended not to see him. They were already two hundred yards away with their back to the marina when the officer reached the end of the dock. The cop yelled and waved his arms above his head in vain and finally threw his hat on the ground in defeat.

"Stay cool now," barked the Captain. "No hasty maneuvers. Got it? We don't want suspicions." At the same time, he motioned nonchalantly for Collin to remain where he was.

The Captain smiled proudly as the men worked the sails, ropes, and rigging on the deck, while he steered the boat out of the harbor as fast as its engine would allow. Once they cleared the breakwater, the crew unfurled and hoisted all sails, and before he knew it, Collin's personally chartered sail boat was moving along at an amazing clip. He came up to the deck at the Captain's bidding and stood near the stern, clutching the railing.

The Captain claimed it had a top speed of nearly twenty-four knots when the wind was right. "And the winds are favorable this morning," said the Captain with pride. "Yes, this is the fastest charter boat on the island. We can take you to Jamaica faster than any of them." His hand swept toward the marina behind them.

Collin couldn't gauge their speed, but the wind rushing through his hair and the sea spray wetting his face told him they were moving fast. His senses were alive. All of them. A sparkling, glittering sea of turquoise and the synchronized, almost orchestral movements of the four crew members dazzled him. His ears heard the rush of the warm air as they sliced a path through the water and the flapping of the mighty sails as they captured the wind and turned it into speed. Adrenaline coursed in his veins, tightening his muscles. Exhilaration spread through his chest at the thought of having outfoxed his pursuers again. His primal need to survive had kicked into high gear and was now guiding him down a previously unconsidered path. An unlikely path, given his Lukas-inspired want for planning and precision. Collin kept checking behind them, watching the harbor become smaller and smaller as the distance from the shore steadily grew. So far, so good. No one coming after them.

"We're near top speed now. Twenty-one knots at the moment," said the Captain, as he surveyed the GPS monitor.

"That's good. Thanks," Collin said, not sure what else to say. Would it be fast enough? Was anyone coming after him? Now that they were away from the island, speed meant little to Collin because the destination meant nothing.

Collin stood in silence, his brow knit and his forehead creased. The Captain studied his face and grinned.

The Captain was wise. He knew things. It showed in his eyes. He occupied himself with the usual captain-like activities, checking the compass, the GPS, and the radar. He eyed the masts and the sails and barked a few nearly incoherent orders to his crew, who were lounging on the bow.

Settling back into his chair, the skipper glanced over at Collin and said, "Everything's good. Nothing to worry about, man," he declared.

"I wish that were true," Collin muttered.

The Captain must have heard it. His eyebrows spiked up and the corners of his mouth turned down, but he said nothing.

Collin began to fidget. Sure, he was outdoors and they were moving, but there was nowhere to go, really. He turned his face into the wind and closed his eyes for a moment, taking in the warm, salty air in long, deep breaths.

The silence was broken by the Captain's baritone voice. "My name is Gordon Sewell. Welcome aboard the *Admiral Risty*."

Collin's eyes popped open, and he turned his head toward the sound, as if surprised. He saw the Captain's outstretched hand and grasped it. "Collin Cook. Pleasure to meet you."

"Was that fast enough for you, Mr. Cook?" "Oh, yes, yes. Very fast. Very fast indeed." "Worth $15,000?"

"The money. Do you need me to pay you the rest now?"

"No, that's not what I'm asking." The Captain chuckled, an amused smile spreading across his jet-black face.

Captain Sewell's warmth eased the tension, but Collin's face was still twisted in confusion.

"Look, man, it's none of my business. I get paid to take people sailing. You pay me lots, we go sailing fast. No problem. My crew and I can go fast, as you have seen now."

"Yes, and I thank you for that. Fantastic job." Collin regarded him cautiously.

The Captain returned his gaze with a look of concern. A moment later he said, "You know, I see some crazy stuff sometimes. Crazy stuff. Lots of it. It seems to find this place." Then with a flash of his white teeth, he added, "Like you."

"What do you mean, like me? I'm not crazy."

"No? You sure about that, man? You jump out of that taxi all excited and willing to pay big money to get off the island. You think that's not crazy?"

"When you put it that way, sure it seems crazy. But I'm not. I'm quite normal. I just want to sail to Jamaica."

"Yeah, man. That's right. You just need to sail to Jamaica right now, and you need me to forget I ever saw you. Cops come speeding up behind you. Yeah, that's not crazy."

"OK. I needed to get off the island, and I'm willing to pay $15,000 to do so. I've got my reasons, even if it seems a bit crazy." Collin felt the need to deflect the attention from himself and move to another topic. "What's the craziest thing you've seen?"

With only a moment's pause, the veteran seafarer came back with a story. In his heavy Caribbean accent, the Captain unwound a tale. "I lost a boat to pirates once. That was crazy. They came up, two of them speedy boats. One on each side. They yelling and screaming. They was crazy, I knew it right away. I just do what they say." The Captain looked off in the distance, gazing at nothing in particular but squinting toward the horizon. "They look through my boat, searching for drugs or money or other stuff they can use. Then they burn it. Burn it, I say. Just like that."

"How'd you get away?"

"I used the dinghy. They let me and my crew get in the dinghy—four grown men in a tiny rubber boat in the middle of the ocean. That was a bad day, man." He chuckled, but behind the chuckle was a grimace. He drew in his breath through clenched teeth, shaking his head. "Yeah, that was a crazy bad day."

Collin searched for the right thing to say, but before he knew it, he was uttering the words, "Wow. That must've sucked."

The Captain's countenance dropped; then his gaze turned to Collin and fixated on his mouth for a moment. His face grew tense as he surveyed Collin. He squinted hard and bit his lip. All of a sudden, he let out a boisterous laugh. "You damn right, man! That really sucked! Like you wouldn't believe, it sucked!" he blurted out between chortles.

The two men laughed together for several minutes. Collin laughed because the Captain was laughing. He laughed harder when he realized how horribly wrong this exchange could have gone. The laughter didn't come easily at first. He hadn't laughed much in the past ten months.

Once the jocularity subsided, Collin asked his next question, "How'd you get through it? I mean, how long were you out there, and how'd you, you know, make it?"

The perceptive Captain went on and told the story. His voice was soft, and it reminded Collin of the way his dad often told stories, slowly and deliberately, making a point. Captain Sewell explained that they spent one very long day and an even longer night bobbing at sea before they were spotted and picked up by a fishing boat. Luckily for them, the seas were calm that day.

He put in a claim with the insurance company and got this boat, like new, paid for mostly by insurance money. Now, business was better than it had ever been. This boat was larger, more stylish, faster, and much, much prettier to look at. This, he was sure, helped him attract the rich American and European clients.

"So, I guess, them pirates helped me. That day sucked, but better days came because of it." Captain Sewell stopped, letting the last sentence sink in, then turned and studied Collin's face before asking a question of his own. "What brings you here? Why Cayman?"

Collin was slow to respond, his mind still caught on what the Captain had said about his life being better since his run-in with the pirates. His life going forward, Collin had come to believe, would amount to nothing more than running from unknown people. Survival in a game of hide-and-seek. That was it. That was all he could see. Finally, he worked out an answer to the Captain's question.

"I don't know. I just like it. Always have, ever since I first heard about it when I was a kid." Collin looked back at the man who was obviously waiting for more. "Well, you know, they advertise it a lot in the dive shops, and when my buddies and I were getting certified for SCUBA, the Cayman Islands were talked about as 'the place' to dive. So, I decided that one day when I had the money, I'd come here."

"That's rubbish, man. Pure rubbish. You know what I mean. What are you doing here?"

Collin struggled with what he should tell a stranger. But he needed an ally, and this guy was reaching out. He looked up from his shoes and met the Captain's eyes. They were not harsh, critical eyes. The man was curious and seemed to genuinely want to know more. "I find myself unexpectedly single and with enough money to travel in style. So here I am. Seeing the world."

Captain Sewell nodded his head knowingly and winked an eye. "Okay. Let me show you a little bit of our world. It's beautiful, no?" He swept his hand in an arc and smiled proudly.

Collin smiled, too. A new relationship was forming. The first new relationship in a year.

It felt good.

The sense of safety and peace returned. If only for a short time.

CHAPTER SEVEN

LONDON, ENGLAND
MAY 3

Nic Lancaster hustled into Alastair Montgomery's cramped office. At twenty-eight, Nic was the youngest and most ambitious investigator on Alastair's handpicked team of corporate crime geniuses, but that was only part of the reason he was chosen for this special, potentially high-profile task. Always eager to further his career, Nic had caught his boss working around the rules, taking advantage of his position, and had threatened to hold it over him. Alastair knew the kid was bright. Bright enough, perhaps, to make them both look good fulfilling what seemed like a dreadful assignment. He decided last night, after his third drink, to give the kid the chance he was looking for. Maybe then Lancaster would stop hounding him.

"Nic, I have a special assignment for you," he said as he waved his hand in the direction of a chair on the other side of the desk. "There's an American on the loose in Europe that may have ties to the Komodos—the group from Southeast Asia that blindsided RBS last week. I need you to find him and bring him in. What do you say?"

"Right, boss. Finding an American in Europe is a special assignment?" said Nic.

"Well, yes, in fact, it is. He hasn't been seen in half a year. Not until five days ago, that is," said Alastair, ignoring Nic's skepticism.

"Right. I'll drop everything to find this chap who's lost his way. It's got all the elements of a monumental international crisis." Nic's voice dripped with sarcasm.

"Look here, chum. The FBI called from Los Angeles and asked for our cooperation. Top priority it is. They think he might lead us to some bigger fish."

"Oh, really? Like how big a fish?"

"Real big. The kind of big fish that could launch one's career if he plays his cards right."

"Now we're talking. Who is this guy that can lead to the big fish, and what do we know about him?"

"His name is Collin Cook. We know that he disappeared from his home in Northern California back in November after his family was killed in a traffic wreck. Horrible thing, really. Must've turned him to the dark side. Regardless, two days before the RBS thing, he's photographed with the top man from this Asian crime ring that we have been trying to get our arms around. These photos surfaced Tuesday," Alastair said as he turned his computer monitor toward Nic and clicked his mouse. "They were taken at a pub in Kings Cross on Monday. This guy is Pho Nam Penh, the big fish I mentioned. An evil bloke bent on destroying Western lifestyle. Been branded a terrorist but hasn't been seen much. Keeps a very low profile ..."

"Wait a minute," said Nic, wagging a finger at the image on the screen. "That's the bloke connected to all those penny-skimming scams months ago, isn't it? He skimmed from dozens of European banks for months until we shut it down. Apparently, he's stepped it up, eh?"

Alastair's eyebrows lifted and his head nodded. "You know about this guy, do you?"

"A bit, yeah. But I'm sure there's more I don't know," said Nic. "Well, then you might also know that our investment banks have suffered the wrath of his attacks, as have others in Germany, France, Australia, and, of course, the United States. He's slick, real slick. He's made us look like fools for months now."

"You want me to go after Pho Nam Penh and break up his operation?" asked Nic, rubbing his hands together. "Sounds quite high profile. I like it."

"I know you're ambitious, Nic. But for now, just find the American. Follow him, try to figure out the connection, if there is one, and let him lead us to Penh. Shouldn't be that difficult really. This guy was nothing but a salesman a year ago."

Nic stroked his chin, a look of warm satisfaction spreading across his boyish face. The lights were on and the wheels were turning. His lucky break. As he stood, he looked again at the photo on the screen and said, "I'm on it."

*　*　*　*

Nic strode purposefully down the hallway back to his cubicle, chin up and chest out. Nic wasn't big on exercise and didn't see the sun often. As a child, he had been rather sickly. The result was an unimpressive physique that was pasty white and thin as a tent pole. The thinning hair didn't help, either. What he lacked physically, he made up for in effort and cunning. He wiggled and stretched his fingers as he sat in front of his computer. "Here we go. Collin Cook, you're mine now," he said out loud. Alastair's warning that there was no evidence against Cook went unheeded.

The clicking of his mouse and keyboard continued nearly unabated until late afternoon, searching and reading and learning all he could about Collin Cook, Pho Nam Penh, and the Komodo syndicate. The news stories about the cyber-attacks were vicious in their treatment of Interpol and Scotland Yard, calling them "an incompetent lot" and "asleep at the controls." Their reports decried it a disgrace that the culprits were still at large after bringing one of Europe's preeminent financial institutions to a grinding halt for nearly a day. Billions of pounds of lost income and lost opportunity had yet to be punished.

No one seemed to know much about this Pho Nam Penh chap or his band of operators, known as the Komodos. The news outlets never mentioned him by name. The intra-agency bulletins made reference to the group as suspects in various cyber-crimes and hack attacks, including the penny-skimming scam. As of yet, no law enforcement agency had collected the kind of solid evidence that could support a warrant for any arrests, cease and desists, or other sanctions. Penh and the members of his enigmatic band had proven so elusive that surveillance and tracking were not possible.

Turning his attention to another enigma, Nic searched Collin Cook online and found a trove of news articles. As he read, Nic discovered Collin's tragic but well-chronicled story on the local Bay Area news stations' websites. He learned that Amy Cook and her three children were returning to their Petaluma home after celebrating the Fourth of July at her family's Lake Tahoe cabin. A semi-truck hauling twenty tons of rock from the highway construction project on Interstate 80 lost control and tumbled onto the minivan Mrs. Cook was driving. The pictures were horrifying. The Toyota Sienna was flattened. Nic paused to catch his breath. Curiosity piqued, Nic continued to read. Another article reported that Collin Cook was hospitalized after being found unconscious on his living room floor in a pool of his own blood and vomit by a California Highway Patrol Officer investigating the accident. The officer was dispatched to the Cook home when Mr. Cook did not answer CHP calls. It was discovered through phone records that Mr. and Mrs. Cook were on the phone to each other at the time of the accident. Nic stopped again. He couldn't help but feel for this guy. No wonder he came unhinged.

The last article he read summarized the mysterious disappearance of the same Collin Cook. It recapped the tragedy and quoted the concerned parents of Mr. Cook who asked for help bringing their son home. That was shortly after Thanksgiving. Mr. Cook reportedly received an insurance settlement estimated to be more than $25 Million, according to unnamed sources.

I guess he took the money and ran, thought Nic. Why not? Seemed like a nice enough guy according to all accounts, but don't they all, up until they cross the line?

With his findings on the two men fresh in his mind, Nic tried to surmise the mysterious link between Penh and Collin Cook. Why? Why would an average Joe like Collin Cook start colluding with an enemy like Pho Nam Penh? Nic had to make sense of it, but none of it fit together. Yet.

*   *   *   *

Alastair Montgomery had spent the entire day in and out of meetings with his superiors and his subordinates. Non-stop status updates on this RBS thing. It was enough to drive a man insane. There were too many demands, too many opinions, and not enough credible information to act on. All the media frenzy, all the accusations, all the commotion had taken its toll. His head felt like it might explode. He needed a drink.

As Alastair draped his coat over his arm and hefted his computer bag, Nic Lancaster swept breathlessly into his office waving a stack of papers. "Sir, I think I'm onto something," he said.

"What have you got there, Nic?" said Alastair. His eyebrows rose, but his facial expression remained unchanged.

"This is a list of banks in the Caribbean that have received an influx of electronic funds transfers into numbered accounts during the three days after the RBS attack. I've eliminated all but those that received at least $1 million in a single transaction."

"That's great, Nic. What do you plan to do with that information?"

"I've informed these banks that we're tracking down the funds that were stolen from RBS."

"And what's that going to do? You don't expect them to jump up and say, 'Oh, yes, we'd be glad to give your money back'? Is that where you're going with this, Mr. Lancaster?"

"No, sir. But, with your permission, I'd like to put a temporary freeze on all electronic transfers out of those bank accounts without verification of identities of the accountholders," Nic said, his eyes pleading.

"What makes you think they'll cooperate? We don't have that kind of jurisdictional authority."

"Maybe not, but it should give them a pretty good scare. I'm willing to bet some will cooperate. Who knows, maybe I'll catch a lucky break. I figure I'll send out that photo of Collin Cook, the American you wanted me to track down, and see if I get any bites."

"Fine, Nic. Good luck with that," Alastair said as he moved toward the open door. "Time you be getting home, too. It's past eight o'clock."

"Right, sir. I'll just finish up a few things here, then head out."

Alastair gave Nic a quizzical look as the young investigator spun and headed down the hallway.

Nic checked his watch as he marched back to his cubicle. It was still mid-afternoon in the Caribbean. He could reach at least half the banks on his list before they closed. Maybe he would get lucky. It was worth a try.

* * * *

NEAR KINGSTON, JAMAICA
MAY 3

As the *Admiral Risty* approached the outer harbor at Kingston, Jamaica, seagulls circled above, cawing and squawking, their white bodies gliding effortlessly overhead against the backdrop of blue sky. Captain Sewell stood beside his chair in the cockpit and surveyed the area near the docks through his high-powered binoculars, scanning back and forth. His countenance grew stern. "There is an unusual amount of activity on shore, over there, near the commercial fishing dock," he said as he pointed with his finger. "I'll go check it out, make sure everything's OK." He handed the binoculars to Collin and continued to indicate the area of concern.

"I've never been here, so I don't know what's unusual for this place," said Collin.

"I'm telling you, that crowd and all that activity is different." Turning to his crew, he ordered Tog and Mickey to prepare the dinghy. He returned his focus to Collin. "Might be nothing. Who knows? For your own safety, you should stay here until I return."

Collin's face turned serious. "I guess, if you think that's best," he said, running his hand through his hair. He did not want to step into another trap.

"The three of us will go ashore to see what it's all about. You stay here with Rojas and Jaime. But, you must stay out of sight, below deck, until we return. Rojas, show him the hiding place, just in case."

* * * *

Below deck, Collin switched on his phone for the first time since boarding the boat. He wanted to save his battery with no signal at sea. As the phone powered up and locked into satellite reception, three message alert chimes sounded. All from Lukas, of course. The first one read: *Sorry I missed your call. Busy with another urgent matter. Did you land safely?*

The second one read: *Where are you going? You should be at the Comfort Inn.*

The time stamp on the last one was roughly twelve hours after the second message. It read: *The money in Grand Keys Bank is not safe. Need to move it right away.*

Relieved to have something to keep him occupied so he wouldn't feel like a captive, Collin opened his laptop and used the signal from his phone to get on the Internet and do some research of his own. He read bulletins on a few reliable web pages for information but found nothing pertinent to Grand Keys Bank. *London Herald*, however, quoted a source close to the investigation into the Royal Bank of Scotland fiasco as saying that Interpol was examining all of the major banks in the Caribbean, looking for suspicious activity. They had, in fact, ordered an injunction against all non-verified electronic transactions out of the banks until Interpol could sort out the origination point of the monies in question.

After reading two other articles that alluded to the banking situation, Collin rang Lukas. "What do I need to do?" he asked as soon as Lukas answered.

"Whoa, you're OK? That's great. I was worried," said Lukas. "You've been off the grid a long time. What happened?"

"Are you referring to the cops in George Town?"

"Yeah. That was an unexpected coincidence, I'm afraid." "What do you mean?" asked Collin.

"The cops over there got a tip that a fugitive from Europe was on his way to their island, so they were searching all inbound flights from the continent to find a foreigner wanted for embezzlement. Anyway, it's a good thing you got out of there. The cops are pretty antsy," said Lukas.

"Yeah, I noticed that. I barely slipped through."

"The large police presence is not altogether surprising. The guys at Interpol are really stirring things up. They are getting slaughtered in the British press, so they're scrambling to make an arrest ASAP. And the banks in Grand Cayman make a tidy living catering to wealthy British businessmen and corporations. This RBS thing has created a panic in the UK, and I'm sure the West Indies are feeling pressure to cooperate. So, how'd you get out of there, anyway?"

"Chartered a private sail boat," said Collin.

"Good thinking, my friend. Take to the seas. There are a million boats out there. Hard to track. That's brilliant."

Collin gave Lukas a brief synopsis of what had happened and how he escaped. "We're anchored a mile from the mouth of Kingston Harbor. There seems to be quite a bit of activity on shore. Any ideas on what's going on?"

"No, but you don't have time to go ashore, anyway."

"Yeah, I saw your last text. What should I do?" asked Collin.

"You need to get back to George Town and get your money out of the Grand Keys Bank. My sources tell me that the new directive from Interpol is to lock down all electronic transfers that have come into the banks since the RBS attack. Didn't you just move some money into Grand Keys Bank last week?"

"Yeah, about $1.5 Million on top of the $1.3 I deposited there originally. It seemed like a safe place."

"It is. Or *was*. Now all these offshore banks are being scrutinized. Especially the ones with strong ties to the UK. It'd be best to get your money somewhere safer," Lukas said. There was the familiar sound of keys tapping in the background.

"Any suggestions?"

"My operatives in the field have always used The InterCon Bank in Panama City. It panders to uber-wealthy Americans and those who have a need for secrecy. You'll fit their client profile perfectly. I'll alert my contact there to your impending arrival."

"Wow, such royal treatment," quipped Collin.

"After a couple of close calls, you need something to go smoothly. The difficult thing will be getting your money out of Grand Keys. You'll have to take a cash withdrawal and move it physically to Panama. Can you do that?"

"I think so," said Collin, scanning the walls around him, knowing something of the secrets this vessel contained. From what Rojas had shown him about the boat's special features, Collin felt some assurance.

"Going by boat seems the best option. You trust the people you're with?"

"Do I have much choice?"

"Not really. But you better get back to George Town as quickly as you can. There's no time to waste."

"Got it," Collin said without hesitation. He had no idea how he would pull this off, but he didn't want Lukas to worry unnecessarily. "But it'll be dark here soon."

"Then sail through the night." "You're not kidding, are you?"

"No, I'm not. And call me as soon as you're done."

"No problem," Collin said, continuing the illusion that he knew what he was doing.

The next ninety minutes went by faster than he could have hoped, mainly due to his preoccupation with researching and recording details, gathering the information he would need to protect the only two things he had left—money and freedom. Captain Sewell and the others pulled up in the dinghy just as Collin finished his planning work. He was anxious to get back to Grand Cayman to execute his plan. It took some convincing and another $10,000 to persuade the Captain and crew to sail through the night. Once the financing was settled, they were anchors up and heading back the way they came. The sun was a glowing orange ball hanging just above the horizon as they set their course north by northwest for Grand Cayman.

Collin hoped to arrive without the police welcoming committee this time.

CHAPTER EIGHT

CARIBBEAN SEA
MAY 4

Collin was roused at midnight for his shift. He, the Captain, and Jaime would man the controls for the next four hours. Collin had watched and learned several of the many tasks required of a sailor. He also recalled much of what he had learned about sailing as a youth.

With only two sails deployed for a nighttime voyage, the boat was traveling much slower than it had on the way to Jamaica. There was not much to do between tacks. The moon overhead cast its white light across the water, creating a tranquil ambiance.

Collin stood amidships and fussed with a length of rope, knotting it and unknotting it repeatedly as the Captain watched in the moon's glow. "Where'd you learn to tie knots like that?" he asked.

"Boy Scouts," Collin replied without looking up.

"I knew you were different. Not like most clients."

"Oh, really? What are most of your clients like?"

"Most are rich, spoiled, and rude. But not you. You're just rich."

"What makes you think I'm not spoiled and rude?"

The Captain chuckled. Then, pointing at the rope in Collin's hand, said, "Not many of them can do that."

Collin just shrugged and tied another knot, which brought another chuckle from Captain Sewell.

"And not many of them make me sail through the night for that matter," said the Captain as he checked his GPS monitor. The glow from the screen illuminated the Captain's face with an eerie, purplish light.

"See? I'm spoiled." Collin looked out over the dark horizon and turned his face into the soft, warm breeze. "But look at what a beautiful night it is. Perfect for sailing."

This elicited another chortle from Sewell. "And that's another thing I noticed. You see the good. You don't complain. That's different, I tell you. Different than most of my passengers." The Captain studied Collin for a moment. "Why are you running, Mr. Cook? What kind of trouble finds such a decent man?"

Collin set the rope down and held onto the rail as the boat pitched into a swell. Wiping spray from his face, he replied, "The usual trouble, I guess."

"Be straight with me, Mr. Cook. I know you are not a criminal. But you behave very peculiarly. What's your story, man?"

"My story? You don't want to hear my story."

"Sure I do. Come on, what brings you here? What makes you run?"

Collin turned back toward the man piloting the boat. *Tell him or not?* The Captain was nothing if not a captive audience, Collin considered. But there was more to it than that. Although his skin was a different color, this man was much like his father. Business-like, yes. Hard on the surface, yes. But inside, Collin could tell, this man was one that could be counted on and trusted for his wisdom and honesty. There was an inner kindness the Captain could not hide. He was not a big talker, but he had experience and would only dispense advice when it was sought from him. He had already helped Collin and seemed willing to continue. With all that swirling around him, Collin knew it couldn't hurt to make this man an ally. Maybe it was time to open up.

He had only recounted the story in bits and pieces, never in its entirety. No one had heard the sad tale beginning to end. Sure he had been interrogated during a deposition in his attorney's conference room, bombarded by representatives from both the construction and the insurance companies. It was recorded. Cameras and microphones pointed at him; question after question was asked, then rephrased, and asked again. It was excruciating. Not something he ever wanted to experience again. He did not like the fact that he had been forced to talk, forced to answer inane questions, and forced to break down over and over again. It was a humiliating sob fest. Something he would never repeat.

And still, there were parts of the story that no one knew.

In the ten months since the tragedy, he had not spoken of it in depth to anyone else—not even his own parents or siblings. His best friends in the world, Rob Howell and Lukas Mueller, knew most of the story but not all.

Shifting his weight, he turned his eyes outward to the ocean and his thoughts inward. In that moment, Collin realized for the first time how completely he had shut off the outside world. He hadn't talked much to anyone. Nor had he felt the need to share with anyone. It was painful. Disturbing images, in hauntingly graphic detail, bubbled up from within every time he thought about what happened.

He shuddered and faced the Captain, whose eyes were wide, searching, and full of curiosity, not judgment.

Collin spoke slowly and recounted the whole thing, starting with the fight before Amy went to Tahoe for the Fourth of July week. He explained how the pressures of his crummy sales job and the strain of their financial situation had led to near constant tension in their marriage. He spoke of Amy and her beauty, her energy, and her caring spirit. He praised her for being his strength and his staunchest supporter for so many years. He blamed himself for dropping out of college and for not knowing what he wanted to do with his life and never having a job that satisfied him or their family's growing financial needs.

"So, what happened? Now you have money, but where is your wife?" asked the Captain.

Collin grew quiet again, searching his thoughts and choosing his words. "I was an idiot. I almost threw the whole thing in the garbage." Collin's gaze was far away, pointed at the horizon ahead, but focused on nothing. For some reason, he wanted the Captain to have the full picture, to know what was going on inside as well. He shook his head as a wave of shame passed through him, then continued. "I had this friend, a female friend. Actually, she's more than a friend. She was my girlfriend in high school. My first love. The girl I always thought I'd marry. She dumped me after graduation, which wrecked me. Amy saved me a year later." Collin paused and surveyed the Captain's face. Without words his expression begged Collin to continue the story.

"Her name was—is—Emily. She called me and said she was in San Francisco and wanted to invite me and Amy to dinner."

"Your ex-girlfriend invited you and your wife to dinner?"

"Yeah, believe it or not, the three of us were friends, although my wife was always wary of Emily."

His heart sank to his toes as the memory of that evening snailed its way through his conscience, starting with the words he had uttered on the phone that evening ten months earlier: "Sure, that sounds good. I'll see you around eight."

It was supposed to be —harmless—two friends having dinner together. Problem was this was Emily Burns, now Dr. Emily Burns, who could've become Dr. Emily Cook. She was mesmerizing in every way: gorgeous, brilliant, and fun to be around. Even her voice was captivating. Hearing it had actually made his heart skip a beat.

The other problem was that Amy had been at Tahoe all week with the kids. It was supposed to have been a family vacation. But with his job on the line, he had to close the Renfro account or be fired and that would only compound the misery. It was the end of a long, lonely, and difficult week. Not the best time to hang out with his ex.

The restaurant lived up to the rave reviews. The food was the best he had ever tasted and the conversation was engaging. Emily was passionate about her work and enthusiastic about her hobbies, several of which she and Collin shared. They reminisced about high school and relived some of the pranks they pulled and the fun times they had together.

As the evening wore on, Emily accepted every offer from the waiter to top off her glass of wine. As the alcohol took effect, the conversation became more personal, more emotional, and more intimate. She told him how none of her relationships had worked out. None of the men she had dated seemed to have their act together. She confessed that none of them measured up to the standard Collin had set. "There's no one like you left out there, Collin," she had said. He struggled to recover from that comment. It was as if his heart had shifted within him and now beat in a strange, but oddly familiar, new rhythm. She was in a silly mood, giggly and flirtatious. It scared Collin.

Inch by inch, Collin felt himself being pulled into the tantalizing orbit of Emily Burns. Everything about her was exciting, exacerbated by his weakened and lonely condition. In many ways, he felt his life was crumbling around him while she seemed to generate a certain magnetic charge that pulled him closer.

The candlelight, her perfume, the soft music in the background, and the good food they had enjoyed, all worked together to create a very pleasing glow, a palpable sense of belonging and closeness. Alarms were going off in Collin's head, but he pushed them aside, rationalizing his choice to stay by telling himself she really needed a friend right now.

When Emily started to slur as she flirted with him, Collin put an end to the conversation.

"I need to go, but first I'll help you to your room so you can sleep this thing off," he said as he stood and held out his hand for her.

Emily heaved a sigh and gripped his outstretched hand as if it were a rescue buoy being thrown to a drowning victim. Her hands were soft but her grip was firm. She didn't let go, even after gaining her balance. It felt good, and a thrill ran through him. She needed him; she really needed him. As a friend, he told himself. But it felt good. As he pulled her up from her seat, she eased up against him and leaned her head on his shoulder. Before he knew what was happening, he found his arm wrapped around her slim waist, and the two of them were striding out the door onto Polk Street. She was staying at the Sir Francis Drake Hotel, just around the corner. At $500 a night, it was apparent she was doing very well.

Despite that fact, Emily was lonely and needy and drunk. She leaned on him for support, in more ways than one, as they walked through the opulent lobby. In the elevator, she draped her arm over his shoulder and by the time they made their way down the hall to her suite, Collin was practically carrying her.

Always neat and organized, a quick dive of the hand into her designer purse was all it took for her to produce the card key, even ine-briated. As Collin opened the door and helped her into the room, she was increasingly amorous. Her vulnerability was in itself intoxicating. Her touch, her movements, her very presence was a turn-on. This was a dangerous place to be. His heart was pounding in his chest, and he was starting to sweat. It was even hard to swallow.

He hesitated after helping her through the doorway, propping the door open with his outstretched leg. Emily gave a squeeze, pulling him closer to her. Collin was already off balance, so with her tug, the door swung shut. He was in forbidden territory and he knew it. The will to escape the situation was draining from him with every beat of his heart.

"So, what happened with this friend?"

The Captain's voice pulled Collin out of his memory-induced daze. His eyes focused briefly on the Captain, then fell to the deck of the boat.

"I'm ashamed to admit what happened next."

"Did you sleep with her? Can't say I'd blame you if you did, but you don't seem like that kind of person."

"No, I didn't sleep with her. That would have been a complete disaster." Collin closed his eyes and let them memory run its course as he narrated. He remembered the conflicting feelings that gripped his heart like octopus tentacles when she wrapped both arms around his neck and pressed her slender body against his.

Her embrace felt good—too good. Her steel gray eyes locked onto his and froze him in place. There was so much in those eyes. He couldn't look away, let alone move. She pulled him in for another embrace, breathing against his neck and talking in a low, sultry voice. She wanted him to stay and keep her safe. She didn't want to be alone, she confessed. Neither did he, but he didn't tell her that. He wanted so badly to stay with her. The conflict within was paralyzing him and sending her the wrong message.

She kicked off her shoes as she looked him in the eye with that seductive gaze. He was trembling but couldn't look away. Their eyes were locked and their mouths were moving slowly toward one another.

Collin felt like a passenger in a speeding car with no brakes. Things were happening so fast he didn't have the ability to stop himself. His brain couldn't calculate, couldn't unwind, the swirling emotions within him. At the same time, it felt as if he were in slow motion. The moment was thick and ripe, the tension palpable.

The boat lurched and Collin stumbled as the bow plowed through a swell. Collin shook his head to clear the thoughts. "We had dinner. We talked. She got a bit tipsy. I walked her back to her room. We kissed. That's it, but it was enough to bring back old feelings and memories. It was wrong and I knew it, but I let it happen. I think we both wanted the evening to continue, but I finally got control of myself. It took every ounce of will power to pull away and leave before we got too carried away."

"You're a better man than most, Mr. Cook."

"I don't know about that. I should never have gone there. I should have left after dinner, but I didn't. I was too weak."

"What did she do?"

"She just sat down on the bed, covered her face with her hands, and started to cry, saying, 'I'm so sorry. This is all my fault.' She's not that type of person, either. I think we were both just in a bad spot—together at the same time, unfortunately."

"Okay, but that doesn't explain why you're here and why you now have money."

Collin sucked in a deep breath. This was the hard part. Even harder than explaining the darkness of his weakest moment. "Amy called me on her way down the mountain the next afternoon." He paused remembering how hard he worked to clean the house, hoping that by clearing the clutter he could also erase his misdeed in the process. "We had a good conversation. We apologized for the argument and agreed to work on patching things up and getting our marriage back on track. We talked about how much the kids missed having me there at the lake." Collin blew out a long breath as he struggled to control his voice. He spoke slowly in clipped sentences, battling emotions as he narrated the events that altered his world forever. As he spoke to the Captain, their last words ran through his mind.

A few moments passed while they each imagined how nice it would be to connect again. Collin broke the silence by asking, "Where are you now?"

"About halfway down the mountain. Just coming up to Colfax," she said.

"What are the kids doing?"

"Watching *The Princess and the Frog* again. They're mesmerized. I don't know how our parents did it without DVD in the car."

"I hear you. How are the roads?"

"Not too bad. There are more cars than I expected, though. And now we're slowing down for all those twisting curves. Oh, dear ..."

Collin heard her gasp. She came back, her voice shaky and breathless. "I came around one of those curves and everyone was stopped. I had to slam on the brakes and swerve to the right so I wouldn't ..."

Collin's blood turned to ice and his heart froze in place at the sounds he heard next. The high-pitched squealing of tires, the whine of a big rig's brakes when they are locked up and trying to stop a heavy load, followed by the screech of metal against metal. Rustling, rumbling, jarring sounds of large machinery toppling and scraping at high speed and a loud metallic crunch. The last thing he heard was Amy's panic-stricken voice scream at full force.

Then the line went dead and everything in Collin's world turned black and silent.

Reliving that moment nearly suffocated him, gripping his heart and lungs in an icy, vise-like lock. Each breath and each heartbeat was labored and agonizing afterward, an eternity passing before he could breathe normally again.

When he had recovered sufficiently, he summed up the story by mentioning the insurance settlement. He left out the dollar amount but indicated that he had enough money to live the rest of his life however he wanted.

"The only problems I have now are that I don't have anyone who needs me, and I have some really nasty people, including my own government, hunting me down. That's why I run."

Captain Sewell listened intently. When Collin looked at him, the Captain reached across the cockpit and put a hand on Collin's shoulder. He said, "As you wander, you're always welcome on my boat. You know how to help, and I know how to hide."

Collin uttered a soft thank you. He realized he had been talking nonstop for thirty minutes. His muscles had grown taut and were now aching.

CHAPTER NINE

Sarah was anxious to get on her way. She was never late for anything and did not want to start now. When she heard the garage door open, she rushed out, knowing Henry had returned. As he got out of the car, Sarah was holding the car door, eager to climb in. The silver Lexus had been washed, gassed, and had the tire pressure and oil level checked, Henry explained. As he stood, he wrapped an arm around her waist and pulled her into an embrace. His calm assurances that the car was ready and that she would be just fine gave her an undeniable measure of comfort. "Oh, and the restaurant's address is already plugged into the GPS," he added as she sat and swung her legs under the steering wheel.

She smiled at him as she shut the door and leaned out the window for a kiss. "You're so good to me, Henry," she said. "What would I do without you?"

Henry managed the details as if she was driving across the country when in reality the jaunt to La Jolla would take barely an hour. It just seemed longer because of her nerves. There was so much riding on this meeting, so much potential hope, so many unknowns. When she arrived in the parking lot, Sarah uttered a silent prayer before opening the car door. The café Emily had chosen was situated atop a hill, overlooking La Jolla's famed shopping area. From the number of cars in the parking lot, it appeared there was a crowd for lunch. The aroma in the air was rich with smells of fresh baked bread and grilled meat as Sarah entered the front door. She stood, waiting her turn at the hostess podium, when she spotted Emily weaving her way through the dining area. Sarah adjusted her purse on her shoulder, clasped her hands together in front of her, and tried to smile as naturally as possible.

Emily smiled, too, and threw her arms open wide for a hug. Sarah obliged stiffly. "It's so good to see you, Mrs. Cook," she said. "I'm so glad you came."

"Oh, please, call me Sarah. It's good to see you. Thank you for taking the time to meet me. I know you must be busy," Sarah said. She couldn't explain her nervousness if she tried, but Emily's sweet disposition had already helped calm her down.

"Oh, of course. It's my pleasure."

The two women made their way to the table, where they spent several minutes catching up on news and happenings. The conversation never veered toward Collin. Sarah was interested in learning about Emily's job, and Emily was excited to share with Sarah the recent break-through she and her research team had made.

After they placed their orders with the bubbly, young waitress, Sarah leaned forward. Her brow was knit, signaling a shift in tone, and she said, "Henry and I never had the chance to thank you for finding us in Alaska and informing us of the accident. That must have been quite a feat." A lump formed in Sarah's throat as she recalled the day last July when her and Henry's names were broadcast on the loudspeaker of the cruise ship, summoning them to the concierge office. The memory of Emily's shaky voice and her obviously memorized script came back in a flash.

"You know, with Facebook and Twitter, it didn't take long to find out from friends and neighbors where you were. I just did what anyone else would've done." Emily's tone matched Sarah's. It was somber and reverent. "I'm not so sure about that. But I do know that was a difficult task for you."

"It was. I hated to be the one to tell you, but I knew someone had to do it. It was the right thing," said Emily.

"Well, just know that Henry and I appreciate what you did. But, I have to admit, I have wondered what happened to you after that phone call. We didn't see you at the funeral or hear anything from you until just the other night." Sarah's eyes searched Emily's face but not in a judgmental way. Just honest curiosity.

Emily held her gaze. A twinge of guilt and sorrow passed behind her expression as she let out a sigh. A moment passed before she answered. "That was a difficult week for me. I was torn. I didn't know how to handle the situation. I was there in the hospital with Collin until the Armstrong's arrived. Then I felt in the way, so I left. I came back for the funeral but did not want to interfere. There were so many people ... I figured that it would be best if Collin didn't see me. He was confused enough when he woke up in the hospital and saw me there instead of Amy." Emily's eyes dropped to her hands, which had begun to fidget on the table.

"I didn't mean to make you uncomfortable, Emily. I'm just trying to understand why Collin took off," said Sarah.

"Why he *what?*" said Emily with a look of genuine surprise. "You didn't know that Collin was gone?"

"No, what do you mean 'gone?'" asked Emily.

"I mean, we haven't seen Collin for six months. He just vanished all of a sudden, and we don't know where he is."

"That's so unlike him. He's the most family-oriented guy I know …"

"Henry and I thought so, as well. We were stunned when we couldn't reach him before Thanksgiving. I realized the holidays would be especially difficult for him, but it tears my heart out to think that he spent them alone, without his family and friends around to support him."

"Certainly, you've heard from him, haven't you? Hasn't he explained where he is, or why he took off without telling anyone?" asked Emily.

"We get an occasional e-mail, but he never mentions where he is, or what he's doing, or why he left so suddenly. I assume from your reaction that you haven't heard from him, either."

"No, I haven't. This is all news to me. I find it very strange."

"You and I agree on that. I've wondered so many times what is going on in his mind. I just thought maybe you would know something more than we do."

"I wish I did, but I haven't spoken to Collin since the hospital."

"I guess I never figured out why you were there and why it was you who called us in Alaska," Sarah said. Her face showed her puzzlement as she wondered out loud.

Emily paused, trying to decide how much to tell Collin's mother, while feeling the burden that needed to be lightened. She knew she needed to explain her presence that day. "Well, you see, Collin and I had dinner together the night before the accident, so the police found my number in his phone and called me. They wouldn't tell me anything, though, so I was just as confused as Collin was. I had to piece things together. Then I felt I had to reach out and tell you. But after that, it was awkward."

"In what way?" asked Sarah, more directly than she intended.

Emily stopped. Her head drooped and she clasped her hands on the table in front of her. Her gaze shifted from the table to Sarah's face. "I don't know how else to say this, and I hope you don't take this wrong. Collin and I realized we still had strong feelings for each other. I guess we just rediscovered those feelings that night during dinner. I'm sorry …" Her voice trailed off and her eyes shifted again.

Sarah's mouth opened; her eyes widened. "I … I didn't know …"

Emily shifted in her seat, her hands toying with her silverware. "It's not like that," she quickly added.

Sarah fixated on Emily's fidgeting hands. "That would perhaps help explain some of Collin's behavior."

"Now, Sarah, you must understand. Nothing happened. Collin was a total gentleman. It was my fault. I kissed him and I shouldn't have. But that's it. He didn't let it go on. He left right away." Emily's voice was soft and full of self-accusation.

Sarah's face froze. "Oh my," she gasped. One hand went up to her ear and fussed with her hair as she looked away.

Emily's fingers fumbled with her spoon until it dropped and hit her plate with a loud clank. Sarah jumped in response. Emily grabbed the spoon and returned it to its place. "Please don't blame Collin, Sarah. I had too much wine that night and, well, I guess I was too forward. It's just that I realized during that conversation what a great friend he is, and I felt for the first time in a long time that someone actually cared about me as a person, for who I am. He sees me as *Emily*, not as Dr. Burns. That's just so refreshing, so comforting. I felt a connection with something other than my work, a connection to a human being, to a friend that I have really missed. It's terrible what I did."

Sarah sat up straight and breathed in as she squared her shoulders. Her brow was knit and her countenance stuck somewhere between shock and pain. An uncomfortable quiet ensued for what must have felt like an eternity for Emily. Finally, Sarah broke the silence and spoke with a steely, stoic voice. "Well, that explains a few things." She took another moment to reflect before she continued. Her voice was softer now, more contemplative. "Now, Emily, we mustn't dwell on our mistakes. It's in the past now."

Emily considered Sarah's words, taking in her expression and her tone. She exhaled and Sarah wondered how long it had been since she last breathed in. "You can imagine why I felt uncomfortable and had to go. Poor Collin had a lot to deal with as he regained consciousness. He didn't need me around making matters worse. After I contacted you and the Armstrong's arrived, I figured my being there would do nothing but complicate things for him. That's why I left without saying goodbye and why I stayed in the background at the funeral. I assumed Rob would have told you I was there."

"No, Rob didn't mention it. In fact, we haven't heard much from Rob, either. But he's always traveling, it seems." Sarah paused a moment, then changed course. "Emily, I have tried everything I know to convince Collin to come home. He won't respond to my e-mails when I plead with him. I can't call him. His old cell phone number has been given to someone else now. And he hasn't friended me on Facebook yet. I know he must be hurting, but he doesn't seem to be coping very well on his own. I think his disappearing is a symptom of something more serious. He needs help, professional help, but he won't listen to my suggestions."

Emily sat still. Her hands were no longer fidgeting. Instead, they were clasped together on the edge of the table as she leaned forward against them. "Maybe this is what he needs—to be away from everything familiar for a while. This is just his way of working through things. I'm sure he'll come home as soon as he feels he's ready to handle being around people."

Sarah considered Emily's words for a moment, her head slowly nodding as she did. "You may be right, Emily. Maybe what he needs is time. I wish I had that luxury."

Emily's face twisted before she asked, "What do you mean by that, Sarah?"

"I don't want to break the news to Collin in an e-mail, and I don't want him to come home just because of it. I want him to come home because he wants to be home—with his family."

"Okay, I would agree with that, but what news are you referring to?"

Sarah's eyes were gentle but resolute. "I was diagnosed with cancer two weeks ago."

Emily tried to mute her astonishment, but she let out an audible gasp and uttered no under her breath.

Sarah continued, "Yes. We're treating it aggressively and hoping we can beat it, but we're unsure yet how well my body will respond. If it doesn't work, I may only have a few months to live."

CHAPTER TEN

GEORGE TOWN, GRAND CAYMAN
MAY 4

The *Admiral Risty* slid quietly into its slip at George Town Marina before five o'clock a.m. Collin prepared himself by reviewing his carefully devised plan on his computer, a plan put together without any help from Lukas. In the predawn darkness, Collin memorized, from his meticulously detailed fact sheet, the names, phone numbers, addresses, and account numbers he would need.

At 6:30 a.m., Collin emerged from below deck with a clean set of clothes that made him look like a wealthy tourist. The sky above was an azure blue with the golden sun just beginning to push its way above a line of silver clouds on the eastern horizon. A slight breeze blew from the southwest, warm and fragrant. The smell of the sea mixed with the island flora to create that uniquely Caribbean scent. The marina was full of majestic sailboats and proud yachts, lines and pulleys clanking gently in the morning breeze. As he looked around, he could see no one else moving about.

For the first time since he began his life on the run, Collin walked without his computer and its carrying case on his shoulder. He didn't need it and felt it would only slow him down. The Captain was an honorable man and promised to remain at the marina until Collin returned. He also promised to guard the bag and the computer. A trust had been forged, and Collin knew he had nothing to worry about.

Collin told the Captain he'd be back by eight o'clock. He felt quite bare without his computer bag despite the trust in Captain Sewell and his crew. In fact, all he had on him was a wad of cash and a forged passport with a fake name. Nonetheless, he carried himself with a sense of confidence and purpose.

Collin was lucky enough to find a cab parked near the docks as he strode toward the main road that led back to town. His mind was focused and all synapses were firing, planning for contingencies.

Acting like every other impatient and entitled American tourist, Collin approached the taxi. He woke the sleeping driver and explained that he had to make several stops. The taxi driver grumbled about being awakened, but Collin shrugged that off and promised to make it worth his while, holding two one hundred-dollar bills between his fingers.

The first stop was at the large outdoor market area. The shops were closed and wouldn't open for a couple of hours the cab driver informed him. But after Collin illustrated his urgency by waving another hundred-dollar bill, it turned out there was a friend of the driver's who owned an army surplus store. He would open early if there was a reason convincing enough.

"Perfect," said Collin. "Take me there, please".

The army surplus store was only a few blocks away, and the driver forewarned the owner with a brief phone call. Collin was able to settle his business with the man quickly, leaving him smiling broadly and giving his friend, the cab driver, a thumbs-up.

The second stop wasn't so much a stop as a drive-by. He ordered the driver to pass through the downtown area so he could scope out the bank that he would soon be visiting. He wanted to make sure no one was there. Early on a Saturday morning, he knew that was unlikely, but he had to erase any doubts. From there he asked the cabbie to drive him to the wealthy part of town, where garish white and columned mansions hid from sight behind massive walls, imposing gates, and stately trees. They wove their way through the neighborhood, the houses growing larger and farther apart as they climbed up a hillside. Once the correct house was located, Collin jumped out and handed the cab driver the two hundred-dollar bills, which produced a large, toothy grin from the heretofore grumpy man. As the taxi drove away, Collin pulled out the cheap cell phone with the pre-paid minutes he had purchased at the surplus store and dialed a number from memory. He connected as the cab disappeared from view.

"Mr. Catangan, sir?" he said with all the authority and clout he could muster. "You don't know me, but I have approximately $2.8 million dollars deposited in your bank. I have reason to believe that my security and the security of my money have been compromised. I need you to meet me at the end of your driveway and take me to your bank right away. You have sixty seconds to comply."

"Who are you? And how did you get my personal cell phone number?"

Ignoring the question, Collin continued, following the script from memory. "Like I said, I am one of your clients. Your bank has had usury of my money for nearly two years." This was a stretch and he knew it, but it sounded better than six months. "I believe this has been a benefit to you. If you do not want the United States government combing through your records, you will come out here immediately and take me to your bank."

"I don't believe your story. Why would I?" the bank president protested.

"Because the federal government of the United States is anxious to find and tax offshore accounts. I understand Interpol is doing the same. They are searching for accounts such as mine and people who aid and abet people like me. They can and have shut down others. They can and will shut you down if you don't comply with my wish. All I have to do is tip them off. You know that I'm right, sir. I mean you no harm, and I expect you to treat me with respect and understanding as one of your clients. All I ask is that you escort me to your bank and help me withdraw my money so that you and I can both avoid a lengthy and uncomfortable investigation. If I can't get to my money, sir, I'll make sure that you and your bank suffer the consequences. The authorities would be more than willing to listen to my story. Is that reason enough?"

"I'll be right out."

The gamble paid off.

The heavy wrought iron gate shuddered momentarily, then began its arduous sweep inward toward the finely manicured lawn. The driveway curved slightly to the left toward the house. Collin followed it impatiently, not knowing what to expect. Maybe an armed guard, maybe a vicious dog. Instead, a very calm and dignified man, tall but portly, stood five feet above him on the whitewashed porch. He wore a white, nylon, Nike warm-up suit that was tight across the midsection and bright red Nike jogging shoes. His skin was dark and his countenance even darker. Thick arms crossed his chest; beady eyes watched Collin intently.

"This is highly unusual," came the booming voice of a man who clearly held the upper hand as Collin approached the steps.

"My life is highly unusual these days, sir," Collin responded quickly. These words and Collin's calm, non-threatening demeanor caught the bank president off-guard. Collin assessed this immediately and continued his narrative with a conciliatory, analytical tone. "What I said on the phone is true. You know it. I know it. Otherwise, you would not be standing here talking to me. Neither of us is in a very good position right now. With an election approaching in the United States and the recent cyber-attack on RBS, we both know it's only going to get worse."

The man nodded and unfolded his arms. Collin had stopped at the base of the steps to the porch. He had to tilt his head upward to make eye contact. The bank president squinted down at him through narrowed eyes. "Why not come to the bank during business hours?" asked Mr. Catangan.

"I was followed to George Town yesterday. The authorities know I'm here and are looking for me. I couldn't take the chance. It would have compromised my security and brought unwanted attention to your fine institution."

"So you did it for my protection?" Catangan said with a sarcastic chuckle.

"More for mine, to be honest. But this way you avoid embarrassment in front of your clients," explained Collin.

Catangan pondered for a moment as he eyed Collin up and down, taking in the whole stature of the person who was so bold and so clever as to find him at his home and to threaten him—no, his livelihood—in such a direct and disturbing way. Yet the man at the base of his porch did not appear to be a physical threat. There was no sign of a weapon, nor any talk of such. He was not large, imposing, ill-tempered, or aggressive. No, it was a much more intelligent threat, and that scared him sufficiently. This man, this invader, wore a flower print, button up shirt, khaki pants, a straw hat, dark Tommy Bahama sunglasses, and functional trail sandals. He looked like any other well-to-do American tourist. The only odd thing about him was the empty backpack hanging loosely from his shoulders.

"I suppose there's no harm in it," Mr. Catangan finally admitted, as he gave an ever-so-subtle gesture with his hand and eyes toward one of the windows at the far end of the porch.

In that instant, Collin realized there was someone watching them. Probably more than one person, too. This could have gone horribly wrong had he tried brute force.

"We go alone, just the two of us, to your bank, and we go now. Otherwise, I push *send*, and a very incriminating e-mail goes to the Commission on Banking and Commerce here in your country and the Federal Trade Commission in mine." Collin held his phone out with his thumb hovering over the screen.

"I understand. There is no need to get excited. I will comply with your wishes. I have no interest in provoking any investigations that could adversely affect my business. Now come with me."

Mr. Catangan nodded again nearly imperceptibly toward the window, then descended the stairs quickly and gracefully. Collin started backing up as soon as Catangan began to move but was surprised at how nimble and agile he was for such a large man. In an instant, the bank president was within a yard of Collin, and it was easy to see that he could close that distance in a flash if he wanted to.

This close, Catangan looked less fat and more athletic, though older. There were hints of white in the closely trimmed hair and beard that Collin hadn't noticed before. Probably about fifty, give or take a couple of years.

The bank president strode along the curving driveway, beneath the abundant foliage of a line of trees that hid his home from plain view of the street. Collin fell into step several paces behind. As he reached the garage door and began punching in a code, Mr. Catangan turned to Collin and asked, "Why don't you just transfer the money electronically? That's how the money got to my bank in the first place, isn't it?"

"Yes, it is. But it's those transactions, especially in large amounts, that Interpol is looking for."

"Do it in small amounts, then, over several days' time."

"I don't have that kind of time. They're here on the island, probing. Neither of us wants to draw their attention now, do we?" countered Collin.

"If you're worried about large transactions, doesn't it seem peculiar to pull out $2.8 million in cash? Don't you think that will raise some red flags?"

"It would if it weren't for the fact that your bank is well-known for its discretion, for protecting the privacy and identity of its customers. That's why I put so much money in your particular bank. You've earned a reputation and I'm sure you're motivated to keep it intact."

"You've done your research. Very well, have it your way. But be warned: the risk of walking through George Town with currency is great." "That's another reason we're doing this now and not during regular hours."

* * * *

After a short ride through town to the Grand Keys Bank of Grand Cayman, the two men climbed out of the sleek, black Land Rover and entered the bank through the back entrance long before any other employees arrived. Within twenty minutes, Collin exited the bank with his backpack full of US currency. $2.8 million dollars' worth.

He took off the silk button up shirt, revealing a well-worn, white T-shirt with a washed-out logo. Under the khaki pants, Collin sported faded cargo shorts. Swapping the wide brimmed, straw hat, he covered his head with a tattered baseball cap. He was now dressed as many of the American regulars on the island, including the sandals and the dark sunglasses. His hair was long enough to stick out in all directions from underneath the hat, covering his ears and his forehead. The sunglasses concealed much of his face, and the dark brown stubble helped disguise the rest of it. The backpack he had purchased at the army surplus store looked similar to what many locals and foreigners alike toted around.

Taking the money out was a risk Collin had to take. His research told him that the authorities were freezing suspicious accounts. That was not an acceptable alternative. The money meant much less to him than his family, but he knew it was vulnerable. He had to keep it away from the dreaded Komodos, if at possible.

The realization that this game was becoming increasingly danger-ous scared and thrilled him at the same time. With his own survival on the line, Collin's brain was engaged like never before. He felt alive instead of alone. He felt vital instead of miserable. Twice in two days he had outsmarted and outmaneuvered his pursuers and, although he was not entirely safe yet, his confidence was at an all-time high.

After walking a few blocks through the streets of George Town with a forty pound backpack bulging with concealed cash over his shoulders, catching menacing glances from several men, Collin's confidence evaporated. He could hardly hear anything except his heart beating, his pulse pounding in his ears. In that moment, he questioned the logic behind his decision, which only made things worse. Despite his attempts to relax, he could not control his head from pivoting all around and his eyes from darting in all directions. Carrying $2.8 million in a backpack had a way of messing with one's mind.

He scurried away from the bank, feeling like a wanted criminal on the run, knowing that Mr. Catangan only needed to pick up the phone and all hell would break loose. Collin could only hope that his threats to unleash catastrophic information to the authorities would dissuade the wise banker from doing so.

Walking briskly, Collin crossed the street and headed north for a block and a half before crossing again and going west, where there was a busy street with some early morning traffic. He hailed a cab. Stuffing the backpack in first, Collin climbed in the back seat and asked the cab driver to take him to a bakery two miles away—one that Collin had spotted earlier and noted because it seemed to be full of Americans. As the cab pulled away from the curb, two police cars, sirens blazing, rushed past them, taking a hard right, heading in the direction of the bank he had just left.

Collin tried not to panic, but he gasped audibly and swiveled his head to watch the passing patrol car. The cab driver studied him in the rearview mirror, which only added to his mounting angst. He couldn't read the driver's expression, so he wasn't sure if the man was suspicious of him or just curious. It felt like a very long ride to the bakery.

Once inside, he began to settle down. The store was full of Caucasians in their island apparel. They buzzed and chirped and were generally an excitable bunch. From the accents, intonation, and high-strung energy they emitted, Collin knew the majority of these people were from New England. They looked like they belonged to the leisure sailing crowd. Most were dressed much like he was at Catangan's house and were obviously well acquainted with the island. These were people who spent months, if not years, sailing through the Caribbean, like some sort of modern day explorers. He listened to their conversations and realized something: These people seemed to not have a pressing care in the world—no schedule, no bosses, no demands on them. They talked about where to dive that morning and whether they would be able to catch something tasty for lunch. They obviously had few real worries.

What a way to live, thought Collin. Carefree and unencumbered. No stress, no worries. No one chasing you. No memories haunting you, stealing your sleep, your sense of self, your ability to enjoy life.

Collin moved through the small crowd to the counter and bought a dozen donuts and orange juice for the crew, trying to shake the demons in his head that were screaming to be acknowledged. Memories from his penniless but happy former life battled with anxiety over what he carried on his back. Worries that the cops would pull up any second to cuff him and turn him over to the FBI also clamored for a share of his mind space. His hands started to tremble, and a bead of sweat formed on his brow.

Breathe deeply. Again. Exhale slowly. Control the impulse to run.

It was time to go. Maybe these people noticed his odd behavior; maybe they didn't. He couldn't take the risk. Time to get out of that shop. He slipped out the front door, turned left, and walked three blocks to find another cab. Once again, all senses were awake and alert, checking for anyone watching, or following, or even paying attention to him. Luckily, there was none of that. Nothing. Almost a ghost. He liked it that way. *Keep it together.*

Just for good measure, he changed cabs twice before making his way back to the marina. It was 7:45 a.m. when Collin arrived at the slip. The Captain and crew were ready to once again set sail. Collin approached hurriedly and asked permission to board. With a nod and a smile from the Captain, he stepped aboard and moved quickly toward the cabin.

"Thank you, Captain."

"My pleasure, sir."

"I brought donuts and juice." This produced smiles from his crew mates.

By eight o'clock, the *Admiral Risty* and its mysterious passenger cleared the harbor and were once again on course for the open sea.

Below deck, Collin sat on the edge of the berth he'd slept in, holding his face in his hands. He breathed deeply and ran his fingers through his thick hair, wiping the sweat from his brow and upper lip several times as he decompressed from his nerve-racking adventure.

*   *   *   *

Shortly before the Grand Keys Bank opened at 9:00 a.m., the bank president received another call. This time it was in his office and came from a young Interpol agent in London, asking about an American whose description was pretty generic. Not sure so soon after his episode with Collin whether this phone call was a test from the mystery invader, he decided to play dumb. Why risk it? The man was coy and smart and way too confident to brush off. Out of fear of reprisal, Mr. Catangan chose to delay any discussion of his encounter. He played it as cool as he could as he spoke to this Agent Lancaster.

Didn't they all look about the same? The banker said he had dozens of clients that met that description. The agent explained that this man was suspected of cyber-attacks that had crippled many European banks. The British agent asked for his cooperation, which Mr. Catangan agreed to give. The agent pressed upon him the urgency of the search for this suspect. Mr. Catangan, wanting to stay in the good graces of Interpol, promised to call if he noticed any suspicious activity.

The bank closed at 1:00 on Saturdays. But today the dignified president of Grand Keys Bank decided to return to the bank in the evening and make a phone call to London. He was now convinced that the early morning intruder, along with his idle threats, was long gone. Since it was imperative to keep the British government, the overlords of the Cayman Islands, happy, Mr. Catangan determined to do all he could to prevent any problems from the other side of the pond. He would only report the fact that a fellow meeting the suspect's description had come to his bank and hope this Lancaster fellow didn't probe deeper. Maybe it would assuage him; maybe it wouldn't. He had to make the effort, for his own best interests, if nothing else.

The message went like this:

"Yes, Mr. Lancaster. This is Harold Catangan from the Grand Keys Bank in George Town, Cayman Islands. I have some information that may assist you in your search for that missing American. At your earliest convenience, please return this message."

CHAPTER ELEVEN

GEORGE TOWN, GRAND CAYMAN ISLAND
MAY 4

The *Admiral Risty* cleared the breakwater that separated the George Town Marina from the open sea, propelled by its ninety-horsepower engine. The crew had filled the water and gas tanks and restocked the supplies of food, drink, and other necessities, always ready to serve the next wealthy client.

Captain Sewell, having overseen all the preparations, smiled and called through the open doorway into the cabin below, "Where are we heading, Mr. Cook?"

Without hesitation Collin hollered back, "Panama." He was busy wrapping stacks of bills in duct tape and packing the stacks in black garbage bags. $2.8 million in $100,000 stacks, each four and a half inches thick. Twenty-seven of those "bricks" and ten stacks of $10,000 each. That was the game plan. Halfway there.

"What are you talking about, man? We can't go to Panama. I've got a business in George Town. I can't just leave it behind," protested the Captain.

"Yes, you can. I'll pay you well for your service," said Collin, sticking his head out the door.

"You want us to take you all the way to Panama? You know how dangerous that is? I'm telling you, I can't do that!" the Captain said.

"But Captain, you miss the dangerous stuff. I know you do. You can do dinner cruises anytime. But helping a guy like me get away from the bad guys, now that's an opportunity you can't pass up." Collin didn't break eye contact. He was neither begging nor apologizing. He was offering something he knew the Captain, deep in his salty, old heart, wanted to do. And he smiled as he spoke. It surprised him how easily he was able to channel the swagger of yester-year when he needed it most. He acted with a confidence he hadn't felt in years. Probably since high school.

"You don't know what you say, man. There are pirates, storms, drug runners, Coast Guard, and ..."

"So, what's the price?" Collin asked evenly.

"$50,000," said the Captain.

"What? How long is it going take?"

"That depends on the wind and weather conditions. Could take a week."

"That's a lot of money. How about $25,000?"

"You paid $15,000 to get from Grand Cayman to Jamaica. Panama is more than twice that far."

"Yeah, but it's still excellent money. I'm sure it's better than what you typically make from your arrogant American tourist clientele. I'm just guessing here, but I figure I'll cover pretty close to three month's income with these two deals."

The Captain kept a steely stare focused on his newest and best client. "Look here, you need me. I don't need this kind of foolishness. This is dangerous territory. We could all die." He paused, looked at the floor, then back to Collin's face. Turning to his map, he studied it for a few moments before restarting the conversation. "I know some folks, and I know some safe spots to go. I take you there, but for no less than $40,000."

"Make it $35,000 and you got a deal, Captain. But I'll need you to stay in Panama for a day or two while I take care of business. That's got to be part of the deal."

Without missing a beat, the Captain added, "Fine. That'll be another $10,000."

"You mean $5,000? Fine."

The two men smiled at each other, and the Captain shook his head slightly as Collin stepped forward and extended his hand to seal the deal with a handshake.

The Captain gathered his crew and told them the new plan. The men looked at each other, shrugged, and agreed. The six men aboard the *Admiral Risty* were now bound for Panama. There wouldn't be much else to look at for the next seven days or so except water, sky, and each other.

* * * *

LONDON, ENGLAND
MAY 5

Nic Lancaster arrived in his cubicle at 6:34 Sunday morning and logged in first thing, knowing his log on and log off times were being recorded somewhere. Few put in the hours he did. He had a reputation to build and defend. The office was dark and quiet; few of his peers would bother to show up today.

In his eager, over-reaching manner, the young British Interpol agent went through his normal morning routine. Not expecting any surprises, he first got his coffee while the computer worked through its security protocol. When he returned to his desk, he checked his voice-mail, which was typically empty first thing in the morning. Who would call a first-year detective who did nothing but sort through endless lists of forgettable tasks? But on this morning, for the first time in his young career, someone had called him while he was asleep. The quick pulsing sound signaling an awaiting voice message filled him with a renewed sense of purpose. He quickly punched in his passcode, pen and paper at the ready. It was Harold Catangan from Grand Cayman.

Upon hearing the message, Nic Lancaster's mouth gaped open in disbelief. Maybe this case was going somewhere. Or, more correctly, this case might elevate him in the eyes of his section chief. His day took a sharp turn away from the mundane toward the completely unexpected.

He was keen to share the news with Alastair Montgomery, his direct supervisor. But Alastair was not yet in his office. The RBS fiasco demanded extra effort from everyone, including the sacrifice of weekends. Alastair usually showed up around seven thirty but wasn't approachable until after eight, when the coffee began to ward off the effects of another difficult night. At 8:05 a.m., Nic rushed into his boss's office, foregoing the normal morning pleasantries. "Listen to the message on my phone," he insisted as he picked up the receiver and punched in the codes to open his voicemail box.

Alastair Montgomery listened with one hand over his eyes, rubbing them gently. He sighed when the message finished and said, "That's very good, Nic, but that message is now several hours old. Your man could be anywhere by this point. Have you contacted this

Mr. Catangan yet?" said Alastair as he pointed a bony finger at the phone. "I need a progress report by noon. I want to know where Cook is and have a plan in place to apprehend this bloke. We need to crack this case. Immediately. We need whatever information he's got on Pho Nam Penh before the next attack."

"I can give you a progress report right now. No need to wait till noon for your head to clear. I've been working on this since I arrived here at six thirty. In fact, while you were sleeping off another bender, I contacted several dozen shops near Mr. Catangan's bank and asked for surveillance camera footage. It should all be available to me in the next thirty minutes." He practically glared at his boss, whose blurry eyes told it all. How this man maintained his high position was beyond Nic. No wonder there were no arrests made on this case. With all of its publicity and press coverage, the section chief couldn't manage to stay sober long enough to provide the real leadership this group needed? It was unbelievable to young Detective Lancaster.

Alastair's head popped up, blood-shot eyes opened wide. He straightened in his seat and cleared his throat. "Very well then. Let's have a look at those video feeds when you have them. Good work."

Nic tried to suppress a huff. "Right," he said and hastily exited his boss's office.

This case now had legs. After just two days with the case, Nic had gotten his first break. This might be the chance to prove himself he had been waiting for. Wouldn't it be brilliant to be the one to make an arrest in this RBS investigation? The media would eat it up. His name would be broadcast far and wide. The higher-ups would have to take notice of his keen detective work. Collaring this Collin Cook guy would earn Nic his first promotion, far ahead of schedule. And perhaps bump ol' Alastair out of his way in the process.

Twenty minutes later, Nic had the surveillance footage he needed. Although Collin Cook kept his face away from the cameras for the most part, he found a handful of nearly perfect frames, undeniably identifying his quarry.

He worked through a list of shops in George Town and pressured each of the owners to expedite the release of their surveillance feeds from that morning, hoping to establish Cook's escape route.

Nic presented his findings to Alastair an hour and a half after their initial meeting. Alastair, looking as though he could use some good news, half-smiled as he congratulated him, and gave him the number for Reggie Crabtree. He picked up his phone, punched a few buttons, then, covering the receiver, said, "Tell Agent Crabtree I assigned you the case, and I'm sorry I'm not available at the moment. Not to be rude, but my time is better spent dealing with the other leads we're chasing." Alastair had apparently kick-started his internal engine and was dialed in, acting more like the man in charge now.

As he headed back down the hallway, Nic wondered how long it would take before others noticed the inconsistencies in Alastair's behavior. Nic checked his watch as he marched. It wasn't even 2:00 a.m. in Los Angeles, so he left a voicemail message for Agent Crabtree, introducing himself and explaining where and when Collin Cook had been seen. "According to the bank president, Mr. Cook is carrying $2.8 million dollars in a backpack. If he survives the day, he shouldn't be too hard to find. Might end up in a hospital somewhere on the island. Local police have been alerted."

Nic spent the next several hours calling every business in a two-block radius of the Grand Keys Bank, asking questions and making threats. He enjoyed using his Interpol authority and was pleased to garner what clues he could. This exercise proved productive. Several store-owners sent feeds from their surveillance cameras. With a healthy dose of patience and persistence, Nic found what he was looking for: a brief segment showing Mr. Collin Cook getting into a taxi. A call to the cab company, along with a few more threats, and Nic learned where his quarry had been dropped off. When Agent Crabtree returned Nic's call late that afternoon, Nic knew just what to ask for.

A satisfied smile spread over his face as he hung up the phone and leaned back in his chair. "I've got you now, Collin Cook."

* * * *

SOMEWHERE IN THE
WESTERN CARIBBEAN SEA
MAY 5

With one full day of sailing now behind them, Captain Gordon Sewell calculated that it would take another four or five days to arrive in Panama City's harbor. So far, the winds were steady, though not strong, and the seas calm. Despite working against the current, they were making good time. The weather report looked fair for the next few days as well. As a matter of habit, he monitored several communications channels, including the Coast Guard's frequency, to gather as much information as possible.

No stranger to the hazards of the seas, both human and natural, Captain Sewell was prepared for most dangers. He had learned a few things since losing his boat to pirates a couple of years prior. That was not going to happen again.

Thinking of nothing more than protecting his money and depositing what he had taken out of Grand Keys Bank, Collin had not calculated the potential peril they could face on this Caribbean crossing until he stumbled down the steps into the cabin late that afternoon.

"Whoa," he said as he found the Captain cleaning a large rifle and adjusting a very ominous-looking scope. Next to him sat several similar weapons.

"We are entering dangerous territory, so we must prepare ourselves, Mr. Cook," Captain Sewell said without looking up. "There are pirates in these waters. And drug smugglers. Dangerous people. Readiness is the key to survival out here."

Still in shock, Collin stated the obvious as if thinking out loud. "I guess we should try to avoid them."

"That's not always possible, my friend. That's why we carry these," he said as he lifted the rifle and nodded his head toward the other weapons lying next to him. "We can't always outrun them, so we prepare to defend ourselves. They may choose to approach, but they would be very unwise to attempt an attack," explained the Captain, examining the rifle he had just cleaned.

Collin nodded in agreement, staring at the guns. His mind ran a couple of frightening scenarios as he recalled the Captain's story about the pirates. As he looked at the weapons spread out in the cabin, he asked, "So where did you get these guns? They look pretty sophisticated, not what you can buy down at the local sporting goods store."

The Captain let out a soft chuckle. "No, these are not from a store. They're military grade. Let's just say I have some friends who have some friends. Understood?"

"Of course," Collin said. No need to explore the details. He noticed they were equipped with laser scopes and a mechanism that the Captain explained allowed the handler to determine if one bullet or two would be fired upon a full squeeze of the trigger. The metal had an uncommon finish, far different from any guns Collin had handled as a teen.

Clearing his throat, the Captain regained Collin's attention and continued. "The best plan, as I have learned from fellow captains and from experience, is to stay out of the way of other boats. Give up the right of way. Tack behind approaching vessels. Don't get too close. I have not had any problems in a very long time using this strategy. But I don't often venture this far from the islands."

The Captain's hands moved expertly across the black metal of the next rifle to clean and dismantle it while Collin watched. His movements were smooth and graceful. It was obvious to Collin that he was thorough, meticulous, and well-practiced. Like everything else on the ship, the rifles were well-maintained.

Collin watched carefully, learning.

Once finished, the Captain went topside. Collin moved down the narrow aisle to the right of the steps to the bunk where his backpack was stashed. He did an inventory of his belongings and counted the stacks of cash. As he worked, he questioned Lukas's instruction to physically carry the money to Panama. Maybe he forgot how bulky and awkward it was to carry that much cash. None of this seemed logical. But Lukas was nothing if not logical. Lukas had guided him safely for the last six months. No reason to start doubting him now.

Just then, there arose a cry from Miguel, the crew member who spent most of his time on the lookout, binoculars in hand. "Five o'clock. Coming fast. Cigarette boat. Four guys. They got guns."

A mad scramble of excitement erupted on deck as the Captain began

barking out orders. Within moments, the ship was at full sail and veering southward. While the crew scurried into position and manned their
stations, the Captain burst into the cabin and began pulling out the guns
he had just cleaned. Collin was frozen, not sure what to do. Without
a word, the Captain handed him two guns and motioned for him to
take them up top. After handing the guns to Rojas, he returned. The
Captain handed him two more guns and told Collin to stay below deck.
The Captain carried an armload of ammunition clips to his men. Each
man snapped the loaded clips into place and took up positions around
the deck. Collin stood on the steps, watching the activity. It was like a
well-choreographed ballet. There was movement, urgent and serious,
but it flowed. Each performer moving independently and with purpose.

Miguel positioned himself at the stern. Holding onto the railing in
a sitting position, the gun in his right hand, a pair of binoculars in his
left, while his feet and legs held on tight. He scanned the horizon to the
rear of the ship and relayed what he saw loud enough for the Captain
and crew to hear. "Incoming vessel at six o'clock. Two miles out and
closing."

Collin felt helpless as each of the other men performed his prescribed part while he watched, motionless and uncertain.

"Captain," cried Miguel. "They are in uniform. Navy, I think. Yes,
they are US Navy."

The feeling of being hunted like wounded prey reemerged inside
Collin, along with the accompanying sense of vulnerability. The swagger evaporated like water droplets on a hot skillet. Breathing became
short and labored. An overpowering flood of emotions paralyzed Collin.

Still standing below deck, clutching the handrail, face and knuckles
white as the clouds above, Collin was unable to move as he watched the
cigarette boat closing in on them from the northeast. The closer it got,
the louder the roar of its engines. Deep, throaty, and powerful.

Aboard the *Admiral Risty*, the men watched silently, their rifles
pointing upward. The Captain ordered them to stand down and do
nothing that would cause alarm. The wind whipped the sails, and they
fluttered and snapped loudly as they harnessed the power of the ocean
breeze. Water sprayed out from the leading edge of the hull with each
wave and swell she cut through. However, she was no match for the

approaching speed boat.

No one spoke.

The cigarette boat was a mile behind them, leaping through the swells, lurching ever closer. Suddenly aware of Collin's presence on the steps, the Captain turned to him and barked, "Go below decks *now* and hide. In the spot Rojas showed you. Get out of sight, and stay there until I give you the signal. Hurry." His voice was commanding but not panicked.

Collin understood the directions and the reason for them. He didn't question. He just obeyed. It seemed logical, even comforting. He finally knew what to do and could take some action.

During Rojas's tour, Collin learned that the Captain purchased this boat at auction in Miami. It was owned previously by a drug smuggler who had designed some special features into the hull and the cabin. In every other way, this boat was identical to its peers of the same model. The exceptions were few but critically important for its designer's line of business. And of course, none of these "upgrades" were documented.

The first special feature was in the head. Hidden behind the toilet were two buttons, one on either side, that allowed the toilet and the floor around it to pivot forward on hinges, exposing a compartment that was no larger than a mid-sized suitcase. That was the perfect place for Collin to stuff the contents of his bulging backpack. With some exertion, he squeezed each garbage bag into place. Devoid of its contents, the backpack folded up so it could be wedged into a gap in the front of the compartment. Collin had to push and poke to make it fit so he could close the hatch.

The second feature was cleverly hidden in the otherwise normal-looking galley. Collin swung the small oven's door open and removed the rack. He felt along the corners where the top panel met the side panels for two concealed buttons that released the back of the oven. The buttons were the same charcoal gray color as the inside panels, so they blended in perfectly. Behind the back panel was a compartment just the right size to conceal Collin's computer bag. With some effort, he was able to make it fit, but he could not secure the back wall into its original position before his attention was diverted by the commotion on the deck.

He strained to hear what was going on, but the only sounds he could make out were Miguel's high-pitched yells. Everything else, other than the noise of the water lashing against the hull, was too faint and muffled to make out.

"Five hundred meters and closing. Men … Driver is …" was all he could hear from Miguel. The other words were drowned in the commotion.

A loud squawk boomed from a PA system aboard the other ship. "This is the United States Navy. Prepare your vessel to be boarded for inspection." The Captain barked out orders, but Collin couldn't make out the words. Immediately, he heard the pounding of feet on the deck above him, followed by the whirring of ropes through their pulleys, the rippling and flapping of the heavy nylon sails, and the clanging of those metal pulleys against the masts and cross bars. From the sounds, he knew the men were bringing down the sails and securing the riggings. The mighty sailboat slowed to a drift. A long way away from their destination. A long way from anything.

Panic set in and he froze in place. This wasn't supposed to happen. Collin remembered the instructions the Captain had given him and tried to unglue his feet from the floor. But they felt so heavy he could hardly move them. His body was not responding. His brain was stuck, anticipating his doom. Exerting every ounce of energy he had, he darted into the bottom bunk and began to work.

Maneuvering into this cramped and smelly space, especially with so little time and the need for silence, required precision and focus. From the lower bunk, he had to pull up the corners of the mattress and feel for a pair of release buttons. When he found them, he pushed against the wall of the cabin and it gave ever so slightly, pivoting from a hinge concealed by the edge of the upper bunk. It swung toward the outside wall just enough for him to roll into the hideaway, suck in his breath to make himself as skinny as possible, and slide into the tiny space between the inner and outer walls of the boat. He had to pull his legs up, squeeze them through the tight opening, then extend them again so he could push with all his might to get the trap door back in place. There was just enough room for him to compress his shoulders against the outer wall so the door would swing shut again. This hiding place was designed for much smaller people.

This chamber was parallel to the lower bunk and less than a quarter of the width. The door of the hatch barely closed as it scraped across his belly, chest, and face as he lay on his shoulder, his body at the same angle as the side of the boat—not quite vertical, but sloping up and out—keeping himself as flat as he could. It was at that very moment that he heard the footsteps pounding down the stairs. He managed to get the door closed but not secured. He could still see light coming in around the three edges of the panel, which meant it wasn't tight and could be seen from the other side. All it would take was a close look to see the outline of the hatch.

He had to reposition his body to snap the latches shut tightly. Doing this under pressure and in cramped quarters presented a formidable challenge that tested Collin's ability to fight off his phobia of being locked up. It was imperative that he be as silent as possible. He hoped the water slapping and lashing the side of the boat would cover the clicking sound. When the latches caught with a loud snap, Collin held his breath and strained to listen for a reaction. His heart was racing, his lungs were burning, and his head was aching, making it difficult to hear anything except his own pulse. Over the drumming in his ears, he heard the thud of footfalls moving toward him. They stopped. Two more thuds moved closer. A muffled voice hollered something Collin couldn't make out, followed by a response from outside. The heavy thuds moved again, this time away from him, toward the bow.

It was all he could do to prevent his arms and legs from thrashing and flailing in hopes of escape. He squeezed his eyes closed and forced himself to relax by imagining himself lying in the sun on the deck above.

In the pitch black, hot, and stuffy space, Collin tried to slow his pulse and breathing. Beads of sweat covered his face, arms, and legs. Rivulets ran down his neck, behind his ears, down his chest, and into his armpits. His whole body itched as the perspiration trickled along his skin. He wanted to wipe it off to stop the tickling, but he couldn't.

Collin's body went rigid and motionless upon hearing a new noise. It was banging and thumping on the walls, the cabinets, and floors. The racket grew louder as the pounding sounds approached the bunk area. Collin wanted to scream or run or shrink to the size of a termite. Then it all stopped as if a discovery had been made. The unfamiliar voice was just beyond the wall that concealed him, asking questions forcefully. Collin remained still and uttered a silent prayer for deliverance.

Another stomping sound on the floor. Then another. A knock on the bulkhead that supported the bottom bunk. A rustling that sounded like the mattress on the lower bunk being moved about. A metallic sound that Collin recognized as the latch to the storage area under the bed. More bumping and thumping as things were moved around within the storage area. Collin felt the vibrations through the fiberglass wall that separated him from the items in the storage compartment.

The seas picked up and the waves tossed the two boats about, causing them to knock and clang as they bumped and bounced into the rubber bumpers hanging between them. Another wave hit and the sound of bodies bumping into walls followed.

Collin heard the unfamiliar voice bark out more orders. The voices topside gave short responses, which Collin was nearly certain were, "Aye, aye." The thudding of footsteps clamored up the steps as yet another wave crashed into the sides of the two boats. Voices were now high-pitched and urgent but growing more distant. More pounding on the deck as several pairs of heavy footsteps moved this way and that, then vanished altogether. The next sound was the throaty purr of the powerful speed boat's engines firing up. Within seconds, those sounds were moving away at an ever-increasing pace until they faded completely.

Time passed, but Collin had no idea how much. As if in the distance, he heard the all-clear signal—a rap-a-tap-tap-rap on the push away wall. It repeated. Then again. Coming out of a haze, he felt thick-headed and sluggish, finally responding with a similar rap-a-tap-tap-rap. Jaime pushed from his side, and the trap door opened just enough to reveal Collin's flushed and contorted face, his clothing dirty and soaking wet. But he smiled faintly as he breathed in the sweetness of the fresh air that rushed to greet him. The Captain and crew cheered and congratulated Collin as they pulled him out of his holding cell.

CHAPTER TWELVE

OFF THE COAST OF PANAMA
MAY 11

Sailing through the Caribbean has a way of melting time and worries. Six days had passed since the Navy team boarded the *Admiral Risty*. The winds had cooperated, aiding their journey. Collin was as relaxed as he had been in years—ever, perhaps. Nothing but a vast ocean of turquoise, warm breezes, a few laughs with the crew, and enough work to him engaged. Since divulging his troubles to Captain Sewell, Collin's mind was freer and less encumbered. No need to hide secrets anymore. Instead, he focused his energy on watching and learning everything he could about sailing, using the navigation equipment, and predicting the weather. Observing the crew members and Captain Sewell kept him occupied, as well. When there was work to be done, Collin jumped up and helped, happy to pitch in with any and all duties aboard. His willingness and ability to work, along with his cooking skills, endeared him to his fellow shipmates. Before long, he was treated almost like one of the other crew mates. There remained, however, a certain level of deference because he was a paying client.

Being helpful and staying busy was second nature to Collin, but it also helped his mind from slipping back into pain he was trying to push away. Because nighttime was the most difficult part of the day for Collin, he volunteered for the late shift, preferring to nap during the day and busy himself when darkness fell.

Late that afternoon, the Captain announced that they would arrive in Panama the next day. "We can take you to the city of Colón. There's a very nice, very modern port there. It will have every accommodation you need," he said to Collin.

"Yes, I read about it. Sounds like it's a major hub for commerce through the Canal."

"It is. But because of that, officials are careful and meticulous, if you know what I mean."

"Are you worried about going there?" asked Collin.

"Friends of mine tell me the entry into Panama can be dicey," said Captain Sewell. "They follow every rule in Colón. Nothing gets past them. That's why I wonder if it might be best for you to enter the country somewhere less crowded, less popular."

"Any suggestions?"

"With your recent experiences, I think it best to sail southeast of the Canal to the island of El Porvenir."

"Never heard of it," said Collin.

"That's the point. It's small, remote, and, by some standards, uncivilized."

"I see where you're going with this. That could work to our advantage," said Collin, snapping his fingers in recognition of the brilliance of the idea.

"Yes, I'm sure you would like to draw less attention to yourself than you did in George Town."

"That's for sure."

Pointing to the digital map on his navigation screen, Captain Sewell showed Collin Isla Porvenir, a small island among the Kuna Yala chain, which stretched eastward from the mainland into the Caribbean south of the Panama Canal. "These islands are inhabited by the Kuna Yala Indians, and they control their own Customs and Immigration office. I understand that they are much less rigorous than in Colón," said the Captain.

"How can you be sure?" asked Collin.

"I have been here once. I found the Kuna Indians to be warm and friendly people. They still speak their native language and follow many of their native customs. A very interesting people—very proud and independent. They don't care too much about the rest of the world. Their life is simple, and they like it that way."

"Do any of you speak their language? It won't help us too much if we can't communicate with them."

"There are some who have learned Spanish. Those are the ones that have all the good jobs, like in the government offices. That kind of job brings status. But, they still like doing things their own way, and they thumb their noses, whenever possible, at the Panamanian government. That is why many sailors prefer to go there to get into the country."

"Excellent," said Collin with a sense of satisfaction and relief. "Sounds like my kind of place."

* * * *

ISLA PORVENIR, PANAMA
MAY 12

The sun glowed pinkish orange through a band of silvery clouds highlighted in purple on the western horizon, just above the land mass that was Panama, as the *Admiral Risty* sailed into the outer harbor of Porvenir. Palm trees swayed in the gentle breeze, and the sound of waves skimming along the sand greeted the weary sailors. On the radio, the Captain tried to make contact with the local authorities, but no one responded. It was a Sunday evening, after all. He positioned the boat in a semi-protected cove, a hundred yards off a rocky outcropping at the harbor mouth. They would handle the formalities in the morning. According to local custom, it could be ten o'clock before officials made their way over.

With nothing else to do, the six men onboard the *Admiral Risty* sat on the bow and soaked it all in—the sound of the waves and the birds, the last rays of the sun before it hid itself behind the western horizon, and the stillness, glad for a respite after their long journey. This was indeed a tranquil paradise. They shared stories late into the night.

* * * *

ISLA PORVENIR, PANAMA
MAY 13

Collin woke the next morning with the sun, eager to begin the next phase of his mission. He dragged his bags out from semi-darkness below deck to the cockpit so as not to disturb the others. To get into character, Collin pulled out his supplies and went to work. By the time he was finished, his fake blond hair was dark brown to match his rather full beard. Per Lukas's fastidious instructions, he traveled with home hair coloring kits in colors to match the pictures in each of his passports.

His hair had become long and unkempt, which fit the British passport he carried bearing the name of Nigel Spencer.

Using his electric razor, he trimmed the beard, then donned a pair of round-rimmed glasses, and equipped the pockets of his knapsack with falsified documents that would verify his status as a Research Fellow with the Archaeology Foundation of England. Brilliant forgeries put together by Lukas's shadowy team of helpers. He also put on the requisite long, nylon, cargo shorts and multi-pocketed, long-sleeve shirt of a field scientist, complemented by hiking sandals. The red bandana and the beaded necklace around his neck added to the costume. A regular British naturalist.

When the local authority finally appeared in a small patrol boat, Nigel Spencer surprised his crew mates by speaking fluent Spanish. He introduced himself and explained, when asked, the purpose of his visit to Panama: "To explore and study the ruins of LaVieja for the Archaeological Society of Leeds under a grant from Archaeology Foundation of England." Collin's matter-of-fact explanation, combined with his mastery of Spanish and convincing persona, gave the customs agent little reason to inspect the boat or its contents any further. He poked around the boat, asked questions about how long and where he would be staying in Panama, but he hardly listened to the answers. A cursory examination of Collin's pack and computer bag lasted scarcely twenty seconds. Collin talked non-stop, trying to divert the man's attention as he explained in breathless detail the goals of his archaeological expedition and his eagerness to get started. His excitement was not contagious. In fact, the man seemed impatient and ready to leave, so he escorted Collin and Captain Sewell onto the Customs boat and took them to the office at the far end of the harbor.

Collin jabbered the whole way.

After nearly two hours of waiting, explaining, filling out papers, explaining some more, and waiting again, the Customs Master invited them into his office. He signed Collin's entry papers, granting him permission to enter Panama. He promptly dismissed them to return to their boat. The problem was the *Admiral Risty* was anchored a mile away, necessitating the exchange of US currency in order to pay for Captain Sewell's return trip to his vessel.

Before they parted, Collin programmed the number for Captain's satellite phone into his iPhone. It was only the second contact saved in his address book. He promised to call him within twenty-four hours to let him know if he would need a ride out of Panama.

Collin thanked the Captain for bringing him safely to this point. "I left your payment in the secret compartment behind the microwave. It's all there with a little extra to share with the crew."

Captain Sewell held out a hand, and when Collin reached out to shake it, the Captain pulled Collin in for a brotherly embrace. "It's been a pleasure, wanderer. You take care of yourself and be careful." As Collin pulled back, he added with a big smile on his face, "You were right about one thing."

"Oh, yeah? What was I right about?" asked Collin.

"I miss adventure … and danger … and helping the good guys."

Collin flashed a crooked smile. "Good. I'll keep that in mind." He turned and walked down the dock toward the island. The confidence he displayed was mostly for show. The next steps in his plan, though spelled out in his elaborate spreadsheet, felt very uncertain. But he knew the Captain was watching him, so he put on a good show. Toward the end of the dock, he stopped, turned, set down his computer bag, and with one last gesture, waved a hand above his head to the Captain. The Captain, in return, doffed his cap, then climbed aboard the patrol boat.

The big backpack was full and weighed about fifty pounds. It was bound to his body with a heavily padded belt and two padded shoulder straps. Collin had repacked most of the money into it amongst clothing and supplies. He also carried the smaller pack and his computer bag, one in each hand. After paying the Captain and crew and keeping some out for spending, he was down to $2.7 million of cold, hard cash. Enough to make him wince as he schlepped it through town.

It was time to check in with Lukas.

"You're wise to enter Panama that way. Much safer," Lukas said after they exchanged greetings. "That Captain knows what he's talking about."

"Yeah, but now I have to get from here to Panama City with all this cash. I feel like a slow-moving target."

"Won't be a problem, my friend," said Lukas. "On your end, you

just need to get on a plane for Panama City. According to our operatives, things are pretty loose and casual down there. The Kuna people
have little concern for the government's rules. Plus, they have immu-
nity, thanks to a long-standing arrangement between the Kuna tribal
leaders and Panama City. The native people on the islands are self-gov-
erned and don't give a rip what the Panamanian authorities want. So
don't worry yourself."

"Okay, that's only half the problem. What if I get mugged?"

"What if? That's not going to happen, either. They are a peaceful
people that wouldn't hurt a person just for the sake of money."

"Okay, let's suppose you're right, and I have no trouble here on the
island. What next? What happens when I land in Panama City?"

"Don't worry about that, either. We've got contacts set up there. I'll
have everything in place for you. For now, just get yourself there, and
text me your flight number, OK? You're burning daylight, and you've
got a lot to do in a very short time," said Lukas.

"What do you mean?" asked Collin.

"I mean the EU and US governments are clamping down hard on
offshore accounts and monitoring large transfers. We've got to consoli-
date your funds, all of them if possible, into InterCon Bank. At the rate
they're going, it's got to be today. We have no time to waste."

"How do you know I can trust InterCon?"

"The US is not going to audit the bank that handles the funds for all
of their covert operations in Central and South America. Trust me, they
do not want to open that can of worms," Lukas said. Collin found this
information disconcerting. The more of these tidbits he picked up, the
more he realized he didn't know—about the world, his own government, and life beyond the little sphere he had lived in for thirty years.

Lukas then outlined the game plan for his stay in Panama City. Parts
of it sounded easier than others. Some parts sounded downright frightening. He had to trust Lukas.

From the dock at Porvenir, Collin walked through the tiny village,
looking for transportation. Life on this little Caribbean island was indeed
slow-paced. Nothing, it seemed, was urgent. Plus, it wasn't laid out like
any town he had visited, either. There were few streets per se. There
were huts and shacks and a few stores down near the water, separated by

tall palm trees. Right next to the Customs and Immigration building where they had filled out their paperwork was a museum celebrating the culture of the Kuna Yala. Beyond that it was hard to identify a downtown or a shopping district. Even finding the main boulevard took effort.

Throughout the village, Collin noticed contrasts. Some of the buildings had stucco walls and tiled roofs. Others were built in the traditional Kuna way with mud walls and roofs made from palm fronds. Since he did not want to call undue attention to himself, Collin tried to slow himself down but found it to be no easy task. He was geared up for the mission ahead of him. Carrying $2.7 million in cash on his back wasn't helping him to relax, either. Despite Lukas's assurances, he continued to glance over his shoulder.

His mind was filled with steps from the meticulously constructed plan, a checklist of things he knew he needed to do to accomplish his goal of repositioning all of his money, not just what he was carrying. There was another $27 million out there. Some of it was safe in banks that Lukas had determined were not on the law enforcement radar. Another $9.5 million in various banks would be easy to transfer to InterCon Bank because the accounts were each under $1 million. Collin's primary concern today was to physically move the $7 million dollars from other banks in Panama City to InterCon.

Concerns about guarding his fortune and following the outline from Lukas swirled as he maneuvered between the huts and brick buildings of Porvenir.

Sliding in and out of Panama without detection was paramount. So far, so good. Thanks to Captain Sewell, getting into Panama had turned out much easier than he had anticipated. Landing here in the Kuna Islands and dealing with the affable native people in Porvenir was a stroke of good fortune that he hoped would continue.

Next goal: Get to Panama City.

He had to get to the local airport, which necessitated finding a taxi, which were not plentiful. The town was so small and so poor, there was hardly a vehicle in sight other than hand-carved boats and rickety bicycles. The first and only cabbie he found required some convincing, oddly enough, but he came around when Collin showed him he had a stack of Panamanian currency.

The airstrip looked more like a long-neglected sidewalk. It was about as wide as a two-lane alley. Cracked concrete with green clumps of grass pushing through, patched in several places, and two sets of yellow Xs marking the ends made up the landing strip. One small building with a make-shift Formica counter served as the airport's nerve center.

Collin swallowed hard as he surveyed the scene. A pang of discomfort rose inside him and squeezed at his sternum. A few deep breaths and a quick bit of research on his phone helped restore a sense of calm. Apparently, everything worked. Planes came and went without incident several times a week. No reports of crashes or fatalities on the Internet.

He also learned there was an outgoing flight from Porvenir to Panama City with empty seats at 12:40.

Things being lax as they were on this obscure island, Collin was able to pay cash for his ticket and walk onto the twelve-seat, twin-engine, commuter plane without question, let alone a search of his person or bags. Lukas had not steered Collin wrong, which added to his confidence.

Next obstacle, however, would be clearing customs in Panama City. As a foreigner coming through Kuna Yala, there would be a higher risk of drawing attention. Lukas assured him he would take care of the details by the end of the twenty-minute flight.

As he walked off the plane in Panama City, Collin's palms were sweaty, as was his brow. He had to maintain control and play it cool.

The secret to getting through unfamiliar situations, he knew, was to act like you had done it a hundred times before. Confidence was the magic ingredient, the thing that made it all work.

Collin summoned the courage he needed to exude confidence. He donned his sunglasses and secured his bags in his grip. He painted a determined look on his face, steely and convincing, as he walked through the terminal with an all-business swagger. No problems.

Out of compulsion, he dug his phone out and did the one-handed texting thing. *Anything I should know?* he asked Lukas.

Inside the terminal, there were crowds of people of all sorts, mostly Latin Americans, but there were quite a number of Europeans, Americans, and other white people. There were tourists, business people, college students, and local merchants moving this way and that. The bulging backpack, however, made Collin feel conspicuous. No one else was wearing such a large, conspicuous pack. He felt like he was standing out, and he didn't want that.

The phone dinged. Lukas's reply: *My contact will meet you at Line 4. Have some US currency with your docs. $200 should be plenty. Nothing to worry about. You'll be fine.*

Collin followed the instructions and made his way to Line 4. The man behind the glass seemed no different than any of the other customs agents. Taking a deep breath, Collin stepped forward when the agent motioned for him, mustering all the serenity he could as he presented his papers. The man's hands were quick and adept. The money slid discreetly from Collin's passport under a loose piece of paper. As the man looked at Collin's passport, not a trace of interest on his face, he said without so much as looking up, "It is an honor to welcome you to Panama, Señor Spencer. We wish you the best on your expedition." The thirty-something-year-old official managed a smile and a nod of his head as he took in Professor Spencer and his large backpack. He then flipped the pages of the passport, pounded a stamp onto one of them with gusto and authority, and handed it back to Collin. "Next," he said as he waved to the person behind Collin. Exhaling in relief, Collin picked up his bags and moved swiftly toward the exit, eager to get away from the crowds, the security, and so many unknowns.

He turned a corner and came upon a short man wearing a three-piece suit and chauffeur's hat holding a plastic placard that read: Welcome Nigel Spencer.

Collin walked right past it, lost in a tangle of complex thoughts. When it finally dawned on him several paces later, he turned to the man and introduced himself. The limousine took him to The Executive Hotel. Uniquely positioned in the heart of Panama City's thriving financial district, the hotel towered above the bustling city. Every bank he needed to visit would be in walking distance.

He fired off a text to Lukas as he stood outside the front lobby: *Nice touch. Seems a little overboard.*

Not for a guest of the govt was the reply.

What? Collin shot back.

Part of your cover. It'll work. Much safer, too.

Preferable to Collin would be a small budget hotel with free Internet, where he could come and go unnoticed. But, trusting Lukas, he tipped the chauffeur and reached for his overstuffed pack and the smaller backpack. He clutched the computer bag in the other hand. Within seconds, two friendly bellhops were at his side, offering assistance that Collin was not used to. His resistance was useless and short-lived. He had to pause when the young bellhop asked his name.

"I shall take this to your room, Señor Spencer."

When they arrived at his room, Collin tipped him with American money and thanked him for his help. Instantly realizing his mistake, Collin's eyes opened wide and his words caught in his throat. Collin was supposed to be a Brit. Why would a Brit be carrying US currency? Plus, he had forgotten to use the proper accent, his Yankee pronunciation flowing out before his brain could catch up.

"Gracias," said the young bellhop who gawked curiously at the money. Too many people paying him too much attention and two mistakes that could haunt him. He had to get his work done and get out of town.

It was already two o'clock in the afternoon. The bank would close in three hours.

He had to prepare the money for deposit. Pouring the cash wrapped in duct tape onto the bed, Collin stopped to take it in. It was a big pile—more money than he and Amy had ever dreamed of. He pulled out his pocket knife and began ripping open the gray bricks, pushing away the thoughts of what he'd lost in exchange for it. His knees gave way as her face flashed in his mind. This time, though, it wasn't the pretty, smiling face he liked to remember. This time it was the face with worry and dread painted on it after paying bills. He caught himself on the edge of the bed and slumped to the floor. With his face in his hands, he broke down, unable to restrain the pent-up angst. "I'm so sorry, honey. I'm sorry we never had enough," he mumbled just above a whisper.

CHAPTER THIRTEEN

Collin awoke with a start when the incessant knocking at the door finally registered. Quickly checking his surroundings, he jumped to his feet but struggled to maintain his balance. Seeing the stacks of cash spread out on the bed, he stopped in his tracks. His mind clicked on, and he remembered where he was and how he got there. The knocking continued, accompanied by a gentleman's lightly accented voice. "Señor Spencer? Is everything all right?"

Blinking hard and rubbing his eyes, he zeroed in on the clock to get his bearings. It read 2:48. "Yes, yes, I'm fine. I'll be right with you," Collin stammered in his best British accent, trying to hide his uneasiness. Scrambling to the side of the bed, he grabbed the large pack and swept the stacks of money into it, dropping it in the closet as he walked to the door. "So sorry to keep you waiting. I'm afraid I dozed off there for a few moments," Collin said, playing off his scattered demeanor.

The man introduced himself as the manager of the hotel and told Collin what an honor it was to have someone so prominent staying at his hotel. Hosting guests of the government was not something they took lightly. Collin thanked him and modestly deflected the compliments. "I'm just a curious professor searching for links between the ancient Mayans and aboriginals of the Caribbean islands," he said.

"I see," said the manager. "It's just that we usually have more than a few hours' notice of the arrival of such distinguished guests. We did not have adequate time to prepare one of our presidential suites."

"Right. No apologies necessary. My office, I'm afraid, must have missed that particular detail."

"Yes, yes, perhaps you are right. Or, perhaps it is because you arrived by boat at Isla El Porvenir," the manager said, his head cocked slightly. "It is so difficult to predict the wind and the seas." His eyes narrowed in anticipation of Collin's response.

Collin was caught completely off-guard. Again, he consciously maintained a cheery, naïve smile. However, he knew his eyes widened and his chin dropped as the man spoke. He felt exposed and it was difficult to conceal his discomfort. "Yes, we had a change of plans that necessitated alternate travel arrangements." He turned away and cleared his throat.

"No matter the purpose for your visit, your business is welcome here at The Executive Hotel and much appreciated, Señor Spencer. I trust your stay here will be peaceful and trouble-free. We wish to provide you a token of our hospitality."

The manager's face was like a mask, completely unreadable. His choice of words obviously meant to convey a level of wariness. He motioned behind him, and another man pushed a small cart holding a silver bucket of ice and champagne into view. The manager moved out of the way, and the cart-pushing attendant looked to Collin for approval. The hesitation was momentary but noticeable, he was sure. He awkwardly motioned for the man to enter.

"You are too kind, my dear sir. Muchas gracias," he said with terrible pronunciation.

The manager and the cart pusher each gave a slight bow as they exited. "We hope you enjoy your stay, Señor Spencer," the manager said. Then he backed away.

Thoroughly flustered, Collin closed the door and moved to the center of the room to survey the cart. He circled it twice, peering at it from every angle. Lukas had instilled in him a high level of skepticism, perhaps bordering on paranoia, so he pushed the cart into the bathroom and closed the door. If there was a camera on the cart, it would record nothing but darkness.

One valuable hour had elapsed. Collin scrambled to gather his paperwork and pack. He felt ill-prepared, but time was running out. As a precaution, he shoved the computer bag into the in-closet safe. He grabbed the backpack and headed out because he didn't have time to buy a more business-like briefcase to carry the cash.

Walking the streets with $2.7 million was a scary proposition anywhere, but even more so in an unfamiliar place. Even though he only had to walk two blocks to his destination, it felt as if it took an eternity. His head swiveled about continually, expecting an attack.

He exhaled in relief as he walked through the front doors of InterCon Bank. Once inside, he was escorted by a young-looking vice president to a private office halfway down a corridor that required a key to enter. As Lukas had promised, the transaction went smoothly and quickly. No prying questions were asked of him, and no scrutiny of his person or papers took place. The most difficult part was finding the obscure office which housed the bank. With the transfers he initiated on his computer earlier, he had already consolidated nearly $11 million in a numbered account at InterCon. This deposit brought his total over $13.5 million.

His watch said 3:37. Two more banks, both within three blocks, held large amounts of his money. He politely requested the young VP to allow him time to return. The vice president promised he would personally attend to all of Collin's transactions.

His first stop was at another well-kept secret of the ultra-rich. PanAmerican Global Assets was a favorite off-shore shelter used primarily by American and Brazilian multinational corporations. Without so much as a sideways glance, the operators there allowed Collin to liquidate $4.15 million dollars, which caused every pouch of his pack to bulge. As he wrestled the pack onto his back, he estimated it to weigh about ninety pounds.

At 4:17 p.m., Collin pushed the electronic buzzer at the entrance of InterCon Bank. The same young man let him into the otherwise empty office. Fifteen minutes later, Collin had an electronic verification that his funds had been received into his account.

One more bank to visit. One more favor to ask of his new friend at InterCon.

"I cannot let you in after five o'clock. The doors lock, and my code will not open them again," the manager informed him.

The second bank was much closer—around the corner and halfway down the block. It held another $2.25 million. Collin couldn't risk leaving his funds in banks that were on the target list for Interpol and the FBI. It would feel akin to leaving one of his children alone in the car at the mall. Since electronic transactions were being monitored, direct withdrawal, while fraught with tangible risks, was his best option.

Despite his ability to correctly code in his nineteen-digit account number from memory, Collin's request raised the eyebrows of the assistant manager who was called to help with the transaction. Collin was escorted into a back office and asked to wait for the bank president.

As he sat, a line of perspiration formed on his upper lip. He squirmed in his seat and fidgeted with the straps on his pack. When the bank president entered the room, Collin half expected the National Guard to enter with him it had taken so long. The man's face was stern, his gaze penetrating. He huffed as he took his seat in the high-backed leather chair opposite Collin, a ponderous mahogany desk between them. "What is the reason for your hasty withdrawal from our bank, Mr. Stevens, is it?"

"Yes, it is. I guess the reason is simple. I'm paranoid. There are too many reports that the security and anonymity of accounts like mine have been compromised in recent days," said Collin. His voice was steady, though his stomach was not.

"I resent the implication of your statement. You cast doubt upon our security measures."

"Not necessarily. But ever since RBS was hacked and millions of dollars went missing, I am rightfully protective and worried. I know you serve your clients well. I chose your bank because of its fine reputation, and once this blows over, if there are no untoward reports concerning this fine institution, I shall redeposit this money and, perhaps, more."

The president's eyebrows arched in response, but he said nothing. His eyes burrowed through Collin's, but Collin held his gaze and continued his hastily contrived story. "You see, I must be more cautious than others. This sum represents more than my life savings. I keep it here because I must hide it to avoid detection by my government, who wants to steal it from me. I cannot afford to lose any portion of this money. Unlike some of your other clients, I don't have the ability to make back this kind of money, even if I work two lifetimes."

"This is a very large cash withdrawal. You realize how dangerous this is, don't you?"

"I do. But I have made arrangements to keep it secure until, like I said, this whole thing blows over."

"Why not transfer it out electronically?" asked the banker.

"They have computers that look for those kinds of large transfers."
"If it's done right, you avoid the risk of carrying cash."

"Maybe, but I'm more comfortable doing it this way," Collin said, checking his watch. It was 4:52.

"I see you checking the time. This is an urgent matter for you?"

"Yes, it is."

"You can see that I am in a rather difficult spot, Mr. Stevens. I am asked to trust you despite the fact that I cannot verify your identity. Your money was transferred in electronically. We have no signature. We have no fingerprints. We have no retina scan. Those would be our normal security protocols when amounts this large are withdrawn. How do I know you are who you say you are—just a paranoid accountholder?"

"I understand your security concerns, but who else might I be?"

"You could be a criminal, a very clever thief. With all of the hacking lately and all the government scrutiny, it pays for someone in my position to be extremely careful, does it not?"

"If I was that clever, I would have moved my money and more a long time ago."

"Or you could be a government regulator coming to monitor the handling of unusual transactions."

"I could be. But I would not be in such a hurry if that were true."

The bank president leaned back in his chair and crossed one leg over the other, studying Collin. His eyes darted to his computer screen and back to Collin. "I believe you. You have an honest face, and I do not want to scare away a good client. Your withdrawal is ready. Please keep our bank in mind for your future needs, Mr. Stevens."

"You have made a very nervous man feel much better. I will indeed bring my money back when the time is right," said Collin as he stood and held out a hand. The two men shook hands, and Collin exited the office. He was promptly greeted by a shapely young lady holding the handle of a roller bag, which she offered to him.

Collin's watch said 4:56 as he rolled the small fortune out the door. On the sidewalk, he picked up the pace until he was running, the wheels of the suitcase clacking on the sidewalk behind him. A sense of sweet relief bubbled up as he rounded the corner and made his way toward InterCon Bank. After he concluded the last transaction, Collin made sure to provide the kind and diligent VP a special reward for going the extra mile.

When Collin returned to The Executive Hotel, the head bellhop approached him with a look of concern on his face. "Señor Spencer, what happened to you? You look distressed and your pack, it is now empty. I believe it was full when you left, was it not? Is everything all right?"

Collin shook his head and said, "No ... I mean, yes, I'm all right. Thank you."

"What happened to your things? Were you robbed?"

"Nothing like that. I had to take some supplies to a colleague, that's all." Under pressure, he somehow was able to pull out a credible story.

"But you look very stressed, if you don't mind my saying."

"I'm fine, I assure you. Just tired." Collin was aware that his accent was not holding up. He wiped the perspiration from his forehead and smiled thinly. "It's been a long day for me. I've had much to do in preparation for my expedition," Collin said as he continued awkwardly past the bellhop toward the elevator. He turned just in time to see the bellhop give a gesture across the lobby to a fellow worker who shrugged, then pushed through the large glass doors to the outside

A dinging sound chimed as the elevator door opened. Collin stood frozen in place watching this exchange. A man in a gray suit entered the elevator ahead of Collin and impatiently punched the buttons, prompting Collin to step forward just before the doors closed. For a moment, he could not even remember what floor his room was on, feeling the glare from Mr. Gray Suit as he hesitated to speak.

Even after returning to his room, Collin struggled to control his breathing and to stop sweating. His nerves felt like they were on fire. There was something troubling about the interaction with the hotel staff. First, the manager and the mysterious bottle of champagne. Now the bellhops. It left him feeling anxious. Maybe Lukas would know something.

He checked the bathroom to see if the cart was still there. Yep, no one had moved it. Maybe it was bugged; maybe it wasn't. Taking chances was not a good option at this point, however. He draped a bath towel over the cart as a precaution, then closed the door again, unsure what else to do.

Lukas did not answer his phone, so Collin sent him a text: *Something's not right here. Not sure what to do. Pls advise.*

Hunger was stabbing at his stomach. He had been so preoccupied with the business at hand that he had forgotten about lunch. A quiet meal in his room sounded nice, but with all the weirdness in this hotel, the idea of room service was disquieting. But so was going out to eat because he'd have to cross the lobby and risk interactions with the bell-hop, *twice.*

Then a thought came to mind. He set up his computer because with all the security protocols Lukas had installed, he felt more comfortable using it to browse the Internet. Within a few minutes, he found a place that would deliver sandwiches and soda. He placed an order over the phone to avoid having to give his e-mail address. But that got him to thinking about e-mail, so after ordering, he opened his e-mail for the first time since leaving Germany. As expected, there were several e-mails from his mother, a few from friends, and plenty of special offers on products he had no use for. But there was a surprise—a Facebook notification informing him that Emily Burns had sent him a friend request. Emily Burns. His beautiful ex-girlfriend. A wave of pain and confusion swept through him, stealing a breath and causing him to blink hard several times until it passed. He sat back and stared at the screen for a long minute, trying to figure out what to do. Finally, curiosity led him to the Facebook login screen. After three attempts, he was able to remember his password and get to his notifications page, where he clicked on the one with her name.

There she was. A picture of her stared through the screen at him. Still gorgeous and sultry, somehow looking both stunning and smart. She was reaching out to him, and it made him feel good but panicky. And curious at the same time. How had she stayed single and disen-tangled? The recollection of that last kiss, the forbidden kiss, haunted him anew. Fresh waves of guilt and the familiar ball of nerves wound tightly in the pit of his stomach as the memory twisted its way through his mind. He was sick and excited simultaneously. Jittery, elated, and nervous.

He stalked her page for a few minutes, noticing that there were very few photos and even fewer details about her life. The photos revealed her passion for her work, wine tasting, and eating at fancy restaurants. Also, somewhat ironically, the outdoors. Trim, athletic, and gorgeous as ever, Emily still made him swoon.

He opened a new browser tab and went to the bank site to check on his electronic transfers in an attempt to get his mind off Emily Burns. But the hook was set. He couldn't stop thinking about her. Nor could he stop going back to stare at the photos. She was really something else. Even after so many years and so many twists in the road, she had a hold on him.

As he traced his most recent transactions on the bank website and recorded them in his spreadsheet, a Facebook message alert popped up on his screen. He went to it and read the innocuous message from Emily: *Hey stranger, long time, no see. How are things? We should catch up sometime soon.*

He pondered his response, not wanting to seem too eager, but not wanting to blow her off, either. Just then, the distraction he needed arrived in the form of a knock on the door. It was his dinner being delivered. As he ate, he continued to stare at her picture, trying to figure out what to say to her. He was consumed with these thoughts when a text came in from Lukas. *Can't talk now. Too much going on. Will call in an hour.*

Collin never fully understood what Lukas did and didn't care to know. It was far too technical and top secret. But he trusted him implicitly. Part of that trust was born of their long-time friendship and the numerous times Lukas had bailed him out of a jam with homework since middle school and through all three semesters at college. It's not that Collin wasn't bright enough or capable enough. It was, perhaps, because the beach was so close that he could practically hear the waves calling to him from the open window of his upstairs bedroom two and a half blocks away. A bad day of surfing was so much better than a good day at school or grinding away at homework.

But there was something more about Lukas that created such deep and abiding trust. He was supremely intelligent, which made it easy to believe in what he said. In typical Austrian fashion, he was thorough, careful, and precise. He didn't make statements unless he was certain of the facts. These traits were coupled with an innate kindness and a puppy-like loyalty. Yes, he was loyal like no one else Collin had ever known.

Sure, Rob Howell was a loyal friend, but he was more like part of the family and had been since his father suddenly left when Rob was only seven. From that time forward, Rob spent more time at the Cooks' house than at his own, which forged an unbreakable bond between him and Collin. Lukas, however, earned trust because of who he was. Only a very few people really knew who he was deep down. Collin was one of them. Rob was another.

Lukas's loyalty ran deep because Collin was the first person to befriend the awkward thirteen-year-old when he arrived in Huntington Beach, California, fresh from the quaint Austrian town of Villach, half-way through their seventh-grade year. Lukas looked so out of place, out of style, and painfully out of sorts, as the teacher introduced him to the class. While other kids snickered and pointed fingers, Collin stood up and shook his hand and introduced himself. Following Collin's lead, Rob Howell, one of the most popular boys in the school, did the same. The laughing stopped and Lukas became a near-instant celebrity at Isaac Sowers Middle School.

To Collin it was a simple act, something he hoped someone would do for him if in the same situation. That simple act altered Lukas's trajectory, changing his outlook on America and Americans and the world in general. It was the beginning of a relationship full of positives, built on the basis of profound respect and mutual appreciation.

As he ruminated about his friends, Collin's heart began to ache in a new way. He missed them. For the first time since the accident, he realized just how much as he sat at the desk in this five-star hotel room in Panama, his life completely unrecognizable from what it was a year ago. He himself was nothing more than a hollowed-out shell, looking for a place to hide from people who meant him harm just because he had the gall to sue them for taking away everything precious to him. Their negligence, or that of their client, ripped his family away from him. Now they hunted him for the money that was rightfully his. He would happily trade in the exotic travel, the excitement, and adventure—along with all the money—and resume his former struggle for survival if he could be with Amy, his children, and his friends again.

Life continued to be unfair.

As daylight waned and darkness waxed, an urgency to remove himself from the watchful eyes of the hotel staff grew stronger, but he couldn't figure out why. With each minute that passed, the restlessness increased. The need gnawed at him, compelling him to move.

He was pacing the floor when his phone finally rang.

"Look, Collin. I don't have time to explain it all, but the manager of the hotel—the guy I usually deal with—was replaced two days ago. The whole banking community in Panama is on high alert. So is the government. The Panamanians are making every effort to soothe frazzled nerves at home and abroad. I fear some of the hotel staff may even be undercover agents," Lukas said. His voice carried a hint of exasperation and apology.

"Who planted them? Our government or Interpol or who?"

"Not sure yet. Doesn't matter. The important thing right now is that you follow my instructions."

"As long as it involves getting out of here, I will. This place just doesn't feel right."

"My driver, the same one that met you at the airport, will pick you up in front of the coffee shop down the street from the hotel—on the corner of Avenida Ricardo Arango and Avenida Federico Boyd—at one o'clock a.m. Got that? That's about four hours from now."

"Yeah, I know right where it is."

"Good. One o'clock sharp. Just lay low; stay out of sight until then."

"What do I do if they come to my room again?"

"Play it as cool as possible, and try not to get flustered."

"Okay. I'll do my best."

"You'll be fine. The driver will take you to a remote airstrip where one of our bush pilots will fly you into Cali, Colombia."

"Colombia? Are you serious?"

"It's the best I can do on short notice. We do a lot of this, so it's more or less routine."

"Sounds crazy, but I'm in. It beats staying here. One question: how are you able to do all of this?"

"I'm dead. Remember?"

"Yeah, but that doesn't explain much."

"It's better that way," said Lukas. "Simply put, it's a perk of the job. I help a lot of people stay alive and out of trouble, and I get some favors in return. Let's keep it at that."

"Got it. Thanks, pal. You're the best."

"One problem, though," said Lukas.

"What's that?"

"Once he drops you off in Cali, that's it. That's as far as he can go. You'll be on your own from there. I'm going to have to lay low for a while, and so will you."

"On my own? What does that mean?"

"That means I have to go on radio silence for a while," said Lukas.

"How long is a while?" asked Collin. His stomach dropped to his toes, and he suddenly felt very weak and vulnerable again.

"I'm not sure. Could be a few days. Could be a few weeks. There's too much activity surrounding the growing threats from a mounting number of hostile groups. I'll be on the go round the clock dealing with crises, so stay small and inconspicuous, like I taught you."

"Yeah, I know. Blend in with the tourists."

"Want my advice?" asked Lukas.

"Of course, I do."

"Make your way to Peru. Lots of tourist attractions, therefore lots of tourists—most of them rich, white Americans. Plus, the Peruvian people are very nice."

CHAPTER FOURTEEN

In typical fashion, Emily showed up to work before seven thirty a.m., ready to review the data collected overnight on her current experiment. She donned her lab coat and pulled her hair back in a ponytail. Her three-mile, morning run along the coast had invigorated her brain cells, helping to bring a new perspective to her research. She had scarcely logged in when her boss leaned into her office, coffee in hand, and asked her to meet with him for a few minutes. As this was not unusual, she thought nothing of it and followed him silently into his glass-walled office, still pondering an enzyme manipulation that came to her during the run.

Mike Zimmerman was a reserved introvert in his early fifties with high marks for science, but low marks for sociality. Pleasant and easy to work for, he nonetheless didn't know how to make small talk or show interest in another person. His primary concern was in advancing humankind's ability to use gene therapy as a way to cure the world's deadliest disease. Without preamble, he launched into his remarks as if he were giving a small but meaningful press conference. Only, his voice lacked the volume and confidence usually associated with such events. "Our recent article about enhanced cell implantation into pancreatic tumors has created a lot of buzz out there, Dr. Burns. I've been asked to present your team's findings at the upcoming BioMed Conference in Chicago next month. But I prefer that you do the presentation."

These words pulled Emily out of her cloud. She shook her head quickly as if she didn't understand what she heard. "But Mike, you're the one they invited," she said.

"You know and I know that I'm not good at public speaking. I'd be so nervous I would botch the whole thing. Plus, it's your team's findings that we used in the article. I contributed relatively little."

"Yeah, but you're the one with the credentials, the experience. You're the one everyone wants to hear, not me."

He looked directly at her, albeit briefly, for the first time since the conversation began. His eyes were kind, if not confident. They darted to and fro as he continued. "I already have an assignment to speak on the patterning of irregularities within cancerous lesions on the liver. I don't think it would be wise of me to attempt a second presentation on such short notice. Besides, it's your turn to receive the credit you deserve, Emily. You've been working on this for eighteen months. You put in the time. You applied the science. You did the calculations and analysis. You should be the one at that podium, not me."

Emily rested her arms on the armrests of the padded chair and stared back at her boss. "You want me to present at one of the biggest conferences in our business? Next month?"

"Yes. Actually, it starts three weeks from yesterday."

"Three weeks from yesterday?" she said as she exhaled. "That's not much time."

"I know, and I apologize. I've been considering my options. You are the clear choice. I should have asked you sooner, I know. Forgive me."

"What makes you think *I* won't botch it up?" she said, a tremor in her voice signaling her growing angst.

"I know you well enough to know that won't happen." His eyes met hers for another split second before darting back to his computer screen.

"But I feel so unprepared. And just three weeks to put it together?"

"Well, actually, they have requested a copy of your slide show a week in advance so the technical guys can work out any bugs before the conference begins. So, make that thirteen days."

"But how can I do that?" Her fingers were now wrapped in a death grip around the end of the armrests.

"Easy. Just review your notes and findings from the trial stage, the ones you used for the article, and put that information into a slide show."

"Still, that's going to take some time, Mike."

He looked at her blankly and said, "No one on the planet knows this stuff better than you, Dr. Burns. No one. I know you can do it."

Emily sat back in the seat, realizing her boss had no empathy. Not that he was mean, but because he was 100 percent committed to his job and expected that she would feel the same. "Mike, I don't know what to say."

"Just say you'll do it and you'll do the best you can. I'll help out if you need, but I doubt you will. This is your baby, and you know your stuff better than anyone else."

* * * *

CALI, COLOMBIA
MAY 14

Collin awoke when the engine of the small, twin prop Piper began to slow just before starting its descent toward the tiny mountainside landing strip. Exhaustion had gotten the best of him and pushed aside all anxiety, at least for a couple of hours. A dark, thick, uneven, green blanket of trees spread out just below them. To the east, the first grayish streaks of sunlight began to show themselves above the mountains. The pilot, seated on Collin's left, was focused on his instrument panel, but as Collin began to stir, he spoke for the first time since takeoff.

"Not many people know about this place. See it there? It's that patch of grass in the trees down there. Those who do know about it are probably nowhere to be found. They're operatives like you."

He returned to his work, his eyes focused ahead, his tongue poking out between pursed lips. Collin's heart skipped as the tail of the aircraft bumped something and the plane momentarily went sideways. The hyper-focused pilot made a series of corrections, then barked, "Damn trees grow taller and make this harder every time I come here."

Collin gulped hard. He searched the area where the pilot's finger had pointed. In the pale morning light, he began to make out the thin strip of grass they would use as a runway and asked, "When was the last time you landed here?"

"About three months ago, but everything grows fast in this part of the world."

"Glad you know what you're doing."

"That doesn't always help down here. Part of it depends on some luck, too. Especially these near-dark approaches," said the pilot. Collin could feel his blood turn icy and his heart rate increase. He peered through the front window, watching for hazards. The small aircraft glided just above the trees tops as the pilot reduced the airspeed and adjusted the trim.

Before he knew it, the plane hit the ground and bounced, causing Collin to grab a handle with one hand and the bottom of his seat with the other, his whole body tense. Now they were rushing toward a copse of trees at high speed. The pilot, tongue out again, made a calculated turn to the left, just missing the trees, before turning again to the right where another hundred yards of grass continued with a gentle upslope. They stopped with a jerk just a few feet from the edge of the jungle foliage, and the pilot calmly continued his narrative, pointing with a pen he had pulled out to jot down notes on a pad.

"There's a small village about five miles to the south. You should be able to get a ride from there to Cali and from there a bus to wherever you're going. Here, you'll need this." The pilot retrieved a worn passport from the pocket of his camouflage jacket and handed it to Collin. "It's got an entry stamp into Colombia already."

Collin thumbed through the pages, noting more stamps into and out of several countries. However, there was no photo on the front page. His mouth turned down as he contemplated this dilemma. "I see it's a generic version," he said.

"Yeah, you'll need to put your own photo in it, of course. Standard procedure. I assume you know the drill," said the pilot as he climbed out to check the fuel level. "Hey, before you go," he called over his shoulder, "I'm going to need your help turning this thing around."

After collecting his wits as well as his belongings, Collin helped the pilot lift the tail of the plane and, with some exertion, the two men were able to pivot its nose one hundred eighty degrees so that it was heading back the way they came. He then handed the pilot an envelope with $5000 cash, as Lukas instructed, and thanked the man for his service. Slinging his two bags over his shoulders, Collin disappeared into the overgrowth, following the nearly imperceptible trail the pilot pointed out. A hundred yards into the bush, he stopped to consult the map and compass he had been given. Using the flashlight from his phone to see, Collin double checked to be sure he was heading the right way.

Through the foliage, he heard the plane's engine rev up as the pilot gunned it for takeoff.

The last remnants of the day's sunshine were fading when Collin stepped off the rickety, old bus in a dodgy part of Cali, Colombia. His clothes were smudged and sweaty, his face grimy and grim. His hair clung in long strands against his forehead, temples, and cheeks. Rivulets of perspiration dripped from them. It had been an adventurous day to say the least. His head was pounding and his stomach roiling from the bouncing and swaying of the ancient, multi-colored bus that had just carried him along winding mountain roads from the village, stopping at five other collections of huts along the way.

It felt like a thousand miles worth of sickening curves, but the map indicated the distance was roughly sixty. A short walk from the bus terminal, he spotted a taxi stand. Many of his fellow passengers were making their way toward it, so he followed, practically staggering. Not knowing what was available, and feeling rather ill, he asked the taxi driver to take him to the nearest hotel. That was a mistake. It took only a few minutes to get there, which was good, but nothing else about it was.

As soon as he walked in, his skin began to crawl. Bolting for the door did not seem to be a good option, based on the fast-approaching darkness and what he had seen of the surrounding neighborhood on the way to the hotel. It appeared there was nothing else remotely close by, so he decided to go with it. Large bugs scurried under the flimsy furniture as he walked through the dimly lit lobby. The fat lady behind the counter watched him the whole way, curiosity painted all over her face.

In heavily dialectical Spanish, she asked, "Where's your woman?"

Now Collin was equally as curious. "What do you mean?" he asked in a much purer form of her native language.

"Are you alone?" she asked incredulously.

"Yes, I am," he said. "If it's a problem, I can go somewhere else."

She laughed out loud at him. "Where are you going to go? There's not another hotel within ten kilometers of here, and no taxi is going to come to this part of town at night. So, if you want to walk, go ahead," she said with a shrug.

"No, thanks. This will be fine."

"One hour minimum. How many hours would you like?"

"Hours?" he asked. "I don't know. Until morning, I guess."

"Do you want me to send in a woman for you?"

"No, no," said Collin, trying not to look or sound disgusted. "I just need to get some sleep. I've had a long day."

"Are you sure? You'll sleep better." Her smile was devilish and her laughter boisterous as she cackled at him.

"Yes, I'm sure. I just want to sleep. Alone. Thank you."

"I'll charge you for eight," she said, informing him of the amount due. He paid with some of the Colombian currency the limo driver had provided back in Panama City, and then made his way up the creaky stairs to his room. The hallway was dark, the carpet threadbare and stained, and the doors and walls paper thin. Muffled grunts and moans and shrieks of exaggerated pleasure escaped from several of the rooms as he made his way down the long corridor. The smells of stale beer, cigarettes, and an assortment of other unpleasant odors combined to create a repulsive thickness to the air that Collin hardly dared to breathe.

His room wasn't much better. The carpet was not as dirty, but insects scattered when he turned on the light. The room was more like a closet with a cheap, twin bed shoved in it. The only place to set his bags was a wobbly desk barely big enough for his computer and a painted wooden chair, both squeezed into a corner at the foot of the bed. There was just enough room to walk around the bed. No night stand, no clock, no TV. The only saving graces to this palace of roaches were the private bathroom and free Wi-Fi. Although he hadn't eaten all day, he had no appetite. Besides, he dared not venture outside. Nor was he in the mood to take any chances on delivery food.

He wore two pairs of socks in the shower to avoid unseen fungi and enjoyed nearly three minutes of lukewarm water before it turned icy. Checking his watch after he got dressed, he realized he had to endure seven and a half more hours pent up in this grungy cage before the sun came up. Despite the fact that he wasn't especially squeamish, lying down in that bed was beyond him. He knew he couldn't possibly close his eyes with the number of creepy crawlies inhabiting his space. It would be difficult to keep himself occupied and awake in his current condition, but he knew he didn't have a choice.

His first order of business was to affix his photo into the new, fake passport the pilot gave him. He rummaged through his backpack for the supplies he needed, then went to work meticulously cutting, pasting, and laminating his picture into place. Lukas had shown him how, giving him the opportunity to doctor six of his own counterfeit passports before his journey began, and suggested he always keep the items he would need on hand.

Another hour burned. Six to go.

It was time to catch up with the rest of the world.

After running the secure login routine, his computer was ready. Collin searched the Internet for stories about the RBS attack and the hunt for the culprits, including himself. Wanting to study it more carefully, he enlarged the photo of him and Pho Nam Penh taken two weeks earlier in a London pub. The chance encounter that had sent his already altered life into a frenetic cascade seemed so long ago now.

Penh's face was partially obscured by shadow, but he recalled the brief exchange. The man was cavalier though quiet. He exuded an unnatural air of confidence and panache as he approached Collin through the crowded bar, asking if he could sit at what appeared to be one of the few available seats in the place. Collin stared at the face on his computer screen. This was the man who wanted his money and wouldn't mind killing him to get it. This was the man who engineered the chance encounter that put Collin in the crosshairs of an intense international search for the alleged perpetrators. Regardless of the lack of evidence, Collin's safety and security had been taken from him, as well as his reputation, and that made him angry.

He seethed as he stared at the shadowy face, filling in the details from memory. The cheekbones, he remembered, stood out more than most Asians. His skin was smooth and youthful. There was a break in his right eyebrow, perhaps a scar of some sort. His eyes were dark and intense; that he remembered vividly in retrospect. And the man was dressed impeccably, wearing a silk suit, dark shirt, and striped tie. Collin assumed at the time he was some sort of business tycoon, a real high roller. The uneasiness he felt back then returned and left him wanting fresh air, same as he had shortly after the man sat down next to him in London. Collin left that pub in a hurry because of that uneasiness.

Turning his attention back to his present situation, he wanted to check in with Lukas, although he knew Lukas was on radio silence. He just didn't know how long, so he sent him a private message through the secure messaging system on his laptop to see what would happen.

Lukas did not respond, but Collin decided to give him an update on his travels anyway.

Despite the fact that he had not taken any pictures, Collin also updated his travel journal with the details of his adventures since leaving Captain Sewell's boat. His story would make Amy cringe, he knew, but he spared no detail, knowing she loved a good tale.

When he finished his latest and longest journal entry, he checked e-mail and responded to his mother with a vague reference as to his activities, mentioning only that he had tried sailing again and loved it and was enjoying the scenery. He assured her that his health was good, and he was safe. She needed to hear these things he knew.

Next, he responded to an e-mail from his buddy Rob, which said, "How's it going, bro? Enjoying your little getaway?"

Collin's response: "You know it. Nonstop party. Rocking it hard. Still alive. Still on tour." He knew Rob would be in touch with his family, and would get the details from Lukas, so he kept it brief but positive, despite the storm of anger that was rising inside. Thanks to his need to run and hide, Collin couldn't enjoy the company of his best friend, who could surely help him deal with his loss. He wondered what Rob would do in this situation. The thought made him even more homesick. Better think of something else.

It was 1:13 a.m. He had thankfully lost track of time. Four hours left. He remembered that he had not responded to Emily's Facebook message in Panama City, so he logged in and found another message from her dated earlier in the day: "Any chance we can meet for coffee and just talk sometime soon? I want to make sure you're doing OK, especially after the condition you were in last time I saw you. I wish I could have stayed there at the hospital with you, but I felt out of place. Let me know when we can get together."

His heart sank, sensing her anxiety and concern.

He responded, "Sorry, I've been traveling and didn't have Internet access. Yes, I would enjoy chatting again in person, but I won't be available for a while."

He contemplated what to say next when a reply chimed in. "You're traveling? That's good, I hope. Tell me more."

He decided to remain vague. "Mostly in Europe. Saw some really cool stuff."

Her next message didn't come in for quite some time, and he wondered what she might be thinking. Finally, she responded and said, "What kind of cool stuff did you see over there?"

"I loved London. Saw Westminster Abbey, Tower Bridge, rode the London Eye. You know, all that touristy stuff. But it was cool." He wanted to keep some distance in both space and time, just in case this communication fell into other hands.

"That's great. When do you plan to come back to CA?"

"Not for a while. I've got a few things I still want to do." He tried to leave adequate time between each message so she wouldn't think he was too eager. Plus, he had to consider her reasons for these questions. So far, it seemed to be a normal conversation. She acted interested in what he was doing, so he reciprocated. "Tell me more about your work. I know you love it, but what are you working on?"

Just after he hit send, another message came in: "How long is a while? Are we talking next week, next month, next year?"

Her inquisitive mind, he remembered, always thought up a million questions. He knew he had to answer her, but he also knew he couldn't be specific. "Not a year. Maybe a month. Hard to say. I'm taking care of some personal stuff, so it will probably be a week or two, at least."

Now the messages were getting disjointed, as she responded to the previous question. "I'm working on a new gene-sequencing experiment to engineer proteins that will hopefully fight cancerous cells within the pancreas and potentially in certain types of other cancers. It's promising, but we're taking baby steps at this point."

"Sounds complex and exciting. You must really be into your work." He pushed send and got another response immediately after.

"I see. Too busy to have coffee with a friend, eh?"

"No, it's not like that. I just have some things I'm working on, and I don't know how long it will take me to finish. That's all," Collin said.

The timing continued to present challenges.

"Yeah, it's just boring science stuff. Us lab rats aren't very interesting until we score a major breakthrough."

"I think your work sounds exciting. I mean, how many people get to really help others the way you can."

"OK. If you don't want to talk face to face, I get it. It's just that I want to be there for you. But I don't want to be a pest."

Collin paused so they could get on the same topic at the same time. "You're a good friend, not a pest at all. Don't worry about that. I would love to meet up sometime. Let me figure out when and how. Believe it or not, my life is very complicated right now." There was a long pause. Collin worried that he had put her off or offended her, so he changed the subject. "You do anything outside of work?"

It seemed like an eternity before Emily came back with a response. Had he pushed her away? Her next message felt more sterile, less chummy. "Admittedly, I'm really into my work, but it's starting to pay off. My colleagues and I are on the brink of a breakthrough, I think. But you might not find biomedical research super exciting like I do."

"I always knew you would do great things. I'm really glad to hear it. I'm happy for you," he wrote.

"Thank you."

"Does this mean you're going to cure cancer?" "I wish. That would be a dream."

"You've always had that dream. I admire your persistence."

"Thank you."

"It wouldn't surprise me if you were the one to find a cure."

"We're a long way off still, but every step, I guess, moves us closer to that goal." Her messages were coming in much faster now. That meant she wasn't thinking so hard about what to say, which, Collin thought, was a good thing. He wanted to keep things light and stay on a subject she felt confident about.

"You'll get there, I'm sure. Knowing you."

"Wanna hear something I haven't told anyone else?"

"Of course."

"My boss asked me to speak at the BioMed Conference in Chicago. He wants me to present the findings that we published in last month's *Cancer Researchers Journal*. I have to admit, I'm pretty nervous."

"You shouldn't be nervous. Just relax and be yourself. You'll do great."

"I appreciate the encouragement. It means a lot to me."

The two high school sweethearts continued their conversation for another hour before realizing it was late—nearly one o'clock in the morning for Emily.

"Keep in touch and let's meet up soon" was her final line.

After Emily signed off, Collin spent the next ninety minutes learning more about the BioMed Conference in Chicago, the Scripps Institute, and the article Emily had published. Her career was on fire, it seemed. She was doing important work and making a difference in the world, just as she had dreamed about when they were dating.

Their lives had diverged for many years and in many ways. Collin was never sure why she was so motivated and focused while he had no idea what he wanted to be. Nothing ever grabbed him the way the world of medicine and science grabbed her. He never finished college; she had a PhD. She had never had a real relationship, other than the one with him. But that was a dozen years ago. Since then, he had loved so deeply and desperately that the loss of that love had nearly destroyed him. Now, from half a world away, he felt closer to Emily, more intrigued by her than he had been since his senior year.

It made him miss home and his friends.

Thankfully, dawn was breaking outside. His release from this filthy cell was imminent.

*   *   *   *

It took Collin a total of six days to work his way the eleven hundred miles across Colombia and Peru to Lima, hopping from one obscure village to another by bus, covering as few as eighty and as many as three hundred miles a day. Each segment of the journey was a grueling and exhausting event, much like the first one. The buses were crowded and stinky, most of them mechanical nightmares on wheels. In a few of the towns, he was able to find a clean motel with Internet access so he could continue his online dialogues, mostly with his mother and Emily, and get some real sleep. But most of them were run down and dirty and backward.

It seemed that things were changing back home. For no apparent reason, his brother, Richard, and his sister, Megan, began to drop e-mail notes to keep him up-to-date on the happenings in their rather ordinary lives. He found this both intriguing and ironic, especially the timing. Why did they all of a sudden start showing concern? They had each expressed their frustrations with him during the holidays but hadn't shown much interest in him since. Megan had said she felt like he was punishing the family for his problems by not being home for Christmas. Since then she had written him a grand total of four e-mails. Richard had accused him of being a coward and running away when the going got hard and hadn't written another thing since New Year's Eve. Why had they decided simultaneously to forgive him? After their separate rants and deliberate distancing, they were now worried? Their e-mails expressed concern for his well-being and let him know their mother missed him terribly and wanted him home. Patiently, he explained that he couldn't do that right now. He had some urgent matters to take care of. But, he promised, when he got all of his business taken care of, he would return.

As he suffered through one cramped and nauseating bus ride after another, he found his mind alternately thinking about his mother and Emily and plotting vengeance against Pho Nam Penh. The more physical hardship he had to endure, the more he felt a desire to communicate with the women who meant the most to him and to strangle the man who hunted him. These thoughts helped him survive the tedium of his travels. Thoughts of bringing down his nemesis energized him when he needed it most. All of these emotions, the positive and the negative, swirling inside also served to keep his mind off of Amy and his children, keeping his sorrow at bay that much longer.

Throughout his journey to Lima, Collin found that he looked forward to sending messages to his family and friends and was eager to read their replies. They were interested in his doings, which caused him to tell more and more. The particulars of his locations and travels remained purposely vague, but he described, in broad brush strokes, the scenery and the people and the food so they could appreciate that he was having new experiences. Sharing brought a measure of joy that had long been absent.

Lukas managed to finally respond to Collin's message. His response was brief and stressed the need for caution and watchfulness. Pho Nam Penh still had a score to settle. His stirring of the hornet's nest with the photos in London, Lukas assured Collin, was just an opening salvo. Surely the game was only beginning. And surely Collin had yet to see his best moves. Despite Lukas's calls to vigilance, Collin saw few white people and even fewer people who even gave him a second look. To the hard-working natives he encountered, he was just another shaggy-haired, bearded American wandering through their world. Despite his ability to speak their language, these rural coffee farm laborers and small-town merchants had little time or concern for someone like him.

He didn't mean to grow complacent and take his personal safety for granted; it just happened. Perhaps it was the constant and repetitive bone jarring he had to endure for long hours each day as he traveled on buses that would be deemed safety hazards up north. Maybe it was the ho-hum responses from everyone around him. Or it could have been the lack of restful sleep. Whatever it was that prompted it, by the time Collin rode into Lima, he had one overriding thought on his mind: comfort.

At the suggestion of the taxi driver, Collin decided the JW Marriott, right on the coast, would be the perfect place to unwind from a week of hardship through the backcountry. Staggering into the opulent lobby, lugging his computer bag and knapsack, looking bedraggled and desperate, he was met by hotel security before he reached the front desk. It hadn't occurred to him that his dirty clothes, unkempt hair, and beard would cause concern. After the places he had stayed the previous six nights, it had completely slipped his mind.

The two men in snappy uniforms approached from behind and startled him, causing him to let out a high-pitched "Whoa," as each guard grabbed an arm. Collin struggled and twisted, ripping his arms out of their grasp.

This brought even more unwanted attention. Conversations stopped, heads turned, and eyes peered, all curious to see how the homeless American would react. He spun around and backed away a couple of steps.

"I'm sorry, sir, but do you have a reservation here?" asked the taller security guard with a forced kindness.

"Not yet, I don't," stammered Collin, still edgy.

With a valiant effort at a sincere smile, the tall security guard cocked his head and asked, "Do you plan to stay with us tonight, sir?"

"Well, I was thinking about it, but if this is the way you're going to treat me, then maybe I won't." Realizing he was on full display and there was no graceful way to sneak out now, he decided to play the indignant card. And it worked. He slipped into a character he had read about in the newspaper. Pretending to be an Internet tycoon on sabbatical, he huffed, "Do you know who I am? I deserve better treatment than this. I was featured in *The Wall Street Journal* in February after selling my company to Google. Despite my appearance, I am a respected businessman—not a criminal—and I demand an apology."

The guard stammered. "Please, forgive me. I had no idea. Come right this way, sir," said the tall one, as he waved an arm toward the front desk. "I am so sorry. Please, follow me."

Little did Collin know that of the dozens of people gawking at this scene, one was a journalist who captured the whole thing on video using her smart phone. She uploaded the clip to YouTube before Collin made it to his room.

CHAPTER FIFTEEN

Nic Lancaster's confidence was shaken but not his determination. Two near misses within the same week left his ego bruised. When the Navy vessel reported finding nothing unusual aboard any of the sailboats they searched in the Western Caribbean, he was dumbfounded. The videos from George Town had clearly shown a man resembling Collin Cook going to the marina. The taxi cab company confirmed a white American with brown hair was dropped off there that same morning. Nic was miffed and mystified by this average guy and his ability to elude him. That was the first.

The second failure came after an Interpol informant in Panama had reported that a man who matched the description of Collin Cook had arrived at his hotel, pretending to be a British archaeologist. Photos were sent to confirm his identity. Nic thought he had struck pay dirt. He coordinated a raid the next morning with the Panamanian Public Forces. However, it proved embarrassingly fruitless. His quarry had once again vanished into thin air. Hotel surveillance cameras produced video evidence that was strong but not 100 percent conclusive. The long hair and beard, combined with the low-quality video stream, produced an 88 percent match on facial recognition software. But in his gut, Nic knew it was Collin Cook and knew he had just missed him—again. Damn that Alastair Montgomery for not giving Nic the authority he needed to sign off on the raid. Having to wait for Alastair's approval cost him time, valuable time, which allowed Collin to sneak away in the middle of the night.

Nic was determined not to let that happen again. No more enduring the water cooler jokes about chasing down pleasure cruises or raiding empty hotel rooms. Maybe it was time to use his prime weapon: blackmail. Nic mulled this over as he sipped his morning coffee, alone at his desk, at 6:55 a.m. His wheels were just starting to turn, devising a devilish scheme, when a dialogue box popped up on his computer screen.

It was an instant message over Interpol's internal system, coming from one of the few basement-dwelling techno-geeks who had proven useful. "Hey, mate, I might have something for you. Come check this out."

Full of impatient energy, Nic took the stairs down four floors to the "dungeon," as the techies liked to call their quarters. The low ceiling and uneven fluorescent lighting accentuated the prison-like atmosphere that earned the IT department's work space its nickname. Peter had weird hair, an earring, and wore lots of black. Not the type Nic normally hung out with, but since Peter was a team player who exhibited real genius, Nic liked him all right. "You got something for me?" he said as he entered the eerily dark cubicle.

"Yep. You gotta see this," said Peter. His fingers tap-danced across his keyboard until a YouTube screen appeared. "Remember that bearded American bloke you wanted us to identify?"

"Of course. Collin Cook. Been trying to nab him for weeks. Why?"

"Well, I took the liberty of using some of the photos we collected along the way and created a filtering algorithm that scans the Internet for his face or anything with an 88 percent match. You remember that was the best we could do with the footage out of Panama, right? 88 percent?"

"Yeah, yeah. Get on with it."

"Well, we got a hit on this particular clip that was uploaded to a Peruvian news site's YouTube channel. Watch." He clicked on the play arrow.

Nic watched in rapt fascination as Collin Cook bluffed his way out of the hands of two security guards, who begged his forgiveness, despite his grungy appearance, at the JW Marriott in Lima.

"Check this out," said Peter. "One of the nicest hotels in the city, and this guy walks in looking like a hobo and gets the red-carpet treatment. Unbelievable."

The video was unsteady, and the audio was unclear because of background noise. They ran the clip three more times. But it was good enough for Nic. He was certain that was his man. "That's brilliant, Peter. When did this incident take place?"

"Looks like it was yesterday evening in Peru; just about eight hours ago. That would make it approximately half past midnight this morning GMT."

"Can you go frame by frame?"

"Sure can," said Peter. Some more taps and clicks, and Collin Cook was moving very slowly.

"Good. That's *him*. Right there. I can't believe this. He just shows up willy-nilly out of the blue in Lima, Peru. How did he get there, I wonder?" Nic's voice elevated an octave or two above its normal high pitch. "No matter. Can you zoom in on the face?"

"Yeah, I can do that, too. It's not the best quality, given the distance and the lighting."

"That's quite all right. We'll work with it. Can you adjust the focus?"

"Will do." Peter typed in some commands, and the image slowly became clearer.

"Brilliant. Can you save that on the shared drive in the Cook folder?"

"Of course."

"Send me the YouTube link, as well, would you?"

"Sure thing, highness."

"Good work, Peter. I'll see to it that you get promoted."

"Right you will," said Peter, but Nic was already halfway to the door. Calling over his shoulder, Nic added, "As soon as I get promoted."

Nic knew he had to hurry. It was already 7:13, according to his flashy wristwatch. That meant 2:13 a.m. in Lima. Cook would be sleeping. Alastair had a meeting that started at eight, so Nic needed to catch him before that. Most mornings when Alastair had to attend meetings first thing, his mood was foul. Nic decided to just plow through it and hope to start Alastair's day with some good news. This time he would get the authorization he needed, and Collin Cook would not escape. They had Cook where they wanted him. Time to lower the boom. On Alastair, too, if need be.

Nic contacted the secretary down the hall. Alastair checked in with her every morning. It was part of his routine. Nic asked her to let him know the moment Alastair walked in because he had some good news that required urgent attention.

While he waited, Nic made half a dozen phone calls. By the time he hung up from the last call, the trap was set. He had the intel and the cooperation he needed. The hotel management and the Peruvian police agreed to assist in the raid. The last piece of the puzzle would be Alastair Montgomery's approval to set in motion the wheels of justice that would arrest Collin Cook for high crimes against the United Kingdom and other sovereign states.

Nic's career was about to take a leap forward. He rubbed his hands together in anticipation.

His phone buzzed. He picked it up. The secretary informed Nic that Mr. Montgomery had just left her office. Nic popped up from his seat and wove his way to the outer hallway where Alastair's office was located. He rounded a corner coming the other way and got there a step ahead of Alastair, who carried a load. A worn leather briefcase in one hand, the morning paper stuffed between his elbow and his rib cage, a cup of coffee and his phone balanced delicately in the other. He jumped with a start when Nic appeared suddenly before him. "Good Lord. Are you mad? You could give a man a heart attack."

"Sorry about that, but I've got some news you need to hear before your meeting this morning."

"Yes, about that. Give me a status update on that Cook fellow, would you?"

"Precisely. We've got him. Right where we want him. He's in a hotel room in Lima, Peru, as we speak. It's the middle of the night there, so the bloke is fast asleep, I'm sure. I've already called the Peruvian authorities and the hotel. Everything is ready to go. We just need your authorization to move in and capture him."

"My approval? Why not Crabtree?"

"I don't know, sir. Why Crabtree? Isn't this our investigation now? Aren't we running the show?"

"He's no longer on our continent. I don't see why we should."

"Look, sir. With all due respect, there's no reason not to jump on this right now. We know where he is. We know what he's done. He has info that we need to catch the bigger fish. Remember? That was my assignment. You gave it to me, but now I need your approval to cinch this thing up. Will you make the call?"

Alastair stopped and scanned the area as he thought things through.

He was keenly aware that they were in open space. Office doors were open all along the hallway, and the cubicles just to his left were most likely occupied. He must take action and be decisive. "Didn't you say this the last time I signed an order to capture this guy? Didn't you say we had on good authority that he was at The Executive Hotel in Panama City?"

"Yes, sir, I did."

"Didn't we barge into an empty room?"

"Yes, but I can explain—"

"And the time before that, weren't you certain that this chap was aboard a sailboat just off the coast of Grand Cayman? What happened there?"

"Well, that was—"

"The point is, Nic, this is getting bloody ridiculous. We look like the Keystone Cops here. It's embarrassing. I don't know if I want my name on another order until I have some proof."

"Fine. I'll show you. Come this way." Nic spoke through gritted teeth, trying to keep his tone in check. Alastair could be a real curmudgeon, especially in the mornings, but Nic did not expect this much harassment. He moved quickly to Alastair's computer monitor and tapped on the keys, logging in.

"What are you doing?" Alastair asked, the annoyance in his voice undeniable.

"I've got a video you need to see. Bear with me while I get to it."

Within seconds, Nic had the YouTube video loading. After it played, he showed Alastair the close-up photos of Collin's face from the video and compared them to the photos they had on file. For further proof, Nic played back an audio recording of his phone conversation with the woman at the front desk of the hotel. She confirmed that the man involved in the altercation last night was in room 2321. To drive his point home, he played back another recording of his call with the police chief in Lima, who agreed under some pressure from Nic, to instigate a raid, but only if the directive was from the section chief.

Nic turned to his boss and glowered There you have it. We know it's him. We know where he's at. Now all we've got to do is go get him. What do you say, Section Chief?"

"I say don't cock this one up." Alastair's eyes narrowed as he said it. Nic knew he was serious, but he also knew he had another video file of old Alastair, one he stored in a safe place on his phone that would be his hall pass if ever Alastair became an obstacle. Maybe Alastair needed a reminder. He held off for now. The right moment would present itself eventually.

* * * *

J W MARRIOTT HOTEL, LIMA, PERU
MAY 20

This is comfort, thought Collin as he walked through his twenty-third floor suite. Thick carpet, soft lighting, every modern convenience and luxury he had ever imagined, and then some. Everything was so clean, so fresh, so modern. A flat screen TV, leather couches, fancy artwork. But the crowning feature was the view of the ocean. It was spectacular. He gazed out the full-length window, taking it all in—the cliffs, the protruding peninsula to the south, the moon as it shimmered on the water.

When he finally finished gawking, he felt even grimier than before. A long, hot shower made him comfortable and relaxed. Dressed in his favorite sweatpants and worn out T-shirt, he stretched out on the bed. He wanted to close his eyes, but he didn't feel sleepy. Instead, he lay there and pondered the events that had taken place downstairs. It was probably no big deal. Nothing would come of it. He forced his eyes shut and let his head sink into the down pillows.

But sleep would not come. The image of making a spectacle in front of all those people kept sweeping across the stage of his mind, followed by the words Lukas had said so many times. "Stay low. Stay small. Blend in." The incident had blown over just as quickly as it had started, so he forced the thought out of his mind by thinking about more pleasant things, like his Facebook conversations with Emily. Since sleep eluded him, he went online to see what was happening and to continue the communication with his dear friend.

At two o'clock in the morning, after emailing his mother, his siblings, and Rob, and messaging back and forth with Emily, he decided it was time to get some sleep. It had been a long, difficult day. And week. He needed to catch up on his rest to stay sharp. He signed off and climbed in the soft, inviting, king sized bed, gathered up the pillows, and settled in for a cozy night of luxury.

At 4:07 a.m., there was a pounding on the door. Then more pounding. When no one answered, a key card was inserted into the lock. The door swung open. Lights on. Eight military commandos stormed into the room, rifles at the ready, swinging them into every nook and cranny of the suite. Within twenty seconds, the man in charge called out, "All clear." Over his cell phone, he confirmed his announcement. "I'm sorry, Agent Lancaster. The room is empty. There is no one here."

"You sure you got the right room?"

"Positive. We double checked with the front desk that this is the right room, 2321."

Nic let out a string of profanity, revealing his bitter disappointment. Hot rage boiled behind his eyes and in his chest. He panted like a dog and hissed like a viper. "You mean to tell me that man from the video, the one that looked like a beggar, never checked into his room? Even after making such a fuss?"

"No, sir. It looks like someone was here. The bed has been slept in, and the shower has been used. Someone was here but not anymore. There is no luggage, no personal items left behind."

Another series of expletives. "Then get me camera footage from the lobby. We've got to find this man. He's an international criminal, and now he's loose in your country. Find him."

Twenty minutes later, as he poured over the video footage from the hotel lobby, Nic continued to curse and fume. He clearly saw, from a different angle, Collin Cook's performance with the security guards and his checking into the hotel. He watched him cross the lobby to the bank of elevators after the front desk staff excitedly flapped over him, practically kissing his feet. Nic fast-forwarded through hours of video. There was constant activity until midnight, then it slowed considerably. The crowds dispersed and disappeared at eight times normal speed. From about twelve thirty on, the lobby was mostly empty, save the occasional couple holding hands as they strolled through or small groups moving at a leisurely pace from the entrance to the elevators.

Nothing interesting until the time stamp in the lower corner showed 3:23 a.m. That's when he saw a lone man, wearing a dark sweatshirt with the hood pulled down to hide his face, walk purposefully through the lobby, head down the whole way. The man had a small backpack on one shoulder and a computer bag on the other. The same pieces of luggage Collin Cook had when he checked in at 7:47 p.m.

Nic slammed his palms on his desk and clenched his jaw so tightly he almost broke a filling. "How in the bloody hell does he do it? Every bloody time."

Too restless to sleep, Collin had gotten up and paced the floor of his suite for another twenty minutes, trying desperately to reach Lukas. When he didn't answer and didn't respond to texts, Collin gave up and followed his own best instincts. He packed, dressed, and exited the building as quickly and quietly as he could. He turned north out of the front doors and worked his way through the deserted city streets in search of a taxi. When he finally found one in front of a downtown night club, he asked the cab driver to take him to the Best Western on the other side of town. He knew there would be budget-minded American tourists there.

Perhaps he was being silly, paranoid even. But he couldn't shake the nagging sense that he had drawn too much attention to himself. He didn't like that feeling and feared a repeat of what happened in Panama City. Sure, he had spent five hundred dollars for a few hours of luxury, and he hated wasting money, but it would be worth it to feel safe and completely anonymous somewhere else.

At least he had enjoyed the view while he could.

* * * *

SAN DIEGO, CALIFORNIA
MAY 20

The clock on the display monitor in her late model BMW showed 9:41 p.m. Emily had stayed late, again, working on her presentation and trying to manage two, simultaneous, interdependent experiments, the results of which could add that much more punch to her performance.

This was the fourth day in a row she had put in fourteen plus hours, and she needed to find another gear, something other than work, to take her mind away.

After backing out of her reserved parking stall at the Scripps Research facility, Emily decided to use her ten-minute commute productively. It was time to call Sarah Cook. With the BioMed Conference looming and the burden of her first-ever professional presentation weighing heavily on her mind, Emily had neglected to keep in touch with Sarah for over a week. This conversation would be different than most because this time she actually had something significant to report.

Sarah was so happy to hear from Emily and thanked her for the good news. It sounded like Collin was interested in rebuilding the friendship, they both agreed, and this gave them hope. Sarah was pleased that Collin had picked up his communication with her as well, although he purposely avoided telling her anything substantive about his doings.

Emily gently turned the conversation toward Sarah and her health by asking how she was feeling.

"I'm on my third dose of chemo, and as I'm sure you know, it gets harder and harder. I'm exhausted for several days after a treatment, and then just as my energy begins to come back, it's time for another dose. It just wipes me out," Sarah explained.

Emily did her best to empathize, but rather than responding emotionally, the scientist in her started asking questions that Sarah didn't know how to answer. When her queries yielded little information of value to Emily, she asked, "Will you do me a favor and have your doctor contact me? If you're OK with it, I would like to take a look at your lab results and just see what is going on."

"Of course, that would be all right. I'll call him tomorrow."

Emily approached her building and explained that she might lose cell service in the basement garage, so they signed off with a promise to stay in touch. Sarah wished her luck on her presentation and assured her that she would be the star of the show.

What Emily failed to notice as she talked and drove was a blue sedan mirroring her every move several hundred yards behind her. As she slowed to turn into her parking garage, the blue sedan kept going and parked under a large tree in front of her high-rise condominium.

In her top floor condo, Emily dressed in nothing but a well-worn, cotton Padres shirt. She stood in front of the picture window in her living room, clutching a steaming, oversized mug of potato soup, looking out over the mighty Pacific, wondering where her friend was and what he was doing. It was eleven o'clock, and she had just signed off her computer after another long conversation with Collin. It was enjoyable but exhausting.

She stood to stretch her legs and think while she ate.

The full moon shone on the glassy surface of the ocean in bumpy streaks that stretched toward her. The muffled roar of the surf below brought a sense of calm that drowned the encroaching loneliness. As she thought about Collin, she felt at once empty and grateful. Grateful for so many memories that still made her smile. Grateful that he let her back in his life at a time when she was most desperate for friendship. Grateful that now she had a chance to return the favor and be his friend when he needed one most. Empty because of his decided absence.

While she was pleased that Collin continued the dialogue and shared his experiences, albeit with the most indistinct descriptions imaginable, she wanted more. Maybe it was because he was a guy and didn't communicate in the language of emotion. Maybe he was masking something. She didn't know, nor could she. Not with his frustratingly vague, bare bones style. She wanted to know, really know, where he was and what he was doing and how he was feeling. She wanted so badly to talk to him, to see him, and, if he would let her, to hug and comfort him.

At the same time, she worried about Sarah and her health. She was sworn not to breathe a word of it to Collin, or anyone else for that matter, but she ached for the ailing mother who longed to see her son.

CHAPTER SIXTEEN

He found an empty seat by a window halfway toward the back of the bus and listened to the chatter. Excited voices with thick mid-western accents went on and on about what a thrill it was to actually be on their way to Machu Pichu, the famed Incan site high in the Andes Mountains. It seemed that no one on board the sleek, new Prevost tour coach could believe that this was happening, that they were about to see the ancient and mysterious city in the clouds.

Collin's hair was now short and black, hidden by a baseball cap. Dark sunglasses covered his eyes; headphone wires dangled from his ears. His beard was gone, as was his British accent. Based on the conversations of the groups huddled around the tables closest to his at the hotel breakfast room, he had decided to sign up that morning for the same five-day tour as the other hotel guests. He changed his persona to be a high school teacher from suburban Chicago, who had saved up to visit the sites he had only seen in books. It would be a convincing story anyone could believe.

He was able to purchase one of the last tickets, according to the gal at the agency two doors down from the Best Western, but he counted at least five empty rows.

Most of the people clumped together in groups of four to eight, but there were a few couples on their own, too. As far as Collin could tell, he was the only solo traveler on the bus. But no one seemed bothered by that fact.

Following Lukas's advice, Collin was blending in with the tourists. During the daytime, he took dozens of photos and listened to Eduardo, the tour guide, and asked searching questions, trying to learn all he could about the mysterious ruins he explored with the group. At night, he updated his photo journal and communicated electronically with his friends and family back home, always careful not to divulge too much.

Whatever assignment Lukas was on, it must have been important and all-consuming. Collin received very little in terms of communication from him, most of it rather superficial in nature. But there was no real need. Except for the scene in Lima, Collin was keeping a low profile, just as Lukas had instructed.

In his conversations with Emily, he learned how stressed she was about her presentation but also about a new direction she was taking her experiments. She had three days to send in her slideshow but wanted to include the latest data. She fretted about getting it all done in time. She told him about a lovely patient who was going through chemotherapy. Emily had become acutely interested in that patient's case. Her goal now was to find a way to personalize a treatment based on that patient's exact needs. Targeted gene therapy, she called it. Other cancer labs did it as a matter of routine, but Scripps had always been more removed from the actual treatment, more esoteric. She hoped to get permission soon so that she could help this patient. It was clear to Collin that she was passionate in her resolve to make a difference for this woman.

"You're amazing Emily," he had said in his most recent message to her. "You really care about saving lives, don't you? Even if it's just one at a time."

Her response was, "Of course, I do. Everyone matters. Everyone has something to offer, so why not do my best to save them?"

By the end of his five-day tour with this group, Collin was at ease. The experience had far exceeded his expectations. The feelings of awe and wonder could only be expressed in his journal to Amy, not with any of his friends or family. During this time he had become part of the group—more than just another face in a crowd. Folks were kind and hospitable, but no one pried into his business, and he was comforted by that. He didn't try to avoid contact or conversation, but he didn't readily engage in it, either. The group accepted him as a studious school teacher on a quest to learn.

At noon the fifth day, the tour came to an end. Most of his new friends loaded onto a chartered bus bound for the airport. Collin waved good-bye and headed for the express bus terminal, where he caught a bus that would take him through the majestic and stunning Andes to Puno, Peru, a popular tourist attraction on the shore of Lake Titicaca, close to the southeastern border shared by Bolivia. At the recommendation of several travel blogs, he headed to the Qelqatani Hotel and settled in for a quiet evening. It was comfortable, clean, and had wireless Internet.

He spent his first night there searching transportation options through South America. He imagined himself taking another month or so to wind his way through Bolivia, Chile, Brazil, and Paraguay, eventually ending up in Buenos Aires, Argentina. Things felt safer in South America. Calmer. Slower. Less threatening. The people were unassuming and generous. They let him be, paid him no mind, never intruding nor interfering. It was all so new and different than what he had expected from South America. It was an adventure. An eye-opening adventure. He was soaking it up.

Collin toured Puno the next day, enthralled with its natural beauty, taking pictures for his photo journal. As he moved among the people, seeing sights and learning history, Collin practiced his South American Spanish. He asked touristy kinds of questions, ordered food, and discussed current events—all in an effort to improve his accent and become familiar with the place. A shopkeeper recommended a visit to an island called Isla del Sol, which lay at the southern end of vast Lake Titicaca. The lake was enormous, like a tranquil ocean twelve thousand feet above sea level. Rugged snow-covered peaks rimmed the lake and valley, providing a formidable boundary of protection, which attracted the early inhabitants. Collin wanted to learn more about this "Island of the Sun," where legend taught that the Incan god of the sun rose from Lake Titicaca to claim his kingdom. Late in the day, as he strolled down to the docks, a boat full of tourists had just returned from Isla Del Sol and began to filter into town, chattering about the amazing ruins and the spectacular views.

Collin found a kiosk and picked up a brochure.

As he read the brochure, he wandered back toward the tourist section of town and his hotel, planning in his head to visit the island the next morning. The sun was perched just above the peaks to the west, casting an orange beam of dancing light across the glassy surface of the lake and causing his shadow to stretch out long and skinny in front of him. His stomach was growling, reminding him of the neglect it had endured since mid-morning. Night was coming on, and a chill wind blew off the lake. He ducked in a taco joint popular with the tourists to grab a quick bite before returning to his room. There he could blend in with fellow Americans. The front of the restaurant was open, allowing him good visibility, and a back door through the kitchen was a possible escape route. Yes, he decided, it would be OK to eat out tonight. He would spend some time among other humans instead of holed up in his tiny room.

He pulled his iPhone out and checked for notifications as he waited for a table to be made ready. No text messages, a few new e-mails, and a notification on Facebook from Emily, responding to his earlier message. He read it, trying to decipher his feelings about the attention she was paying to him. Smiling to himself, he reread her message, oblivious to anything else.

The small taco bar had an upbeat atmosphere. Young people, mostly American and European tourists, filled the place with noise, laughter, and activity. It felt good to relax and absorb the youthful energy, even though he kept to himself at a small table in the corner.

He enjoyed the atmosphere late into the evening, chatting via Facebook with Emily on his phone, cocooned by the crowd, lost in the online conversation. All day, thoughts of her popped into his head at random times, no matter how many other interesting things he tried to stuff in it. The pictures, the conversations, and the feelings they produced kept rolling through his head, churning up embers of a long-forgotten fire. Why couldn't he stop thinking about her?

A memory from his brief stay in the hospital percolated to the top of his stream of thoughts.

Collin's eyes flitted left, then right, before they finally opened. The left one wouldn't open all the way. It was swollen and painful. Everything was blurry at first, and nothing was familiar. Too much white and a strange antiseptic smell. Panic set in, but his body didn't respond to his impulse to jump out of bed. Was he glued down? Breathing heavily, he fought to focus his vision and figure out where he was. He could just make out an image to his right, hovering attentively over him. It hurt to turn his head, like his brain was sloshing to the side and slamming into the wall of his skull. He closed his eyes again and tried to swallow, but there was nothing to swallow. His mouth was as dry as a desert, and his lips throbbed with a dull ache.

The figure next to him was holding his right hand and saying something softly. He could feel the squeezing and hear the sweet voice, but the words didn't register. His arms felt as heavy as lead and disconnected. The voice grew more insistent, beckoning him onward. It was as if he was being urged to climb a ladder with a heavy pack on his back. Everything went dark momentarily.

Through the din, he could hear the voice more clearly now, calling his name and pleading for him to look at her. Yes, he could tell now that it was female. It must be Amy. *Thank Heaven she's okay. Must've been a terrible dream.*

Gravity had a firm grip on his whole body, pushing his limbs and torso into the bed and holding his eyelids down, but he battled until his eyelids held their ground. The image of a woman gradually came into focus. High cheek bones, steel gray eyes, sandy hair pulled back in a ponytail. It wasn't Amy after all. It was Emily. Confusion swarmed his mind as he blinked several times in disbelief.

"It's okay, Collin. I'm right here. Talk to me."

He couldn't form words, but his mouth moved and emitted a guttural sound. His tongue licked his lips, which felt like sandpaper, in a vain attempt to moisten them. He felt another squeeze of his hand and fingers under his chin, stroking his cheek. It brought a nice sensation, making him realize he wasn't dead.

"Your eyes are open. That's good. Let me take a look," Emily inspected his forehead, eyes, and jaw. "You're going to be all right," she said in measured words.

That was reassuring, but why was she here, and where was Amy? These thoughts floated by and he tried to grab them and make use of them, but his efforts fell short. He forced out the only word he could form: "What …"

Emily's overly sweetened and excited voice showed Collin how awkward she felt as she rattled off a chain of non-stop thoughts. "What happened? Well, you know, that's a bit difficult to say right now. I'm hoping you can tell me, since no one else will. I mean, I've been here— what?—four hours now, and no one will tell me anything. I'm more than frustrated. In fact, I'm getting angry because I feel like I don't know what to do or what to say. Know what I mean? It kinda sucks.

Anyway, I'm talking too much again, I know. Nervous habit. Now, do you remember what happened?"

Collin was dizzy from her barrage of words, but he could not let go of the one question on his mind. Another word, forced and dry, "Where …"

"Where are you? You're in Petaluma Valley Hospital. It appears that you fell and hit your head. I guess the police found you in your living room. Of course, they won't tell me anything more. In fact, I had to pry just to get that much out of them. But the doctors say you're going to be fine. Just a concussion and some stitches. Thirteen to be exact. I got that much out of them."

"Amy?"

Emily paused. Her eyes narrowed as she watched his face. When she spoke, her voice was gentle and soft and much slower. "I wish I knew, Collin. No one has told me anything." She drew in a breath, then changed course. "You need to rest, Collin. I should go."

"No. Stay." He felt lost, but he knew she would figure things out and help him understand what was going on. Plus, he did not want to be alone in this foggy-headed condition. Everything felt so heavy, so thick. He closed his eyes, wanting to forget what he thought he already knew.

That was the last time he saw Emily.

He left the taqueria around nine o'clock and made his way through Puno's open air market en route to his hotel. It was dark and cold and his sweatshirt did little to keep him warm, so he pulled the hood over his head and walked briskly through the rows of vendors huddled around small fires burning in metal buckets near their stands. As he approached the Qelqatani Hotel there was an unusual amount of commotion on the street. Loud noises, yelling, screaming, crying. People were running toward the sounds, others ran away. Despite the commotion, he continued walking toward the still unfolding scene on the lakefront avenue, directly toward the fray. His instincts told him to stay in the shadows, observe from a distance. His gait changed, becoming catlike. But the noise and confusion continued to draw him in as curiosity cast its magnetic spell.

From behind the line of people that pressed their way forward for a better look, Collin listened to the yelling. He picked up on some of the chatter between the young people nearest him and came to understand that the federal authorities were aggressively questioning several shopkeepers and workers from the hotel about an American. The police were accusing this American of something that he couldn't understand, saying he had done something that sounded awful. He didn't know those words. The Federales wanted information. That much he understood. They used intimidation and threats in front of the gathered crowd to instill fear and inspire cooperation, thus underscoring the importance of their mission.

Tingles ran up and down Collin's spine; the hair on his neck bristling. As the yelling of the authorities grew louder and more incessant, Collin heard words that made his blood run cold and his breath stop short. Words like "Americano" and "ladron" and "peligroso" hung thick in the air, causing the crowd to gasp and whisper among themselves. "Thief." "Dangerous." His guts began to twist and tighten as if being constricted in a vice. A nearby group of teens was all abuzz about this "international criminal" who had come to their town. From their fast-paced chirpings, Collin understood the Federales were looking for an American who was wanted for something to do with banks and taking a lot of money. The teens wondered if he had the money hidden right here in Puno. Wouldn't that be cool?

The twisting inside intensified.

The throng of people pressed in tightly when the chief inspector raised a color photo of the suspected terrorist high above his head, turning slowly so all could get a glimpse. Collin could only make out a white face and brown hair, so he moved in for a better view. Peering between shoulders and heads three layers back in the crowd, his horror was confirmed. His own face stared back at him. Taken three weeks prior in the Grand Keys Bank, the photo was clear as day. For the moment, he forgot that he had cut his hair and changed its color.

The street near the hotel was electrified. Groups of women huddled, hands over their mouths, shaking their heads. Merchants and workers craned their necks to get a closer look, nodding agreeably. The teens were amped up, some of the boys becoming animated and excited, some eager to find the treasure, others wondering out loud if there was a reward available. Many of the girls were terrified and crying. The crowd was anxious, fueled by fear, uncertainty, and morbid curiosity.

He tried to run, but a paralyzing dread crashed down upon him, shackling Collin's very soul and shattering the short-lived sense of security he had enjoyed since leaving Lima. The accusations made by these men in uniform stung like a thousand wasps. The blood ran out of his head, leaving him dizzy and faint, as his mind caught hold of the ramifications of what was happening. Fear made it difficult to breath. No wind, no strength, and no thoughts. He was incapacitated.

Collin staggered toward the shadows at the crowd's fringe, struggling to stay upright, reeling under the weight of a changing reality. It was all caving in on him. Again, he tried to run. His legs would not cooperate.

He was falling. He could feel his body swaying, but he was powerless and began descending toward the sidewalk. As he fell, he grabbed hold of a chain link fence, causing a loud clattering and clanking. The teens standing atop a pile of rocks only fifteen feet away let out a cacophony of laughs, heckles, and shrieks of terror at what they thought was a drunk. They hadn't noticed him until now, having been too caught up in the drama unfolding on the street. Their commotion was loud enough to draw the attention of the officers, who looked over and scrutinized the man who could hardly stand. The officer in charge nodded to the one closest to Collin and signaled with a toss of his head for him to go investigate. Collin wobbled, even as he clung to the fence, unaware of the approaching policeman.

* * * *

HUNTINGTON BEACH, CALIFORNIA
MAY 27

As Henry and Sarah Cook prepared to eat dinner that night, Sarah was struck with a sudden sense of melancholy. No, it was more than that. There was an urgency behind it. Something tugged at her heart, but she had no idea why. Dark and foreboding, she could not shake the feeling. Instead, it grew stronger and more pressing. Her countenance showed the strain she was experiencing inside. When she dropped the paring knife against the granite countertop and braced herself with both hands, Henry moved quickly to her side and wrapped an arm around her waist for support.

"What's the matter, dear? Are you all right? What's going on?"

"I don't know. Something's wrong. Something's horribly wrong."

"What is it? Shall I call 911?"

"No, it's nothing like that. It's something else. One of the kids is in trouble," she said in a faint voice.

Henry knew from years of experience that his wife had an uncanny knack for sensing when her children needed her. Thirty-eight years of marriage had taught him that. "Which one?" he asked without thinking. Of course, he knew.

"Collin. It's definitely Collin. Let's pray for him. Right now, Henry. Let's pray for our son," she said. Her voice was much stronger now, determined, and full of faith.

Henry reached for Sarah's hands, facing her, head bowed. She followed suit, clutching his large and gentle hands, feeling his warmth and strength. He started the prayer. "Dear Lord, we know that you know all things. We know you love your children. We know you have watched over us and our family continually. For all of these blessings, we thank you, Lord. Now we ask you to reach out and extend your hand of protection in the care of our son, Collin. We know not where he is or what he is doing, but we fear he is in real danger. Please deliver him. Send your angels to be with him and give him strength, comfort, and inspiration. Help him to know we love him and are praying for his safe return home. This we pray, dear Father, in the name of your Holy Son, Jesus. Amen."

The Cooks stayed in that position, holding hands, heads bowed and eyes closed. Each silently repeated a similar prayer, sending love and strength. Their desire and their faith united and powerful.

* * * *

PUNO, PERU
MAY 27

In the same instant, Collin felt a power rush through his body. His mind cleared enough for him to hear, or maybe sense, the footsteps coming toward him. He had to move. Now. Although his stomach remained tied up in knots, his mind scrambled and raced, the fog within lifting. Strength returned to his legs. They began moving unsteadily, taking him away from the crowd, down the block, and into the shadows of a darkened street, staggering like a drunk. The officer continued to follow for a few paces before giving up. Why bother? There was a much more important matter to attend to.

A courtyard wall across the street provided an unlit place for Collin to retreat. He followed the barrier to the next intersection at the end of the block. He turned right and picked up the pace. Even though the air was thin at twelve thousand feet, he broke into a fast jog and maintained the pace for nearly a mile. He didn't think. He just ran and ran. Block after block, running. At the edge of town, only a few streets from the bus station, he stopped, realizing that he couldn't leave. He had nothing with him but his phone and a couple hundred dollars. He studied the map on his phone and knew what he had to do. And it scared him.

Because Collin had allowed himself to slip into a comfort zone, he had left two important items in his hotel room: the computer and backpack. They were essential to his survival. The two bags contained about $70,000 cash, in a variety of South American currencies and US dollars. All of his fake IDs were in them as well. Plus, his laptop contained all of his important, personal information. There was no other option. He had to go back and get them. Without them, he was done for.

Two weeks in South America had made him much too lax. He had not followed Lukas's strict protocol, the instructions that had kept him ahead of his pursuers for so many months. That realization ran through his veins, like coursing shards of glass, causing pain the entire length of his body from the inside out. At the same time, it brought instability, putting pressure on his fragile mind. He felt memories invading, their powerful tentacles embracing him, squeezing tightly, and he knew he had to switch gears internally if he wanted to survive another day without capture.

Stay in the moment or you die, he thought.

Exerting all of his mental energy, recalling the sudden burst of strength from minutes earlier, Collin focused his mind on the situation at hand, concluding that these federal agents were not the brightest set of detectives. There they were making a public scene with shopkeepers that would have had a limited amount of interaction with Collin instead of searching the hotel for clues. What were they doing and why? Despite their dominant presence, he knew he had to get his stuff and get out.

He sprinted back to the hotel, slowing as he approached to catch his breath.

When he returned, Collin found the scene still teeming with people. The yelling had stopped, and the authorities had disappeared somewhere. Collin moved cautiously closer to the crowd, listening to what they were saying. He was able to discern that the hotel staff were being interrogated inside by the federal police because of all of the tourists staying there. Many of the guests had been questioned as well. The crowd was anxious, expecting more action. Those staying in the hotel wanted to get out of the cold night air.

Amid the commotion outside, Collin moved warily, wanting to hear but not wanting to be seen. His hood covered most of his head and face. His hands were thrust deep in his pockets, and he moved as casually as he could. Seeing a fellow American tourist standing alone at the edge of the throng, Collin approached him guardedly.

The young man leaned against a wall, observing the crowd. He was younger than Collin, maybe in his mid to late twenties. He wore long cargo shorts and a long sleeve thermal shirt. His hair was long and straggly and stuck out in all directions under a beanie cap. He hadn't shaved in a few days. He seemed as likely as anyone to be friendly. "Hey, man, do you know what's going on here?" Collin asked.

As he turned toward Collin and took him in, his eyes grew wide with recognition. "Dude, they've got a picture of you. At least, I think it's you. Your hair is different, but the eyes and face are the same. You're the one they're looking for!" The man didn't raise his voice. On the contrary, he spoke just above a whisper as if in some sort of hushed conspiracy.

Collin knew this already, but it still made his stomach drop. He tried to contain the panic that gripped him. But the color drained from his face, and his knees felt weak. Collin braced himself against the wall and looked the man in the face imploringly. "Why? Why are they looking for *me*?"

The young man recoiled. "That I don't know, man. My Spanish isn't that good. All I know is that they seem to think you're dangerous and—"

Collin cut him off. "I'm not. I can promise you that. I am not a dangerous person. But the people coming for me are. Look, for your own sake, you never saw me, OK? Keep yourself out of this, and you'll be OK." As Collin turned toward the hotel, with its yellow and white façade, wood-trimmed windows, and rock accents, the young man began to yell and wave his hands. He was calling out to the Federales and pointing at Collin. "Hey, look. Over here. This is the man you're looking for."

Collin shot the young man a dark look as he clenched his jaw and shook his head. The buzz from the crowded street drowned the man's cries. A few local police seemed to take notice of the man waving his arms, but Collin was gone, weaving and ducking through the throng of people to the front entrance of the hotel. The lobby that had seemed quaint and cozy was now too small and cramped to maneuver through. Cops everywhere, talking to hotel staff in every corner. He'd never make it through. How could he get to his room? There had to be a way.

A side door that led to a hallway with phones, restrooms, and a staircase started to open. Collin made his way over to it for a closer look. Behind the door was one of the nice older ladies that worked there, peering out into the street. From what he could tell, she was the cleaning supervisor. Collin had been polite and friendly with her and the other staff members since his arrival. In return, she always smiled back. Short and stout with black hair and weathered skin, she had a serene demeanor.

The woman saw Collin and pushed the door open slightly. She looked him up and down, concern spreading across her typically square, native Peruvian face. Her brow pulled together as she mumbled something to him, but he couldn't make out the words. She said it again, louder this time. "Get your things and go. It's not safe for you here." She jabbed a thumb repeatedly toward the stairway, hurrying him along.

Collin followed the prompts, slipping silently past her into the dim hallway. He dashed up the stairs and spun to the right. His was the third door down. As he scampered toward it, he fumbled for the key and dropped it on the floor at his feet. As he bent down to retrieve it, he heard voices coming from the opposite end of the hallway, along with heavy footfalls, he guessed from thick-soled boots that carried an air of authority. They were coming up the other set of stairs at the far end of the building.

He managed to grab the key and open the door before the boots made it to the top of the stairs. Closing the door silently, Collin made his way through the dark room. Closet on the right, bathroom on the left. Closet ends, room opens up. Bed to the left, dresser to the right, window straight ahead. Small desk to the right of the window. He pulled the curtains open to allow light from the street lamps below to illuminate the space as he unplugged the laptop, shoved it in the computer bag, and fumbled for his backpack. The boots were coming down the hallway outside his door. He could hear them pounding on the thin carpet that covered the wooden floor. His fingers did a quick inventory of the contents of the backpack. Passports, bundles of currency wrapped in rubber bands, boxes containing hair coloring kits, medicine, and toiletries. Contact lens cases. Bottles of lens solution. Glasses cases. Two wallets. Combs, toothbrush, toothpaste, electric shaver. It all seemed to be there, so he zipped it up and slung the pack over his shoulder.

The boots sounded like they were only two or three doors down when they came to a stop. Collin held his breath and listened. Silence. Then a knock at a door. Some loud, demanding words, a door opening, followed by more stomping. The door closed, and the voices and stomping stopped. It was evident from the sounds that the boots had gone into another room. This was his chance.

Collin bolted for the door, opened it quietly. He poked his head out and looked to his left. No one. Good. He slipped out the door and tiptoed to the same staircase he had climbed just moments before. His door slammed shut as he took the sharp left U-turn and began to descend, taking three stairs at a time. The big voice became audible again. The door down the hall had opened and the sound of the boots emerged and began stomping toward him. Never hesitating, he vaulted down the remaining stairs, through the narrow back hallway, to the side door where the square-faced old woman stood with her foot holding open his passage to freedom. He nodded and whispered gracias as he bounded into the tumult on the street.

Returning to the safety of the darkness from which he had emerged minutes before, Collin retreated as fast as he could, fear and adrenaline propelling him to run, backpack and computer bag bouncing against his body as he fled the chaos into the shadows.

Leaving a trail of evidence, such as fingerprints and hair, in his room was not what he had planned, but under the circumstances, he had no choice. Reluctantly, he had to flee the beautiful little town of Puno, Peru, forever.

CHAPTER SEVENTEEN

PERUVIAN-BOLIVIAN BORDER
MAY 27

His eyes glazed over as he stared out the dirty window of the lumbering, old bus. Although the sky outside was pitch black, he was aware that he was traveling through mountains. Only outlines of jagged peaks were visible in the pale starlight. Trees blurred as they passed. The bus teetered and swayed as it rounded one curve after another, alternately speeding nearly out of control on long, downhill stretches and whining as it labored up another hill.

After retrieving his belongings from the hotel, Collin had sprinted to the bus terminal on the outskirts of Puno and caught the next bus out of town. Lima was the only place he didn't want to go. As luck would have it, he was on his way to La Paz, Bolivia.

Collin wondered what was next. Now that they had found him in this remote part of the world, he knew they could find him anywhere. He felt vulnerable and confined. His world was shrinking; hiding places vanishing. The mounting stress was putting pressure on his fragile mental state.

Maybe it was time to try a different strategy, try something unexpected to catch everyone off-guard.

His thoughts meandered, eventually settling on Emily. He wanted to talk with her. Actually talk. This electronic communication thing was great, but not as good as being there, in the same place, at the same time. The more he thought about her, the more he wanted to see her, to have a real conversation. A conversation with someone he knew, someone who cared about him, would be novel. Since meeting Captain Sewell, he longed to have a friend again. He wanted contact. He wanted a real connection. Why not with Emily?

A dark feeling ran through him as he recalled kissing her that night in her hotel room. It felt like a barb had been plunged into his heart, causing him to gasp and cough. His near miss with infidelity and the guilt that shrouded him afterward returned, pressing against him, stealing his breath. It took several minutes to unwind the coil that had wrapped itself around him. He told himself that it was a mistake; it had no bearing on the accident. Emily had been drinking, and he was not in a good place at the time. He reminded himself that he had been strong enough to remain faithful to his wife and that Emily was just a friend. A good friend with whom he shared some of the best times of his youth.

Wouldn't it be good to see her? And wouldn't it be fun to surprise her? Once this idea caught root, nothing could stop it from growing. His shattered soul needed something that it didn't have in his current situation and, like a hungry person craving food, it didn't matter what was set before him; he would take it. His mind was fixated on surprising his friend, on reestablishing a link with someone familiar. He knew he couldn't go home. Not yet. His presence would endanger his family. But a quick visit to Chicago might be the next best thing. Chicago was a big city. It would be easy to go undetected there if he did it right.

This distraction, this idea of actually seeing Emily, with its heightened level of difficulty, could help his aching mind, which, when left idle, threatened to unravel. If his grief caught up to him, a meltdown could render him helpless. With his enemies close behind, that was dangerous.

Having a mission, a vital task to complete, always helped him stay focused on something other than his loss. New scenery, a new plan, new challenges to overcome had helped in the past. Maybe it would help again now.

Collin's flashbacks had become less frequent and less severe than they had been a month ago in Europe. He credited his adventures and new-found friendship with Captain Sewell, as well as the change of scenery.

Ah, the thought of Captain Sewell brought a smile to his face. What a cool cat. He had proven to be a great help in so many ways. He had programmed the Captain's satellite phone number into his cell phone. He knew he'd use it someday.

These thoughts occupied him as the bus ride dragged on. He struggled to ward off memories of his past and what he had lost. His beleaguered body wanted sleep, but he couldn't allow it. He tried everything to prevent a meltdown, but his mind grew weary, unable to focus.

The screeching brakes and droning engine disrupted his concentration, exacerbating his fatigue.

Somewhere during the early morning hours, Collin lost the battle and dozed off. During this brief and shallow sleep, they found him—vulnerable, physically exhausted, mentally drained. Like wisps of smoke creeping through the crack under the door, memories of his beautiful wife and children entered in the form of an innocent dream. In the dream, which was really a memory replayed, his sweet daughter Jane, who was about four years old at the time, was enjoying an ice cream cone on a hot summer day. The ice cream was melting faster than her little tongue could lick it. Sticky, blue streams rolled down the cone onto her little hand and chubby fingers. Her furrowed brow showed her concern that her parents would be upset about the mess. She looked up at her daddy with apologetic eyes. Collin just grinned at her, kissed her little nose, then began licking the ice cream from her hand. "Daddy!" she started to scold, then burst into a giggle fit as he tried to stuff her entire hand in his mouth. "You can't eat my hand, you silly!"

"Why not? It tastes so good! Like bubble gum ice cream!"

"But that's *my* hand. What will I hold my ice cream cone with if you eat my hand?"

"You've got another one, you know."

"But Daddy, I need both my hands so we can play basketball together."

"You're right, sweet girl, maybe I should just bite off your cute little nose instead."

"Noooo, you can't do that either! How will I smell?"

"Well, if you didn't have ice cream on it, I probably wouldn't want to eat it."

"Why don't you eat your own ice cream, Daddy?"

"I did. But I'm still hungry."

"So, eat Mommy's."

"Mommy won't let me. Besides, she's way over there on the other side of the table. You're right here, and it's just easier to eat your yummy fingers and nose."

"Oh, Daddy. You're silly." Playful giggles and the sweet laughter of an innocent child rang in his head.

The bus slowed to a stop, and the image of his precious little one abruptly vanished as he jolted from sleep. A second later, it all came back to him—where he was, why he was there, and what was happening to him. Unable to control himself, he stretched out an arm, grabbing at air, and released a pained noooo, awakening the dozen other passengers onboard. His sweet Jane was gone, and he couldn't pull her back, no matter how much he wanted to. He would never share an ice cream cone with her again. His ears would never again hear her lovable, playful giggle. His eyes would never behold that precious smile, those golden ringlets, or those pudgy fingers. The cruel reality gripped him like an electric charge, causing a fit of grief and pain. Burying his head in his hands, he struggled to control his breathing and his emotions.

A minute later, he regained his composure and apologized to his fellow travelers. Waving his cell phone in the air, he explained that there was some bad news coming from his family. It would be fine, he assured them. He just needed to get home and see them again.

His story and his accent were apparently believable. With sincere concern in their voices, a few of the older women, after briefly conferring among themselves, promised to pray for him and his family. They crossed themselves, bowed their heads, and mumbled inaudibly. Then, looking up to Heaven and mouthing amen, they each turned toward Collin, one by one, and said, "Vaya con Dios."

His instincts had kicked in to make up a plausible story on the spot and win the hearts of the ladies on the bus. Now, he had to avoid the scrutiny of the border patrol officer that was boarding the bus. He wasn't sure he could withstand too much interrogating at the moment.

A young uniformed guard stomped up the steps, a stern look on his hardened face. He cradled an AK-47 assault rifle across his chest, muzzle pointed up, with one hand, a large flashlight with a powerful beam in the other. Puffed up with importance, the guard tramped deliberately down the aisle, scrutinizing each face and visibly relishing the fear he inspired. He interrogated a few about where they came from or where they were going, followed by queries regarding what they were carrying with them.

As the guard approached, Collin dabbed his eyes with a tissue. He did this while leaning down and away as if he was adjusting his socks, trying not to be noticed. The guard caught the motion and jerked the beam of light at Collin. "You there! What are you doing?" he barked in Spanish.

Collin replied with an unsteady voice, "Tying my shoe."

This enraged the young soldier and he stormed down the aisle. Collin looked at the tissue in his hand and wanted to scream in horror. The white tissue was streaked with brown. The tanning lotion he had applied to his face and hands in the bus terminal restroom to help him look more Latin was rubbing off. There was no time to check it in the mirror. No time to re-apply. No time to think. The soldier stood over him, glowering down, the beam of his flashlight darting all around.

"Identification," he demanded.

Collin's hand shook as it moved toward his shirt pocket. He couldn't help it. The strain was taking its toll. His fingers pulled at the passport, but he lacked the control to grip it tightly. It fell to the floor. The soldier huffed and Collin apologized, finding the strength to hold it this time. He presented the requested document with his trembling hand. Collin kept his face down, looking at his lap, the tissue wadded tightly in his fist.

The guard flipped each page with exaggerated drama.

"Why are there no markings for entry into Peru?" he demanded.

Collin didn't have an answer. He couldn't say why, so he just shrugged. "What were you doing in Peru?"

"Business."

"What kind of business?"

"I sell cleaning products to restaurants and hotels. Sometimes when I go to countries—Peru, Brazil, Uruguay—they don't stamp my papers. Sometimes I don't see the border patrol. I cannot say why. I don't question," Collin explained in a feeble, weary voice.

"Where did you visit in Peru?" demanded the guard.

"Just Puno," answered Collin.

"How long were you in Puno?"

"Just for the day."

"Did you see or hear about the American they are looking for in Puno?"

"I saw the commotion, but I did not see the American. I know nothing about it."

"Is the Qelqatani Hotel one of your customers?"

"No, not yet," Collin said.

"Did you visit there today?"

"No, I did not. The manager said he did not have time for me today. Maybe next time."

"Who did you visit while in Puno?"

Collin paused, searching his memory for names, any names, which he could throw out. "Atajo, IncaBar, Los Uros—"

"OK, OK. I've heard enough. Where do you live?"

"Buenos Aires."

"Where are you going next?"

"I will visit hotels and restaurants in La Paz."

"For how long?"

"Two days, maybe three."

The young guard paused, considering his words, then slapped the booklet shut and thrust it back toward Collin. Without another word, he spun on his heels and marched back down the aisle. At the edge of the steps leading down to the exit door, the guard turned once more to face the group of blurry-eyed passengers. He glared at them, especially Collin, before clicking his heels and stamping down the steps.

The ordeal was over. Hot sweat had formed under Collin's shirt, at the back of his neck and, most dangerously, at his forehead and temples. As he dabbed the sweat, more brown patches appeared on his tissue.

His chin dropped to his chest, his hand lay still in his lap, and exhaustion kicked in. His situation appeared increasingly precarious with two near misses in less than six hours. He was flirting with disaster.

The door squealed as the bus driver pulled the handle in a long, sweeping motion toward himself. Sleep did not return, nor did he want it to. Not worth another breakdown in front of strangers. He needed a new plan. He had to talk to Lukas. Sooner would be better, but he knew it had to wait until he was off this bus and alone. That would be another five hours. A very long five hours.

* * * *

HUNTINGTON BEACH, CALIFORNIA
MAY 28

Sarah Cook had been fretting since the day before when she had that strong feeling that Collin was in danger. Of course, in his most recent e-mail he said everything was fine, even when she quizzed him about why she would have had that prompting. His answer, as casual and vague as ever, was simply, "Yeah, I had a bit of a scare and thought I might faint, but I'm all right now, Mom. Thanks for the prayers. They definitely help." She felt he was skimming over some important details. Thanks to the Internet, as well as Agents Crabtree and McCoy, she wasn't as naïve as he perhaps thought. Collin was wanted by the FBI. She saw the picture with the sinister-looking Asian man and knew everything was not all right with her son. It bothered her that he wouldn't tell her the truth.

As she sat staring at her computer screen, Henry walked up behind her and put his large, gentle hands on her shoulders. Without saying a word, her husband gave her comfort and strength. She squeezed a hand and pressed her cheek against it as she began to sob.

Henry knelt down beside her and pulled her close. He was a man who chose his words carefully and spoke them sincerely. His opinions were based on facts and heartfelt convictions.

Holding his wife, with her face buried in his chest, Henry found the words to console her. "Dear, the good Lord is aware of our son and is watching over him, wherever he is. He's a smart, resourceful young man. He's a survivor. I trust that he knows what he's doing, and there is purpose behind it."

Sarah's weeping subsided. He wiped away a tear, then added, "Try to stay positive. He's going to be OK; I know it."

His words and the conviction in his deep, baritone voice gave Sarah comfort because she believed whole-heartedly what he said. He was steady and sure, the rock of his family, the one they all turned to during the storms of life.

Henry added, "I'm sure there's a reason for his not sharing more details with us. He's being protective, I'd say. When the time is right, he'll tell us the whole story." Henry knew Collin as well as anyone, perhaps better than Sarah ever would. It was a father-son thing, wrought from many long talks during those critical teenage years, some of them late at night over a bowl of cereal at the kitchen table, some of them watching a bonfire burn at the beach after a round of catch with a Frisbee or a football, some of them in the car on the way to or from a baseball game. He couldn't explain it fully to his wife, but he trusted Collin's judgment.

* * * *

LA PAZ, BOLIVIA
MAY 28

In downtown La Paz, Bolivia, Collin Cook, under the name of Jorge Silva, checked into the Columbus Palace Hotel, one frequented by tourists and business travelers alike. The hotel had wireless Internet and good food, according to the online reviews. It was midmorning when he arrived, but, for an extra twenty dollars, the clerk allowed him to check in early.

He hurried to his room and dropped his bags, grateful to have gotten across the border using a fake passport, without landing in a Bolivian prison, awaiting a thorough investigation.

The stress of the past twelve hours had his mind spinning. He felt the need to talk to Lukas and to Emily and, strangely, his mother. Time and distance had disconnected him from the important people in his life. He hated being isolated, hunted, and stuck in a strange land. Loneliness and longing set in like an anchor tied to his heart. He paced the floor, trying to ignore the tugging inside. He texted Lukas. No reply. Twenty-five minutes of additional pacing and still no reply. Hunger and fatigue begged him for food and rest. He relented. After a pizza and salad from the restaurant downstairs, he fell sound asleep, fully clothed, on top of the covers.

* * * *

SAN DIEGO, CALIFORNIA
MAY 28

Emily arrived home late again, expecting to settle into another night of typing a conversation with Collin while the Oxygen channel ran in the background. When she logged on, there were no messages from him on Facebook. Nothing in e-mail. No texts. Nothing from Sarah, either. *Sleepless in Seattle* was on again. One of her favorites. She halfway paid attention to it as she cleaned and straightened. Her ultra-modern, stylishly appointed condo never looked messy. The one advantage to living alone. She liked things to be tidy and organized. As she scooted about, dusting this and rearranging that, her thoughts turned once again to the happiest times in her life: high school. After reliving a few good memories, her mind went to that night, after graduation, when the good times ended.

It pained her to think how badly she had hurt Collin, when he was young and sweet and just living in the moment. It seemed so long ago now. That night Collin had planned a celebration. He prepared a special meal that was fabulous, but the conversation grew awkward. Collin had put together a magnificent spread in the pool house behind his parents' home, complete with his mother's fine china, candles, flowers, music and decorations.

Collin had obviously spent hours on the food and presentation. He'd thought of every detail to make the evening perfect. It had taken Emily only minutes to ruin the whole thing.

She recalled how everything came crashing down when she opened her untrained, teenaged mouth—the mood, the relationship, and the hopes of a tender, teenage boy.

"What's the matter?" Collin had asked in his innocent, naïve manner, seeing as how she was quiet, pensive, and distracted. The hopeless romantic was ambushed with little warning.

"I have something I need to tell you," she started, her voice tight with emotion. Her speech, practically memorized, sounded more like a book report than a break-up. "This is not going to work," she began to explain to an increasingly bewildered boy.

"What are you talking about?" he sputtered.

"You and me. It's not going to work," she continued. At this point, the stunned, teenaged Collin put down his utensils and sat back in his chair. He was wide-eyed and quiet. "We're two different people who want totally different things out of life. We have different approaches and different ambitions. It will never work out."

When he looked away, she finished her prepared remarks. "I think it will be better for us both if we just end it now and not pretend this relationship is going to last. I mean, it's obvious, isn't it? You like surfing and sports and movies. I like math and science and music. I would rather go to the opera or a play. You would rather go to an Angels game. I want to be something and somebody. Make a difference. Stand out. Contribute to the advancement of mankind through science. You don't even have the foggiest idea what you want to do or become. All you know is you're going to live at home and go to Sac State. That's the level of your ambition? That's the sum of your career planning? That's pathetic. We're just not right for each other. It's time we face the facts and move on."

She spun out of her chair, ran out of the pool house, and exited through the side gate.

Try as she might, Emily could never erase those words or take back that moment in time.

Thinking of that evening now, standing in her La Jolla condo, overlooking the Pacific Ocean, she wondered how, when she was only eighteen, she managed to sound so much like her mother. Her mother, who she had always considered mean. Despite her many accomplishments and her satisfying career, Emily felt empty. Even as she surveyed the trappings of her success, there was so much missing from her life.

Her parents had insisted that Collin was not good enough for her. He lacked ambition. Collin, they said, would hold her back. Better to end it before it causes either of you more pain down the road.

Now thirty years old and feeling unfulfilled and lonely, she reflected on the judgment they passed on the boy who stole her heart. Why was she so susceptible to their persuasions?

And for what?

They were gone now. Killed six years ago in a car crash on the way home from one of their high society parties with the elites they were so eager to impress. Her father was drunk but so good at hiding it. He failed to negotiate the steep and windy road that led down the hill upon which the host's ostentatious mansion was perched, high above Los Angeles. Their new Mercedes ended up in a crumpled heap at the bottom of a steep ravine, having skidded off the road less than half a mile from the party. No one knew about it until morning, when someone noticed tire marks on the curb and a flattened bush.

Why couldn't she see then how wrong her parents were about Collin?

CHAPTER EIGHTEEN

BUENOS AIRES, ARGENTINA
MAY 31

After fifty-four hours of bus rides, Collin arrived in Buenos Aires, Argentina. He chose to take the first-class express buses this time for speed and comfort. It required several bus changes and stops every four to six hours to eat and stretch, but it was much faster and more comfortable than the economy bus lines. During the long trip, Collin kept his mind occupied by reading a spy novel, reviewing and enhancing his written plans and preparations, and listening to music. He tried everything to prevent another meltdown.

He scripted every foreseeable encounter during his journey from Bolivia to Chicago, anticipating various scenarios. Every detail of his assumed identity, he knew, must be firmly lodged in his mind in order to be convincing and believable.

A heightened terror threat worldwide meant travelers were scrutinized. But Collin was ready for it. Traveling under an identity Lukas had created and uploaded to the federal database, Collin planned to re-enter the United States via Toronto, Canada. Lukas had guaranteed him safe passage through any airport with this particular passport. He was instructed to use it sparingly. Despite this and his thorough preparations, the prospect of returning home, where he was wanted as an international criminal, sent a chill up his spine.

Before leaving his hotel in La Paz, Collin changed his hair color back to brown, scrubbed off the fake tan, and inserted blue contact lenses. In addition, he wore round, wire rimmed glasses and a new suit he purchased at an upscale men's clothing store. His persona was that of a high-priced computer network consultant. His fake passport contained stamps from several South American countries, including Peru, Brazil, and Argentina, with date stamps showing he had traveled into and out of these countries several times over the previous two years. Collin felt confident in his carefully constructed identity. Now he just had to keep himself together and not allow the stress to cause a mental collapse.

The money was concealed in special pockets in his computer bag lined with a thin, high tech, magnetic membrane that would project a false image of the contents to the scanners. The technology was experimental and used predominately by clandestine agencies, but Lukas was in a privileged position which enabled him to acquire several of these devices for Collin. Without them, carrying $70,000 in cash across international borders would be impossible.

In his hotel room in the Buenos Aires Airport Marriott, Collin donned his new charcoal gray wool suit, tossed his hair with some styling gel, and inserted a set of prosthetic teeth which changed the shape of his jaw line, thus completing the disguise. He inspected his new look in the mirror, then blew out a long breath. It was time to begin the scariest journey of his life.

The next two hours were critical to his survival. The magnitude of the risk he was taking began to weigh on his mind, causing him to wonder more than once why he was doing it. The scene in front of Qelqatani Hotel in Puno flashed across his mind, followed by the guard on the bus at the Bolivian border. South America was no longer a safe haven for him. It was time to move on, anyhow. He might as well test his ability to enter the States.

Acting like every other frequent flyer was imperative. He had to put on the almost bored countenance of one who spends much of his life in airports and on airplanes while remaining keenly aware of all that was happening around him. During the shuttle ride to the airport, Collin's heart palpitated and his breathing grew erratic. His hands trembled and his palms wouldn't stay dry. He pinched his eyes shut and exerted calm upon his nerves by recalling the tranquility he felt in his surfing days as he bobbed in the swells, waiting for the perfect wave.

By the time the bus stopped at the curb, Collin felt markedly better. With forced assurance and poise, he made his way through security and onto the plane problem free. No unusual searches. No probing questions. No issues with his carryon bags, his shoes, his belt, or his laptop. And no one following him, looking at him, or chasing him. This was all good. Everything was going according to plan.

Because he was posing as a hot-shot, high tech consultant, Collin treated himself to business class. He enjoyed the wide, reclining seats, the generous leg room, foot rests, and the over-the-top service. Outside, he was calm and poised. Inside, the butterflies fluttered and spun.

Collin occupied himself for the first four hours of the flight by reading the local paper and *USA Today* and reviewing the outlines of Plan A, Plan B, and Plan C on his laptop—all done up on a beautiful spreadsheet, a throwback to his previous life. When his attention began to wane, he put the computer away and pulled out the spy novel, hoping to learn something that would either validate or enhance his game plan. Thirteen pages in and the labors of the past few days caught him. During that time, he had pushed his mind and body to the limit with his planning and preparation, with bus rides and identity changes, with plans A through C, and a script to memorize. Through the flurry of activity, he had pushed aside the memories that lurked in the background, waiting to come out. Eyelids grew heavy and drooped. He tried to shake it off and continue, but after three more pages, he was fast asleep.

Ten minutes later, the flight attendant bent over his seat and inserted a pillow between his head and the wall, closed the window shade, and covered him with a blanket. He didn't notice any of it. He was in dreamland, being carried away—possibly in a canoe, maybe a rickshaw—to a peaceful place where he felt warm and safe. The anxiety melted like frost in the morning sun; his cares gave way to a surreal sense of home. Of belonging. A feeling he had not had in a long time. In his dream, he walked in warm sand for what seemed to be a very long time. The walk was pleasant; the surroundings both unfamiliar and unremarkable. Amy appeared from nowhere, off in the distance ahead of him, holding Eliza in her arms. Sweet baby Eliza, all of two years old, had her arms wrapped around her mother's neck, her head resting comfortably on her mother's shoulder. She looked happy and peaceful. When her mother whispered in her ear, she looked up and saw her daddy. With the pure joy of an innocent child, she smiled her wide, toothy smile and stretched out her arms toward him. Amy put her down, and she began to run toward him, giggling and bouncing all the way. He tried to run to her, but his legs wouldn't move. They were stuck. Try as he might, he couldn't walk, let alone run. Eliza didn't notice and didn't care. She continued to bound toward him, laughing and calling, "Daddy, Daddy," until she stopped abruptly. She came to a ledge. A deep, dark canyon opened up between them. Her happy face turned to a frown, then she burst into tears. Collin was on his knees in the sand on the other side, now desperately trying to reach across to her as the gulf between them opened wider and wider, calling her name and crying out, "Don't worry, baby girl. Don't be scared. Daddy's coming."

With a terrible jolt and a blood-curdling scream of anguish, Collin shot upright in his seat, thrashing about wildly. He found he could move his legs but couldn't get anywhere because of something low and tight across his hips. He yanked open the buckle, then stopped cold. He felt the gaze of dozens of eyes on him. He was panting, barely able to catch his breath. His heart was galloping, its beat ringing in his ears, drowning out other sounds. As the dream faded, he surveyed the upstairs business class cabin, trying to figure out where he was and why he was there. Looking around at the bewildered and concerned faces of the other passengers and the flight attendant, he remembered boarding the plane and taking his seat. A half second later, he recalled his plan, and the fact that he was heading to Canada.

"What happened?" he asked the middle-aged woman in uniform hovering over him.

She was trying to comfort him, saying, "You're OK, sir. It's all going to be all right. Just relax. Breathe. It's going to be OK." Her French accent was soothing, and Collin was able to slow his breathing, regain his bearings, and realize, much to his embarrassment, he had had another outburst. Try as he might to contain it, the dam that held back his sorrow was breaking. His grief wanted out and clamored for expression.

"You were screaming in your sleep, sir. A nightmare, perhaps?"

"Oh, man," he whispered. "I'm so sorry. What was I saying?"

"You were very agitated, very worried, I would say. Yes, you seemed very concerned."

"But what did I say?"

"I think you said, 'Daddy's coming.' Yes, monsieur. I think that's right."

"Oh, great. Thank you. I'm so sorry for all the trouble. It looks like I frightened the others." He half stood and, gesturing with a hand, said loud enough for the other passengers to hear, "I'm so sorry."

"It is all right, sir," said the flight attendant. "They, we, are startled; that's all. The question is: Are you OK, sir? You've experienced something terrible, yes?"

"No. No, I'm fine, I think," he muttered in her general direction as he looked around his seat. Luckily, the seat next to him was empty. His mind cleared enough to put together a plausible explanation on the fly that would satisfy her and the others and diffuse the situation. "Just a bad dream about my daughter. That's all. She's been ill while I was away. I guess I'm more worried about her than I thought." This he said loud enough for the people in his immediate vicinity to hear.

"Is there anything I can get for you?" the attendant asked with a gentle smile.

"Maybe you could tell me how much longer until we land?"

"Yes, of course, sir. I believe we have almost seven hours until we land in Toronto," she said, checking her watch. "Let me bring you something to drink. Would that be nice, yes? Maybe some nice wine?"

"No, no. Not wine. No alcohol. Just water, please. That would be very nice. Thank you. I think I'm going to use the restroom first, if that's all right."

"Of course, sir. It's located up front." She gestured with her hand. He nodded politely as he passed all the people he had just frightened.

Locked away in the bathroom, Collin splashed cold water on his face. The images of Eliza were so clear, so beautiful, so real. Oh, he wanted to hold her tight and kiss those perfect little cheeks and caress her soft, silky hair and tell her how much he loved her. The image of that gulf opening up, moving his precious Eliza farther and farther away, haunted him. That helpless, powerless feeling lingered. That sense of failure was connected to every thought and memory he had of his past life. Helpless to change anything. Helpless to save the people he loved most, the ones that depended on him. Powerless to bring them back. These emotions haunted him, chased him, and today had cornered him on a plane full of people who had no idea what he had lost.

Feeling unsteady, he sat down on the toilet, the lid closed, and put his head in his hands. Like a tsunami overrunning a small island, he realized the surge of memories couldn't be controlled. Many minutes passed. Collin lost track of the time. He washed his face again with cold water, trying to reduce the puffiness in his eyes. It was minimally effective. Nonetheless, it was time to get out of this cramped space.

Mortified, Collin hoped many of his fellow business class travelers would be sleeping again or too involved in the movie to pay him any attention. For the most part, his wish came true. Only a few wary glances as he emerged from the restroom and tiptoed back to his seat.

A tall glass with ice water awaited him on the tray at his seat. He took the glass and continued to the back of the business class section, where there was a magazine rack. The nice flight attendant who had helped him was busy preparing meals in the galley area beyond the reading material, chatting with the other attendant in French. Collin only picked up a few words as he approached. "Pity" and "trauma" were two of the words he could make out from that far away. He tried to smile at them, then headed down the stairs. They smiled back. Neither of the ladies tried to stop him. The economy cabin was about two-thirds full—a mix of Latin Americans, Asians, and Canadians, he surmised as he looked around at the faces of the passengers, who were occupied with either sleep, the movie, reading material, or their computers. Collin made his way to the last row, which had several empty seats. He settled in and tried to watch the movie. It was no use. His body was left with little energy and his mind was much the same. Within minutes, Collin dozed off, but this time there was no dream, no panic, and no screaming.

Collin slept until he heard the engines slow down, signaling the plane's descent into Toronto Pearson International Airport. He pretended to sleep all the way through landing and taxiing. When the plane came to a stop at the gate, he sat and waited for the other passengers to clear out. He did not want to see any of those people from business class again. When it was empty, he went upstairs. The stewardess with the French accent had his coat ready for him. She gently touched his arm and told him she hoped all would be well at home when he got there.

Thanking her for her kindness, he collected his book from the seatback pocket, his backpack from the overhead bin, and his computer bag from under his seat. As he made his way off the plane, a line of flight attendants thanked him for flying Air Canada and wished him a good day.

The most difficult part of his journey was now upon him, and he felt less prepared than ever. His game plan, though memorized, began to feel inadequate. His confidence and swagger were gone, thanks to his meltdown. He scrambled mentally to pull himself together as he walked through a set of doors that slid open automatically. Beyond those doors were long rows of people waiting to be processed and admitted into Canada.

Collin gulped and stared at the crowded space. Behind him, the automatic doors closed. There was no turning back. There was only one way out. His stomach knotted and his mouth went dry, but he adjusted his bags and plodded toward the line for foreigners.

Collin had to remind himself of his routine, the one he had used so many times in almost every major airport in Europe. He just had to stay in character, act like this happened every day.

Anonymity was his friend and conformity his disguise. Unlike his past life where he was always trying to stand out and be noticed, he now wanted to blend into the scenery. Being nameless, faceless, and indistinguishable aligned perfectly with his current set of ambitions. There were no promotions to get, no raises to vie for, no competitors to outperform, and no bosses to suck up to. Money was no longer an object and reputation a casualty of the game he was unwittingly pulled into. He was out of that rat race and happy to be, except for the fact that he was alone. All alone. Not a soul in the world to share his burden, no home to return to each night. Collin would gladly go back to his past life and live the work-a-day routine he once dreaded if it meant he could get back what he lost.

But that was impossible, so he had to convince himself he was glad to be free from the corporate world that so many of the men and women moving through this airport were in. They were like he was back then: hard-working, opportunistic, motivated to keep his job and make a buck or two.

Collin had exited that adrenalin-fueled fast lane the moment he heard that horrific sound over the phone—the screeching tires, the thunderous impact, followed by instant and eternal silence. Collin changed in that split second, never to be the same person. Never to live a normal life again.

His pursuers expected him to crack and fold, but he was determined to hold it together and win this battle. Isolation was a terrible thing to endure at such a precarious time in his life, but he knew he had to hold on. Lukas would figure out a strategy, and they would take these guys down.

In this pack of weary travelers, he was just another prisoner waiting to be freed. He inched forward, checked his watch frequently, and wondered how things might have been. His mind was caught up in analyzing his predicament, struggling to make sense of the senseless, when an impatient voice called out, "Next, please."

Perched in his little booth a foot above those he was admitting into his country, the hawk-like customs agent scanned Collin as he approached. He seemed more like a magistrate handing down rulings than a customs agent. In that moment, Collin felt unprepared for the impending appearance and subsequent judgment but managed to keep his astonishment to himself, trying to recall how he had gotten to the front of the line already.

The pale-skinned, dark-haired judge in the booth began to wave him forward more impatiently as Collin hesitated. Collin lurched forward and handed his fake passport to the man behind the bulletproof, plexiglass cage. "I'm sorry, sir, just a bit out of it today."

"Yes, I see." The customs officer seemed mildly annoyed but efficient. He raised his eyebrows and did a double take at Collin's passport.

"Martin Smithers?"

After a long pause to collect his thoughts and run through the plan he had rehearsed so many times, Collin blurted out, "Yes, sir, that's me."

"I see," the man said again, his French-Canadian accent on full display. "And what is the nature of your business?"

Gaining confidence as his memory kicked in, Collin replied, "I'm a computer systems consultant."

"I see," he said for the third time. These two words and the high-minded tone with which they were uttered were enough to make Collin uncomfortable. "You're American, yes?"

"Yes, sir, I am."

"Arriving from Argentina, yes?"

"Yes, sir, I am."

"And what brings you to Toronto at this time?"

"Business, sir. I have a meeting with the Information Technology manager of the Chrysler plant in Brampton. I am presenting my proposal to overhaul their data backup and restore system."

"Is that so?"

"Yes, sir. It's a big meeting for me. Huge potential ..." Collin said as he glanced over his shoulder.

"I see," he said yet again. Collin determined that the aristocratic French accent intimidated him more than anything about the way the man used this phrase.

The agent punched some keys on his computer, spent a few moments studying his screen, then considered Collin one more time. He picked up the phone and spoke in hushed tones. Collin could neither hear nor understand a word. His pulse quickened, and his stomach churned. He looked away to avoid eye contact with the man while he took a deep breath. The phone conversation continued and the man behind the glass pointed to his computer screen. When Collin turned back toward him, after composing himself, the man cupped his hand over his mouth.

Collin checked his watch, then scanned the crowd for any sign of approaching policemen. The man in the booth was watching him closely. Collin pasted a condescending look on his face, as he checked his watch again.

The consultation ended. The agent placed the phone back in its cradle and proceeded to stamp the passport in front of him with much ceremony. His eyes narrowed as he slid Collin's passport through the metal box. A look of disdain briefly crossed the man's countenance before he called, "Next," and looked beyond Collin.

Breathing a hidden sigh of relief, Collin proceeded to the next line where a machine would inspect his bags. The laptop and the contents of his pockets were put into a plastic tray in tight formation with his computer bag and backpack. He was quizzed about the contents of his bag and whether it contained any fruit, vegetables, plants, or seeds from outside Canada. When he answered no, he was dismissed and instructed to proceed.

Although he slept on the plane, Collin was jet lagged and ready to lie down in a warm, clean bed. Using his phone, he booked a room at the Radisson Hotel in Brampton. He rented a car at the airport and made the short drive to his hotel using the GPS provided in the car. No one followed him.

His arms and legs felt as though they had been filled with wet sand. Every movement came with great effort. He mustered his remaining energy to hoist himself out of the car, gather his bags, and propel himself through the automatic doors and across the lobby to the registration desk. The clerk smiled as she welcomed him.

It was a struggle to get to his room at the end of the hall. Every step seemed a chore, but he plodded on. He felt like a marathoner at mile twenty-two, his arduous journey nearly complete.

He needed to prepare for another important day of travel. In the morning, Collin would enter the United States for the first time since he started running from Pho Nam Penh and his henchmen.

He was home, sort of.

CHAPTER NINETEEN

LONDON, ENGLAND
JUNE 1

The suspicious and ambitious mind of Nic Lancaster could not rest. Only a handful of cubicles in the immense, third floor cube farm had lights burning on a Saturday morning. Of course, Nic's was one of them. He paced in his cubicle as he clicked a pen and tried to unlock the secret of the disappearance of Collin Cook. Twice in two weeks he had him trapped, and twice the little bugger had managed to get away. Cook could be anywhere but was most likely hunkered down somewhere in South America, afraid to show his face. If the Peruvian police hadn't gone in so heavy handed, Nic was sure they could have apprehended him in Puno. Video footage showed a man meeting Cook's description exiting a bus in Puno the day before the police raid. But that was almost a week ago now. No other reports had come in since.

Nic grudgingly had to admit this guy was good. He knew all the tricks and knew how to disappear. Collin Cook was smart, cunningly smart.

Nic had posted Collin's name, photo, and background on Interpol's online priority bulletin board. He didn't know when or where Cook would show up or when he would make a mistake, but Nic knew he would eventually. Nic would be ready.

Getting Collin Cook was Nic's top priority, despite the other assignments that had been placed on his desk. He would not allow an amateur like Cook to embarrass him again. Nic worked longer and longer hours. The cyber-crime team needed a win within Interpol, and the agency especially needed a win with the British press. Personally, Nic needed the publicity, the promotion, the raise. And, of course, the recognition of his hard work and dedication.

Right now, however, he just needed a break in the case.

* * * *

CHICAGO, ILLINOIS
JUNE 2

Emily fidgeted in her seat, waiting patiently for the plane to start moving. The sooner they could be in the air, the sooner she could open her laptop and review her presentation again. Not that she hadn't already reviewed it a hundred times, but she felt that there was no substitute for stellar preparation, which would settle her nerves. It was her first ever conference presentation and, if it went well, it might lead to others. And if it were to lead to others, it would mean that she was accomplishing what she set out to do: make a difference in the world through medical science.

She had four hours on the plane, another couple of hours tonight in the hotel, and perhaps another hour or two in the morning before the convention started. Would it be enough? Her colleagues had all assured her she was ready. Her boss, Mike Zimmerman, had reviewed it with her and sat in an empty conference room while she rehearsed. His comments, surprisingly, included a suggestion to start off with some humor, something funny that would make her presentation stick out in the minds of the attendees. Mike, of all people.

Emily was focused, making her unaware of things happening around her. She didn't realize someone was watching her when she checked into her hotel in Chicago. She blithely went about her business, replaying her slideshow in her mind as she strolled through the lobby to the elevators.

She ate dinner with Mike, and they talked about their respective preparations. He suggested breakfast together to do a final run-through. He seemed more nervous about her presentation than she did. After dinner, she hit the hotel gym for a three-mile run on the treadmill and a few laps in the pool to help burn off her anxious energy. She paid no mind to the observers. Not even the man from the lobby, who watched her from behind the cover of a thick book. Her mind was elsewhere, and she had no reason to suspect a thing.

* * * *

BRAMPTON, ONTARIO, CANADA
JUNE 2

"Are you out of your mind? What are you doing in Canada?" Lukas asked as soon as Collin picked up the phone.

It was 3:38 a.m. Collin had no idea where Lukas was or what time zone he was in, and he didn't ask. He sat up in bed, cleared his throat, and tried to think of the most succinct way to explain things to his most trusted friend and security advisor. His mind was instantly activated, alarmed by the harshness in Lukas's tone. When he finally spoke, his voice was gravelly. "They found me in Peru, twice. I had to get out of there."

"Why didn't you tell me? We should have discussed this first, especially with the recent changes."

"I called. I texted. You didn't respond. I figured you were too busy working on more important things, so I came up with my own plan."

"I am busy, I admit, but there is nothing more important than keeping you safe. Now I'm afraid you've put more than just yourself in danger."

"What are you talking about?"

"I'm talking about Emily. That's the change I needed to tell you about. Why didn't you respond to my texts?"

"What texts? I got nothing back from you, Lukas. I called; you didn't answer. I sent you texts; you didn't respond. What do you want me to do? Just sit here like a slow-moving target?"

"No, of course not. Just respond to my texts."

"I turned my phone off for the flight and just now turned it back on."

"I sent you texts yesterday. Are you telling me you haven't turned on your phone since then?"

"I didn't see your texts until I got to my hotel here in Toronto."

"Still, you could have responded."

"Do you know how much work it is to travel through South America by bus? I just wanted to sleep."

"Terrific. You're tired, so you ignore your own safety?"

"Back to Emily—what did you mean?"

"Someone has hacked both your mom's and Emily's Facebook accounts. I don't think it's the FBI or Interpol. They still seemed vexed as to what you're up to."

"They should be. Even if they've been snooping around and reading our Facebook conversations, they wouldn't have learned anything. I've given away nothing in terms of my location or my intentions."

"I fear, nonetheless, that you have put the two of them in danger, as well as yourself, by coming back here."

"I'm nowhere near home—"

"I know that, but I also think I know what you're up to."

"I swear this will work, and when it does, I'll be back on a plane heading to Osaka as soon as I can. I'm thinking train ride to Vancouver, then Vancouver to Osaka early next week. Think I can lie low in Japan for a while?"

"I don't know, Collin. Everything seems a bit shaky right now. There's a lot of activity. More than I can tell you, but I doubt you'll be able to get on a plane again anytime soon."

"Why not? I just flew from Argentina to Toronto without a problem."

"You got lucky this time. I doubt you would be that lucky again. Not with this Interpol bulldog on the case. It would be wise for you to stay underground for a while. You've had two near misses recently, and the guys at Interpol are pissed. They're stepping things up."

"What do you suggest then?"

"Stay away from Chicago, first of all. Find yourself an out of the way place there in Toronto, and stay inside until things die down."

"I doubt I can do that, Lukas. You know I hate staying inside."

"Yes, I know, and it keeps getting you in trouble."

Collin thought back to his escape from Germany and the incident in Lima, both places where he was supposed to stay out of sight. Before that, he had refused to stay indoors in London. Someone had been on his tail ever since. "I hear you, but I've just got to see Emily. That's all. I need to see someone I know. Just one quick visit with a friend, then I'm gone, underground, for as long as it takes."

Lukas blew out a breath. "I get it. You want to see her, but I'm sure you don't want to put her in danger. You don't want to get her messed up in all of this, do you?"

"If they're hacking her Facebook, it sounds like they've already made her part of it. Now I have to warn her and, without Facebook or, I assume, e-mail, I have no way to communicate with her other than direct contact."

"It's too risky, Collin. Think about it."

"I am thinking about it. If they're watching her already, I have to warn her. I have to tell her what's going on. I can only do that by talking to her. I have to see her."

"Don't do it, Collin. You'll put both of you in danger, and I won't be able to protect you."

"I've done all right on my own lately, no thanks to you."

"What's that supposed to mean?"

"It means you go silent for weeks, and I figure out how to stay safe on my own all that time, then you pop up and tell me what to do again. Do you have a better way to keep Emily safe? Are you going to call her? Or visit her? You think that will work better?"

Lukas sighed into the phone. "It's not like I forgot about you. I knew where you were. I expected you to stay out of sight. But this? You got lucky. For her sake, stay away from Emily."

"Not gonna happen."

"Collin, don't get all stubborn on me. This is serious."

"Don't tell me it's serious. I know it is, and if I don't tell her what's going on, she'll be in even more danger. They'll follow her, corner her, who knows what they'll do."

"I don't like this. I don't like this one bit," said Lukas.

"You don't have to like it, but this is what has to be done. I don't see a better choice here, do you?" He waited for a response. When there was none, he continued. "That's what I thought."

Before he hung up, Collin was developing a plan. He got dressed in a hurry, putting his disguise back together, and was on the road by four o'clock in the morning, speeding west by southwest toward the border crossing at Port Huron, Michigan, hoping for less traffic and an easier time getting through there than at Detroit. By nine o'clock he was back on US soil for the first time in seven months.

Then Chicago by sundown.

* * * *

LONDON, ENGLAND
JUNE 3

Nic arrived in the office earlier than usual. But he wasn't alone. Before he even made it to his cubicle, he was intercepted by Peter, the techno-geek from the dungeon. "You're going to love me for this one," he said with a measure of pride. "I found your man again. That Cook fellow. Remember him?"

"Of course, how could I forget?"

"Seems you're not the only one who caught grief over the last episode. I can't say he's sitting there in a hotel room again, but at least I know where he landed yesterday."

"Oh yeah. What have you got?"

"My little algorithm is still chugging away, inspecting everything that comes through. Remember our formula?"

"What, you mean the 88 percent match?"

"That's right. It pulls off all images with an 88 percent match or better and sticks it in a file for review. I got a hit yesterday but didn't think much of it. It was borderline. Rounded up to 88 percent. But then, this morning I get here, and there are two more texts telling me there've been two more hits. The one yesterday is from Buenos Aires International Airport. One from this morning was taken at Toronto Pearson; the other from the camera at the car hire counter at the Toronto airport. Wanna see them?"

"Sure, show me what you've got." Peter opened a file on the shared drive for Nic, who studied the images thoroughly, rewinding and replaying the video several times. "It definitely looks like him, doesn't it? But he looks different than last time."

"Right, he does," said Peter. "That's why we're only getting an 88 percent match," said Peter. He clicked and tapped on the mouse, and a second image appeared. "See here. These are the measurements from the original photo. And these here are from this one," he said, pointing to a set of white numbers that appeared on the screen between the two photographs. "The measurements of the distances between the eyes, the ears, and the nose are all the same. The main difference is in the color of the eyes—easy to change with contacts, right? —and the measurements of the jaw line. With prosthetics, it's possible to alter these measurements enough to throw off facial recognition software."

"Are you saying he used prosthetics?"

"If that's your man, then yes. That's what I'm saying."

"That's a pretty crafty criminal, I'd say."

"I'd say so, too, but I'd hate to have another fiasco like last time,

CHAPTER TWENTY

CHICAGO, ILLINOIS
JUNE 3

Emily Burns paced the floor outside the packed room where she would momentarily be the guest speaker. This was something she had worked for, anticipated, dreamed about, and prepared for over the course of her career—the chance to present breakthrough results of her laboratory successes. This was exciting stuff, but her insides felt like they were being twisted in a vice. She knew her material and knew it well. There was no need to panic, just focus and relax. And practice that opening line one more time.

The door swung open, and one of the convention volunteers smiled at her and nodded. It was show time. Once she entered the room and heard the applause, confidence replaced fear. She climbed the steps and strode to the podium, smiled, and delivered her opening line.

"Research tells me there's a doctor in the house." The chuckles helped her relax a bit more. "And the doctor tells me to take two enhanced enzymes and call him in the morning."

From there she launched with grace and charisma into an explanation of the oddities within the protein chain she and her team had isolated. The dissertation was expert, the delivery impeccable, the results riveting. Emily was in her element and the facts and figures seemed to flow smoothly.

At the end of her presentation, the crowd erupted in enthusiastic applause. Many attendees lined up to shake her hand, congratulating her on the excellent work, and thanking her for sharing.

One man waited for the crush of people to dissipate, watching intently as she smiled and thanked the last well-wisher. She gasped as she turned and saw the bearded man moving purposefully toward her. Putting her hand to her mouth and looking toward the door with a slow-building sense of panic, Emily wanted to scream but couldn't. Or wouldn't. The man, though alone and watching her every move, was not threatening. She lowered her head and began to hurry toward the exit.

"You seem pretty sure that your enhanced enzymes stopped the growth of the tumors. Are you sure it's not the elevated toxicity of the environment post-injection? It could be just a temporary lull in the tumor growth," the man said as he continued to draw near to her.

Without stopping, Emily spoke confidently but continued moving toward the exit. "Definitely not. Once we isolated the enzyme and ran our tests, it became obvious to us, based on the reactions to the reagent, that it was not temporary, despite some elevated toxicity from the injection. Everything since then has pointed toward adherence to the enhanced enzyme," she said.

"I see," said the man, adjusting his hat and glasses. He explained how he had read her paper and analyzed her conclusions. He praised her work, which, he said, spurred him to this conference. Nothing else was as interesting to him as her and her research.

Her inner senses were ablaze, and she was half-paralyzed with fear, half-intrigued by the interest the handsome attendee displayed. Emily was caught somewhere between the desire to run and the desire to speak further with the curious visitor. His voice was soothing and sincere. As he spoke, her senses calmed. She felt as if this stranger wasn't so strange. There was something warm and familiar about him. The more he talked, the stronger that feeling grew.

Without any forethought, she blurted out, "Where did you say you're from?"

An awkward pause followed. "Oh, I'm sorry," said the man. "I didn't properly introduce myself, I'm afraid. I'd like to do so but, perhaps, over a cup of coffee, unless you're otherwise occupied."

"I'd like that. I'm free until Dr. Nicolson's speech at four o'clock."

The handsome stranger cocked his head to the side as a wry grin spread across his face. "May I walk with you?"

Flattered, she tried to conceal the blush that she knew was warming her face. "That would be very nice. Thank you."

This was the closest thing she had had to a date in a year. Dr. Burns felt nervous and excited, guilty and honored all at once. She wasn't prepared for this. She stopped in the ladies' room to freshen up. Her beauty was natural and didn't require much effort. At this point in her life, she was not looking for too much attention from the opposite sex. She was more or less happily married to her work. She also had thoughts of her friend and former sweetheart, Collin. No one else had ever caught her attention. Until now. This caused some guilt, but she shrugged it off. It was just a meeting to discuss science over coffee.

She finished in the ladies' room and headed to the coffee bar with the stranger.

As they strolled down the long corridor, the man made casual conversation until they arrived at the counter and placed their orders. With their coffee cups in hand, the two found an empty table. A true gentleman, the man held her chair out and helped her scoot in before sitting opposite her.

She stared at him for a moment, not sure how to restart the conversation. The man returned her gaze and smiled. He removed his glasses and set them on the table. "I owe you an answer to your earlier question," he said, reaching for something in his pocket. He placed it on his thigh, turned his face toward his lap, and began poking his eyes with a finger. Then he fiddled with his mouth. When he sat up, he continued. "I, like you, am from Southern California. A nice little surfer hangout called Huntington Beach."

Her mouth fell open, and her eyes went wide. "Collin? Is that really you?" She stood and threw open her arms, working her way around the small table.

He couldn't hold back. He opened his arms wide and received her embrace; he returned it with the first hug he had given anyone since his wife's and children's funeral nearly a year before, holding on longer than the prescribed time. Emily's cheek pressed against his, stirring old feelings in his barren, neglected shell. A sense of familiarity and connectedness ran through him like warm water. The reaction surprised him. Shocked him, really. He expected there to be hesitancy, or maybe reluctance, on her part. He didn't expect this sort of reception. Not in this stodgy, clinical setting. Emily was unabashed. Her long-lost friend, wounded and aching, had returned from a mysterious sojourn. She told herself to tone it down so as to not scare him away. She had no idea what he might be feeling or what he had gone through over the past several months. Pulling back from their long embrace, she looked him over.

"You look great, Collin. Different but great."

"You didn't recognize me when you saw me earlier?"

"Not really. But at the same time, you looked so familiar." With a quizzical look, she added, "Why did you do that?"

Collin motioned for her to take her seat, then responded as he sat down. "Well, I guess I wasn't sure how you would react to me. I knew you weren't expecting me … and I didn't want to get in your way before your big speech." He kept to himself the fact that he also wanted to observe her without her knowing he was watching. He wanted—and was able—to see her behave in a natural way, in her element, without him around, and without knowing she was being watched. "You were terrific, by the way. I was really proud of you. I'm so impressed with the work you've done and the way you talk about it."

"Thank you. That means so much to me. The fact that you read my research is really quite flattering."

"Well, I had some extra time while I was traveling and wanted to see what you were so excited about. I can't say I understand it, but what I understand is that your work is pretty amazing. It's incredible what you've done," he said.

"Thank you. That means a lot to me. It really does."

"You're doing it, Emily. You're making a difference, just like you said you would."

"I don't know. There's still a long way to go." She shook her head slowly. "I still can't believe you're here. There's so much to talk about." Emily reached out to touch Collin's arm as her words came tumbling out. She prattled on about how good it was to see him, how surprised she was, how she had worried about him, and how sorry she was about what happened. It must have been awful for him. Then she stopped, mid-sentence, and realized what she was doing. She was acting like a teenager with no impulse control. She breathed in, held that breath, then exhaled slowly. "There," she said. "I think I'm over my shock and ready to proceed in a more adult-like manner." Her false seriousness was spoken with a hushed voice and a playful grin that spread across her face.

Collin watched her with amusement. She was still energetic, bubbly, and oh-so beautiful when she was excited. Her gray-blue eyes danced as she spoke. He tried not to stare, but it was hard not to. She was still mesmerizing, even after all these years. Collin shifted his eyes to his hands.

Forcing his mind to get back on task, he latched onto the memory of his plan and began reviewing it in his mind. After a moment of reflection, he realized that Emily had stopped talking and he had not responded. Sheepishly, he glanced up at her face, which was full of expectation as if she had asked him something crucial and was waiting for his answer.

"Sorry. My mind wandered off for a moment," he said. "It's just that it's so good to be here with you. I'm having trouble believing it myself."

"I was mostly rambling. But I did ask what your plans are while you're in Chicago."

"Truthfully, I can't stay. I'll be heading out after this."

"Heading out? No. You've got to stay. We can go to one of those jazz bars after my dinner with the bosses."

He paused, rubbed his chin for a moment, then said, "Sold. I'll stay for that."

Collin asked her more about her work and Emily, animated and vivacious, told him all about it. He enjoyed every word, although most of it went right over his head. Just hearing her speak, watching how passionate she was, and hearing her lovely, gravelly voice again, made the long, arduous trip from the depths of South America—and the risks involved with re-entering the United States—worthwhile.

Emily paused, then asked, "Where have you been all this time?" It was not a harsh question, but one spoken with the concern of a good friend.

"I told you, I've been wrapping up some business."

"You don't expect to get away with such a brush-off answer, do you? Not with me?"

"You probably wouldn't believe me if I told you."

"Try me."

Collin let out a sigh. He should have expected this; it was so like Emily to go straight to the hard questions and not back down until she had learned what she wanted to know.

"Before we talk about me, can I just thank you for tracking down my parents and telling them about the accident? I'm sorry I was so out of it when you left. I think it was the pain medication. All I know is that the nurses didn't know where they were or how to find them, but you tracked them down in Alaska. That's pretty incredible."

"You can thank the power of social media for that little bit of research success."

"You're being modest. I'm sure it took quite a bit of effort. Thank you."

"Glad I could help."

"I was barely aware that you had left the hospital, but I realized why when I woke up and saw my in-laws there. I mean, they're wonderful people and all, but I'm sure it would have been awkward. I never had the chance to say thanks and tell you how much that meant to me."

"It was nothing. I wish I could have done more. I'm sure you would have done the same for me." Emily thought back to that moment when she learned the truth of what happened to his wife and children. She had had to push aside the guilt, steel her emotions, then search for his parents, eventually finding them on an Alaskan cruise, and explain to them the awful circumstances surrounding their youngest son. When she had finally found a moment to rest at the side of Collin's hospital bed and laid her head next to his hand, Amy's parents pushed open the door and jumped to the nearest conclusion.

"Things have been pretty rough for me ever since that day," he said, looking at his hands on the table.

Emily's tone was reverent. "I can only imagine."

"My life has been turned upside down," he said. His voice was low and somber.

"I have worried about the role I played. I was so out of line that night, the night before it happened. I feel so terrible about what I did and the extra burden that must have caused you."

"Look, that was my fault."

"No, no. I was the one drinking and getting sloppy. I had no right to be so forward. It was stupid of me. I am so sorry, Collin."

"Don't worry about it. What happened happened," he said, still looking at his hands.

"I appreciate you being such a decent man. That night and always."

This was not where he wanted this conversation to go. He had to get back on point and break the news about her Facebook page being watched by the bad guys. He looked up, glancing all around, and continued with a lower voice. "The truth is, Emily, I'm now a wanted man."

"Wanted? For what? By whom? How can that be?"

"It's a long, complicated story. I'll tell you the whole thing someday, but this isn't the right time or place. But, to answer your earlier question, I have literally been all over the world. You name it: Europe, the Caribbean, Central America, South America. I've been to a lot of places that I never ..." His attention was diverted by someone three tables away, to his left.

The man sat with a conference program held in front of him, peering over it now and then. He was just within Collin's peripheral vision and became of such intense interest to Collin that he stopped speaking. When Collin glanced his way, moving his head slowly to the left, the program went back up and the man shifted in his seat.

Collin rocked in the chair across from Emily, his elbows on the table, his arms folded over each other, his hands gripping his biceps. He was trying to control an involuntary shaking that was growing more pronounced. The grip tightened, his arms flexing in an effort to override the tremors. He didn't utter a word or change expressions.

Emily, too, was now in danger. He had to figure out a way to get her out of this mess. He looked back at her and found her eyes peering into his own, searching. He felt something deep inside that had long lain dormant. It felt so good to be with her, to hear her talk, to look into her eyes. He wanted it to continue but knew it couldn't. There were things happening around him. Around *them*. Something was brewing, and he didn't like it. The calm before the storm was coming to an end.

Collin's eyes darted from Emily's face to the guy with the program. Something wasn't right. He couldn't stand it any longer. He had to get both of them out of there.

Collin arose so suddenly and so forcefully that as his legs extended, they sent his chair tumbling behind him, creating a thundering crash as the metal chair collided with the marble tile. Emily let out a shrill scream. Turning in all directions to survey the startled crowd, Collin made haste to collect his things. He checked to see who moved in his direction as he put his arms through the straps of his backpack and slung the computer bag over his back.

The man with the program jolted forward in surprise, his mouth and eyes wide open. He watched Collin intently but didn't move. There was movement in the crowd, coming from beyond the man. A face concealed behind the heads and shoulders of other moving bodies in the crowded walkway was aggressively moving toward him. Time to get out.

Collin grabbed Emily's hand and pulled her through the aisles of chairs and tables until they reached the more open space of the main corridor. Most of the people in the corridor were oblivious to the commotion Collin had created. Emily resisted, but he didn't let go. He weaved through the crowd with Emily in tow until they reached the nearest exit to the street. She was asking questions that he didn't have time to answer.

As he pushed through the doors, he angled his body to look behind them, searching for signs of his pursuers.

"Where are we going, Collin?" she asked for the tenth time when they reached the sidewalk outside, pulling her hand away.

Collin turned to face her. "We've got company. They somehow found me here. I'm so sorry, Emily. I didn't mean for this to happen. We have to go."

He snatched her hand again and started to run, searching for a taxi. There were none in sight, so he headed down Michigan Avenue toward Navy Pier. This was not going to work with her in a skirt and heels.

"I don't understand, Collin. Who found you?"

"Not sure who they are, exactly. I just know they're after me. They want my money. And they'll kill me to get it."

He kept looking over his shoulder at the doors they had just come through. They burst open just as Collin and Emily reached the corner. He looked back and saw a tall, bald man looking up and down the sidewalk. He spotted Collin and came running while talking into his sleeve.

Emily gasped as she noticed the big man racing toward them. "You weren't kidding, were you?"

"No, not this time. Get away from me. Act like you're mad. Get in that taxi and go to Bloomfeld's. Meet me in the men's department," he said.

The taxi took off, and Collin saw the look of terror on Emily's face.

He looked over his shoulder. The man was ten yards from him. He turned and sprinted across the street, dodging traffic. On the other side, he checked over his shoulder to make sure the big guy was still in pursuit. Using his speed, he darted around the corner and raced down the block, his computer bag bouncing against his hip. He turned another corner and spotted a taxi that was dropping an old woman off in front of an apartment building. He arrived just as the cab began to pull out. No sign of the large, bald man.

A few minutes later, he reunited with Emily in the men's department of Bloomfeld's. He knew he had to explain things quickly yet thoroughly. He had to make her understand the situation but not panic. He had to answer her questions but not give away too much, or it could completely paralyze her with fear. Collin told her about her Facebook and e-mail accounts being monitored and how she had to be careful, but he would not leave her on her own. He presented a plan to keep them both safe, overcoming her skepticism, though just barely.

Fifteen minutes later, another taxi dropped him off a block from the front entrance of the convention center. He ran to a spot across the street, not far from where he last saw the bald guy, and waited. The taxi with Emily stopped, and she got out. He spotted the bald guy keeping watch. As she approached the building, Collin emerged from his hiding place and ran, crossing between cars, to catch her just as she opened a large, glass door. He tried to grab her arm, but she pulled away, yelling loudly at him to leave her alone and that she didn't ever want to see him again. Collin persisted until a couple of observers approached as if they were Emily's sworn protectors.

"Fine," Collin yelled back. "We're done."

"Good," she said and walked away, leaving Collin standing just inside the entrance of the building. The bald guy spoke into his sleeve again. Collin waited until he was near the entrance, approaching from the outside. As the man opened one of the large doors, Collin moved to the farthest set of doors and bolted outside, sprinting at full speed back the way he came. As he turned down the sidewalk, he checked to make sure the bald man was following him and not Emily. He was. Collin led the chase a few blocks, keeping the man in his sights, but once he noticed a car in pursuit with at least two more men in it, he cranked up the speed and, with some evasive maneuvers, picked his way through buildings and parking lots that the car could not enter. Sweating and out of breath, Collin found a taxi stand, jumped in the first available cab, and sped away.

CHAPTER
TWENTY-ONE

CHICAGO, ILLINOIS
JUNE 4

Emily tried to restore her confidence as she strode away. She smoothed her hair, then her skirt, and put on a look of indignation as she marched across the large, open corridor, her heels clicking in a steady rhythm as she picked up speed. A stranger approached from her left and excused himself for butting in. He wore a dark blue blazer with a nametag that identified him as a conference attendee from the Harvard School of Medicine. His name was Alec Parchman.

"Aren't you Dr. Burns? From the Scripps Institute?" he asked.

"Yes," she said. Because of the conversation with Collin, she was instantly wary and guarded, never slowing down.

The young stranger matched her pace and continued. "Again, I'm sorry to intrude, but I couldn't help noticing the trouble just now. Is everything OK?"

"Yes, everything's fine. Thank you," she said without breaking stride. She had already forgotten his name.

"I attended your lecture today and was very impressed." "Thank you. That's very kind of you to say."

"I wanted to ask you a few questions afterward about your conclusions, but I noticed you left the lecture with that same man. I didn't want to interrupt you," he said, jabbing a thumb toward the door she had come through.

"That's very thoughtful of you. I don't mean to be rude, but I'm trying to get to another session—one my boss wants me to attend with him."

"I understand. Can I buy you a cup of coffee after the session? I'd like more details on the preparation of your specimens."

Emily's mind was racing, more cautious and more alert than it would have been ordinarily. Was this guy one of those people chasing Collin? Or was he stalking *her*? An admirer? The idea that he could be just a driven scientist wanting to gain insight for scientific purposes registered—only after her initial suspicions. "OK. Meet me in the central food court at five o'clock. Is it all right if my boss joins us? We're supposed to meet up with his boss at six."

"Of course. I'm sure Mike Zimmerman could add much to the conversation."

Her back straightened involuntarily at her boss's name. This guy knew too much to be a casual observer. The thought scared her, but she controlled the gasp that welled up inside her and pushed down her rising anxiety. She swallowed hard, shaking her head slightly. Perhaps he was a very serious scientist. Or maybe he was a skilled spy. Or a pathological creep with a perverse crush on her. Her pulse quickened, and her eyes widened, but she kept moving forward. She fought off the urge to run away, and instead employed her rational, calculating brain to make the decision to keep friends close and enemies closer. She would ascertain which he was later. "Would you care to join me and Mike at Dr. Nicolson's lecture?"

His eyes lit up, and a smile spread across his face. "I'd love to, thanks."

Maybe he wasn't the enemy. Even if he was, she would use his presence to her advantage.

* * * *

The taxi let him out and sped away. The buildings that lined the street were old and dingy and stacked tightly together. Most had heavy bars across the windows. Some had neon signs advertising services such as pay day loans, tattoos, and cheap car insurance. He ducked into a beauty salon and was greeted with incredulous stares. "Can I get my hair dyed?" he asked with cheerful, exaggerated naiveté.

All conversation stopped, and all eyes turned to stare at, perhaps, the only white person within blocks of this place. A heavyset woman stood slowly and lumbered across the stained linoleum floor. "You got something in mind?"

"Yeah, let's go blond, just for fun." If Collin was nervous at all, he hid it from his audience. Three of the four chairs were occupied, hairdressers standing over their clients. One woman, probably in her twenties, was having her hair braided. A forty-something-year-old was trying to hide the gray. The third appeared to be finished but remained seated, watching it all.

The round woman eyed him warily. "What makes you think I have blond hair color?"

"Why wouldn't you? I'm sure you have other clients that want to give it a try."

Her eyebrows arched, and she drew her breath in through her teeth. "Let me go check the back." She shuffled across the floor and disappeared into the back room, returning a few moments later with a box of hair color. Fifty minutes after that, Collin bid his new friends adieu and exited the salon, heading up the block to a used car lot. It was encircled with twelve-foot fences, the tops adorned with razor wire. In another thirty minutes, he was speeding southward on Interstate 90 toward Gary, en route to Indianapolis in his newly purchased wreck, bought with cash under an entirely false, but never verified, identity.

The 1991 Ford Mustang was not exactly comfortable and had not been well-maintained on the inside or outside. The paint was faded and spotty. The velour seats were riddled with cigarette burns. The dashboard was cracked, exposing the sunbaked foam inside. There were all manner of creaks and groans that accompanied sharp turns, potholes, and heavy braking. However, the engine seemed to run fine. For the $1200 he had spent, he was assured it would easily outlast the sixty-day warranty. Just to be safe, Collin kept his speed below seventy-five miles per hour.

If it survived, it would be someone else's problem in just three days.

With stops for rest, gas, and food, he figured he would be in Key West in about two and a half days. Collin realized that he had never been on this kind of road trip—alone in a car with fifteen hundred miles of open road in front of him. And a deadline. Glancing again at his watch, he recalled his brief conversation with Captain Sewell. "I need a favor," he had told the Captain. "I need to get out of the country without detection. You and your boat came to mind first."

The good Captain chuckled. "That will cost you."

"Of course. I'm good for it. Just tell me where to meet you."

"You know there's a hurricane heading our way, don't you?"

"No," said Collin, "I haven't been paying attention to the weather."

"I want to be far away when it comes. But if you can be in Key West no later than noon on Friday, we might have time to outrun it."

"Okay, I'll be there," said Collin.

"Find Rojas at the marina. Bring burgers and beer," the Captain said with a laugh.

The Captain never asked where he was or how long it would take him to get there. Little did he know how far Collin had to drive. Collin checked his iPhone again. The GPS app indicated twenty-two hours and thirty-seven minutes of driving remained. He blew out a long breath. It was Tuesday evening already. He could make it, but it would be tight.

Running his fingers through his newly blond, freshly cropped hair as he checked himself in the rearview mirror, Collin wondered if Rojas would recognize him and hoped the cash supply in his two bags, which had dwindled to roughly $48,000, would be enough.

*   *   *   *

Halfway through Dr. Nicolson's presentation, something buzzed and chirped inside Emily's purse. She didn't recognize the sound; it was different than any of her phone's programmed settings. Harvard boy raised an eyebrow and cocked his head as she fumbled through her purse to make it stop. Mike Zimmerman, sitting on the other side of her, glanced over, too, no doubt wondering why she had not shut her phone off before the meeting began. When she finally located the noisemaker, she struggled to find the power button. The phone was completely for-eign to her. She had never seen this device and wondered how it got into her purse. It was one of those cheap phones that wireless carriers practically gave away. Not wanting to draw attention, she shoved it into the purse. Emily sat back in her seat and refocused her attention, at least outwardly, on the speaker. Inwardly, she was puzzled and a bit shocked by the knowledge that she had somehow picked up an extra cell phone. She smoothed her hair and crossed her legs, fighting the temptation to explore this new mystery and solve it.

The remaining twenty-five minutes of the speech dragged on. Emily hardly heard a word that was said. When Dr. Nicolson finally concluded, she excused herself, saying she needed to freshen up. In the ladies' room, she ducked into a stall and turned the mystery phone back on. With some effort, she found the call log and saw a Chicago number she did not recognize. That same number had left her a text message that read: *This is Collin. Sorry about the hassle earlier. Call me back at this number when you're alone and can talk. Keep this phone our little secret. It's better that way.*

She pondered this and the mystery grew. There wasn't enough time to delve into a conversation now. Mike and Harvard boy were waiting for her. She texted a quick response: *I'm busy 'til after dinner. Call you then. Need to know what's going on. Very confused right now.*

Harvard boy proved to be a legitimate scientist or, at the very least, a convincing imitator. She continued to have her doubts but needed to use him to diffuse the situation with Collin in case she was still being watched. He and Mike spoke at length and in great detail about Mike's presentation and the paper she and Mike had published. He was fascinated. After forty-five minutes of talk and mind probing, his motivation was revealed. He asked Mike about possible positions at Scripps. He was a fan of the work they were doing and hoped, after finishing his PhD, to find a mentor and a team environment where he could pursue his passion for research and learn more about the fascinating work with enhanced enzymes.

Emily was impressed. Mike seemed to be as well. The kid knew how to network. During the conversation, Emily found herself scanning the area, looking, as Collin had instructed, for anyone watching her. She wasn't trained in this sort of thing, so she felt vulnerable. And scared. It felt like everyone was watching her, like everyone was an enemy. Each huddled group in the area was a potential threat. But the two loners nearby made her breath catch in her throat.

Emily checked her watch. "Mike, we'd better go. We have that dinner meeting at six."

"Yes, that's right," said Mike as he stood. Extending a hand to their guest, "It was a pleasure to meet you, Alec. Best of luck in your studies. Contact me. We'll continue this conversation." Mike gave him a business card and readied himself to leave.

Alec thanked him and promised to touch base. Turning to Emily, he said, "Hope you're all right after that little incident earlier."

This took Emily aback and her mouth dropped open slightly before she recovered. "Yes, I'm fine. Thank you." She stole a glance at Mike, who looked puzzled.

Harvard boy continued blithely. "Wasn't he the same guy who knocked over the chair in the food court earlier?"

The thought that Harvard boy had been watching her and Collin was unsettling. It took her a couple of beats to control her reaction. When she answered, she spoke loud enough for the few people seated nearby to hear if they wanted. Collin said it was possible for there to be people planted in the building who would track her every movement and listen to her every word. For them, she tried to be convincing, but Harvard boy became her prime suspect.

"That was a guy I used to work with, trying to take credit for my—our—research. He's terribly insecure." Alec shot her a curious look, and Mike's face grew more puzzled. She quickly added, "I didn't realize that he had a thing for me and has never let it go. I wasn't interested then, nor am I now. I have no time for a relationship, especially one that requires so much energy." She extended a hand and gave Alec a firm handshake, signaling their meeting was over.

As Emily walked with Mike through the convention center concourse and into the adjoining Hilton Hotel, she caught a glimpse of a large black man following them. By the time they found Mike's boss in the swank restaurant on the second floor, he had vanished. She scanned the area, still feeling watched, but could not locate him again.

Mike's boss, Phil, greeted them warmly and invited them to sit, thanking them for the presentations they had each shared. The three scientists enjoyed dinner and conversation that lasted almost two hours. Their exchange was light and chummy. Congratulations and praise were heaped upon Emily by both bosses. Sitting there talking with the two of them, she felt safe and appreciated. She didn't want it to, but the meeting eventually ended.

Being June, pale and orange-tinged sunlight still lingered over Chicago at eight o'clock. The days were long and warm. It would be a fine time for a run along Lake Michigan. Under normal circumstances, that's what she would have done. But, since her encounter with Collin and all she learned from him, nothing felt normal. It had been a long day, full of firsts and surprises. She just wanted to take a long, hot bath and relax in her hotel room.

As she walked in and dropped her purse on the bed, she remembered Collin's request to call him when she was alone, so she pulled out the secret phone and hit the call back button.

"Emily, I'm so glad you called. Are you OK?" Collin asked. His voice was raised above the excessive background noise of the car and the road. "I guess. I'm just spooked. You have me so freaked out; I think everyone is out to get me. I don't like this feeling."

"Welcome to my life," said Collin. "You'll get used to it."

"Get used to it? Is that what I'm supposed to do? Get used to it?" Her voice was elevated, barely under control.

"Look, Emily, things didn't work out quite the way I had planned. No one was supposed to find me at the conference."

"But, Collin, why would you take such a chance? If you knew, as you said, that you were a wanted man, why would you come back to the States?"

Collin sucked in a deep breath. "They found me. In Peru, of all places. I did the best I could to hide in obscure places, but they found me anyway. I didn't feel safe, no matter where I went, no matter what I did to elude them. Coming here felt no riskier than staying where I was." He paused until the rumbling of a big truck faded. "But I realize now how stupid it was of me. I never wanted to put you in harm's way." Another pause. "I just wanted to see you. That's all. I wanted to see you, and talk to you, and be with a friend for a change. I'm sorry."

The words and the soft, pathetic tone in his voice melted her inside. She sat down on the bed and heaved a sigh. "Oh, Collin, I hate to see you in this mess, whatever it is. I wish I knew what to do to help you."

"You've done it already."

"What do you mean?"

"I needed to see a friend, and I saw you." "But I didn't do anything."

"You were you. That's all I could ever ask for. And now I know why I need to stay away. I have to protect those I care for by not being near you or them. At least, not for a while longer."

"But Collin—"

"Listen, Emily." His voice was stronger now, more in control. "You need to be careful from now on. I'm really not sure who those guys were this afternoon, but there's this Asian syndicate who can hack anything, like I said. I think the guys today are working for them. In any case, as I told you earlier, there's a good chance they've hacked your Facebook and e-mail accounts and are monitoring our communication."

"They hacked my Facebook? Oh my—"

"I told you, these guys can and will hack anything to get what they want. Right now, they want me, not you. I think they somehow figured out that I would try to meet you here. I don't know. That's my best guess."

"How can they—"

"They're clever, very clever. But with them hacking into every-thing, it means this phone you're using now will be the only way I can communicate with you. So, don't use it in public, and don't use your everyday phone to contact me. OK?"

"Speaking of, how did I get this phone, anyway?"

"I slipped it in your purse when I caught up to you outside the con-vention center this afternoon, just before our little mock breakup. Nice job with that, by the way. I see an Academy Award in your future."

"Not even. But when did you have time to buy a phone?"

"I bought it on my way into Chicago before I even saw you."

"That took some forethought."

"Yeah, I wanted to be able to communicate with you, so I bought two cheap phones with, like, a billion prepaid minutes."

"A billion?"

"Yeah, I knew you'd have a lot of questions."

"Very funny. OK, let's be serious for a minute. This scares me, Collin."

"I know. It scares me, too. I've been thinking about how I could keep you safe, and I think maybe you need to talk to the FBI. Ask for the main guy handling my case. Ask them for protection. They'll prob-ably try to strike a bargain with you, so give them what they ask for. Just don't tell them about this phone. This is my lifeline."

"But what about you? Won't that make things worse for you?"

"I don't think so. I've still got some tricks up my sleeve. I'm going to disappear until I can clear my name and prove my innocence."

"Can't you talk to them and explain things? Wouldn't they believe you?"

"I wish it were that simple. They have photos and other evidence that points to my involvement with these cyber terrorists. They think I'm to blame for some nasty hack jobs on some of the world's biggest banks. Can you believe that? They think *I'm* capable of hacking into and stealing money from multi-billion-dollar companies. Unreal. But, until I can unwind that tangled mess, I'm stuck hiding."

"I wish there was something I could do to help you."

"There is. Go to the FBI, tell them what you know, and ask them to protect you."

"No way, Collin. I'm not going to do it. I'm not going to rat you out."

"I thought you might say that, so I've made arrangements to keep you safe."

"You've done what?"

"I know some people that know some people, and they are going to make sure nothing happens to you."

"Collin—"

"You should expect to see a large black man carrying a sign with your name on it tomorrow after the conference. His name is Benson. He'll be your limo driver and will make sure you get to the airport safely. At the airport, there will be a lady; her name is Genevieve. She'll take you from Chicago O'Hare to San Diego Lindbergh, where a black Tahoe will take you to a safe house for a few days. Got all that?"

"Are you joking, Collin?"

"No, I'm not. I just transferred a hefty sum of money to pay these people, so let them do their job."

"How do I know I can trust them?"

"They were highly recommended by someone I trust, who knows all about security. I trust this guy with my life and my freedom. You can, too."

"Geez, Collin. This is weird. I don't know what to think."

"Think this: My friend Collin is very sorry for the disruption he has caused in my life. This is his way of making it up to me."

"You're a nut."

"I've been told that before … and I'm starting to believe it."

"That part of you hasn't changed. You still manage to crack jokes in tense situations. But can we be serious again for a minute? I really, really want to help you. Something other than trying to pretend that you're not my friend and that I want no part in your life. I don't think I can keep that charade up for too long. Isn't there something else I can do?"

"When I figure out what that might be, I'll let you know. For now, you've done a lot. Believe me. Seeing you today reminded me of how much I miss home, despite all the changes in my life."

"You really have changed—a lot. One minute I think you're just the same old Collin. The next minute you're spouting things that make you sound like some sort of espionage king or something." Emily paused and an image of Sarah crossed her mind. "You need to come home. I think it would be good for you and for your family if you were able to be with them. They miss you, Collin. They want you home."

"I know. I miss them, too. And my friends. Like you. But I can't put you or any of them at risk again. You're right. I have changed. My whole life has changed. But these changes were not my choice. They were forced upon me because I won't just lie down and become a victim again. I won't let these guys win without a fight."

"I don't understand who you're talking about."

"I'm fighting against some very twisted but brilliant people who want to—who have already done a lot of damage to our country. They're terrorists. A new breed of economic terrorists. Cyber bullies. Punks who want to bring down Western civilization. If they win and take all that I have away, they'll use it to hurt more people. There's no one else who can stop them."

"What makes you think you can stop them, Collin?"

"That's a good question. Why? Why do I have to be the one to stop them? I think it's because I've pissed them off. They tried but couldn't steal their money back from me, so they're out to get me however they can. Releasing photos of me with their nefarious leader is just the opening act, I'm afraid. And I'm one of a very small number of people who has seen him up close. To this point, I've been lucky enough to stay one step ahead of them. With some help, I've out-smarted them. Little ol' me and my genius helper." As he spoke, his thoughts crystallized, and he became more determined than ever to stay alive, to stay free, so he could help Lukas find Penh and his lackeys. "Listen, Emily. You have to distance yourself from me as soon as possible. Unfriend me on Facebook. Write me a nasty e-mail about how you don't ever want to see me again. How you want me to stay out of your life and stop trying to derail your career. Stuff like that."

"Do you think that will work?"

"I don't know for sure, but it can't hurt. If these guys are spying on you like my sources tell me they are, you need to do everything you can to throw them off and make yourself uninteresting to them."

"That's going to be hard for me to do, Collin, when I want more than anything to make sure you are OK."

"That's why you have the cell phone you're using. I'll call you whenever I can. Please relay messages to my parents, let them know I'm all right. I'll check in later."

CHAPTER
TWENTY-TWO

LONDON, ENGLAND
JUNE 5

In the dungeon, Nic and Peter watched surveillance video from the conference center in Chicago. They observed Collin elude their man and dash away. They listened to the voice message from the field agent explaining how Collin outran them and went through buildings to evade them. He disappeared, but the search continued.

"You know what, Peter? I hate this guy. He keeps slipping through our fingers. Without enough backup, this *salesman* keeps getting away from trained agents," Nic said. "This is supposed to be a high priority case, but no one is willing to provide adequate manpower because this guy is supposedly an easy target. Easy? None of them has tried their hand at nabbing this chap, have they? It's bloody embarrassing, I tell you." He was slumped down in a chair, staring at the screen in utter disbelief.

What Nic didn't tell Peter was how he had gotten the FBI involved. Peter had asked. He was sharp and always asked the right questions, but Nic didn't give him the full answer. The answer he gave was that he had a signed requisition from Alastair. That was true. The part he left out was the part about finding Alastair out of the office at noon just two days ago. Sure, Alastair had told his secretary he was heading out to a meeting. But Nic, suspicious as ever, followed him. What he saw was not a meeting with the Chief of Investigations over at Scotland Yard. No. It was a rendezvous with a young woman, probably half his age, in a two-bit flat on the other side of town. What Nic saw was an opportunity too good to pass up. He waited outside for an hour. When Alastair emerged, Nic shoved some papers in front of him and told him to sign. Too shocked to protest, too embarrassed to cry foul, Alastair signed and slunk into a waiting taxi.

The signed papers got the FBI involved, despite Nic's two recent embarrassments with other international agencies and Alastair's refusal to take another bad risk. This time should have been different. The FBI were much more adept than either the Panamanians or the Peruvians. Certainly, with all the intel he and Peter had provided, they should have apprehended this amateur. Once again, Nic came up short. Once again, Collin Cook slipped through Nic's grasp.

Nic seethed and fumed as he climbed the stairs to call Alastair. Collin Cook would make a mistake, and when he did, Nic would make sure he paid for it.

* * * *

SOUTH OF LEXINGTON, KENTUCKY
JUNE 5

Barreling down Interstate 75 in Kentucky, half an hour south of Lexington, Collin struggled to stay awake. The old Mustang was holding up better than he was. It showed no signs of slowing, but Collin's eyelids grew heavy. His mind wandered. That was dangerous, and he knew it. There was no time for a meltdown. No room for error.

He had stopped for a late dinner in Louisville, and, realizing it was past midnight, he took a nap in the car. His intention was to just rest for an hour. To his horror, he overslept. It was six thirty in the morning when he got back on the road. The tight schedule grew even tighter. With the storm coming, the sooner he could get to Key West, the better. For everyone. Sleep was a luxury he could ill afford and it could cost him dearly.

By ten o'clock, the sun was glaring, and the forest around him was awash in radiant sunlight. He passed the town of Williamsburg, Kentucky, and was winding his way through the gently rolling Cumberland Mountains. Collin's eyes were dry and sensitive to the light. Despite the long nap, the increased stress level was enervating. Worries about Emily and guilt over dragging her into his darkened reality knocked around in his head. His body and his brain teetered on the verge of collapse, but he pressed on.

The old Mustang rattled and shook with every bump, but the engine purred along heading south at seventy miles per hour. That purring had a hypnotic effect. His body was relaxing, melting into the scarred, velour seat. He blinked hard to moisten his eyes, but they stay closed longer than he intended. There was thumping, followed by a grinding sound. Neither registered with him. The next moment, he became aware that he was spinning, hurling out of control. Something slammed into him. Glass shattered. Tires squealed. Horns blared.

In the span of his extended blink, the car veered to the left, rubbed along the concrete K-rail in the median, hit an obstruction, and spun twice before getting rammed by a passing pickup. The Mustang came to a jarring stop perpendicular to traffic and straddling two lanes. Collin's eyes, now wide open, frantically scanned his surroundings. His head was throbbing, his heart pounding, nerves pulsing with electricity. But his body wouldn't move. His surroundings went dark, then came back to light, then went dark again.

Cars behind his screeched to a halt and strangers approached him. Warm rivulets of blood ran down his cold, pale face. He was too stunned to move, his thoughts thick and sluggish. Worried but unknown faces now appeared in his windows, asking questions and expressing concern, wide-eyed and eager to help: Was he all right? Don't worry; we've called 911. An ambulance is on its way. Just stay right there, son, don't move.

I can't stay here, he said to himself. *They'll find me.*

"I'm okay. I'm not hurt," he said, waving a hand dismissively. He pushed through the mental fog and began to calibrate his circumstances. "Let me just move this car out of the way." The concerned faces protested, but the car started. Collin threw it into gear. It *moved.*

The throng of onlookers gasped in horror as he gunned the engine, squealing the tires, and pulled away. The mangled Mustang picked up speed and disappeared over the hill.

From his rearview mirror, Collin could see the bewildered faces, arms waving, some running in vain toward him. Small piles of glass lay in the roadway where he had come to a stop. A reddish streak of paint and a thick black stripe decorated the concrete K-rail. His side window was broken out where his head had collided with it, and the cool morning air swirled and rushed through the cabin, causing the open wounds on the side of his face to sting all the more. The windshield was cracked but still serviceable. The Mustang had survived amazingly well, despite the ground-down left side and the caved in right rear panel. The steering was now loose, and the car pulled to the left. He knew he had to get out of sight fast, so he kept the accelerator on the floor. The concerned citizens behind him had informed the authorities of the accident. They would arrive on the scene momentarily, sirens screaming. Collin had to put some distance between himself and the accident sight, but he also had to get off this highway as soon as possible. His sense of self-preservation was very much intact.

The damaged car would rule out "blending in." Time was of the essence. It wouldn't take long before the state troopers were on his tail. He would be easy to spot.

The sign ahead indicated he was coming to the town of Jellico, the first exit he saw and the first town on the Tennessee side of the border.

After turning off the highway, Collin turned right on Main Street and drove to the nearest gas station. A tanker truck was in the driveway, the driver just unhooking the hoses. He parked the car behind the small building, out of sight. However, a dozen people witnessed the Mustang pull in as they stared in disbelief.

Mouths agape as their curiosity took over, the spectators watched as Collin slammed his shoulder into the driver's side door until it opened with a loud bang, followed by a raucous, creaking noise from the damaged hinges. Collin swung his legs out, planted his feet on the ground, and rose slowly, using the door as a crutch. Standing made him light-headed, but he managed to gather his backpack and computer bag out of the backseat before attempting to walk. Stars burst in a pattern of intense, bright colors behind his eyelids as the backpack slammed against his rib cage. *Must've cracked a rib or two.* He held his breath as he limped, ignoring the pain and dizziness. Collin managed to pry open the glass door of the convenience store. The plump, blond cashier watched him warily. She, like the customers in the store and at the pumps, could not take her eyes off the stranger with blood running down his forehead.

"You alright, sir?" she asked with that soft Tennessee drawl. "You don't look too good."

Collin shrugged. "I'm fine. Can I borrow your bathroom?" "Sure can. It's at the back of the store, on the right."

"Thanks."

"You sure you don't need nothin'?"

"I'll be fine. Just a little bruised, that's all."

He shuffled past the counter to the restroom as best he could, his head feeling like it was stuffed full of cotton. When Collin emerged, his face and hands were washed, his movements a little more fluid, his clothes fresh and clean. The blood was gone but not the throbbing pain. He thanked the cashier, who hushed up when she saw him. Collin, feeling the weight of many stares, limped out the front doors to the tanker truck's driver, who was preparing to leave. Every eye in the store followed him. Collin hobbled around the truck, spoke to the driver, then climbed into the cab on the passenger's side, wincing as he did.

The pain from his ribs shot through his torso like daggers. The truck driver stared as Collin maneuvered his bags into the space at his feet and hoisted himself onto the seat. "You ain't looking too hot, cowboy. You need a doctor?"

"Just get me to Knoxville. That's all I ask." Collin's voice was raspy and far from full strength.

The gregarious trucker was talkative and curious. He had questions and wanted answers but was friendly about it. Unusual circumstances needed some explaining. "Look here, I don't want nobody dying on me," implored the tall, skinny trucker. His vein-riddled arms were decorated with a plethora of tattoos. He sported a filthy ball cap and a wad of chew stuffed in his cheek. The truck lurched forward, and the driver concentrated as he steered the truck out of the driveway.

Collin squeezed his eyes closed and drew in his breath as he adjusted to minimize the discomfort. "I just need some rest and a ride to Knoxville.

I'm not going to die."

"Whatever you say. Ain't never got a hundred bucks from a hitch-hiker before. What's so important down in Knoxville?"

"Business meeting. People waiting for me." Collin spoke in bursts, sucking in air sharply between each sentence.

"I guess it must be important if you gotta show up in that kind of shape," said the trucker. "Can't you call and reschedule?"

"Maybe, but it would ruin months of work. Timing is critical. Know what I mean?" Collin explained, his breathing still ragged. He realized there was a chance this trucker could be interviewed by police at some point, when people started talking and the police patched together stories. He did not want to give this guy any information that would put his getaway at risk. Nor endanger the amiable trucker.

"I suppose I do. I got a few customers like that. They get all bent up if I'm late. What kind of business you in?"

"It's complicated."

"Oh, you don't think I'm smart enough to understand your business?"

"That's not what I meant. It just hurts to talk."

"I got one more question before you doze off: Why would anyone pay that kind of dough for an hour-long ride? I'm just curious; you in some sort a trouble there, boy?"

Wincing with pain and trying to get comfortable, Collin answered the question slowly and deliberately. "No, but I will be if I don't get there on time. People are depending on me. I gotta take care of things in Knoxville. That's all."

"All right, then, Mister. I'll get you to Knoxville. But tell me this, what happened to you? Looks like you might've fought a bear or something." His curiosity was irrepressible. A toothy grin, complete with tobacco-stained teeth, spread across a face that had not seen a razor in several days. His manner was pure southern—hospitable, warm, and caring. But, at the same time, he was suspicious about his nameless passenger.

It was difficult for Collin to continue putting him off. The man was trying to make conversation. Collin felt he had to give him something so that he would have stories to tell. Everyone back at the gas station would want to hear the details upon his next visit. They would not soon forget this break in the normal flow of life in Jellico. Collin knew people in small towns were connected if nothing else. Connected with each other, the environment around them, and any developments that might affect their community. Collin appreciated the intrinsic beauty of neighborly concern and communal protection. At this point in his life, he yearned for it.

"I got in an accident back there a ways. Must've fallen asleep at the wheel. My car hit the center divider and spun out. Because this business deal is so important, I couldn't wait for the police or an ambulance. If I don't show up on time, things will go from bad to worse for me. Things are tough enough already, know what I mean?" He looked at the trucker to assess his reaction. The man was nodding, a sort of frown developing as his lips pressed together.

"I hear you," said the tattooed driver. "Things have been tough all over." He nodded, and his eyes grew distant.

Collin sensed the trucker had a deep, personal understanding of tough times.

They were out of the mountains and into more populated areas. A sign ahead said Knoxville was ten miles away. The trucker kept the conversation going. "You got a family there, Mister?"

Collin tensed, all expression draining from his face. This question produced more pain than his cracked ribs. Like a DVD played in super-fast motion, clips from his life flashed through his mind. There were scenes of laughter at the dinner table, little Max shooting milk out of his nose as he erupted at something funny. Also, tears in Eliza's eyes when she learned she had to go see the doctor again. Dancing in the kitchen, cheek to cheek with Jane as her feet dangled and her giggles filled the room.

Realizing that the question had gone unanswered and that tears were welling up in his eyes, Collin cleared his throat and leaned forward, clutching his knees. "I used to," was all he could utter.

A long pause. "Geez, man, I don't mean to be nosy, but what happened? You divorced or something like that?"

"No, not divorced. They were taken from me."

"Like, kidnapped?"

"Car accident."

The trucker fell into a reverent silence for several minutes as the scenery continued to change, becoming more urban by the mile. At length, he simply said, "I'm sorry."

They turned off the freeway and headed toward downtown. Collin climbed out as the truck stopped to make a delivery. He thanked the man for his help as he handed him a wad of crumpled bills from his pocket. The one showing on the outside was a one-hundred-dollar bill. Collin had no idea how much the wad contained, but he knew there were several of every denomination, including a couple more hundreds in there. The tobacco-stained teeth showed through the scruffy beard as his jaw dropped. The tattooed driver gazed at the money in his hand. When he finally spoke, he struggled to get the words out. "This is too much. You said a hundred."

"I know," said Collin. "You really helped me. Now I want to help you."

"Are you kidding?" The trucker's voice choked with emotion.

"No. Why?"

"It's just that things have been rough ever since my wife got sick." He fought for control of his voice. "How'd you know?"

Collin didn't have a response. He extended a hand and said, "Do something nice for her, and tell her how special she is. Will you do that for me?"

"Yes, sir," said the trucker as they shook hands, his voice barely above a whisper. "This is an answer to prayer," he said, his eyes moving to the fistful of bills.

Collin turned and hobbled away, feeling a tangible sense of connectedness, a warmth he remembered from his prior life when service played a vital role. His pain receded and his pace quickened as he turned the corner, consulting the map on his phone.

CHAPTER TWENTY-THREE

Alastair Montgomery was reluctant to let Nic win, but he had little choice. His career would go up in smoke, and his already miserable home life would only grow uglier if Nic made his work-time philandering public. The bloody tosser had video footage, so there would be no denying it. That cheeky Lancaster had him over the barrel, and both men knew it. Having received a phone call from Nic demanding his immediate help, Alastair rushed back to the office, arriving at 9:30 p.m. Nic explained that Collin Cook had once again vanished, and it was time for more drastic measures.

The FBI had cornered him in Chicago, but he squirted away, like he had done before. Fortunately, Nic explained, Peter's brilliant algorithm had picked up another hit earlier in the evening. Footage had been uploaded from a convenience store security camera by local police asking for the public's help investigating the accident, and a high percentage match triggered an alert. Nic showed Alastair the clip from the convenience store in Jellico, Tennessee. Both agreed it was Cook, no doubts, despite the short, blond hair. Collin's trail was becoming visible, as were his intentions.

Sitting at his cluttered desk, Alastair punched his password into the computer and went to the interagency requisition page. The first step was to issue an All Points Bulletin for law enforcement agencies throughout the United States to aid in the search for Collin Cook, a man wanted for cyber terrorism against European and American financial institutions. The second step was to request roadblocks along all major highways leading into Florida to apprehend him. A photograph of Collin in Jellico was uploaded. Alastair called Agent Crabtree to compare notes and hasten the process of setting up the roadblocks. Both Alastair and Reggie Crabtree shared the frustration of defeat at the hands of Collin Cook. On paper, they agreed, it looked so easy. Neither man could understand how he managed to escape.

Reggie followed Nic and Alastair's line of thinking, based on the video evidence from Jellico and the statement of the truck driver, that Collin was heading to Florida. The question was where in Florida? It was a big state with hundreds of miles of coastline. Reggie promised to help mobilize resources to shut down Florida's northern borders and apprehend their man.

It was all or nothing at this point. If Collin Cook made it to the coast, as Nic calculated he would, they would lose. Cook would be gone forever. Their best chance of gaining access to Pho Nam Penh would vanish like a rain drop on Saharan sand.

There was no other known associate of Pho Nam Penh, only Collin Cook. The agency desperately needed a win. So did Alastair. Alastair decided to go all-in.

They had a very short time to get all the pieces in place. Suspecting that Cook had used a false identity to buy another used car with cash, they figured he was on the road, looking for the shortest, quickest path back to the Caribbean, where the bulk of his money was stashed. It only made sense. As a precaution, Crabtree alerted the US Border Patrol to monitor all exit points along the Canadian and Mexican borders. Security at bus and train terminals, airports, and harbors needed to be stepped up. The media had been informed, as well. The story, along with pictures of the suspect, was set to be broadcast on the evening news across the southern States.

By ten thirty in London, Nic and Alastair were confident they had done all they could. News outlets from Carolina to Mississippi would run the story at six and put Collin's face all over the airwaves. There would be no place for him to hide. No chance for escape.

*   *   *   *

HIGHWAY 75, GEORGIA
JUNE 5

Racing southward in the faint twilight, following the yellowish headlight beams of the 1988 Chevy Blazer he had acquired back in

Knoxville, Collin felt the pressure build with every minute that passed. He calculated mileage and arrival time in his head as an exercise to keep himself alert. According to the signs and the map on his phone, he still had over thirteen hours of driving ahead of him. Add an hour for gas and food stops and, if all went well, he could arrive in Key West by eleven o'clock in the morning, an hour ahead of his deadline. That would make the Captain happy. At the moment, however, he was making no progress toward his goal. Evening rush hour traffic outside Atlanta had slowed to a crawl, so he decided to pull off the highway, gas up, eat, and rest for a while. No sense sitting in traffic. He was still on schedule.

Back on the highway, night was settling in, and his body was growing fatigued. Even with an hour buffer, he worried about not making his rendezvous with Captain Sewell. So many things could go wrong. No time to stop for rest. He was approaching Macon, Georgia, and already, he was fighting hard each mile to stay awake and to fend off another debilitating meltdown.

Collin's mind was also weary, unable to stave off the memories clamoring for attention. They swarmed him, despite his efforts to resist and push them back. At length, he decided it best to let them entertain him, choosing which ones to relive as a way to combat the fatigue. He absorbed the energy from each moment of his past life as it played in his mind, while his eyes scanned the road.

Those flashbacks included Max's first hit in baseball, Jane's first dance recital, and Eliza's first steps. He thought about picnics and school plays and trips to the beach. He remembered Disneyland, the zoo, and teaching Max and Jane to ride a bike. Collin forced those memories to linger, basking in the pure joy of each moment.

Had he taken those moments for granted at the time? Maybe. Probably. Most people do.

So many beautiful memories. Collin forgot about everything else. He lost track of time and distance. Before he realized what was happening, the few cars and big rigs that shared the highway at ten thirty at night were slowing to a stop. Blue lights twirled in the darkness ahead, the sight of them causing his stomach to tighten and his pulse to race. He scanned the roadway in all directions. There was no place to turn off. He was stuck in the left lane with nowhere to go, cars behind him, beside him, and ahead of him, crawling toward a police blockade. He felt like he was being squeezed and pressed.

As he approached the line of patrol cars, Collin's phone vibrated in his shirt pocket. He pulled it out and read the text: "Trouble brewing. Stay away from FL. Contact Cpt, set up new meet." Lukas's guidance arrived a bit too late.

Collin came to a stop behind a big rig as Lukas's call came in. "Did you get my text?"

"Yeah, just now—"

"Listen. There's an Interpol agent on you," he said. "He's got pictures of you in Chicago and Jellico, Tennessee, and has posted them to the Most Wanted list. Now they've set up road blocks heading into Florida."

The twenty-second burst of information left Collin's mind numb, too full of information he couldn't process. "Not much I can do now," he said. "I'm stopped at a roadblock. I'm about three cars back in line."

"OK, just remain calm and act like you know what you're doing. Have you changed your looks since Chicago?"

"Yeah, just my hair, though."

"Well, put in the teeth and contacts, and hope it works."

"Yeah. Thanks."

* * * *

SAN DIEGO, CALIFORNIA
JUNE 5

Emily didn't talk much on the flight, even though Genevieve seemed to be a lovely person. Emily was not comfortable with the idea of having a body guard. It felt restrictive, almost disciplinary. When she landed, her first thought was to call Collin and make sure he was all right.

With Genevieve sticking so close, she couldn't pull out her secret phone. Genevieve escorted her swiftly into a waiting car and climbed in the back seat with her. The door shut, and the black Tahoe whisked them away.

"Where are we going?" asked Emily as the car headed for the freeway. "We can't take you home. At least, not yet. We'll have a team sweep the interior for bugs and cameras first thing in the morning. It would be too conspicuous to go in this late."

"You're doing what?"

"We have been hired to keep you safe and to make sure you are not being targeted."

The driver interrupted and barked, "Hang on, everybody. We've got a tail. I'm going to lose him." As the Tahoe entered the freeway on-ramp and accelerated, the deep thrum of the engine filled the space inside. Emily grabbed the seat in front of her and cursed under her breath. The Tahoe wove through traffic, tires squealing, darting into unthinkably small spaces and speeding past vehicles. Emily glanced through the back window and saw a dark sedan mirroring their every move. This continued for several miles until the driver banked hard to the right from the far-left lane, almost perpendicular to the flow of traffic, barely avoiding collisions as he crossed four lanes and exited onto eastbound Soledad Freeway. The chase car didn't make the exit.

"Lost 'em," announced the driver.

"Well done," said Genevieve. "Now let's get her to the safe house."

"You got it."

As the Tahoe slowed to match the flow of traffic, Emily began to breathe normally again. Her hands let go of the front seat and raked through her hair. Her head sagged. She collected her thoughts and resumed her line of questioning. "You said you were hired? Why? And by whom? What is going on here?"

"Your friend, Collin, hired us to protect you. He said your Facebook account had been hacked. He believed you were being monitored and were potentially in danger. We're here to make sure nothing happens. Our team will sanitize your condo unit and shadow you for three days, more if needed."

"Sanitize my condo?"

"Yes, to remove any electronic surveillance devices that may have been planted there." Genevieve's voice was matter-of-fact, emotionless.

Emily's mouth dropped open, and she fell silent. "Do you know where Collin is?" she asked. She noticed that the driver had taken several turns and was using the back roads to work his way south and east.

"No. He didn't share any of that information with us. Frankly, our only concern is you. His directive was for us to protect you." Genevieve paused to make eye contact with Emily. "It's best if no one knows where he is or where he's going."

Emily fell silent again, staring out the window. The darkness was broken up by the orange, glowing street lights and the brightly lit parking lots of strip malls.

The Tahoe turned into a neighborhood and worked its way through the tree lined streets, gaining altitude as they went. She knew they were in the general area of La Mesa. Up a steep driveway they went, into an empty garage. Inside, Genevieve showed her a spacious and well-appointed home. She would have her own private quarters on the second floor. The master bedroom with her own bathroom.

Genevieve promised that her stay with them would be comfortable and secure. As soon as it was safe, they would take her back to her home. Emily locked the door as she closed it, still unsure. She crossed to the bathroom and dialed the only number stored in the secret phone, hoping Collin would answer. She had so many questions and needed a chance to talk about what was happening to her and to him. The phone rang and rang. No answer.

She was too antsy to wait, so she dialed Sarah's number and left a message. Sarah returned her call moments later. The conversation with Sarah and Henry brought her a measure of peace and comfort. Afterward she tried Collin again. This time, Collin answered. But she knew immediately that something wasn't right.

CHAPTER
TWENTY-FOUR

A firm tap on the glass startled Collin, causing him to drop his phone in his lap. A State Trooper stooped, flashlight in hand, waiting for Collin to roll down the window. The window didn't move at first, so Collin jiggled the controller and gave it a nudge to get it to descend. Collin didn't try to hide his embarrassment or nervousness. Maybe being flustered would earn him some much-needed sympathy.

"Where ya'll headed tonight?" asked the large patrolman. His high-pitched voice did not match his brawny frame.

From somewhere in the passenger's side foot well, Collin heard the secret phone ringing. The sound was muffled by the contents of the bag. Collin cleared his throat and put on a subtle southern accent. "Winter Haven."

"Winter Haven? What're ya'll fixing to do there?"

"Visit my grandma for her birthday," said Collin.

"Fine, fine. Let's see some identification, please."

In the few minutes, he had waited in line at the checkpoint, Collin had managed to put in his colored contact lenses and prosthetic teeth. He wore glasses and a faded baseball cap. He had also conjured up a believable story. Nevertheless, it was hard not to be anxious with this imposing patrolman watching his every move.

He let his hands tremble as he opened his wallet and pulled out the same driver's license he'd used to purchase the vehicle.

The patrolman studied it briefly. "And the registration?" He looked it over and handed both items back to Collin. "Mr. Waters, where are you coming from?"

"Knoxville."

"What do you do in Knoxville, may I ask?"

"I work at a Sonic Drive-In."

"Ah, yes. And how old are you?"

"I'm thirty, sir," Collin replied, wondering if these were common questions at roadblocks. It was his first one, after all. Collin was doing his best to play the part of a not-so-bright high school dropout. He talked slowly with a mild drawl.

"It looks like you just purchased this vehicle yesterday. Is that right?"

"Yes, sir, it is," Collin said with some pride in his voice. "First time to buy my own car."

"How long have you lived in Knoxville?"

"About a year, I guess."

"I see. And why did you say you're coming to Florida?"

"I'm visiting my grandmother for her birthday. Plus, I wanna show her my new car."

"I'm sure she'll be proud of you, son. You haven't been drinking now, have you?"

"No, sir. Gave that up. 712 days sober, sir."

"Good for you, son. Another thing for your grandma to be proud of."

"I hope so, sir."

"Just one more question before I let you get on with your business: Where does your grandmother live in Winter Haven?"

*   *   *   *

HUNTINGTON BEACH, CALIFORNIA
JUNE 5

Sarah tottered into the downstairs office, where Henry was sitting at the computer. She was in her pajamas, hair matted to the side of her head, clutching the door frame for support. Her first chemotherapy treatment had wiped her out. "Listen to this, Henry," she said, holding out her cell phone.

"What is it, dear?" Henry stood to greet her.

"It's Emily. I didn't answer because the number is from Chicago; I thought it was a marketing call. Listen and tell me what you think."

Sarah played the message with the speaker on so both could hear. Emily's gravelly voice was barely above a whisper. Her words tumbled out at great speed. "Sarah, it's me, Emily. I just saw Collin and need to share with you what I learned because I think he's in trouble, and I don't know how to help him. Please call me back at this number, not on my regular cell phone."

"It's almost eight o'clock here, ten in Chicago. It's not too late. Let's call her right now," said Henry.

When she answered, Emily sounded relieved and let out a burst that could have been either a laugh or a sob. "I have so much to tell you. I almost don't know where to start." She recounted her experiences with Collin and all that transpired in Chicago, including the security team Collin had hired and the fact that she was being sheltered in a safe house in San Diego. "I'm talking to you from inside a closet, hoping no one can hear me," she said. "I don't know what to do."

Henry responded first. "I think it would be wise to go to the FBI like Collin suggested, for your own safety."

"That does seem the best thing to do, Emily," added Sarah. "We want you to be safe. We know two agents who are working on the case. Maybe if we share this new information with them, they will believe he's not a criminal."

Emily remained quiet for a moment. "I guess that makes sense. I just don't want to make things worse for Collin."

"Do you know where Collin is?" asked Henry.

"No, he wouldn't tell me where he is or where he's going. He said it would be better that way," she replied. "I'm afraid I won't have any useful information for the FBI."

"That's OK," said Henry. "We need to worry about your safety at the moment."

But we can't tell them about this phone. I promised Collin."

* * * *

GEORGIA-FLORIDA BORDER
JUNE 5

Collin's heart skipped, and his breathing stopped. He fumbled for his iPhone on the floor and leaned down to get it, but the patrolman quickly barked, "What are you doing there?" as he shined his light at Collin's hands.

Collin threw both hands in the air as his body flew against the back of the seat. "I dropped my phone. Can I get it?"

The officer was in a defensive position, weight on his back leg, one hand holding the flashlight. His other hand was on the handle of his service revolver at his hip. "OK. Please keep your right hand on the steering wheel where I can see it. Move slowly and show me the phone."

Collin, stiff with fear, obeyed the patrolman's command. When he produced the phone, he held it in his left hand as it shook. "I don't remember the address, but I have it in the map on my phone. Can I show it to you?"

"That's fine, son. Go on and show me."

Collin's thumbs came back to life, moving over the phone's screen. Within seconds he had the map open, with the name and address of a retirement community in Winter Haven that he had searched while waiting in line. He held up the phone, and the officer inspected it.

"That works for me." The officer leaned in and studied Collin's face. The officer's brow furrowed, the stern expression hardened. "Ya'll know there's a hurricane coming in, don't you?" Before Collin could answer, the patrolman's radio squawked. He straightened himself and stepped back as he responded, engrossed in the exchange.

Collin strained to hear what was being said, terrified that it could be about him, but he couldn't make out the words. The officer was looking down the line of cars, paying no attention to Collin. Seizing the opportunity, Collin eased his foot off the brake pedal. The Blazer inched forward. As the distance between him and the patrolman grew, Collin watched in his side mirror. There was no reaction. The patrolman continued to speak into the radio at his shoulder. Collin pressed the gas and brought the Blazer up to speed, his heart pounding, his eyes darting between the road and the mirror. Still no reaction from the trooper.

Collin wiped the sweat from his forehead and checked his watch. It was 10:53. He had thirteen hours to drive five hundred ninety miles. Enough time to get there, with stops for food and gas, but not enough time for sleep. The tropical storm the Captain had mentioned was now a hurricane? Great. This would only compound his problems.

The twirling blue lights from the patrol cars at the checkpoint were still visible in his rearview mirror, his heart still trying to punch through his ribs, when the secret phone began to ring again. Collin scrambled to find it. His voice was tight and his breathing ragged when he answered.

"Collin? Is something wrong?" asked Emily.

"Yeah … I mean, no. Things are good here. How are you?" His voice was far away, the words spaced as if strung together haphazardly. His attention was fixed on the line of police cars in his mirrors, watching for movement.

"Tell me the truth, Collin. What's going on?"

Collin cleared his throat and took a deep breath to calm himself. "The less you know, Emily, the better." He had no desire to share information with her that could present a hazard for either one of them.

"I don't think I like that answer. You're avoiding telling me something." As he put more distance between himself and the roadblock, Collin's comfort level increased, as did his focus on the conversation. "Yes, I am, but it's out of necessity. Trust me. Tell me, though, are you back home in San Diego, safe and sound?"

"I am back in San Diego but not in my home. I'm safe. Although the bodyguard you hired is lovely, Collin, I don't enjoy being held like a prisoner."

"Like a prisoner? Are they mistreating you?"

"No, nothing like that. It's just that they brought me to a safe house and told me I can't go home until they *sanitize* my condo, as if it's some sort of health hazard. I can't believe this is happening to me."

"I told you, the guys coming after me will use any means to find me, including spying on my family and friends. I'm sorry they've done this, but it won't last forever. I promise."

"What am I supposed to do, Collin? I don't have my car. I only have the clothes I took to Chicago. How am I supposed to go to work and live my life?"

"You could take a few days off and relax."

"Not really. I have a lot to do."

"It wouldn't hurt to take a vacation, you know."

"This isn't my idea of a vacation, Collin."

"I know. Just saying …"

"Truth is I have an urgent project I need to work on. It's important."

"So is your safety. Right now, it's best to make sure your condo is not bugged and that you're not being followed, OK?"

"I can't just stay here and hide. I have a life. There are people depending on me."

"Aren't there other competent scientists who can handle things while you're out?"

"The project involves that friend I mentioned. She needs my help before it's too late."

"What kind of help?"

"Another group at the lab is in clinical trials on a new therapy, and this friend is a perfect candidate. I have to pull some strings to get her into the case study group."

"Can't it wait a few days?"

"No, these groups fill up fast. A few days and the window could be closed."

"Can't you just make a few calls to make it happen?"

"No, it's more complicated than that. I really have to be there to present her data and be a sponsor for her."

"Is it that important?" Collin said. "You're willing to risk your own safety for this friend?"

"I am," she said. Emily knew she should just leave it at that, but her emotions got the best of her. The conversation with Sarah and Henry was fresh in her mind. Sarah's voice sounded much weaker than it had last time they spoke. And now Collin was pressing her to stay in hiding. She couldn't help but blurt out, "And you should be, too."

CHAPTER
TWENTY-FIVE

LONDON, ENGLAND
JUNE 6

Nic was on the phone with Reggie Crabtree at four o'clock in the morning London time, eight p.m. in California. He had just reviewed another video clip that had been analyzed by Peter's algorithm, which showed a 93 percent match for Collin at one of the roadblocks. He had stayed at the office all night and was wired on caffeine.

Reggie said, "Give me a few minutes to watch the video. It should give us a new picture of our suspect, a description of the car, and a license plate number to share with the Highway Patrol and local news stations. I'll call you back."

Nic paced his cubicle, rubbing his hands together, waiting for Reggie's return call. He checked his watch. Time was ticking away, and so was his patience. Once Reggie sent out the updated photos and information, it would be only a matter of time before Cook was in custody and providing intel on Pho Nam Penh and his syndicate. Nic, the department, and the agency would be redeemed.

It was a long ten minutes before Crabtree called back. "OK, Nic. We've posted new pictures of Cook, his vehicle, and license plate. Local law enforcement and news agencies have the information. Television stations all over Florida will run it as a breaking story during their eleven o'clock news broadcasts."

"Fantastic," said Nic. "Should be quick work to find him."

"I've been around long enough to know you can't count your chickens before they hatch. But, I think our chances have improved greatly."

"The chances should be nearly 100 percent, given the fact that we just gave them completely accurate, up-to-the-minute information. Unless they're totally incompetent, the Highway Patrol ought to nail this guy in ten minutes." Nic's voice was an octave above normal, rising with his intensity.

"It doesn't always work like that, Agent Lancaster. I'm sure you know that by now. There are too many things that can go wrong. But I'll tell you what. My partner and I will be on the next flight to Miami to track him down ourselves."

"That's fantastic. But why Miami?"

"We'll connect out of Miami to Key West. My gut tells me he's heading down there. He'll make his escape by boat into the Caribbean and get himself lost amongst the boats and islands. It'd take us years and resources we can't spare to track him down again," Crabtree said.

"What about this storm? He's not stupid enough to head into a hurricane, is he?"

"He knows what he's doing. Law enforcement resources are stretched thin with this storm approaching, giving him the perfect opportunity to slip through. None of the local departments will have staff to aid in a search at a time like this, so McCoy and I will be there. We'll find him."

"I'm beginning to like our odds," said Nic, his voice pitching higher. "It just seems so easy. We know he can't be too far from that checkpoint. All they have to do is send a patrol car south on I-75, and they'll run him down in no time."

"Hopefully it works out that easily." Reggie's voice conveyed more skepticism than hope. "Either way, we'll be there first thing in the morning."

* * * *

SOUTH OF GAINESVILLE, FLORIDA
JUNE 6

The conversation with Emily rattled around in his head and fueled a nervous energy that kept him awake and focused. Guilt, longing, and fear stirred deep inside him as her words echoed in his head.

"That friend is your mother," Emily had told him. "Traditional treatments haven't worked well on her type of cancer in the past, so I'm trying to get her nominated for participation in a promising, experimental therapy being run in another lab group."

Too stunned to speak, Collin drove in a protracted silence. The words didn't sink in, yet he felt more unmoored than ever. "But why didn't anyone tell me?" he muttered.

"She doesn't want you to worry about her or come home just because she's sick. She wants you home because you *want* to be there," said Emily. "At the same time, she knows you're in some sort of trouble and is concerned."

Collin started to add up things. His brother and sister had started e-mailing him more regularly, urging him to come home and be with the family. Emily had suddenly reappeared. His mother's notes were more pressing, more pleading, in recent weeks. He should have suspected something was wrong. The clues were there. But his life didn't allow him to dwell on the needs of anyone else, and he loathed that fact. Another reason to hate his circumstances. He suddenly felt enslaved by them, much like he had by his job and his financial distress before the accident.

"Collin, what are you thinking?"

"I'm thinking this sucks," he said. "This whole thing sucks. What am I supposed to do? If I go home, I'll be either arrested or dead before I reach Huntington Beach. If I stop running, same result. I have no choice but to stay away from everyone I care about until this is over."

Emily paused. "Don't worry about your mother, Collin. My colleagues and I will take care of her. She is an excellent candidate for this treatment. There's nothing you could do by being here, so don't worry. You do what you have to do, and I'll attend to your mom."

"You said it was experimental?"

"Yes."

"How do you know it will work?"

"We don't, but it looks promising based on lab results."

A long pause. "Emily? Will you do me another favor?"

"Of course."

"Tell my mom that I'm sorry I was rude to her and my dad the last time I saw them. Tell her I love her, miss her, and will be praying for her. I want to be there, but it will make things worse for everyone else if I try to see her." Collin fought through his tangled emotions and got the words out. "I don't want anything to happen to her, Emily. Promise me you'll do everything you can."

"I promise, Collin."

"I'm really glad I have a friend like you. Thanks for using your brilliance to help my mom."

* * * *

LONDON, ENGLAND
JUNE 6

"What do you mean the resources are being reallocated? That's absurd. There's an international criminal on the loose in your state, and that's all you have to say?" Nic was incensed as he spoke with the chief of the Florida State Highway Patrol. His voice ran high with his emotions. "It only takes one patrol car driving down the highway looking for a faded brown 1988 Chevy Blazer. How hard can it be?"

"We're in the middle of an evacuation order. All available units are trying to protect our citizens from an incoming hurricane. We will do our best to look for your fugitive, but that's got to be our second priority behind the safety of our citizens."

"You've had hours to find him on roads that can't be that crowded, not in the wee hours of the morning."

"Look, Agent Lancaster, with all due respect," started the Chief. Then he thought better of instigating a shouting match. "We have patrol cars on alert. If he's out there on our highways, we'll find him."

* * * *

BACK ROADS,
SOUTH OF GAINESVILLE, FLORIDA
JUNE 6

"Did you do what I told you to do?" asked Lukas.

"Yeah, before I stopped for gas and food in Gainesville, I took out the teeth and contacts, took off the hat, and changed my shirt. Then, like you said, I found a mud puddle—not hard to find here in Florida, you know—and drove through it a few times. I almost got stuck, but that was a good thing. The tires spun and coated the sides of this car with mud."

"Good. No trouble, then?"

"No trouble? Ha. I wouldn't say *that*. At the convenience store where I stopped, some redneck told me how I look like a guy on the news. He was pointing at a TV in the corner. It scared the crap out of me, Lukas. My face and my car were right there on the screen."

"What happened?"

"I almost wet myself; are you kidding? Do you know how scary it is to see your own face on TV with the words 'Suspected Terrorist' underneath? You'd freak, too."

"What did the redneck do?"

"He said, 'That guy could be your brother.' So I lied and said, 'I don't have a brother.' He was squinting and staring at me, really studying my face. It was creepy. Then he said, 'Sure that ain't you?' I just said, 'Pretty sure,' and got out of there as fast as I could."

"He didn't call the cops did he?" asked Lucas.

"I don't know, but he did follow me outside, still jawing at me. When he saw me get in my car, he got a funny look on his face. I've been staying off the interstate ever since, sticking to back roads."

"I don't know if you have time for that, Collin."

"I know, it's really slowing me down, but I don't know what else to do."

"Did you change out the license plates yet?"

"No."

"The sooner, the better. You've got to get back on the interstate and make time. Dishonesty can save your life sometimes, my friend."

"If you say so."

Not long thereafter, Collin spotted his victim: a lonely pickup truck parked in a field next to a dilapidated shed just off the highway. He squeezed through a barbed wire fence, tools in hand, and swapped the plates as quickly as he could, using the light from his iPhone for illumination. The pickup's plates were dirty, though not caked with mud like his plates and car, but he hoped no one would notice.

He headed east on the back roads, working his way to Florida's Turnpike. Soon he was doing seventy-five miles per hour again. Patrol cars passed him; some gave him a second glance, but nothing more.

There was enough on his mind to keep him occupied as the miles spun past. He listened to an AM news station for updates on the weather.

The storm was now a Class Two hurricane, aimed right at The Bahamas and projected to sweep across the channel, pick up speed, and hit the Florida Keys twenty-four hours from now. Before he expected, daylight struggled to break through the blackness, bathing the landscape in gray. Collin realized how thick the cloud cover was overhead, ominous and threatening. He also noticed the steady stream of cars moving northward on the opposite side of the turnpike. Very few cars were heading south. People, at least the smart ones, were moving away from the incoming storm. By the time he reached Fort Lauderdale, it was 6:30 a.m., and he needed gas. Collin pulled off the turnpike in an outlying rural town ten minutes south of the city and found a small gas station with a general store. Since there were other people in the store, he went inside to pay and overheard a conversation that may have saved him. The clerk and a cowboy were talking at the counter as Collin searched for milk and packaged donuts. The cowboy was talking about the storm and how he had to hurry down to Key West to pick up his prized horses and get them far enough inland to be safe. The clerk asked him if he had heard about the roadblock on Highway 1 and told him to expect delays going south.

"Are they trying to keep people away from the storm?" asked the cowboy.

"I heard it's to catch a terrorist or something," replied the clerk. "They've had his face on the TV and everything."

When he heard those words, Collin set his items down and snuck out the door. He started the Blazer and moved it to a dirt parking lot behind the store. Grabbing his two bags, he stole to the rear of a long horse trailer attached to a dually pickup parked at one of the pumps. He assumed the truck and trailer belonged to the Key West-bound cowboy inside. He secreted himself between bales of hay and watched the store entrance through the slotted side of the trailer. The cowboy soon appeared and began filling the tank. Collin sat perfectly still and quiet for what seemed to be an eternity, while the pump spewed thick, pungent diesel fumes that wafted into the trailer and hung in the air. Several minutes later, the engine roared to life, and the caravan started to move.

As the truck picked up speed, the wind swirled and kicked up dust and straw that pummeled Collin's face and body. With some effort,

Collin arranged the bales to provide a measure of protection against the wind, then settled in for a long ride. He opened the map on his phone and studied the layout of Key West so he would be familiar with it. After a thorough examination of the town, he fell asleep, but when the truck began to slow, his eyes popped open. He took a furtive look outside. As he suspected, they had arrived at the roadblock.

Collin again moved the hay bales. This time stacking the bales in a crisscross fashion, making a sort of fortress around himself as the truck inched forward. When finished, he slid underneath the cross pieces and pulled his feet in as far as he could. The space was cramped. The air was hot, dusty, and reeked of dry hay. He pinched his nose to thwart any allergic reaction and covered his mouth with his shirt in a feeble attempt to filter the air. With his eyes closed, he shut out thoughts of being confined and focused on listening. Outside there were muffled voices, but he couldn't make out the words. He huddled in his makeshift fort, sweat streaming down his face, neck, and along his ribs, tickling as it rolled. The stop was brief and soon the truck lurched forward again, dragging the trailer and Collin with it.

Once the truck was at speed again, Collin scrambled out from under his itchy hideaway and swiped at his face, hair, chest, and legs, trying to brush off the irritating straw. He checked his watch. It was 9:25. The map on his phone showed a hundred miles and two hours, fifteen minutes to go. His margin had evaporated. Looking through the slats of the trailer, hints of sunshine poked through the gathering clouds. The seas were agitated and bumpy. Northbound traffic was at a crawl.

Impatient and confined, Collin endured the tedium of watching watery scenery and time roll past, the scenery moving too slowly and the clock moving too quickly. Despite the wind blowing through the space, the air was moist and heavy. His clothes clung to his sweaty skin, along with the inescapable stench of horses. At 11:41, the truck slowed markedly and started an unhurried, arcing right turn onto a dusty road, lined with trees and bushes. Collin's phone showed that they were on Stock Island, five miles from the marina. As they moved farther away from the highway, Collin panicked. He knew from his map that this road was taking him the wrong way. He had to bail out. It took some effort to open the gate from the inside, but he tugged at the sliding bolt until it cleared, and the gate swung open. Tall grass lined the dirt road. Now or never. As the truck ambled along, Collin lowered his bags onto the dirt one by one, then jumped out toward the grass on the passenger's side and rolled. In one fluid motion, he was back on his feet, scooping up his bags, and retreating into the tall grass.

As Collin lay low in the grass watching, the truck stopped, and the cowboy appeared around the back, exclaiming aloud, "What the hell?" He checked the gate, the latch, the contents. Collin took the opportunity, while the cowboy inspected the inside of the trailer, to sprint into the trees to better conceal himself, hoping the man would give up and move along. The cowboy reemerged and scanned the area guardedly. Time was ticking, and Collin was growing ever more apprehensive as noon approached.

The cowboy secured the sliding bolt on the rear gate and moseyed back to the truck, still shaking his head, then drove off slowly. Collin sprinted for the main road and headed into town. His clothes were filthy, stained with dirt and grass; pieces of straw clung to them and stuck out of his hair. With only ten minutes to go, Collin couldn't stop. The warm air exacerbated things, causing sweat to pour down his face and body, soaking his shirt anew. But he kept running along a path that paralleled the highway. He crossed a small inlet with seven minutes left and could see that he was approaching the tiny airport on the edge of town. That meant taxis, so he veered across the highway and found one about to enter the roadway, headed toward town. Self-conscious about his appearance and odor, Collin apologized as he jumped in the front seat. "I need to get to the marina as quickly as possible," he said.

"Which marina, sir?" asked the short, Hispanic driver.

"The main one, I guess."

"OK, I take you to Bright Marina."

The taxi sped away and at two minutes before noon, he was dropped off in front of a sign that read, "The Schooner Western Union, Key West Flagship." Collin tipped the driver generously and jumped out, already searching for the First Mate.

Rojas was nowhere to be seen among hordes of moving people. Collin poked his head into the adjacent store. No Rojas.

The waterfront area was brimming with activity. Swarms of people moved with a foreboding urgency. Many were dragging suitcases or coolers. Some yelled into cell phones, tugged on children's arms, or shuttled armloads of supplies.

He scanned the docks, the sidewalks, the parking lot, straining for any sign of Rojas—to the left, to the right, straight in front. Looking over the half-vacated marina, all he could see were the towering masts and hulking yachts that had yet to depart and more people moving to and fro.

From the water, a cacophony of lively sounds filled the air. Crews worked feverishly, preparing to get underway, barking out orders and questions to one another. Engines roared to life. Lines and clips clanged against metallic masts as the wind blew harder. He began to jog toward the docks, scanning in all directions. That's when he saw them. Two men who looked out of place, talking to a small cluster of people, displaying a printed photograph. One was a tall, older, black guy. The other looked like a moving tree trunk, thick with muscle, blond curls atop his head. Both men wore dress pants and button up shirts. They weren't tourists, and they weren't boat owners.

Collin's insides went cold. A shiver ran up his spine, causing his head to do a quick shake. They had to be cops, searching for him. *How'd they know?* He spun around, keeping his face turned toward the water, searching more frenetically for Rojas's familiar mop of hair— long, dark, and tangled. Checking over his shoulder to keep an eye on the detectives, he moved forcefully through the crowds, trying to get his bearings and figure out where Rojas would be. His phone began to buzz in his pocket.

"Where are you, man?" Captain Sewell's voice was calm, the words slipping lazily through the air.

"I'm at the marina, looking for Rojas. Where is he?"

"He's there, looking for you."

"No, he's not. He's nowhere to be found. Did he leave already?"

"No, he's sitting on a bench next to the gas pump."

"Gas pump? Where?"

"It's by the main office."

"I only see a store. Is there an office in there?"

The Captain paused, sucking in a breath. "Which marina are you at?"

"The one that has the sign for the Western Union Schooner."

"Wrong marina. He's down at the next one—Conch Harbor."

"I'll go there now. Tell him to wait."

When Collin turned to find the guys with the photo, they were gone. Not knowing where they were scared him more than knowing they were close. He couldn't wait. He had to move. He opened up the map on his phone, located Conch Harbor Marina, and punched the icon to request walking directions. Half a mile.

His grimy clothes, along with the straw stuck to him, were drawing unwanted attention. Young people stared and pointed at him. Older folks looked on with either pity or disdain. Keeping his head down, he followed the directions on the phone map. His pace was brisk, matching those around him. As he moved through the crowd, Collin heard someone call his name. Instinctively, he turned his head toward the sound. Wrong thing to do, he realized. The two men were now only yards away and closing.

Collin broke into a full sprint, crying out, "Move" and "Coming through," as he ran, knocking into people and pushing others out of his way. His bags slowed him down, but he was still able to outpace his pursuers.

As he approached Conch Harbor Marina, he called at full volume: "Rojas, get to the boat."

Upon hearing his name, Rojas popped up and looked toward the sound. Collin was barreling full speed in his direction, dodging around groups of people as he ran. Behind him two guys were in full chase. Rojas dashed toward the boat. Collin could see his ropey tangles bobbing up and down amidst the crush of people. They disappeared as Rojas headed down the ramp toward the docks. Twenty yards down the dock, Rojas jumped into a rubber dinghy and started up the engine as Collin bounded down the ramp. Collin was on the composite deck and making his turn when the two pursuers hit the ramp. Collin slipped as he tried to negotiate the hard left but caught himself before he slid into the water. "Go, go," he yelled, pointing toward the end of the dock, straight in front of him as he got back to his feet, legs churning like a running back.

Rojas jammed the dinghy's motor in reverse. Once he cleared the end of the slip, he threw the throttle forward and swung the boat in the direction of Collin's flight, quickly drawing alongside him, matching his speed. At the end of the dock, Rojas eased off the throttle so the dinghy was gliding just off to Collin's right and slightly ahead of him, eight feet from the end of the dock. Without pause or hesitation, Collin leaped at an angle and landed on the hard floor of the rubber boat. His momentum carried him forward toward the opposite side, almost pitching him into the water. Rojas acted quickly and grabbed the shoulder strap of Collin's computer bag and leaned hard toward the center of the boat, just managing to keep Collin inside and the boat from capsizing. Collin fell in a heap, and Rojas gunned the little engine, steering into the crowded waterway, weaving through traffic, heading toward open water.

CHAPTER TWENTY-SIX

GULF OF MEXICO, WEST OF KEY WEST, FLORIDA
JUNE 6

"Man, you look and smell like—" Rojas yelled over the high-pitched whaling of the outboard motor racing full-throttle through rough water.

"Yeah, yeah, I know," Collin interrupted. "It's a long story. I'll tell you all when we get to the boat." Collin scanned the water behind them. There were dozens of boats of all sizes plowing lines in the water, the harbor resembling a freeway at rush hour.

Rojas again yelled over the din. "Looks like everyone wants to get out of here."

"What do you know about the storm?"

"Supposed to hit the Bahamas pretty soon, I think. Then South Florida a couple of hours later. They think it will die out when it hits land."

"Where is everyone going?"

"Probably as far north and west as they can."

"What's Sewell's plan?"

"Same thing. Get far away, to the west."

"Think we can outrun these guys?"

"Don't worry, man. No sailboat faster than the *Admiral*."

"It's not the sailboats I'm worried about."

* * * *

CONCH HARBOR MARINA, KEY WEST, FLORIDA
JUNE 6

Crabtree and McCoy watched Collin hit the deck as he turned, so they slowed at the bottom of the grated metal ramp to take the ninety-degree turn more cautiously. Nonetheless, they didn't stand a chance of catching the speedy Collin. They watched from forty feet away as Collin leapt and landed in the moving dinghy. As they reached the end of the dock, Crabtree stopped, hunched over, and grabbed his knees. Between breaths he exclaimed, "Never … seen … anything … like … that."

McCoy, the former football player, remained standing, hands on his hips, kicking at the dock in exasperation. "Not only fast but highly motivated. Wish I had it on video. It'd go viral." He wasn't as winded as his partner, but he was equally as frustrated.

Crabtree remained bent over for a beat or two then reared up and said, "Grab that boat. We can still get him." He was pointing at another dinghy, larger than the one Collin jumped onto, tied up in an empty slip twenty feet away.

McCoy dashed toward the waiting rubber boat. This one had a built-in console with a seat and a steering wheel. A much fancier model than the target vessel. As he untied the ropes, his more experienced partner arrived, as did the owner, yelling obscenities and demanding them off his dinghy. The man was large, tanned, and muscular. He meant business. Crabtree flashed his badge and said, "FBI. We need your boat. We'll return it when we're done."

The man threw his hands in the air and spewed more profanities as the agents tore off in hot pursuit.

✳ ✳ ✳ ✳

GULF OF MEXICO, OFF THE COAST OF KEY WEST, FLORIDA JUNE 6

"Where's the *Admiral*?" shouted Collin.

Each swell they plowed through sent a shower of sea spray from the leading edge of the bow. Collin's sore ribs throbbed with each jarring thump. Wisely, Rojas had brought a large garbage bag to keep Collin's belongings dry. Collin had cinched it tightly, then wrapped it up, and tied it down under the aluminum bench. He knelt in the front section, holding the safety rope attached to the top of the tubular rubber sides, to keep the boat more stable. Although the water was warm, the slashing wind chilled his wet skin. Before long, Collin was soaked and shivering.

The boat traffic thinned out as they cleared the protected harbors of Key West and headed into the open waters of the Gulf of Mexico. Dozens of cabin cruiser yachts and fishing boats of all sizes, shapes, and models—some old, discolored, and barely seaworthy; others large and luxurious enough to call home—spread out in a fan shape, heading north by northwest. Amongst the motor yachts, scores of sail boats, just as varied in their dimensions and ages, unfurled only a portion of their sails to harness enough wind to drive them forward without capsizing. Many pitched and swayed violently, trying to adjust to the gusts and swells. Others plunged through the waves gracefully, gently rolling as the sails filled with wind and propelled them as if in flight.

Rojas dug a handheld device out of his pocket. It was bright yellow and made of what appeared to be a rugged, buoyant material. He checked it and adjusted their course. Using his outstretched hand, he pointed in the direction they were going. "It's about four miles ahead," he shouted.

"Why so far away?"

"Captain wanted to get ahead of everyone."

"Good idea." Collin scanned in all directions. That's when he noticed it. On the horizon behind them, approaching quickly. He pointed to the boat and shouted, "The two dudes chasing me. They're following us"

"Maybe," yelled Rojas. "Watch them."

The little dinghy continued to bounce as it bored through the one-and two-foot swells and troughs. It seemed like an eternity to Collin. He just wanted to get back on the *Admiral Risty* and change into dry clothes. Rojas was calm and focused. Collin was nervous and shivering with cold. The sky and the sea grew dark, angry, and threatening.

Every few swells, Collin ventured a glance behind them, only to find the pursuing boat a little closer. Unpleasant thoughts raced through his mind.

"Up ahead. That's them," called Rojas, pointing.

The *Admiral Risty* bobbed in the growing surf several hundred yards ahead. The pursuing dingy had veered off course. Collin strained his eyes to make sure. Then he saw a little boat similar to theirs with two passengers just to the south of their position, about a mile away, heading toward a large yacht.

When they got close to the *Admiral Risty*, Captain Sewell stood on the stern, urgently waving them in. "Toss me the line," he called.

Collin gave it a heave and the coiled rope floated a few yards in the air, then caught the wind and landed short, splashing in the water. Collin reeled it in, hand over hand, recoiling it on the floor of the dinghy. His second attempt wasn't much better. His third attempt landed the end of the rope right at the Captain's feet. Jaime grabbed the rope and began to pull the dinghy closer, while picking his way along the railing toward the bow. Rojas tossed a rope from the stern, and soon the dinghy was sidelong the *Admiral Risty,* ramming into the thick, rubber bumpers dangling from the gunwale. Collin handed the garbage bag full of his worldly possessions to Tog as he held the railing. The two boats rose and fell with each swell, water washing over the deck of the *Admiral* and over the sides of the dinghy, partially filling it with seawater.

After Collin and Rojas boarded the *Admiral Risty* safely, the other men worked quickly to pull up one side of the dinghy to drain the water. Two of them scrambled to secure a rubberized canvas cover over the small boat, one that fastened onto the bow and stretched to the stern with a heavy gauge zipper along the side rail. With the cover in place, the two men tied the dinghy's bow rope to a cleat on the *Admiral's* stern and lowered the dinghy back in the water. They gave the Captain the "Aye, aye, sir," as they finished. Every man scurried to his post, and, at the Captain's orders, they worked the lines and riggings, sending sails up and booms a swinging. In no time, the *Admiral Risty* was slicing through the waves with speed and purpose, the experienced crew making it look easy.

A mile to the south, the pursuing agents realized their mistake as soon as they caught up to the slower vessel. Neither of the two men onboard was Collin Cook. Crabtree pointed northward to the men tying off a similar, rubber boat to the back of their sailboat. McCoy punched the throttle and raced toward it. Once the sails were aloft and the sailboat began to move, Crabtree shot a look of panic at his partner, who had to deftly work the throttle. The swells had grown. At full speed, the little dinghy became airborne at the tops of each wave. If the propeller were to breach the water's surface with the accelerator engaged, the lack of resistance could strip the gears and seize up the motor. Knowing this, McCoy backed off the throttle as they knifed through the top of each swell, causing them to land with a jolt in the trough, before he gunned it again up the next swell.

The two agents, bracing for each impact, worked their way through the waves, steadily closing on the large sailboat.

Shuddering with cold, Collin was directed by the Captain to go into the cabin and change his clothes. He was dripping wet. The wind and the water had chilled him to the bone. As he stood there shivering, momentarily trying to engage his brain, he heard commotion above. The crew was yelling and clamoring on the deck. There was a new urgency. Collin climbed the steps and held the railing, following the crew's eyes to the dinghy racing toward them. The Captain ordered another sail to be hoisted, despite the strong winds, to help them outrun the oncoming vessel. Men ran to the forward mast and worked the lines. In no time, the *Admiral Risty* gained speed, and the dinghy's progress toward them stopped. Both boats were full speed ahead through the turbulent seas, neither gaining any ground on the other.

The chase continued for over an hour, the FBI agents in the dinghy tailing the *Admiral Risty*, two hundred yards aft. Captain Sewell dared not hoist another sail with the wind gusting over sixty miles per hour. He and the crew had their hands full controlling the boat as it was. Luckily, the winds were blowing predominately from their back.

Captain Sewell monitored radio communications on the Coast Guard channel. He knew the FBI agents in the dinghy had called for reinforcements but that those reinforcements were busy with the evacuation of South Florida. He also knew Hurricane Abigail, currently a Category Two with sustained winds of one hundred miles per hour, had battered The Bahamas and would soon hit the Florida Keys. It was traveling quickly, averaging fifteen miles per hour across the water. He understood his advantage and the other boat's weakness. At some point, the dinghy would run out of fuel. The experienced Captain just hoped that happened before a Coast Guard cutter intercepted them.

Forty minutes later, his wishes came true. The dinghy began slowing, then finally stopped, bobbing and tossing in the swells that had increased to three feet. The Captain listened as the pilot of the dinghy radioed a distress call. A minute later, the response the Captain did not want to hear came through. The Navy was sending help. Using the agents' cell phones as a beacon, they had locked onto their coordinates and were full speed en route. Estimated time of arrival: nineteen minutes.

The Captain called to his men as he continued to navigate through the worsening conditions. Rain had started coming down harder and harder. The crew gathered around their Captain, intent on hearing every word. He shouted over the noise from the wind and rain, directing his comments at Collin, stabbing the air with his long index finger for emphasis.

"Look, the Navy is coming—nineteen minutes away—to pick up those two guys. They'll run us down to capture you. We have little time and few options. You can stay here and hide again. Or, you can take the dinghy and go to one of the tiny islands until the storm passes. I doubt they would find you."

"Do you think it will work again, hiding in the compartment?" Collin shouted back.

"I don't know. Maybe."

Collin could see doubt in the Captain's expression. Using the same trick on the same boat twice was risky. "What are my chances in the dinghy?"

"The storm is coming in hard. Visibility is very bad. They'll never see you if you go now. Get far away from us. But this storm—it is very dangerous."

"I'm OK with that. It's safer for everyone if I'm gone. Where do I go?" shouted Collin.

"I know a place ten or fifteen miles from here. You can use GPS to find it, but it will take an hour or more in these conditions. Very dangerous."

"Doesn't matter," said Collin. "Beats the alternative."

The Captain ordered the crew to prepare the dinghy and load it with fuel. He instructed Collin to retrieve a special, black bag from a hold under one of the bunks and load his things in it. He advised him to throw in as much food and as many water bottles as room in the bag would allow. When Collin returned with the bag stuffed full, he found the Captain scanning the horizon through binoculars, searching for approaching vessels. The Captain showed him how to seal the bag, which was made of a thick, rubbery plastic, to make it water tight. Tough and buoyant, the Captain explained, this bag would protect his gear and food from

the water.

The Captain motioned for Jaime and Rojas to pull the dinghy broadside and secure the bag to the front bench of the little boat, along with a red, plastic, five-gallon gas can.

Pulling Collin by the shoulder as the wind and waves battered the *Admiral*, Rojas handed him the small, yellow, handheld device he had used earlier. The Captain explained to Collin how to use the GPS device to navigate. Collin figured it wouldn't be much different than the one he used for hiking. There were a number of way points listed in a table called "Favorites," with numbers and symbols indicating longitude and latitude, as well as a short nickname for each. Number nine on the list was labeled "spit 3." Collin was instructed to go there.

"This is risky. Are you sure you want to do it?" asked the Captain. "I'm sure I don't want to put you and the crew in further danger. I also don't want to be stuck in that compartment in these conditions," he said, motioning at the high waves.

"You're a brave man, Collin Cook. God's speed," said the Captain as he clasped Collin's shoulder.

With that, Collin gazed pensively out at the angry sea. Wind and waves tossed the boat to and fro while rain slashed at him. Butterflies spun like a tornado in his gut. He steeled himself, grasped the railing, and stepped toward the two men holding the raft at the side of the boat.

CHAPTER TWENTY-SEVEN

GULF OF MEXICO, WEST OF THE FLORIDA COAST JUNE 6

The cover had been unzipped just enough to allow Collin a place to sit in the rear of the raft where the outboard motor was mounted. The *Admiral Risty* and the dinghy slammed into each other as angry waves heaved the two vessels up and down and side to side. Rain slashed in diagonal sheets, carried by the increasingly powerful winds coming from the southeast. Collin crouched next to Rojas holding the railing, surveying his options and planning his exit onto the dinghy. Without warning, a towering wave crested and broke over the side of the boat, knocking everyone off their feet. Collin lost his grip and went skittering across the deck, grabbing hold of the main mast as he did. Rojas and Jaime let go of the dinghy's side ropes as they grabbed the railing and struggled to stay aboard the *Admiral Risty*.

Collin scrambled back to his feet. The dinghy was slipping away as the wind propelled the *Admiral Risty* one way and the waves carried the dinghy another. Knowing his time was up, he took one giant step and launched himself over the side, hurling his body toward his escape vessel. He struck the side of the dinghy near the bow with his chest, arms extended. With the tarp covering the entire bow, his arms couldn't wrap around the tubular side. There was nothing to hold. The tarp was wet and slick. He bounced off, stunned by the sudden burst of pain from his ribs. He forgot about his ribs. He sank into the water, doubled over with his arms wrapped around his torso. Bubbles erupted around him as he screamed underwater. His instincts kicked into gear, playing out the scenario around him, reminding him that his ride was moving away from him. His eyes shot open. He ignored the pain. He had to get on that dinghy or he'd die.

As he kicked his way to the surface, he caught a glimpse of something slithering in the water nearby. It was moving away from him unsteadily, jerking up and down. He reached for it, but it slipped through his grasp. He kicked with his legs and pulled through the water with his arms until it was close again. This time he focused on grabbing it and holding on tightly. With a firm hold on the rope, he pulled himself upward, breached the surface, and refilled his burning lungs with air. He had the bow rope clutched tightly in his hand. He wasn't about to let go.

Struggling to keep his head above water, Collin pulled the raft closer. As he did, he surveyed his surroundings. Through the sheets of rain and wind-tossed waves, he could make out the whitish form of the sailboat bobbing violently in the growing swells, accented by five dark, apprehensive figures bunched along the closest railing, peering desperately in his direction. He pushed the matted strands of hair from his eyes as he clung to the rope, rising with another wave. He mustered the strength to thrust his left arm high above his head to give them the thumbs up. Whistles and shouts, muffled and unintelligible, erupted from the distance as he struggled to maneuver himself along the side of the dinghy toward the stern.

By the time he reached the back of the boat, still holding the bow rope, he could see the sixty-foot mainsail of the *Admiral Risty* in the distance, surging westward. The crew had no time to help him; they had a Navy rescue ship to outrun. And so did Collin.

As he and the dinghy slid down the face of a swell, Collin used the momentum from the wave to swing his right leg over the rear gunwale, his right hand braced against the side of the outboard engine. Collin kept his head low in the water and swung the rest of his body around clockwise to avoid the propeller and outdrive. His legs found purchase so he could leverage the rest of his body into the boat.

He knew he had no time to spare. He pushed through exhaustion and pain that shot like bolts of lightning through his body, starting at his ribs. The boat was unstable with too much weight in the back and heavy seas tossing it about. Ignoring the searing pain, Collin maneuvered himself into a position where he could kneel in front of the rear bench and still reach the motor. Hoping and praying for a miracle, he yanked on the pull cord to start the engine. Nothing. Exerting all of his strength, he yanked again and again and again, until the motor finally turned over once, then died. He tried again. It turned over once more.

Then, with one more mighty pull, the little motor spit and coughed and came to life.

Collin jammed it into gear and twisted the throttle hard. The little engine whined and screamed, but the boat hardly moved. Collin repositioned his hand on the throttle and twisted more, giving it all the gas the throttle would allow. The propeller started to gain traction, and the little boat began to plow its way forward. Water flowed to the rear of the boat. Even with the tarp covering the bow, the dinghy had taken on a substantial amount of water, the weight of which was creating drag and throwing the center of balance too far aft. The nose of the dinghy bobbed precariously out of the water as it climbed up the face of a swell. Collin leaned as far forward as he could while still holding the throttle. The dinghy crested the wave; Collin's weight was just enough to keep it from flipping over backward. He had no time to improve his center of balance before the next wave hit. All he could do was ease off the throttle before he reached the top and lean forward. In the troughs, he scooped and paddled with his free hand, but that did little to solve his weight imbalance.

After several minutes, he realized he had no idea what direction he was headed. He had to stabilize the boat first, then worry about navigating. If he didn't, he would capsize and have little hope of surviving. Desperately, Collin struggled to keep the little boat from turning over. Between waves, he checked the water level at the back. That's when he saw it. His salvation in the form of a white, one-gallon bucket tied to a string, floating in the back of the boat. Collin grabbed it and scooped as fast as he could with his free hand until he neared the top of a wave, then he pitched his body forward on top of the cover to hold the nose down. On the back side of the wave, he bailed out as much water as he could. He repeated this process until the boat was stable enough to ride the waves without fear of being blown over backward.

As he maneuvered through the waves, he managed to pull out the encased GPS unit from the Velcro pocket of his cargo shorts and tighten the strap to his wrist. "Spit 3" was already highlighted, so he punched "Go." The map resolved and showed his location as a blinking red dot with a line jutting out from it at the eight o'clock position, behind and to the left of his current course. He turned the dinghy gradually until he pointed in the right direction. The danger now was it required traveling crosswise to the waves, but he soon figured out how to negotiate the swells to prevent being flipped over by pointing the nose of the dinghy into the crest of each wave, then toward his destination on the downhill side until he was halfway up the next one.

He made slow and steady progress, inching ever closer to spit 3, as the storm intensified. The spit displayed as a lone speck at the bottom of a steel-gray screen. The GPS said he was nine miles away, traveling at a speed of 3.8 knots. Over two hours to get there. He'd never make it in time. The storm would sink him for sure. Collin decided to risk it and increase his speed. With less weight in the boat and more stability, he found he could manage 6.5 knots without too much trouble. Now he had a better chance of arriving on the tiny island before the front edge of the storm hit full-force, he hoped.

With the increased speed, the stronger wind, and more rain, Collin's core temperature was dropping. The cotton T-shirt and cargo shorts not only didn't insulate, they sucked the heat from his body. His teeth clattered as his jaw quivered uncontrollably. The hand on the throttle was now a pasty white, and he could barely move his fingers. He switched hands frequently, keeping the free hand in his crotch for warmth, though there was little to be found anywhere on his body.

His whole frame convulsed. He recognized this as the onset of hypothermia and followed his Boy Scout training, tensing every muscle in his body and holding it for ten seconds, releasing, then tensing again. This got his blood flowing to his muscles, preventing him from losing cognitive function and large motor skills.

As he continued the regimen of tensing and flexing, Collin focused on preventing a capsize and staying on course. With the heavy rain and rough seas, all he could see in front of him was the next wave he had to surmount. This went on for what felt like hours. Checking the GPS, he was relieved to see that he had a mile and a half to go. The relief would have been greater were it not for the driving headwind keeping his speed under six knots. *Another twenty minutes*, he thought. *That's all.*

His relief and optimism were short-lived. A quarter mile later, the engine conked out and wouldn't restart. He had run out of gas. He remembered the canister tied to the front bench, under the cover, but with the wind gusts and the crashing waves, Collin knew he was in peril.

Working as fast as his cold, stiff muscles could work, he fumbled at the zipper. His fingers had so little feeling, let alone strength, the zipper tab kept slipping through their grasp. Each attempt gained him only inches of access. Waves continued to pound the dinghy, pushing it backward and tossing it about like the tiny object it was on this vast, surging sea. Fighting to keep his weight close to the center for maximum stability, Collin's efforts with the zipper were fruitless. The activity was frustrating but had engaged his brain.

He remembered seeing Rojas put a screwdriver in a clear, zippered pouch under the bench behind him. He fought the swells that threatened to capsize his little raft and struggled to get at the long, thin tool. Once he did, his fingers didn't grip it well enough, and it dropped to the floor, and disappeared under several inches of water. Collin lunged into the rear of the dinghy, flailing wildly through the flooded bottom, shouting his frustration until he found it. With his weight in the back, the nose of the dinghy tipped upward as it was thrown to the top of another wave.

Again, Collin lurched toward the center to prevent the boat from flipping backward. His heat-starved body lacked its usual coordination, and he landed awkwardly on the tarp, banging his shins on the aluminum bench. He had nothing to hold. The nose of the boat slapped into the water just as the dinghy reached the top of the wave. Collin bounced and skidded across the slick tarp and over the edge at the front left quarter of the raft. As he slid, his hands flailed in all directions; the three longest fingers of his right hand snagged and wrapped around one of the safety ropes that ran along the top of the dinghy's inflated side tubes. His weight pulled him down as the sea pushed the boat up, shooting sharp pain through his fingers, tearing skin, and causing friction burns on the sensitive flesh underneath. A tearing sensation coursed through his upper arm and shoulder. Despite the pain, his survival instincts demanded he not let go. Like a rodeo cowboy, Collin held on as the boat bucked. His left hand still clutched the screwdriver.

Kicking his legs and left hand—screwdriver, GPS, and all—he worked to turn his body until he could grasp the safety rope with both hands. He pulled his head out of the water and gasped for breath, sucking in rain and sea spray as he did. He sputtered and choked and coughed it out.

Panicked like never before, Collin tried to pull his body onboard from the side. As he did, he felt the boat ready to flip on top of him. He relaxed his arms, letting his body slump back into the water. Instead, he shimmied along, hand to hand, to the nose of the boat and waited until a swell pushed him upward. Ignoring the stinging in his hand and the torn muscles in his arm, he pulled with all his might until he got one arm across the pointed front end and heaved his upper body onto the gunwale. The boat nosed up another wave, pushing his body upward until he sprawled out across the tarp, still holding the safety rope with one hand. He spun on his stomach to get his legs toward the aft. From there he inched backward until he was on his knees in front of the rear bench, where he had started.

Wasting no time, Collin inserted the thin end of screwdriver through the eye of the jumbo zipper tab and tugged it open until he saw the gas can. A yank on the end of the knot loosened the can. Still fighting waves and wind and with rain lashing his face, Collin pulled the can to the rear of the boat and fumbled with the screw top on the floor-mounted tank. He fought to stay balanced. Gasoline splashed out of the spout of the gas can as he jarred it open. Waves threatened to overturn the dinghy, so he steadied himself against the bench. Settling his weight on the floor as close to the center of the boat as he could, he angled the spout of the can toward the tiny opening as the sea continued to jostle him violently. Gas spilled all over until he was able to jam the spout into the opening of the tank. Collin leaned forward to cup his hand over the opening and around the spout as he poured to prevent water entering the gas tank.

When he had gotten what he deemed would be enough in the tank, he closed the spout and screwed the fuel tank cap back on. He dragged the half full can back to the front of the boat and pulled the zipper as far as he could in one effort, bracing for another wave as he did. He turned back to the pull cord starter. Fortunately, the engine started on the second pull. He revved the throttle and engaged the gear just in time to push up the face of a monster wave and avoid getting overturned by it.

After stabilizing the boat, he checked the GPS attached to his left wrist and discovered that he had been pushed back two tenths of a mile. Steeling himself, he twisted the throttle and leaned into the wind and waves, fighting every moment to remain balanced and steady.

The time lost proved critical. The leading edge of the hurricane was bearing down on him. Collin could tell by the erratic and power-ful gusts of wind, howling like a hungry animal on the hunt. Darkness was setting in. He hunkered down, praying silently as he focused on following the course set by the GPS until the island was a just quarter mile away. Though it was reported by the Captain to be only twenty meters in length and eight meters wide, it provided a sliver of shelter from the torrent.

In the shadow of the little spit of land, the waves were half as large and far less violent, allowing Collin to pick up much needed speed. He approached the island from the north and discovered a wall of rock, six feet high, as the Captain had said he would. He had to make his way around the east end to find the sandy, horseshoe-shaped lagoon where Captain Sewell told him to beach the boat. He pushed eastward, toward the storm, around the end of the rocky outcroppings. Turning to his right, the wall of rock continued. As he made the turn a ferocious wall of water greeted him, colliding with the island and amassing two meters above his head. He gunned the little engine full throttle and scaled the wave. The nose of the dinghy went airborne as he broke through the crest and sped down the back side, out of control. The sea pulled back and revealed in the fading twilight, an exposed shoal. He was headed straight for it. He throttled again and banked left, closing his eyes and bracing himself as he did.

He expected to catapult headfirst out of the boat and into the rocks. Or to topple over and tumble onto the jagged surface. Instead, he swung upward again, racing up the face of another giant wave. This repeated several times until an inlet appeared to his right. Veering hard right at the bottom of the next wave, he narrowly avoided another towering rock. He slipped past it into a semi-protected, crescent-shaped cove. A row of sentinel-like spires of rock poked out of the water from the shoals, forming a breakwater.

Collin cut the power to the motor as the water became shallow to avoid damaging the propeller on rock or sand. He slid into the water feet first over the bow, gathering the tie rope as he went. He landed chest-high in the water on a sandy bottom amid a powerful surge that thrust him and the dinghy to the shore, causing him to trip on an unseen rock. Scrambling on hands and knees, Collin dragged the little dinghy up the semi-sandy beach. Another surge pushed it several feet higher up the beach, which was pitched at a steep angle, washing over Collin's head. He sputtered and grasped for a hold as the water receded, dragging him backward, across the sand.

He struggled to get back on his hands and knees when another wave slammed into him, driving him face first up the beach. He held the rope tight, knowing the dinghy represented his salvation. Again, he scrambled to his knees and braced himself. The waves pushed him and the dinghy up the steep incline until he was able to grab hold of a football-sized rock. The waves continued to surge, but he was able to gain balance and traction and move up the beach, beyond the waves. Collin tugged the dinghy until it also reached sand, completely out of the water.

The island was barren. Nothing but rocks and sand from what he could see silhouetted in the darkness. It stood maybe seven feet above the water at its peak and was half the size of a soccer field.

There was not a good place to tie the boat that he could see, except a fat, round rock that looked like a toilet bowl—wider at the top, narrower at the base. Collin tied the bow rope around the base and cinched it tight. That way even if the water rose, the rope should hold. He swung the stern of the boat as far up the beach as he could and tied the stern rope to another rock. The dinghy sat perpendicular to the direction of the waves, but several yards from their terminus, its propeller and outdrive, he hoped, would be spared the pounding against sand or rock.

As he scrambled up the beach toward a jumble of rocks in search of shelter, he remembered the sea bag and its precious contents. He turned toward the dinghy to retrieve it as a potent gust of wind hit him with such force it knocked him off his feet, hurling him toward the ground.

CHAPTER TWENTY-EIGHT

"SPIT 3," GULF OF MEXICO
JUNE 6

Collin felt the wind lift him off his feet. He was hurtling through the air, feeling minuscule and helpless. For the first time in his life, he feared being literally blown away, like a dry leaf. His imagination spun on that for a split second, wondering how far into oblivion the wind could actually carry him, afraid of being blown out to sea with no boat, no life jacket.

He landed on his back, several feet from where he had been walking, with such force that his breath was pushed out of him. His landing spot was a low, bumpy boulder, thinly covered with a layer of fine sand. The impact sent fresh flashes of pain through his ribs, shoulder, and back. His head slammed against the rock hard enough to make him see stars. He lay there dazed, half in shock, trying to regain his breath and wits while the rain peppered his body with more ferocity than he had ever experienced.

For several long moments, Collin struggled to move. Every attempt caused a wave of pain that incapacitated him. He had to get out of the rain and wind, so he rolled to his good side and pushed up to his knees. Staying low to the ground, moving along the clutter of slick rock and sodden sand, his knees wobbly and head bleeding, Collin searched for some sort of refuge. He couldn't see because of the rain and the fast-encroaching darkness and was deafened by the roaring wind and pounding surf, making rational thought impossible. In all his years living in California, he had never experienced rain or wind like this. It brought to mind images of fire hoses knocking down protesters, such was the force behind it. This was raw, natural, fearsome power.

Equally as powerful, though, was Collin's will to survive.

Within a few yards, he stumbled into something promising: a refrigerator-sized rock lying against another, creating a triangular space similar in size to that found under a large desk. Collin squeezed himself in, gathering his legs and torso into a ball and maneuvering until he was sitting with his back against the supporting rock. Rain water dripped and ran into the space, but he was protected from the wind and the pelting. He sat on a jagged, but mostly dry, rock. That's when he remembered the sea bag with his raincoat and the dry clothes he had intended to bring. It was too risky to retrieve it. Instead, he fumbled to remove his shirt so he could wring out as much water as possible before putting it back on. It wasn't much, but it would help. When he was done, he pulled his legs close to his chest and wrapped his arms around them, trying to conserve body heat. He placed his forehead against his knees, closed his eyes, and thanked God for helping him get here.

* * * *

LONDON, ENGLAND
JUNE 7

Nic stared blankly at his computer screen. He had just hung up the phone with Reggie Crabtree and was dreading the meeting that would soon be convened in his boss's office, where he would have to explain that Collin Cook was missing at sea. According to Crabtree, the commander of the Navy ship that intercepted the sailboat suspected of harboring Cook interviewed its captain and crew after escorting the sailboat out of the danger zone.

The ship's captain explained when asked that he did not know his passenger's origins or history. All he knew was that the man was a good-paying customer who asked to tour the Caribbean. Each crew member's statement indicated that Cook had stolen the dinghy and headed south, toward the approaching hurricane. To a man, each reported that Cook seemed wild, crazed, and suicidal as he commandeered their dinghy and raced off into the storm.

The Navy and Coast Guard would suspend search efforts until morning, after the storm had passed, due to safety concerns.

Nic wasn't convinced that Collin Cook was lost at sea. But he needed to persuade Alastair Montgomery that Cook was dead, or the pressure would never let up.

Like a two-day-old helium balloon, Nic's spirit sagged. With Collin

Cook, all hope of tracking down Pho Nam Penh and bringing him to justice for the world to see had disappeared. Wiped away by a Category Two hurricane named Abigail.

Nic knew he would not have his day of redemption, let alone fame and recognition. He would not be shown on *Sky News*, hauling Collin Cook, the international cyber terrorist, into a detention facility. He would not be interviewed by the London papers. He would not be patted on the shoulder by Director McCutchins. His rise through the ranks would be somewhat less than meteoric. He would go back to monotonous days on the phone, chasing down empty leads, filling out reports on mundane criminals and their mundane activities. Living an ordinary life. Having an ordinary career. The thought crushed him.

Nic blew out a breath he had been holding unconsciously, slapped the manila folder against his knees, and stood, pausing long enough to chase away the last lingering shadows of doubt. His twenty-meter walk of shame down the hallway, past the rows of cubicles, would be the longest of his career.

If Collin Cook resurfaced, he would pay for this humiliation.

*   *   *   *

"SPIT 3," GULF OF MEXICO
JUNE 7

When his eyes opened, they were greeted by blinding light. He lay on his side, curled like a fetus. His hands wedged in his armpits; his cheek pressed against wet sand. Rays of golden light sliced through puffy, purple-lined clouds, caressing his face and arms, infusing much needed warmth into his clammy, ashen skin. He didn't remember falling asleep. The only thing he could recall was praying over and over that he would be spared as the surf pounded into the rocky shore, the wind roared, and the rain splattered all around him in an all-out assault on his senses. He imagined this was what it felt like to live through a massive bombing raid, never knowing when the one would drop that would snuff out his life.

With only rocks shielding him from the elements, he shook with cold all night. His wet cotton clothing did nothing to insulate him, so he continually tensed his muscles and rubbed his skin to generate what little heat he could.

As he awoke, he found it hard to move. Every muscle in his body was knotted and exhausted, a whole night of shivering and tensing taking its toll. After several attempts, Collin pushed up from the sand to a kneeling position and crawled out of his shelter, pausing to make sure the storm had really passed. The filtered sunlight beckoned him, almost pulling him from under the rock, eager to claim victory over Abigail.

Collin surveyed the tiny island that had saved him from the storm. His hole was along a rise that jutted no more than seven feet above sea level, littered with car-sized slabs of chocolate brown rock. He could see both ends of the island, which were only twenty yards apart.

Unable to straighten his half-frozen frame, Collin hobbled to a throne-like rock at the edge of the sand. The coffee colored stone had soaked up enough energy to feel warm to the touch, exactly what Collin wanted. He spread across it, making as much contact with the heated surface as possible. Gradually, his muscles unwound. Color replaced pallor. Hollowness gave way to gratitude. Motivation supplanted melancholy. He cried out toward the sky, thanking God for helping him and for sending the sun to chase the storm.

Time passed, though he had no idea how much. The sun broke free from the last of the clouds and poured on him full force. Steam rose from his shirt, patches of which had dried. His mind had thawed as well, and he remembered the sea bag in the dinghy and the dry clothes it contained.

Rising unsteadily from the bed of rock, he worked to loosen the muscles in his legs, back, and arms by flexing and stretching them. Every joint felt locked or rusted. Prying them loose hurt at first, but the movements felt almost as good as the warmth of the sun. To his relief, the dinghy remained tied to the rocks, though the ropes were stretched and frayed. It was full of water, but no worse for the wear. He pulled out the sea bag, grateful to the Captain for making him pack it with food and water. First, he downed a quart of water, gulping the clear, cool liquid. He hadn't realized how dry his throat was. Then he changed his clothes and wolfed some bread and fruit.

He was starting to feel alive again, like a functioning human. His mind replayed the events of the previous night, and he realized how significant and wondrous it was to be alive, to be functioning. It was a miracle. Miracles happened, he had heard, always as part of a grander design. In that moment, he knew there was a reason he survived, a purpose for his life. He planned to fulfill it. He gathered a lungful of fresh, tropical air, clenched his fists, and stretched them upward, more invigorated than he had been since his teenage years. Emboldened, empowered, preserved. Tears of gratitude and relief streamed down his cheeks as he dropped to his knees. Collin Cook knew his life still had meaning and that thought humbled him.

The silhouette from the Internet news story crossed his mind's eye. Asian man he had been photographed with in London just a few weeks ago. The man who had turned his existence upside down, disallowing Collin the chance to mourn the loss of his wife and children. The man he had been running from all this time. The man whose shadow had chased him across three continents.

It was now clear to him that his mission was to save other innocent people from the financial calamities Pho Nam Penh and his band of evil geniuses lay ready to unleash.

The thought brought him to his feet, back to the moment.

He had to get off the island. Most likely the Coast Guard or Navy would scour the area looking for him now that the storm had passed. Surely, they knew about this tiny island and would come searching.

After checking the contents of the sea bag and determining that his computer and both phones still worked, Collin prepared to leave the protection of the island and take his chances once again on the open ocean in his twelve-foot dinghy. He tied down the sea bag and gas can under the front bench and checked the tubular walls all the way around. All were tight, holding air. Another miracle.

Turning on the GPS, he scrolled through the favorites to determine which was closest and to calculate, as best he could, the feasibility of making it there. Dry Tortugas was closest—thirty-four miles away. He topped the tank, leaving the can half full. Judging from the amount of fuel he used the night before to cover roughly thirteen miles, he gauged it to be doable, especially on calmer seas. He pushed the "Go" button on the GPS, and a blinking red dot appeared with a gray line extending almost due south to Dry Tortugas. Wasting no time, he untied the ropes from around the two rocks and dragged the raft down the ravaged beach, into the now calm, but still murky, water of the lagoon.

As he started the motor, he gave the island a long, contemplative look. It was a bleak and barren spot of solid ground amidst miles of water. Not much more than a pile of rocks. One of thousands of such islands in this part of the world; but to him, it was beautiful and hallowed.

CHAPTER TWENTY-NINE

COAST GUARD STATION, KEY WEST, FLORIDA
JUNE 7

After several minutes of haranguing from a San Francisco-based FBI agent named Crabtree, the Commanding Officer at the Southernmost Lifesavers station agreed that as part of their search for two small craft missing since the hurricane, they would search a grid ten miles in radius from the spot where the *Admiral Risty* was intercepted. At first, the CO balked, saying he did not have the manpower to search an additional hundred square miles of ocean. His reluctance was short-lived because of his political aspirations. In exchange for a commendation for providing exemplary interagency cooperation, the Commander acquiesced. He was more willing to oblige than he let on.

The four-ship armada left the Key West harbor at 0500 hours, heading to the search area. Specialized aircraft launched at 0700 hours. All searching for two missing vessels that had called mayday during the hurricane. Finding those two boats and their occupants were their first two priorities. Third on the list was finding the tiny, gray dinghy with a lone, white male, age thirty.

Progress reports came in regularly with no change until 1200 hours, when the thirty-foot cruiser had been located, the white painted bottom of the hull making it visible from the air. It had capsized seventy miles off the coast, two of its three crew members clinging to it. The third reportedly drowned.

The missing fifty-foot schooner had made it to a harbor near Naples under its own power, half of its sails shredded and flapping uselessly. Its location was radioed in at 1400 hours.

Only the twelve-foot rubber dinghy was still missing. There was no sign of it, though the search effort now focused exclusively on the hundred-square mile grid surrounding its last verifiable location.

At 2100 hours Eastern Daylight Time, the Commanding Officer

relayed to Crabtree the message from the officer in charge of the rescue effort that the entire grid had been searched and nothing was found. Their conclusion: the lone man could not have survived a Class Two hurricane in a twelve-foot dinghy. It was presumed that the boat had sunk, and since the man had no life preserver, that he had perished.

When Reggie Crabtree heard that message, he hung his head and let out a long sigh. He had been called into the Coast Guard CO's office so he could deliver the news to Crabtree in person. Reggie knew the parents would be distraught, inconsolable. He knew he and the Bureau would be blamed. He knew he had not heard the last from Sarah Cook.

* * * *

LA JOLLA, CALIFORNIA
JUNE 9

Emily had not heard from Collin since her arrival at the safe house. That was Wednesday evening. She had been driven to her office the next morning, which was awkward; had begun her preparations to advocate Sarah's candidacy for inclusion in the clinical trial phase of the experimental new treatment; had been driven home to her freshly "sanitized" condominium after work; had spent a restless evening, first waiting for Collin to call, then trying to get through to him. She stayed busy at work on Friday, though she felt unproductive.

Saturday morning, she awoke and went for a run, trying to push away the clustered and conflicted feelings that wrestled inside her. The run helped in that regard, but it didn't last long. In the shower, the troubling thoughts returned. She tried him again on the secret phone when she was dressed. Again, no answer. She was half-annoyed, half-worried sick. Thoughts of Collin interfered with everything she did, all weekend long, whether she was doing errands, cleaning her condo, making dinner, or watching TV. She couldn't stay busy enough to not think about him.

As Emily prepared for bed Sunday night, she was emotionally exhausted. She knew she had a long, crucial week ahead of her. She wanted to be fresh and energetic when she presented Sarah's case on Monday, but with so much on her mind, she feared she would fail.

Collin was taking up too much of her mental energy.

Ever since he showed up unexpectedly in Chicago, his face, his voice, even his smell, permeated the majority of her thoughts, her dreams. The lack of response, the absence of communication, was tearing at the fibers inside her tightly constructed sense of well-being. These feelings, like outliers on a plot graph of results, didn't conform to her scientific life. She couldn't explain them, nor could she summarily rule them out. Ignoring them wasn't a solution; it only fueled more questions that begged to be answered.

She knew Genevieve was waiting outside and would follow her to the office in the morning. She knew Sarah would call her and ask if she had heard anything from or about Collin. She was not looking forward to either encounter.

Late Sunday evening, Emily poured hot water into her mug and watched it swallow the tea bag dangling over the edge. The tea, she hoped, would help her relax so she could sleep. She decided to do some research online to occupy her mind, hoping it would provide some answers to put her at ease.

During their conversation in Chicago, Collin had mentioned the FBI and their pursuit of him. He said he was one of their Most Wanted. Maybe there would be an update about Collin online. Why hadn't she thought about that before, she wondered? She opened her laptop and went to the FBI website and typed his name in the search bar. A list of reports filled the screen. She scrolled down the page, reading the captions, stunned at the number of entries about her friend. The one at the top, the one she dismissed off-the-cuff because it seemed too unbelievable, was the one she went back to read more thoroughly. She clicked on the link to read the full write-up. It was brief and to the point.

Saturday, June 8, 21:53 EDT: Collin Cook, the fugitive wanted in connection with cyber-attacks on RBS and many other European banks, eluded FBI agents and local police at two Florida roadblocks and escaped into the Gulf of Mexico in a twelve-foot rubber dinghy late afternoon on Friday, June 7, as Hurricane Abigail approached. Last known location approximately forty-five miles north-northwest of Key West, FL. Navy and Coast Guard personnel and equipment spent sixteen hours searching a hundred-square-mile area of ocean, where he was reported to have gone missing. Search crews and equipment in the water and air found no evidence of Cook or his vessel. He is presumed to have perished at sea. All search activity has been called off.

Emily read the report twice, disbelieving her eyes the first time. Collin was gone. Her mind went numb; her insides felt hollow. She began to weep. She couldn't absorb the true meaning of the words. She was not prepared for it. A melancholy ache worked its way through her core as if a burning poison was being carried through her bloodstream, damaging everything it touched. Emily's head dropped to her hands. Her shoulders heaved; her body shuddered.

Twenty minutes later, she pushed herself up from her kitchen table, walked to her bed, and collapsed.

Monday morning, her music alarm blared at six o'clock. Emily pounded the snooze button, wanting to shut out the world and wallow in her sorrow. Then the thought struck her and jolted her to a sitting position: Sarah depended on her. She had to advocate for her. She had to keep moving forward. She had promised Collin she would take care of his mother.

Emily forced herself to concentrate on getting Sarah's case reviewed for acceptance into the clinical trial. Her presentation was stilted. Even though it was filled with compelling information and a passionate plea, she lost her train of thought twice during the fifteen-minute meeting.

As she left the conference room, it seemed that gravity was several times more powerful inside her chest cavity than anywhere else. She walked slowly toward her office. Mike Zimmerman caught her in the hallway. "What's up with you, Emily? You feeling all right? You don't seem your usual self."

"Yeah, I'm just a bit off today. I've got a lot on my mind, but I'll be OK."

"Just go home. You won't do much good here. Besides, you deserve a break."

At her desk, Emily collected her things; each felt heavy and cumbersome. Her lab coat, her purse, her computer bag, even her phone. Walking through the building and across the parking lot felt like climbing a mountain. Her steps were labored. It required thought to push one foot forward, then the other.

Then it came. The moment she had been dreading since she read those FBI reports. She was almost to her car, key in hand. Her phone was buzzing. The caller ID said Sarah Cook. Her mouth went dry, and her stomach twisted like a pretzel, but she answered anyway.

"I don't suppose you heard the news about Collin, did you?" asked Sarah.

"I actually read it online last night. I don't know ..." Emily couldn't hold back the sob that burst out of her, though she tried to conceal it with a hand over her mouth.

Sarah jumped right in. "Listen to me, Emily. Don't fret. There's no need to cry. Collin is alive. I know it." Her tone was resolute. But Emily thought she detected something different, something unusual. There was a strain, a rasp hidden under there as if she had been crying.

Despite that fact, Sarah's message was so strong that it staunched the flow of Emily's emotions like a flood gate in a canal. She cleared her throat. "How can you say that with such conviction?"

"I just know. My mother's instinct tells me he's alive."

"You've seen the reports, haven't you?"

"Yes, and I received a special phone call from Agent Crabtree. He went to Florida and saw Collin get away on a small rubber boat. He chased him for hours, he said. At one point, Agent Crabtree said he thought he and his partner might die, the storm was so powerful. He told me there is no way Collin could have survived a hurricane in that boat. But you know what? I don't care what he says or what the Coast Guard report says. My son is alive."

Emily wrestled with her thoughts, not sure what to say. The scientist in her looked at the evidence and followed logic to a justifiable and reasonable conclusion. One hundred mile an hour winds, twelve-foot waves, and driving rain. Odds were against survival. But her feminine intuition latched onto Sarah's steadfast pronouncement. "Maybe there's a slim chance, Sarah. Maybe." She stopped as if to put words to a new thought. "If anyone has the pluck and fortitude to make it through something like that, it's Collin."

"That's more like it. I need you to stay strong, Emily. You must believe and pray for him. He's still in danger, but he can make it through.

I believe that like I believe I'm talking to you."

"Wow, Sarah. I don't know how you stay so strong."

"It's not easy, but when you learn to close your eyes and let your feelings guide you, you find that what *can* be trumps what the world says *should* be."

CHAPTER THIRTY

GULF OF MEXICO, NORTH OF DRY TORTUGAS NATIONAL PARK JUNE 7

Billowy, white clouds dotted the sky. The turquoise ocean spread out in all directions like a shimmering field of diamonds as the crests in the water reflected the sunlight. A gentle breeze stirred the thick, heavy air. With the sun beating down on him, he was covered in sweat and felt like he was slowly roasting. Collin had trouble believing that only hours earlier he was in stage one hypothermia, shivering uncontrollably, praying that he would live to see the sun again. Now its glare was blinding him, the heat suffocating.

He had been racing along in the dinghy on a southwesterly course heading toward Tortugas, which was seventy miles west of Key West. He knew nothing about what was there but figured to find food, water, and gasoline, if nothing else. Beyond that, he hoped there might be transportation back to the mainland, although the thought of going back into the United States was unsettling. He was a wanted man there, and if someone recognized him, it could spell the end of his freedom.

The engine had shut off, having run out of fuel. He refilled the tank with the last of the gas Captain Sewell's crew had loaded on the dinghy for him. The five-gallon plastic container was now empty. The GPS showed eight miles to go to reach his destination, so his confidence was high.

To gain some relief from the blistering heat of the late afternoon, Collin scooped seawater with the white bucket he had used for bailing during the storm. He poured it over his head, soaking his hair and shirt. Though the water was quite warm, it felt refreshing to wash away the sweat. Collin was so preoccupied with the gas and the bucket shower that he didn't notice the large motor yacht bearing down on him. It approached at a healthy clip, but Collin didn't see or hear it until it was just a stone's throw away. Although there were people on the fly bridge, one of which sat behind the wheel in the pilot's chair, no one seemed to be watching where they were going. The four of them were laughing and talking and sipping bottles of beer. Collin scrambled to start the engine and maneuver the dinghy out of the way in order to avoid being run over.

About the time he started moving, the pilot of the larger boat noticed him, cut the power to the yacht's engines, and steered to the right to avoid Collin's dinghy. He was flapping his arms and shouting something. Collin thought he was angry. The man hurried down the ladder from the fly bridge to the back deck and hailed Collin toward them. Collin swung around in a loop and approached the stern as the yacht drifted to a stop. Both boats were bobbing gently in the wake the yacht had created.

Collin estimated the yacht to be somewhat shorter than the *Admiral Risty*, which would make it maybe fifty feet long. It was wider and very plush, much like Rob Howell's boat.

"Hey, what are you doing way out here in a dinghy?" called the man, sounding more confused than angry. He now stood leaning over the gunwale with his hands cupped over his mouth. Collin detected a Southern accent.

"I'm heading for Tortugas."

"Alone?"

"Yes. I got separated from the mother ship during the storm."

"Are you OK?"

"Yeah, I'm fine."

The dinghy had drifted close enough for the two to talk instead of having to shout.

"Is your mother ship meeting you in Tortugas, or what is your plan there?"

The pilot was joined on the deck by another man and two women, who listened intently. They all looked to be in their fifties, dressed casually, well-tanned, and relaxed. None of them seemed to have a concern in the world before they saw Collin. The women looked at him with worried expressions.

"I was hoping to get some gas and food and maybe a ride to the mainland."

"You won't find any of that there. There are no services. It's just a National Park with a ranger and some tour guides. You'll learn a lot about the history of the island, but you'll still be hungry."

"No gas there, either?"

"Nothing except a gift shop. And with the storm, I doubt they've reopened yet. It's probably all shut down."

One of the women stepped close and whispered in the man's ear. He nodded as if her idea had never crossed his mind. "You hungry? We've got plenty of food. My wife here is worried about you, kid."

"I've got some food and water. I'm all right."

The woman stepped closer and said, "Why don't you come on board with us and get yourself something to eat? You're a long ways away from anything, and I can't believe you have enough food on that tiny boat."

The man added, "You got enough gas to get you to the mainland?"

Collin shrugged. "I don't know. It depends. I was planning on refueling in Tortugas. Not sure I can make it back to Key West."

"Well, come tie up, and let's get you taken care of," the pilot said with a beckoning gesture, waving his arm toward the yacht. "You're going to need some food, and we got plenty."

Collin started the little engine and maneuvered close enough to throw his bow rope to the second man, who pulled him alongside the yacht. The name beautifully painted on the stern wall in a flowing script was *Ain't Life Grand.*

He was welcomed aboard with words, like "You poor dear" from the women and "I'll be damned" from the men.

After greeting Collin, the two women slipped inside the cabin while the men peppered Collin with questions about how he got there, what he was doing, and what his plans were. At first, Collin wasn't sure how to answer them. The questions came in rapid-fire succession, giving him no time to answer before another one was launched from the other inquisitor. The men seemed less interested in his answers and more interested in asking more questions. Before Collin had a chance to talk, the two were telling their story about waiting out the hurricane in Key Largo. "It was scary, man. The winds were horrific," said the second man.

"Yeah, I was afraid we were going to be stuck there for days," said the first man, the owner of the boat. "But, as soon as the storm passed, we were out of there at first light. I don't like being behind schedule, you know."

When the women returned with a large, well-appointed sandwich, stuffed with meat, cheese, tomato, and lettuce, on a plate with a pile of potato chips and a soda poured over ice in a tall glass, the owner's wife asked, "Where ya'll headed?"

"I don't know at this point. The boat I was going to work on sails out of George Town on Grand Cayman. I suppose I'll try to work my way over there and see if I can join up with them."

The owner and his wife exchanged a glance. Both smiled. "You're in luck, pal," said the owner. "That's our next stop. We do this every few years. We start from our home port in Beaufort, South Carolina— that's where we live—and spend most of the summer making our way to Cancun. We do some fishing and some scuba diving along the way, you know. I have to keep this baby out of the country once every four years for tax purposes. Otherwise the government says I can't call this a second home and can't write off my expenses. We love Grand Cayman. Beautiful diving there, son. You a scuba diver?"

"I am, actually. Love it," replied Collin.

"Good. We'll take you there. You can join us on a dive or two if you've got time."

"I'd like that."

The owner pointed to the fly bridge and started climbing. "We'd better get underway. Join us up top. Let's hear your story." Turning to the second man, he said, "Hey Frank, why don't you tie that dinghy to one of our long stern ropes? We'll tow it beyond the wake."

Once the dinghy was secured, the yacht began to plow westward again. The remaining four climbed up the ladder and found seats on the fly bridge. They positioned Collin in the copilot's chair so he could be heard. Collin took a bite and started to chew as he listened to all the questions.

Upon reflection, he realized he was ravenously hungry. He nodded and said, "Thank you so much. This is delicious." Then he started answering questions between bites, sharing a believable story that was mostly true.

He left out the parts about being pursued by the FBI, explaining instead that he was supposed to work onboard the sailboat but couldn't catch them in his dinghy as they raced to outrun the storm. He said he lost sight of them and, with the wind, couldn't communicate on the radio, so he began to turn back to shore when he realized his mistake. He told his harrowing story of surviving the storm in the dinghy and finding his way to the tiny spit of land as the hurricane approached. His small audience was mesmerized and awestruck.

When he had finished answering their questions and telling his story, Collin marveled at the way things were working out. If he had a doubt about being watched over, it was dismissed by the arrival of his new-found friends from Beaufort.

* * * *

HUNTINGTON BEACH, CALIFORNIA
JUNE 13

The doorbell rang at nine thirty that Thursday morning. Sarah was lying on her bed with her robe on, wrapped in the decorative blanket that usually adorned her reading chair. "Coming," she called. With her strength drained by another round of chemotherapy, the words were so faint they barely made it past the end of the bed, let alone all the way down to the front door.

Henry popped his head in the doorway. "Don't worry, dear, I'll get it."

She closed her eyes and whispered, "Thank you."

Henry returned with a FedEx envelope in his hands. He was already tearing it open as he sat on the edge of the bed next to Sarah. Her eyes fluttered open. "What is it?" she asked.

"There's a note in here, nothing else," he said. Unfolding the single sheet of plain white paper, he read it aloud:

Dear Mr. and Mrs. C.,
Please meet me at The Californian Restaurant in the Hyatt
Regency at noon for lunch. Thanks, and I look forward
to seeing you both there.
—Rob Howell

Henry stared at the paper for a long second. "I wonder what this is all about," he said. He reached over and clasped Sarah's hand and tried to read her expression.

"I can only imagine that it's about Collin. Why else would he send a FedEx package?"

"You're probably right. If you're not up to it, dear, I'll go alone."

"No, no. I'll be fine. That will give me plenty of time to get myself looking presentable."

Designed to look like an old, Spanish colonial villa, the Hyatt Regency Huntington Beach exuded style and comfort. Its thick, white walls, accented with dark stained, beveled timbers and red tile roof, paid homage to the first European settlers in the region. Henry and Sarah surveyed the richly appointed, elegantly furnished interior as they walked through the hotel lobby, trying to get their bearings. The floor was covered with large, square tiles of varying shades of red and orange. Exposed wooden timbers ran along the ceilings and supporting walls. An open hearth with a fire burning divided the lobby into two lounge areas furnished with brown leather couches and chairs. As they gawked, a bellhop approached and pointed them toward the restaurant.

Rob appeared out of nowhere and greeted Henry and Sarah shortly after they walked through the arched doorway of the restaurant, his eyes scanning in all directions. "Please come, sit down. I have a table for us on the patio. I hope that will be all right."

Neither Henry nor Sarah knew what to say. Henry was worried about Sarah, who was conserving her strength. She smiled wanly at Rob as she gripped his hand between the two of hers. "It's so good to see you, Robert. You look so handsome."

Rob leaned down and kissed her on the cheek. "Good to see you, too, Mrs. C."

Rob had that movie star look about him. Casual, yet tasteful. An open-collared, light blue button up shirt under a dark blue, linen blazer. His hand-woven leather Chubasco sandals, earth tone cotton slacks, and two-days' stubble completed the outfit. More than one set of admiring, female eyes watched as they passed between tables to the patio.

Rob double checked their surroundings before he sat down. Their table was under a slat-roofed, private gazebo. Not another table or chair within twenty feet. He pulled out one of the wooden chairs, topped with a burgundy cushion, for Sarah and scooted it in as she sat.

Sarah beamed at him, full of pride. "You were always such a gentleman."

Nodding to Henry as he folded himself into his seat, he said, "I learned from the best." With only a slight pause, Rob continued, "I'm sure you're curious as to why I invited you here, especially given the manner in which the invitation was sent." He checked both of their faces to confirm their amused confusion. "I've been sent here by Collin. He wants you to know that he is safe and doing well. I can't give you the details, but he is being sheltered and fed by some good friends in a safe location." He paused as the message sunk in. The Cooks were silent, stealing glances at each other, a sort of reassurance spreading between them. "Problem is," Rob continued, "he can't come home yet. That would put you in danger. As you've no doubt seen or heard, he is—or was—a wanted man. The FBI has been trying to put him in prison for crimes he did not commit, and Collin is trying to draw out the guy who framed him so he can put an end to not only his nightmare, but the nightmares this sleazebag plans to inflict upon others. Collin's a brave and determined man. He wants justice served and his name cleared, and he won't stop until that happens."

Sarah was silent, dabbing at the tears in her eyes with a tissue.

Henry reached for his wife's hand, gave it a squeeze, and said, "How is he going to catch the bad guy and clear his name?"

"Let me just say he has some very capable people, who are very well connected with the upper echelons of law enforcement, helping him."

"Then why is the FBI hunting him?"

"That is part of the ruse. To draw out this criminal, he has to play this cat and mouse game with the FBI and Interpol. Otherwise, the guy would be suspicious and would never come out of hiding."

"It seems Collin's been placed in a very dangerous situation," Henry said.

"Yes, he has, Mr. C. By no fault of his own, he got mixed up with an offshore insurance company headed by an anti-west economic terrorist."

Henry and Sarah looked at each other. Sarah's face shone with righteous indignation. "What are Collin's chances against this terrorist?"

"Collin has proven himself to be quite deft at eluding him and his group so far. He's got an incredibly brilliant sponsor within the US government's anti-terrorism task force and he's got the resources he needs to live underground for as long as it takes. Besides that, he's really mad now and refuses to let this guy win."

"I don't know that any of what you just told us brings me much comfort, but at least I know he's still the same person he always was, even after the tragedy."

Rob let out a short, amused burst. "You can say that again. Now that it's become personal, Collin is out to win and won't stop until he does."

"How are you involved in this, Rob? You're not working for the government, are you?" Henry asked.

"No. I'm involved because Collin's my friend, and I want to help him. I also have a connection to that brilliant guy I mentioned who wants to keep him safe."

"Have you seen him? Or talked to him?"

His hands were folded across the table in front of him. He leaned forward and spoke just above a whisper. "Not directly, but my friend has. I've told you this so that you know he's alive and safe, but you can't tell anyone, not even those two FBI agents you've spoken to. That would expose my friend and blow the whole operation, making it impossible for me to communicate with you in the future. You have to assume that your phones have been tapped and that your e-mails are being read. In fact, it would be safe to assume that all of your online activities are being watched."

"Why? Don't they think he's dead?" asked Sarah, her brow furrowed and her face contorted.

"That's what they published online. It's an easier explanation. But, since they have no confirmation, they will watch and wait. They believe, since Collin is such a family man, that if he's alive, he will, at some point, return home or make contact with you. They're waiting for him to make a mistake and get caught."

"Oh, dear," gasped Sarah. "That's unconscionable."

"With the misinformation they are going on, it stands to reason. They think he's complicit in a number of cybercrimes that crippled several international banks and embarrassed government agencies."

"That couldn't be," said Sarah.

"You and I know that, but they have nothing else to go on except for the contrived evidence this man has left online, which implicates Collin."

"But can't they sort out what information is false and what is not?" asked Sarah.

"Not without more evidence. As I said, Collin is being helped by some very knowledgeable people in high places. These guys will help exonerate him when this is all over."

"That's good to hear, but what can we do?" asked Henry.

"Your job is to just be yourselves. Don't change what you're doing; just be mindful that they're watching you, and be careful not to divulge anything about this conversation. If reporters come asking for a story, point them my way. I'll handle media relations for the family again, like I did before."

Henry and Sarah looked at each other again. Henry nodded and said, "Thank you, Rob. This means so much to us."

A handsome, young waiter arrived to take their orders. Rob sat back and, from that point forward, steered the conversation to other topics.

* * * *

GEORGE TOWN, GRAND CAYMAN ISLAND JUNE 14

Captain Sewell barked out orders, and the crew lazily responded. Every sail, every line, every pulley, and every boom had to be inspected, tested, and made ready. Every surface had to be cleaned and polished. Every detail had to be right. Each man's skin shimmered with a coating of sweat as they worked. Rojas stopped, pulled a bandana from his pocket, and wiped his face, surveying the surrounding boats and docks as he did. A man stood far off, leaning on a rail, watching them labor from his elevated vantage point. Rojas stuffed the red cloth back in his pocket and turned back. The man was gone. Rojas shrugged and went back to his duty.

A moment later, that same man appeared, walking briskly along the dock toward the slip where the *Admiral Risty* was moored. He wore khaki trousers without a wrinkle on them, a starched, white polo shirt, a cream-colored blazer, and a broad brim hat that matched his pants. Thick, black sunglasses covered his eyes. His goatee was dark brown, neatly trimmed, and gave him a hard-edged appearance. As he approached the *Admiral*, he saluted the crew and asked for their captain.

Gordon Sewell regarded the stranger without moving from his spot next to the mainmast, sensing a potential customer. "May I help you?"

"You may, indeed," said the man in a crisp and proper tone.

Captain Sewell arched an eyebrow and took a step forward. The man removed a thick envelope from an inner pocket of his blazer and handed it to him. The Captain cocked his head and kept a cautious eye on the stranger as he opened the envelope and peered inside. There was a handwritten note on a white index card. It read:

I'd like to rejoin the crew if there's room onboard.
I'll even return your dinghy.

The Captain stared at the note, his face tightened in confusion. Behind the note, a thick stack of hundred-dollar bills. He eyed the stranger again, squinting at him until recognition dawned. Collin Cook had returned.

Then he couldn't contain the smile that enveloped his face. Captain Sewell burst out with a hearty chuckle. His baritone voice boomed as he thrust forth his hand and grasped the stranger's. "We always have room for you, wanderer."

* * * *

Thank you for reading "Off Kilter," my debut novel. I hope you enjoyed the adventure.

Please take a moment and share your thoughts with other readers by writing a review on Amazon by visiting *https://www.amazon.com/dp/B00UA9Z8K8/*

Reviews help authors like water helps plants to grow. Your ratings and reviews on Amazon give other readers something upon which to make their decisions about what to read and allows authors like me connect with new readers.

I would greatly appreciate you leaving a review of "Off Kilter" on Amazon and/or GoodReads.

If you'd like to learn more about my books and where I get my inspiration for my stories, please connect with me at my website, *www.GlenRobinsBooks.com* and sign up for my newsletter. I promise to not clog your inbox. I'll only keep you informed of my next releases and the occasional special offer for deals and freebies and what-not.

Please like my Facebook page, too. *https://www.facebook.com/glenrobinsbooks/*

Continue to the next page for excerpts from "Off Course," the second part of Collin Cook's journey.

PROLOGUE

The room was dark. A thick cloud of cigarette smoke hung over the makeshift conference table. Eerie, bluish light from seven laptop screens bounced off the haze. Small holes in the heavy brown curtains allowed shards of muted sunlight to pierce the gloom. No one spoke. No one dared to. Instead, each man stared intently at his computer screen, afraid to make eye contact with him. These men knew him as their fearsome leader and he wanted to keep it that way. Fear was, after all, a powerful motivator. Fear and respect.

Pho Nam Penh stalked back and forth near the head of the table, trying to tamp down the rising anger. Maintaining control of one's emotions was absolutely paramount, especially in front of subordinates. The seven in the room squirmed under his scrutiny, unsure how to respond to his questions about their quarry. Some gazed intently at their screens, as if riveted by the data displayed there. The rest kept their eyes down to avoid drawing his ire.

He inhaled, with great satisfaction, the scent of fear. Power was an intoxicating drug and Penh relished the control he had over these men. He loved to watch them quiver in his presence. His next goal was to make the entire Western world tremble and quake. With the money he would soon recover from Collin Cook, Penh would increase the size of his team and expand his global reach. He and his Komodos would be feared by their enemies and hailed by their allies.

Penh gazed around the room, reading the body language of each man and surveying the conditions.

The table at which the men worked was really a door held up by two-by-fours. It was surrounded by his hand-picked cadre of computer hackers and technical whiz kids from around the region. They were sought because of their skills, yes, but also because of their allegiance to the cause: the fall of Western capitalism and the filthy, greedy, gluttonous pigs who gorged themselves at the expense of the rest of the world. Every man in the room wanted a front row seat to watch the chaos and clamor as the proud and mighty, the wealthy and shameless Americans and their smug British and European counterparts, sank into economic ruin.

This team seemed also to enjoy the prospect of spreading some of that ill-gotten Western wealth among themselves. Their promised reward had seemed imminent before Collin Cook escaped into the eye of Hurricane Abigail. Frustrated and harried, the team had worked tirelessly to track any sign of the man they sought and his hidden fortune.

An elaborate array of monitors, modems, servers, switches, wires, and power strips crowded nearly every inch of the painted wood surface. The only other items on the table were a handful of overflowing ashtrays, a smattering of white cube-shaped boxes of takeout food with chopsticks stuck in them, and dozens of water bottles, most of them empty.

Penh, clad in a tailored gray silk suit, patent leather Italian loafers, and a dark purple silk shirt, sucked in a lungful of smoke from the cigarette held between his thumb and forefinger. He wanted elegance and sophistication to ooze from his every movement, from his every fiber. Image was all about garnering respect and keeping an edge. He removed the sleek, narrow sunglasses that veiled his eyes, dropped the butt of the cigarette. As he ground the cigarette butt into the pocked concrete floor under his foot, he finally exhaled with an air of satisfaction. A thin vaporous trail of smoke wafted toward the low ceiling, being blown slowly and evenly from the tight crease of his mouth.

His men watched his every move, each of which was calculated to bolster his finely-honed image as a man of means and power.

For an Asian man his features were sharper, more distinct than most of his countrymen. Although only five foot seven inches in height and weighing one hundred forty pounds, Pho Nam Penh's presence was, he knew, enough to turn blood to ice. Study and practice, along with his natural gifts, had helped him craft the persona he projected. Maybe it was his eyes, dark and penetrating. Maybe it was the knowledge that he was a master martial artist or that he held two PhDs that made him so intimidating. In any case, the seven men huddled over their computers remained silent and fearful.

The stench was thick and ripe. A mixture of stale cigarette smoke;

the aroma of the morning's grease-laden, assortment of fried fish, noo-
dles, and spiced vegetables; and the body odor of seven sweaty and
stressed men filled the cramped space. These men had been confined to
the sixteen-foot-long, twelve-foot-wide room for days, trying to track
down the missing Collin Cook and his money, looking for any hint or
clue that would help them pinpoint his location. They already knew
they couldn't drain his accounts. That had been tried repeatedly and
had failed each time.

Collin Cook, the enigma, had grown to become an obsession with
Penh. Never had any target been so mind-numbingly tricky. It was no
longer just about the $30 million that Cook was hiding. It was more
about regaining face.

Cook had been on the run with Penh's money for months, out-
maneuvering Penh and this skilled team. Even the FBI, Interpol, and
law enforcement agencies the world over, called into the hunt surrepti-
tiously by Penh when he posted pictures of him sitting with Collin in
a London pub and shaking his hand in the Bahamas, were baffled by
Cook. Thanks to Penh's clever ruse, Collin was now a prime suspect in
the string of cybercrimes perpetrated by this select team and others. The
chase had spanned the globe from Europe to the Caribbean, to Central
America, to South America, to Canada, the United States, and back to
the Caribbean.

Meanwhile, the money had become invisible. There was only one
way to get it back. They had to find Cook and his computer. Certainly,
the information they needed was contained on its hard drive. If he was
smart—and every indicator suggested he was, more so than Penh would
have ever guessed at the onset—the data on that computer was ultra-se-
cure. Killing Cook, therefore, was not an option—yet.

Despite their dedication, Penh's highly skilled cyber mercenaries
cramped in this sweltering room were essentially being held captive
until his, their master's, bidding was complete. Two old army cots in
the corner were provided for short rest periods. Food was brought in
twice a day. There was a squalid bathroom down the hall, which was
really just a closet with a stained porcelain-lined hole in the floor and
little more than a trickle of water to flush it. No one had showered since
being brought here except for their illustrious leader, who appeared

at random times of day with a bodyguard or two, hissed at them and threatened harm against their families if they failed, then would disappear again.

This time, however, he lingered on purpose, sensing a subtle shift in the atmosphere. It was his longest stay thus far and he hoped it would be productive. His most recent tirade had dissipated, but not his resolve. Without a word, he stopped in front of a grimy glass pane—maybe three feet square—that adorned the outermost wall, pulled back the dark curtain, and folded his arms across his chest. Silent and foreboding, Penh stared at the street vendors squatting and squabbling with customers over their plastic buckets full of produce, sea food, and various animal parts. The chaos of the open-air market below provided a stark contrast to the orderly, systematic way his brain sorted through the myriad options proposed, considered, then discarded. His moment of hot displeasure had given way to a smoldering caldron of wicked contingencies. There would be hell to pay for the misdeeds perpetrated against the cause and Pho Nam Penh vowed to deliver Collin Cook on Satan's doorstep personally to arrange the transaction.

But not yet. Cook still held valuable information.

At length, he spoke. His words projected an introspective calm born of supreme intelligence and imposed self-mastery. "Have you confirmed that it was Cook who withdrew that $500,000 cash from the Bank of George Town? Do we have photographic evidence yet?"

One of the men at the far end of the table stood, bowed in deference to him, the leader, and spoke clearly and assuredly. "We do, sir. It just arrived. I can show it to you if you wish."

"Yes, show me," demanded Penh.

The man turned his laptop to make it visible to Penh, who now hovered over his shoulder, and clicked the mouse. A twenty-three-second video stream rolled. An American dressed in a dark sport coat and a wide-brimmed mesh hat, lugging a knapsack on one shoulder and a computer bag on the other, walked across the marble floor of the Bank of George Town. His gait was brisk and business-like, but it had a familiarity to it. Pho Nam Penh ordered his face to be enhanced and magnified. A few clicks later, he was looking into the eyes of the man that had taken his $30 million and embarrassed him for nearly seven months now.

Penh clenched his jaw, the muscles tensing as he took in the image. "That's him. That's our target. Do we still have men on the island?"

"Yes, sir."

"How many?"

"Four of them, sir."

"Are they properly prepared?"

"They are ready, sir."

"Armed?"

"Yes, sir. They are positioned as instructed and are waiting for the target to appear."

"Good. Send them this video. The target is undoubtedly coming to their location. They are to report directly to me when they make contact. Cook must be kept alive. Is that understood?"

"Yes, sir."

Another man spoke up from across the table. "Sir, I am receiving a text message now from our men in Grand Cayman. It states they have a visual on a man wearing clothing that matches the target in the video. He just exited a taxi near the marina."

"Ah, he has returned, just as I suspected he would," said Penh.

"Wait," said the man, holding up one finger as he read something on his screen. "The target has disappeared again."

"Where did he go?"

"Our men have a limited view from their position, sir. It is very difficult for them to get a full view of the street."

Penh drew his mouth tight. "Nonetheless," he muttered. "Stay with the plan. We know he is heading for that boat."

"Yes, sir." There was a pause while the man at the computer typed a message. Everyone sat still and waited for the ding of an incoming text. "The team leader has acknowledged his understanding."

"Remind him to keep Cook alive until we are finished with him."

Another round of furious keyboard tapping before the man responded. "He acknowledges your request, sir."

"Good. I will check with him later."

Pho Nam Penh and his followers knew much about Collin's life, both before the tragedy and after, but they didn't know everything. They were continually perplexed by how an average guy like Collin Cook with average skills had hidden $30 Million in numbered accounts in some of the world's most secretive financial institutions within seconds of receiving the settlement money from Penh's front company, Tranquil Pacific Casualty Insurance, and without leaving a trace. That took skills that most equipment sales people never needed, so never acquired. Beyond that, Cook had eluded Penh's men every time they got close, slipping into oblivion at just the right time. Even after Penh had lured law enforcement into the hunt, using their vast resources to track and chase his quarry, Cook remained at large and his money safely tucked away, inaccessible to Penh and his skilled team.

No one knew Penh's MIT classmate, Lukas Mueller, was involved. Lukas was supposed to be dead, killed by a roadside bomb in Afghanistan. Therefore, he was never given a second thought. No one knew Lukas was working as part of a deep-cover NSA cyber terrorism task force. Penh and his men only knew Cook had become an aggravating enigma. A cursed and resilient pest. A squirming, looming, irritating threat to his entire operation. No one knew why.

Penh's top priority was to bring Cook's run of good fortune to an end.

"What is the time stamp on this video?" Penh snapped his fingers as if a thought had just struck him.

"It's less than an hour old," the young man stated.

"He is moving very cautiously, as he should," said Penh.

"Yes, sir, but it seems our men have reestablished visual contact with the target, sir."

"What is he doing?"

"He stopped and is leaning on a rail, sir. It seems he is surveying the area, looking for something."

Penh inhaled sharply. "He is nervous. I can't blame him. Interpol has been combing the entire island searching for him. He must suspect them around every corner, especially near that boat."

"Some of our informants reported all but two undercover agents left the island this afternoon, returning to Europe and America," said another man on the other side of the table.

"The government has given up their search, have they? They must not want him as badly as I do," Penh paused, tapping his chin. "Where is Cook now?" he asked the man in front of him.

"Walking, sir, from his vantage point toward the boat."

After waiting for what seemed like an appropriate amount of time, Penh asked again.

"Still walking," answered the man. "It is a very long distance."

"Remember. They must be patient and they mustn't kill him."

CHAPTER ONE

Collin Cook had returned to the only place on Earth he felt at home anymore. Having spent nearly two weeks with the Captain and crew of the *Admiral Risty*—a for-hire, sixty-foot, fully appointed sailboat based in the Cayman Islands—and having escaped his pursuers on two different occasions with the help of the *Admiral*'s crew, it was a comfortable place for him to return. As he exited the taxi on the street overlooking the George Town Marina and surveyed the boat and its surroundings from a distance, scenes from recent experiences onboard the *Admiral* welled up. He stopped and leaned along the railing to watch the Captain and the crew, who had come to feel like a father and brothers to him, clean and polish the majestic sailboat and to check for any sign of a trap. It almost felt like returning home.

Collin strode purposefully down the docks toward the *Admiral Risty*, keeping a keen eye for anything out of the ordinary. Everything he owned fit into a backpack and computer bag, both slung over his left shoulder. He leaned to the right as he walked to keep the bags from slipping off, reminiscing all the way. The reggae music blaring from the boat's speakers, which could be heard from a hundred yards away, and the banter between the crewmates as they worked, helped set Collin's worried mind at ease as he approached. He looked forward to reuniting with them, but he did not want them to recognize him yet.

Collin turned from the main promenade to the narrower access walkway on the port side of the boat and tried to remain cool and calm as he asked to speak to the Captain. When Captain Sewell stepped forward and introduced himself, Collin handed him a thick envelope. His disguise was working so far. The Captain eyed the envelope warily before he opened it and found a handwritten note inside. The note asked if he could rejoin the crew and offered to return the dinghy. The Captain examined the note, then the man who handed it to him. He also examined the wad of cash that accompanied the note. It all clicked into place, causing his face to light up as he welcomed the man aboard the *Admiral Risty* as if he were the prodigal son, a smile stretching from ear to ear as he shook his hand and patted his shoulder, exclaiming, "We always have room for you, wanderer."

But the Captain's jovial smile quickly faded. Collin frowned and shook his head slightly, his index finger to his lips. Collin's demeanor and movements were unnatural and uncharacteristic. Collin could see from the expression on the Captain's face that he was curious about Collin's guarded approach. Collin wanted more than anything to exult in the warmth of their reunion, but he kept a serious countenance as he moved purposefully toward the cabin.

The Captain cocked his head at Collin and looked unsure of how to react. Without a word, Collin pointed down the steps toward the cabin, signaling for the Captain to follow him.

Collin, dressed as one of the elite businessmen of the islands, sporting a dark brown, neatly trimmed goatee, insisted the Captain and crew shove off immediately. His voice matched his looks. Both were hardened, cool, and aloof. Even his accent carried an air of superiority and affluence. Collin's commands, grim countenance, and decisive tone were echoed by the Captain. The crew hesitated, as if unsure of the intentions of this stranger. The puzzled looks on their faces displayed the sudden atmospheric change. The Captain barked again and the men began obeying his orders and preparing the *Admiral* for an immediate departure.

The crew scurried about the deck, attending to their assigned duties, sizing up this new customer. Theirs was not to question; only to follow their skipper's orders. His boat, his rules.

Captain Sewell followed Collin, who had become his best customer, into the cabin below deck. "Why so serious, man? You should be happy. I'm happy. You're not dead," he said with a forced chuckle.

"Yeah, I should be happy, right?" said Collin as he opened the secret compartment in the wall of the lower bunk and began to stuff his bags into it. "You don't mind if I stick this in here, do you?"

"Be my guest."

"I'm a bit leery these days," said Collin as he worked the computer bag into place. "I always feel like someone's watching me, ready to get me. Know what I mean? I guess these last few months have made me paranoid."

"I was worried about you, man," said the Captain, his voice growing serious. "That was a dangerous move, driving the dinghy into the storm like that. I thought that was it. You were gone forever."

When the Captain paused, Collin jumped in, trying to lighten the mood. The last thing he needed right now was high emotion. "You thought you wouldn't ever see the money I owe you." He forced a laugh, but the Captain only lifted an eyebrow and tilted his head.

"We have traveled many miles together. We have shared many stories, many meals, and much laughter. It is not about the money now. You know that. You are part of this family," said the Captain, opening his arms and gesturing toward the men above them on the deck. "You are one of us."

Collin stopped in his tracks, looked the Captain in the eye, and nodded his head as he spoke. "I know. That's why I came back. If I can't be home helping my sick mom, I want to be here, helping my friends. Plus, I never got the chance to thank you and the crew for risking your lives to help me get out of Florida. I'd be rotting in a jail somewhere if it weren't for you guys."

The Captain paused a moment, deep in thought. "Remember how you told me I could do dinner cruises any time, but I would be happier finding adventure?"

"Yeah, kind of." Collin was pulling items out of his bags as he spoke. They were too bulky to fit in the secret compartment. He dropped a worn T-shirt and his favorite cargo shorts on the bed next to his bag and removed the linen sport coat and the fancy button-up shirt. He finished changing while the Captain spoke.

"Well, you were right, man. Always sailing to the same places, serving the same meals, pandering to the rich American and European tourists gets to be very boring. Safe and profitable, but boring. With you, things are different. The men see it, too. Because you help them, cook for them, tell them stories, make them laugh. You listen to them. That is very different from other customers. You treat them with respect. That is why they are willing to do great things for you. You are their friend, their brother."

Collin smiled as he absorbed the sentiment of those words. "I know.

I feel the same way. But this time, there will be no need to do great things for me. This time, we'll relax and enjoy the ride. A real sailing trip. You know, a leisure tour, like your other clients. Only much, much longer."

"Ah, yes," said the Captain with a smile. "That will be nice."

"Perfect. But I do want to get out of here as soon as possible. Is that all right?"

"Of course, man," said the Captain in his customary lilt. "We push off very soon. The question is, where are we going?"

"I don't have much of a preference. I'm fine if we just stay lost for a month or two. I need to stay below the radar for a while, you know, off the grid. I need time to let the dust settle and come up with a game plan. So it doesn't matter much to me where we go. Let's see something new."

"Well, I suggest we head to the east side of the Caribbean. There are thousands of small islands there, full of pleasure cruisers. No one will notice you, my friend. You can remain safely anonymous."

"Sounds great. How much?"

The Captain laughed out loud, waved a dismissive hand at the air, then turned on his heels and climbed the steps up to the cockpit. He switched on his instrumentation as he sat in the padded Captain's chair behind the large steering wheel. "Rojas, Jaime. Are we ready?"

"Aye, Captain," the two said in unison as they hopped to the dock and moved toward the tie lines.

Captain Sewell fired up the boat's small engine so he could maneuver out of the harbor. It chugged and sputtered as it came to life, throwing out a blue cloud of fumes.

"Miguel, Tog. Man your stations," he bellowed in his hearty, baritone voice.

"Aye, sir," they called back one at a time. Each man scurried into position, one at the bow, one at the stern.

Jaime and Rojas untied the ropes from the dock cleats fore and aft and gently guided the *Admiral* out of its slip as Captain Sewell started up the little engine. Neither of them noticed the activity on the boat in the next slip.

After the Captain went topside, Collin pulled the contents out of the computer bag and backpack. He had placed a few items of clothing, the dozen false passports he owned, his laptop, and $500,000 worth of cash into the overstuffed bags before coming to the marina. They were too bulky to fit in the compartment, so he began to repack things into a large waterproof sea bag the Captain had loaned him on their last voyage. Moving quickly, he reloaded his computer, the money, and his passports into the long, cylindrical sea bag, then crammed it into the smuggler's hideaway, as the crew called it. With those items out of the way, he tossed the nearly empty computer bag in a closet.

One of the items Collin had removed from his backpack was a small waterproof pouch which contained his iPhone, a seaworthy GPS unit, and a few thousand dollars in several different currencies. He tugged at its sides and nodded to himself. Collin pulled a cheap cell phone he had purchased in Chicago from the pocket of his blazer and checked that it had a full charge. Its twin was in Emily's possession. The thought of her, his eye-popping high school sweetheart, made him smile. As he squeezed the little phone into the small sea pouch with his iPhone, a strange commotion erupted on the deck above. Loud footfalls on the fiberglass hull at the bow were rushing toward the stern. Commands were barked out by an unfamiliar voice in short, guttural bursts. Sensing danger, Collin grabbed the waterproof pouch and jumped down two steps to the galley. He swung open the door to the microwave oven, reached to the back, pushed on two soft buttons to release the latches, and shoved the pouch in the secret compartment behind the back wall of the microwave.

Captain Sewell had purchased this boat at auction and later learned it had been confiscated by the DEA during a drug bust. Unbeknownst to the Captain at the time of purchase, the original owner had designed features into this boat necessary for his trade. Jaime had shown Collin these secret compartments and he had used them to his advantage on previous occasions.

Both hands were inside the oven when an angry voice barked something he didn't understand. Collin whirled around, slamming the door shut with his elbow, to stare down the muzzle of a snub-nosed, semi-automatic Uzi pointed right at his face. The ill-tempered Asian man carrying it glared disapprovingly at him. Collin's hands shot straight up in the air. There was no other option but to surrender and trust that God would somehow deliver him again.

The gunman approached suspiciously, making as wide an arc as he could in the tight quarters below decks. He wore a flowered shirt and a straw hat, but the rippling biceps and the thick chest indicated he was something more than a tourist. Using the weapon as a pointer, the man motioned for Collin to move toward the stairs, using quick jabs in the air and short, unintelligible grunts. Checking his surroundings, he then maneuvered like a stalking panther in a slow semicircle opposite his prey. When Collin reached the steps, beyond arm's reach, he stopped, obeying the gunman's gesture. The man opened the microwave door and stole a glance inside. Collin's heart was in his throat, unsure if the back wall had snapped shut all the way. If his phones and laptop were discovered, it would be all over. Pho Nam Penh would win because every detail of Collin's finances was stored on those devices. Penh would crack his sophisticated firewall eventually and know the whereabouts of the nearly $30 million stashed in several banks around the world. The lion's share of the money, however, was held in a top-secret bank in Panama City, Panama, used primarily by the US clandestine community operating in the region. Lukas, with his knowledge of deep-cover operations, had helped Collin gain access to this hidden gem. Having the account numbers and pass codes from Collin's laptop, Penh would have much of what he needed to syphon away everything. Collin maintained safeguards, but Lukas had warned Collin at the beginning to guard that laptop and iPhone with his life. Information on those devices, including the instant messages between Collin and Lukas, could also expose Lukas's covert operational involvement in the war on terrorism, thus blowing his carefully guarded existence.

It took only seconds for Collin's already unbalanced existence to shift once again. In that instant, he realized he had placed the life of every man on board the *Admiral Risty* in jeopardy. The feeling of being in total free fall caused him to stagger backward, before catching himself on the bulkhead by the steps. This drew an angry look from the gunman. Collin knew if he didn't play his cards right, they would all die, Penh's terror group would receive a healthy round of funding and enough classified information to help them stay under the radar indefinitely. None of these outcomes boded well for Collin, his friends, or his country.

The stocky gunman peered again into the microwave, pulled out a coffee mug, and sniffed its contents. He dumped it into the sink and checked inside the oven again. As he did, Collin forced himself to remain composed and keep a poker face. Disgusted, the man grunted and slammed the door shut. Startled, Collin let out a nervous cough. The gunman's focus returned to Collin as he climbed the two steps up from the galley.

The attack was swift and sudden. The gunman pounced, closing the distance between them in milliseconds, and smashed the butt of the gun into the side of Collin's head before he could adequately shield himself. The force of the blow snapped his head sideways into the wall on his right, causing his world to go dark.

Three more gunmen stood on deck with Uzis aimed at the other four crew members and the Captain. The *Admiral Risty* had not yet cleared the harbor, but these men boldly displayed their hardware, apparently unafraid of anyone. The gunman closest to the Captain directed him to move out of the way. The green-shirted man fiddled with the instruments in the cockpit for a moment, then pointed to a spot on the Captain's GPS map. "We go there. Now," he demanded.

"Panama? You want to go to Panama?" asked the Captain.

"Yes. We go now."

"OK, you're the one with the gun. But you know it will take a week or more, don't you?"

The lean, long-haired one standing to the Captain's right cocked his head slightly. "You go faster. This boat very fast. You go faster. Three days." His face was like stone and his eyes were hidden behind dark sunglasses. Every movement was calculated and efficient. Every word carried meaning and consequences.

The Captain looked from one armed man to the other, studying their expressionless faces. He had no idea what they might do, but he had to set the right expectations from the start. He knew mean men and he knew they had to be handled with the right balance of firmness and cooperation. It was important to set the boundaries early in these situations, so the Captain held silent for a long moment, showing no fear and no desire to acquiesce to their demands. "That depends on the wind, you know?" he said, waving a hand in the air and looking at the sky around them. "No wind, no going faster."

It was a rather surreal scene. In a matter of seconds these four highly trained, heavily armed Asian mercenaries took control of the *Admiral Risty* and altered its course and the lives of everyone onboard.

Visit *https://www.amazon.com/dp/B01BCP6YQK*
to read *Off Course.*